" The polite crowd drew away from him." (Page 36.)

Pharos the Egyptian.]   [*Frontispiece*

PHAROS

The Egyptian

The Classic Mummy Tale of Romance and Revenge

GUY BOOTHBY

Illustrated by JOHN H. BACON

Dover Publications, Inc.
Mineola, New York

DOVER HORROR CLASSICS

Bibliographical Note

This Dover edition, first published in 2016, is an unabridged republication of the work originally published by Ward, Lock & Co., Ltd., London, in 1899.

Library of Congress Cataloging-in-Publication Data

Boothby, Guy, 1867–1905.
    Pharos, the Egyptian : the classic mummy tale of romance and revenge / Guy Boothby ; illustrated by John H. Bacon.
        pages ; cm. — (Dover Horror Classics)
    ISBN-13: 978-0-486-80315-9 (softcover)
    ISBN-10: 0-486-80315-5 (softcover)
    1. Mummies—Egypt—Fiction. 2. Paranormal fiction. I. Bacon, J. H. (John Henry), illustrator. II. Title.
PR4149.B957P48 2016
823'.8—dc23

2015028997

Manufactured in the United States by RR Donnelley
80315501   2016
www.doverpublications.com

Contents

CONTENTS

List of Illustrations

PREFACE

"MY DEAR TREVELYAN,—Never in my life have I been placed in such an awkward, not to say invidious, position. I am, as you know, a plain man, fond of a plain life and plain speaking, and yet I am about to imperil that reputation by communicating to you what I fancy you will consider the most extraordinary and unbelievable intelligence you have ever received in your life. For my own part I do not know what to think. I have puzzled over the matter until I am not in a position to judge fairly. You must, therefore, weigh the evidence for us both. For pity's sake, however, do not decide hastily. *In dubiis benigniora semper sunt praeferenda*, as they used to say in our schooldays, must be our motto, and by it we must abide at any hazards. As far as I can see, we are confronted with one of the saddest, and at the same time one of the most inexplicable cases ever yet recorded on paper. Reduced to its proper factors it stands as follows: Either Forrester has gone mad and dreamed it all, or he is sane and has suffered as few others have done in this

9

world. In either case he is deserving of our deepest pity. In one way only are we fortunate. Knowing the man as we do, we are in a position to estimate the value of the accusations he brings against himself. Of one thing I am convinced—a more honourable being does not walk this earth. Our acquaintance with him is of equal length. We were introduced to him, and to each other, on one and the same occasion, upwards of twelve years ago ; and during that time, I know I am right in saying, neither of us ever had reason to doubt his word, or the honour of a single action. Indeed, to my mind he had but one fault, a not uncommon one in these latter days of the nineteenth century. I refer to his somewhat morbid temperament and the consequent leaning towards the supernatural it produced in him.

" As the world has good reason to remember, his father was perhaps the most eminent Egyptologist our century has seen ; a man whose whole mind and being was impregnated with a love for that ancient country and its mystic past. Small wonder, therefore, that the son should have inherited his tastes, and that his life should have been influenced by the same peculiar partiality. While saying, however, that he had a weakness for the supernatural, I am by no means admitting that he was what is vulgarly termed a spiritualist. I do not believe for an instant that he ever declared himself so openly. His mind was too evenly balanced, and at the same time too healthy, to permit such an enthusiastic declaration of his interest. For my part, I believe he simply inquired into the matter as he would have done into, shall we say, the kinetic theory of gases, or the history of the ruined cities of Mashonaland, for the purpose of satisfying his curiosity and of perfecting his education on the subject. Having thus made my own feelings known to you, I will leave the matter in your hands, confident that you will do him justice, and will proceed to describe how the pathetic record of our friend's experiences came into my possession.

"I had been hunting all day, and did not reach home until between half-past six and seven o'clock. We had a house full of visitors at the time, I remember, some of whom had been riding with me, and the dressing-gong sounded as we dismounted from our horses at the steps. It was plain that if we wished to change our attire and join the ladies in the drawing-room before dinner was announced, we had no time to lose. Accordingly we departed to our various rooms with all possible speed.

"There is nothing pleasanter or more refreshing after a long day in the saddle than a warm bath. On this particular occasion I was in the full enjoyment of this luxury when a knocking sounded at the door. I inquired who was there.

"'Me, sir—Jenkins,' replied my servant. 'There is a person downstairs, sir, who desires to see you.'

"'To see me at this hour,' I answered. 'What is his name, and what does he want?'

"'His name is Silver, sir,' the man replied; and then, as if the information might be put forward as some excuse for such a late visit, he continued, 'I believe he is a kind of a foreigner, sir. Leastways, he's very dark, and don't speak the same, quite, as an Englishman might do.'

"I considered for a moment. I knew of no person

named Silver who could have any possible reason for desiring to see me at seven o'clock in the evening.

"'Go down and inquire his business,' I said, at length. 'Tell him I am engaged to-night; but if he can make it convenient to call in the morning, I will see him.'

"The man departed on his errand, and by the time he returned I had reached my dressing-room once more.

"'He is very sorry, sir,' he began, as soon as he had closed the door, 'but he says he must get back to Bampton in time to catch the 8.15 express to London. He wouldn't tell me his business, but asked me to say that it is most important, and he would be deeply grateful if you could grant him an interview this evening.'

"'In that case,' I said, 'I suppose I *must* see him. Did he tell you no more?'

"'No, sir. Leastways, that wasn't exactly the way he put it. He said, sir, "If the gentleman won't see me otherwise, tell him I come to him from Mr. Cyril Forrester. Then I think he will change his mind."'

"As the man, whoever he was, had predicted, this *did* make me change my mind. I immediately bade Jenkins return and inform him that I would be with him in a few moments. Accordingly, as soon as I had dressed, I left my room and descended to the study. The fire was burning brightly, and a reading-lamp stood upon the writing-table. The remainder of the room, however, was in shadow, but not sufficiently so to prevent my distinguishing a dark figure seated between the two bookcases. He rose as I entered, and bowed before me with a servility that, thank God! is scarcely English. When he spoke, though what he said was grammatically correct, his accent revealed the fact that he was not a native of our Isles.

"'Sir William Betford, I believe,' he began, as I entered the room.

"'That is my name,' I answered, at the same time turning up the lamp and lighting the candles upon the mantelpiece in order that I might see him better. 'My man tells me you desire an interview with me. He also mentioned that you have come from my old friend, Mr. Cyril Forrester, the artist, who is now abroad. Is this true?'

"'Quite true,' he replied. 'I do come from Mr. Forrester.'

"The candles were burning brightly by this time, and, as a result, I was able to see him more distinctly. He was of medium height, very thin, and wore a long overcoat of some dark material. His face was distinctly Asiatic in type, though the exact nationality I could not determine. Possibly he might have hailed from Siam.

"'Having come from Mr. Forrester,' I said, when I had seated myself, 'you will be able to tell me his address. I am one of his oldest, and certainly one of his firmest, friends.'

"'Nevertheless, I was instructed on no account to reveal his present residence to you,' the man replied.

"'What, then, can your business be with me?' I asked, more nettled at his words than I cared to show.

"'I have brought you a packet,' he said, 'which Mr. Forrester was most anxious I should personally deliver to your hands. There is a letter inside which he said would explain everything. I was also instructed to obtain from you a receipt, which I am to convey to him again.'

"So saying, he dived his hand into the pocket of his greatcoat, and brought thence a roll, which he placed with some solemnity upon the table.

"'There is the packet,' he said. 'Now, if you will be kind enough to give me a note stating that you have received it, I will take my departure. It is most necessary that I should catch the express to London, and if I desire to do so, I have a sharp walk in front of me.'

"'You shall have the receipt,' I answered; and, taking a sheet of note-paper from a drawer, I wrote the following letter :—

"'THE GRANGE, BAMPTON ST. MARY,
December 14*th*, 18—.

"'DEAR FORRESTER,—This evening I have been surprised by a visit from a man named——'

"Here I paused and inquired the messenger's name, which I had, for the moment, forgotten.

"'Honorè De Silva,' he replied.

"'——from a man named Honorè De Silva, who has handed me a packet for which he desires this letter shall be a receipt. I have endeavoured to elicit your address from him, but on this point he is adamant. Is it kind to an old friend to let him hear from you, but at the same time to refuse to permit him to communicate with you? Why all this mystery? If you are in trouble, who would so gladly share it with you as your old friend? If you need help, who would so willingly give it? Are the years during which we have known each other to count for nothing? Trust me, and I think you are aware that I will not abuse your confidence.

" ' Your affectionate friend,

" ' WILLIAM BETFORD.'

" Having blotted it, I placed the letter in an envelope, directed it to Cyril Forrester, Esq., and handed it to De Silva, who placed it carefully in an inner pocket and rose to take leave of me.

" ' Will nothing induce you to reveal your employer's present place of residence ? ' I said. ' I assure you I am most anxious to prove his friend.'

" ' I can easily believe that,' he answered. ' He has often spoken of you in terms of the warmest affection. If you could hear him, I am sure you would have no doubt on that score.'

" I was much affected, as you may imagine, on hearing this, and his assertion emboldened me to risk yet another question.

" ' Upon one point, at least, you can set my mind at rest,' I said. ' Is Mr. Forrester happy ? '

" ' He is a man who has done with happiness such as you mean, and will never know it again,' he answered solemnly.

" ' My poor old friend,' I said, half to myself and half to him ; and then added, ' Is there no way in which I can help him ? '

" ' None,' De Silva replied. ' But I can tell you no more, so I beg you will not ask me.'

" ' But you can surely answer one other question,' I continued, this time with what was almost a note of supplication in my voice. ' You can tell me whether, in your opinion, we, his friends, will see him again, or if he intends to spend the remainder of his life in exile?'

"'That I can safely answer. No! You will never see him again. He will not return to this country, or to the people who have known him here.'

"'Then may God help him and console him, for his trouble must be bitter indeed!'

"'It is well-nigh insupportable,' said De Silva, with the same solemnity; and then, picking up his hat, bowed, and moved towards the door.

"'I must risk one last question. Tell me if he will communicate with me again?'

"'Never,' the other replied. 'He bade me tell you, should you ask, that you must henceforth consider him as one who is dead. You must not attempt to seek for him, but consign him to that oblivion in which only he can be at peace.'

"Before I could say more he had opened the door and passed into the hall. A moment later I heard the front door close behind him, a step sounded on the gravel before my window, and I was left standing upon the hearthrug, staring at the packet upon the table. Then the gong sounded, and I thrust the roll into a drawer. Having securely locked the latter, I hastened to the drawing-room to meet my guests.

"Needless to say, my demeanour during dinner was not marked with any great degree of gaiety. The interview with De Silva had upset me completely; and though I endeavoured to play the part of an attentive host, my attempt was far from being successful. I found my thoughts continually reverting to that curious interview in the study, and to the packet which had come into my possession in such a mysterious manner, the secret contained in which I had still to learn.

"After dinner we adjourned to the billiard-room, where we spent the evening; consequently it was not until my guests bade me 'Good-night,' and retired to their various rooms, by which time it was well after eleven o'clock, that I found myself at liberty to return to the study.

"Once there, I made up the fire, wheeled an easy chair to a position before it, arranged the reading lamp so that the light should fall upon the paper over my left shoulder, and having made these preparations, unlocked the drawer and took out the packet De Silva had handed to me.

"It was with a mixture of pain, a small measure of curiosity, but more apprehension as to what I should find within, that I cut the string and broke the seals. Inside I discovered a note and a roll of manuscript in that fine and delicate handwriting we used to know so well. After a hasty glance at it, I put the latter aside, and opened the envelope. The note I found within was addressed to you, Trevelyan, as well as to myself, and read as follows :—

"'MY DEAR OLD FRIENDS,—In company with many other people, you must have wondered what the circumstances could have been that induced me to leave England so suddenly, to forfeit the success I had won for myself after so much uphill work, and, above all, to bid farewell to a life and an art I loved so devotedly, and from which, I think I may be excused for saying,

I had such brilliant expectations. I send you herewith, Betford, by a bearer I can trust, an answer to that question. I want you to read it, and, having done so, to forward it to George Trevelyan, with the request that he will do the same. When you have mastered the contents, you must unitedly arrange with some publishing house to put it before the world, omitting nothing, and in no way attempting to offer any extenuation for my conduct. We three were good friends once, in an age as dead to me now as the Neolithic. For the sake of that friendship, therefore, I implore this favour at your hands. As you hope for mercy on that Last Great Day, when the sins of all men shall be judged, do as I entreat you now. How heavily I have sinned against my fellow-men—in ignorance, it is true —you will know when you have read what I have written. This much is certain—the effect of it weighs upon my soul like lead. If you have any desire to make that load lighter, carry out the wish I now express to you. Remember me also in your prayers, praying not as for a man still living, but as you would for one long since dead. That God may bless and keep you both will ever be the wish of your unhappy friend,

"'Cyril Forrester.

"'P.S.—Matthew Simpford, in the Strand, is keeping two pictures for me. They were once considered among my best work. I ask you each to accept one, and when you look at them, try to think as kindly as possible of the friend who is gone from you for ever.'

*   *   *   *   *

"So much for the letter. It is possible there may be people who will smile sarcastically when they read that, as I finished it, tears stood in my eyes, so that I could scarcely see the characters upon the paper.

"You, Trevelyan, I know, will understand my emotion better. And why should I not have been affected? Forrester and I had been good friends in the old days, and it was only fit and proper I should mourn his loss. Handsome, generous, clever, who could help loving him? I could not, that's certain.

"The letter finished, I replaced it in its envelope and turned my attention to the manuscript. When I began to read, the hands of the clock upon the chimney-piece stood at twenty minutes to twelve, and they had reached a quarter past five before I had completed my task. All that time I read on without stopping, filled with amazement at the story my poor friend had to tell, and consumed with a great sorrow that his brilliant career should have terminated in such an untoward manner.

"Now, having completed my share of the task, as required of me in the letter, I send the manuscript by special messenger to you. Read it as he desires, and when you have done so, let me have your opinion upon it. Then I will come up to town, and we will arrange to carry out the last portion of our poor friend's request together. In the meantime,

"Believe me ever your friend,

"WILLIAM BETFORD."

*   *   *   *   *

Six months later.

Trevelyan and I have completed the task allotted to us. We have read Forrester's manuscript, and we have also discovered a publisher who will place it before the world. What the result is to be it remains for time to decide.

CHAPTER I

IF ever a man in this world had a terrible—I might almost go so far as to add a shameful—story to relate, surely I, Cyril Forrester, am that one. How strange—indeed, how most unbelievable—it is I do not think I even realized myself until I sat down to write it. The question the world will in all probability ask when it has read it is, why it should have been told at all. It is possible it may be of opinion that I should have served my generation just as well had I allowed it to remain locked up in my own bosom for all time. This, however, my conscience would not permit. There are numberless reasons, all of them important and some imperative beyond all telling, why I should make my confession, though God knows I am coward enough to shrink from the task. And, if you consider for a moment, I think you will understand why. In the first place, the telling of the story can only have the effect of depriving me of the affection of those I love, the respect of those whose good opinion I have hitherto prized so highly, the sympathy of my most faithful friends, and, what is an equal sacrifice as far as I am personally concerned—though it is, perhaps, of less importance to others—the fame I have won for myself after so hard a struggle. All this is swept away like driftwood before a rising tide, and as a result I retire into voluntary exile, a man burdened with a lifelong sorrow. How I have suffered, both in body and mind, none will ever understand. That I have been punished is also certain, how heavily you, my two old friends, will be able to guess when you have read my story. With the writing of it I have severed the last link that binds me to the civilized world. Henceforth I shall be a wanderer and an outcast, and but for one reason could wish myself dead. But that is enough of regret—let me commence my story.

Two years ago, as you both have terrible reason to remember, there occurred in Europe what may, perhaps, be justly termed the most calamitous period in its history, a time so heart-breaking that scarcely a man or woman can look back upon it without experiencing the keenest sorrow. Needless to say I refer to the outbreak of the plague among us, that terrible pestilence which swept Europe from end to end, depopulated its greatest cities, filled every burial place to overflowing, and caused such misery and desolation in all ranks of life as has never before been known among us. Few homes were there, even in this fair England of ours, but suffered some bereavement; few families but mourn a loss the wound of which has even now barely healed. And it is my part in this dreadful business that I have forced myself with so much bitter humiliation to relate. Let me begin at the very beginning, tell everything plainly and straightforwardly, offer nothing in extenuation of my conduct, and trust only to the world to judge me, if such a thing be possible, with an unbiassed mind.

I date my misery from a wet, miserable night in the

last week of March—a night without a glimpse of the
moon, which, on that particular evening, was almost at
its full.   There had been but one solitary hour of paint-
ing-light all day ; short as it was, however, it was
sufficient for my purpose.   My picture for the Academy
was finished, and now all that remained was to pack
it up and send it in.   It was, as you remember, my
eighth, and in every way my most successful effort.
The subject I had chosen had enthralled me from the
moment it had first entered my head, and the hours of
thought and preparation it had entailed will always
rank amongst the happiest of my life.   It represented
Merenptah, the Pharaoh of the Exodus, learning from
the magicians the effect of his obstinacy in the death of
his first-born son.   The canvas showed him seated on
his throne, clad in his robes of state.   His head was
pushed a little forward, his chin rested in his hand, while
his eyes looked straight before him as though he were
endeavouring to peer into the future in the hope of
reading there the answer to the troubled thoughts inside
his brain.   Behind him stood the sorcerers, one of
whom had found courage to announce the baneful
tidings.

The land of Egypt has always possessed a singular
attraction for me—a taste which, doubtless, I inherit
from my poor father, who, as you are aware, was one
of the greatest authorities upon the subject the world
has ever known.

As I have said, it was a miserable night, dark as the
pit of Tophet.   A biting wind whistled through the
streets, the pavements were dotted with umbrella-laden
figures, the kennels ran like mill-sluices, while the roads

were only a succession of lamp-lit puddles through which the wheeled traffic splashed continuously. For some reason—perhaps because the work upon which I had been so long and happily engaged was finished, and I felt lonely without it to occupy my mind—I was stricken with a fit of the blues. Convinced that my own company would not take me out of it, I left my studio in search of more congenial society. This was soon forthcoming; and you will remember, Betford and Trevelyan, that we dined together at a little restaurant in the neighbourhood of Leicester Square, and followed the dinner up with a visit to a theatre. As ill-luck would have it, I was in the minority in the choice of a place of entertainment. The result was disastrous. Instead of ridding myself of my melancholy, as I had hoped to do, I intensified it, and when, at the end of the evening, I bade you farewell in the Strand, my spirits had reached a lower level than they had attained all day. I remember distinctly standing beneath a gas-lamp at the corner of Villiers Street, as the clocks were striking midnight, feeling disinclined to return to my abode and go to bed, and yet equally at a loss to know in what manner I should employ myself until there was some likelihood of slumber visiting my eyelids. To help me make up my mind I lit a fresh cigar and strolled down towards the river. On the pavement, at the foot of the steps leading to Hungerford Bridge, a poor tattered creature, yet still possessing some pretensions to gentlemanly address, came from beneath the archway and begged of me, assuring me most solemnly that, as far as he was concerned, the game was played out, and if I did not comply with his request, he would forthwith end his troubles in the river. I gave him something—I cannot now remember what—and then, crossing the road, made my way along the Embankment towards Cleopatra's Needle. The rain had ceased for the moment, and in the north a few stars were shining. The myriad lights of the Embankment were reflected in the river like lines of dancing fire, and I remember that behind me a train was rolling across the bridge from Charing Cross with a noise like distant thunder. I suppose I must have been thinking of my picture, and of the land and period which had given me the idea. At any rate, I know that on this occasion the ancient monument, in front of which I soon found myself, affected me as it had never done before. I thought of the centuries that had passed since those hieroglyphics were carved upon the stone, of the changes the world had seen since that giant monolith first saw the light of day. Leaning my elbows on the parapet, I was so absorbed in my own thoughts that when a sudden cry of "Help, help!" rang out from the river it was with a sensible shock that I returned to the commonplace and found myself standing where I was. A moment later I was all action. The cry had come from the other side of the Needle. I accordingly hastened to the steps farthest from me, shouting, as I went, in my excitement, that a man was drowning. It might have all been part of some evil dream: the long line of silent Embankment on either side, the swiftly-flowing river, and that despairing appeal for help coming so suddenly out of the black darkness. Then I became aware that I was not alone on the steps. There was another man there, and he stood motionless, peering out into the dark stream, scarcely a dozen paces from me.

I had reached the top of the steps and was about to descend them in order to accost him, when something occurred which stopped me and held me spell-bound. The moon had emerged from its pall of cloud and was now shining clear and bright across the river. Thirty seconds must have elapsed since we had heard the cry for assistance, and now, as I looked, the drowning man was washed in at the foot of the steps upon which we stood. It would have needed but the least movement on the part of the man below me to have caught him as he swept by and to have saved him from a watery death. To my amazement, however—and even now, after this lapse of time, my gorge rises at the very thought of it—the other did not offer to help, but drew himself back. Before I could return my eyes, the wretched suicide had passed out of sight and had vanished into the darkness again. As he did so a pronounced chuckle of enjoyment reached me from the man below—a burst of merriment so out of place and so detestable that I could scarcely believe I heard aright. I cannot hope to make you understand how it affected me. A second later a fit of blind fury overtook me, and, under the influence of it, I ran down the steps and seized the murderer—for such I shall always consider him—by the arm.

"Are you a man or a fiend," I cried in jerks, "that you could so allow another to perish when you might have saved him? His death is upon your conscience, brute and monster that you are!"

So extreme was my emotion that I trembled under it like a man with the palsy.

Then the other turned his head and looked at me;
and, as he did so, a great shudder, accompanied by an
indescribable feeling of nausea, passed over me. What
occasioned it I could not tell, nor could I remember
having felt anything of the kind before. When it departed, my eyes fixed themselves on the individual
before me. Connecting him in some way with the unenviable sensation I had just experienced, I endeavoured
to withdraw them again, but in vain. The other's
gaze was rivetted upon me—so firmly, indeed, that it
required but small imagination to believe it eating into
my brain. Good heavens! how well I recollect that
night and every incident connected with it! I believe I
shall remember it through all eternity. If only I had
known enough to have taken him by the throat then
and there, and had dashed his brains out on the stones,
or to have seized him in my arms and hurled him down
the steps into the river below, how much happier I
should have been! I might have earned eternal punishment, it is true, but I should at least have saved myself
and the world in general from such misery as the human brain can scarcely realize. But I did not know,
the opportunity was lost, and, in that brief instant of
time, millions of my fellow-creatures were consigned unwittingly to their doom.

After long association with an individual, it is difficult,
if not impossible, to set down with any degree of exact-
ness a description of the effect his personality in the first
instance had upon one. In this case I find it more than
usually difficult, for the reason that, as I came more
under his influence, the original effect wore off and
quite another was substituted for it.

His height was considerably below the average, his skull was as small as his shoulders were broad. But it was not his stature, his shoulders, or the size of the head which caused the curious effect I have elsewhere described. It was his eyes, the shape of his face, the multitudinous wrinkles that lined it, and, above all, the extraordinary colour of his skin, that rendered his appearance so repulsive. To understand what I mean you must think first of old ivory, and then endeavour to realize what the complexion of a corpse would be like after lying in an hermetically sealed tomb for many years. Blend the two, and you will have some dim notion of the idea I am trying to convey. His eyes were small, deeply sunken, and in repose apparently devoid of light and even of life. He wore a heavy fur coat, and, for the reason that he disdained the customary headgear of polite society, and had substituted for it a curious description of cap, I argued that he was a man who boasted a will of his own, and who did not permit himself to be bound by arbitrary rules. But, however plain these things may have been, his age was a good deal more difficult to determine. It was certainly not less than seventy, and one might have been excused had one even set it down at a hundred. He walked feebly, supporting himself with a stick, upon which his thin yellow fist was clutched till the knuckles stood out and shone like billiard balls in the moonlight.

Under the influence of his mysterious personality, I stood speechless for some moments, forgetful of everything—the hour, the place, and even his inhumanity to the drowning wretch in the river below. By the time

I recovered myself he was gone, and I could see him crossing the road and moving swiftly away in the direction of Charing Cross. Drawing my hand across my forehead, which was clammy with the sweat of real fear, I looked again at the river. A police boat was pulling towards the steps, and by the light of the lantern on board I could make out the body of a man. My nerves, already strained to breaking pitch, were not capable of standing any further shock. I accordingly turned upon my heel and hurried from the place with all the speed at my command.

Such was my first meeting with the man whom I afterwards came to know as Pharos the Egyptian.

CHAPTER II

A S you are aware, my picture that year was hung in an excellent position, was favourably received by those for whose criticism I had any sort of respect, attracted its fair share of attention from the general public, and, as a result, brought me as near contentment as a man can well hope or expect to be in this world. Before it had been twenty-four hours "on the line," I had received several tempting offers for it; but as I had set my heart on obtaining a certain sum, and was determined not to accept less, you may suppose I did not give them much attention. If I received what I wanted, I promised myself a treat I had been looking forward to all my life. In that case I would take a long holiday, and instead of spending the next winter in England, would start for Egypt in the autumn, taking in Italy *en route*, make my way up the Nile, and be home again, all being well, in the spring, or, at latest, during the early days of summer.

Ever since I first became an exhibitor at Burlington House, I have made it a rule to studiously avoid visiting the gallery after varnishing day. My reasons would interest no one, but they were sufficiently strong to induce me to adhere to them. This year, however, I was led into doing so in a quite unintentional fashion, and as that exception vitally concerns this narrative, I must explain the circumstances that led up to it in detail.

On a certain Friday, early in June, I was sitting in my studio, after lunch, wondering what I should do with myself during the afternoon, when a knock sounded at the door, and a moment later, after I had invited whoever stood outside to enter, my old friend, George Merridew, his wife, son, and three daughters, trooped into the room. They were plainly up from the country, and, as usual, were doing the sights at express speed. George Merridew, as you know, stands six feet in his stockings, and is broad in proportion. His face is red, his eyes blue, and he carries with him wherever he goes the air of a prosperous country squire, which he certainly is. Like many other big men, he is unconscious of his strength, and when he shakes hands with you, you have reason to remember the fact for five minutes afterwards. His wife is small, and, as some folk declare, looks younger than her eldest daughter, who is a tennis champion, a golfer, and boasts a supreme contempt for Royal Academicians and, for that matter, for artists generally. The son is at Oxford, a nice enough young fellow with limpid blue eyes, who, to his father's disgust, takes no sort of interest in fox-hunting, racing, football, or any other sport, and has openly asserted his intention of entering the Church in the near future. There are two other girls, Gwendoline and Ethel—the latter, by the way, promises to be a second edition of her mother —who, at present, are in the advanced schoolroom stage, dine with their parents, except on state occasions, and play duets together on the piano with a conscientious regard for time and fingering that gives their father no small amount of pleasure, but with other people rather detracts from the beauty of the performance.

"Thank goodness, we have got you at last!" cried Merridew, as he rushed forward and gripped my hand with a cordiality that made me suffer in silent agony for minutes afterwards. "But, my dear fellow, what on earth induces you to live in a place that's so difficult to find? We have been all round the neighbourhood, here, there, and everywhere, making inquiries, and shouldn't have found you now had it not been for an intelligent butcher-boy, who put us on the right scent and enabled us to run you to earth at last."

"Such is fame, you see," I answered with a smile. "One should be humble when one reflects that the knowledge of one's address is confined to a butcher-boy. How do you do, Mrs. Merridew? I am sorry you should have had so much difficulty in discovering my poor abode."

I shook hands with the rest of the family, and, when I had done so, waited to be informed as to the reason of their visit.

"Now, look here," said the Squire, as he spoke, producing an enormous gold repeater from his pocket, which by sheer force of habit he held in his hand, though he never once looked at it during the time he was speaking. "I'll tell you what we're going to do. In the first place, you're to take us to the Academy to see your picture, which every one is talking about, and at the same time to act as showman and tell us who's who. After that you'll dine with us at the Langham, and go to the theatre afterwards. No, no, it's not a bit

of use your pretending you've got another engagement. We don't come up to town very often, but when
we do we enjoy ourselves, and—why, man alive! just
consider—I haven't seen you since last autumn, and
if you think I'm going to let you escape now, you're
very much mistaken. Such a thing is not to be thought
of, is it, mother?"

Thus appealed to, Mrs. Merridew was kind enough
to say that she hoped I would comply with her husband's wishes. The daughters murmured something,
which I have no doubt was intended to be a complimentary expression of their feelings, while the son
commenced a remark, failed to make himself intelligible,
and then lapsed into silence again.

Thus hemmed in, it remained for me to invent a valid
excuse, or to fall in with their plans. I effected a com-
promise, informed them that I should be very pleased
to accompany them to the Academy, but that it was
quite impossible I should dine with them afterwards, or
even visit the theatre in their company, having, as was
quite true, already accepted an invitation for that evening. Five minutes later the matter was settled, and we
were making our way towards Piccadilly and Burlington
House.

In the light of all that has happened since, I can only
regard my behaviour on that occasion with a contemp-
tuous sort of pity. The minutest details connected with
that afternoon's amusement are as clearly photographed
upon my brain as if it had only occurred but yesterday.
If I close my eyes for a moment, I can see, just as I saw
it then, the hawkers selling catalogues in the busy street
outside, the great courtyard with the lines of waiting

carriages, the fashionable crowd ascending and descending the stairs, and inside the rooms that surging mass of well-dressed humanity so characteristic of London and the Season. When we had fought our way to the vestibule, I was for doing the round of the rooms in the orthodox fashion. This, however, it appeared, was by no means to George Merridew's taste. He received my suggestion with appropriate scorn.

"Come, come, old fellow," he replied, "we're first going to see your picture. It was that which brought us here; and, as soon as I have told you what I think of it, the rest of the daubs may go hang as far as I am concerned."

Now, it is an indisputable fact that, whatever Nature may, or may not, have done for me, she has at least endowed me with an extremely sensitive disposition. My feelings, therefore, may be imagined when I tell you that my old friend spoke in a voice that was quite audible above the polite murmur of the crowd, and which must have penetrated to the farthest end of the room. Not content with that, he saluted me with a sounding smack on the back, bidding me, at the same time, consign my modesty to the winds, for everybody knew—by everybody, I presume he meant his neighbours in the country—that I was the rising man of the day, and would inevitably be elected President before I died. To avert this flood of idiotic compliment, and feeling myself growing hot from head to foot, I took him by the arm and conducted him hastily through the room towards that portion of the building where my picture was displayed.

Whether the work was good, bad, or indifferent, the

public at least paid me the compliment of bestowing
their attention upon it, and their behaviour on this
occasion was no exception to the rule. I hope I shall
not be considered more conceited than my fellows; at
the risk of it, however, I must confess to a feeling of
pride as I glanced, first at the crowd wedged in before
the rail, and then at the party by my side. George
Merridew's face alone was worth the trouble and time
I had spent upon the canvas. His eyes were opened to
their fullest extent; his lips were also parted, but no
sound came from them. Even the face of my formid-
able friend, the tennis champion, betrayed a measure of
interest that, in the light of her previous behaviour, was
more than flattering. For some moments we stood
together on the outskirts of the throng. Then those
who were directly in front moved away, and my friends
immediately stepped into the gap and took their places.
As there was no reason why I should follow their
example, I remained outside, watching the faces and
noting the different effects the picture produced upon
them.

I had not been alone more than a few seconds, however, before I became conscious of a curious sensation.
It was accompanied by a lowering of the pulse that was
quite perceptible, followed by an extraordinary feeling
of nausea. I battled against it in vain. The room and
its occupants began to swim before me. I tottered, and
at length, being unable any longer to support myself,
sat down on the seat behind me. When I looked up
again I could scarcely credit the evidence of my senses.
Approaching me from the crowd, leaning upon his
stick, just as I remembered him on the previous occa-

sion, and dressed in the same extraordinary fashion, was the old man whose personality had given me such a shock at the foot of Cleopatra's Needle. His face was as thin and as wrinkled as I had seen it then, and I also noticed that he wore the same indescribable look of cruelty and cunning that I remembered so well. One thing was quite plain, however profoundly I may have been affected by my proximity to this singular being, I was not the only one who came within the sphere of his influence. Indeed, it was strange to notice the manner in which the polite crowd drew away from him, and the different expressions upon their faces as they stepped aside in order to give him room to pass. Had he been a snake, they could scarcely have shown a more unanimous desire to withdraw from his neighbourhood. On this occasion he was evidently not alone. I gathered this from the fact that, as soon as he had emerged from the crowd, he paused as if to wait for a companion. A moment later a woman came to his side—a woman who carried herself like a daughter of the gods ; the most beautiful creature, I can safely assert, that I have ever seen either in this or any other country. If her companion's height was below the average, hers was at least several inches above it. But it was neither her stature, the exquisite symmetry of her figure, the beauty of her face, the luxuriance of her hair, nor the elegance of her attire that fascinated me. It was the expression I saw in her dark, lustrous eyes.

It is essential to my profession that I should be continually studying the human face, attempting to obtain from it some clue as to the character of the owner, and learning to read in it the workings of the mind within.

And what I read in this woman's face was a sorrow that
nothing could assuage, a hopelessness that was not
limited to this earth, but was fast passing into the
eternal.

Having once freed herself from the crowd, who, you
may be sure, turned and stared after her as if she were
some rare and beautiful animal, she took her place at
her companion's side, and they passed along the room
together, finally disappearing through the archway at
the farther end. A moment later the eldest of my
friend's daughters joined me. I had never credited her
with the possession of so much emotion as she displayed
at that moment.

"Mr. Forrester," she said, "I want you to tell me if
you have ever seen anything so awful as that old man's
face?"

"I think I can safely say that I never have," I
answered; and then, in an attempt to conceal the
emotion I was still feeling, added, "I wonder who he
can be?"

"I cannot imagine," she continued; "but I'm certain
of this, that I never want to see him again."

At that moment we were joined by the remainder of
the family.

"By Jove! Forrester," said the squire, but without his
usual heartiness, "I don't know what is coming to this
place. Did you see that little chap in the fur coat and
skull cap who came out of the crowd just now with that
fine-looking woman behind him? You may scarcely
credit it, but his face gave me quite a turn. I haven't
got over it yet."

"The girl with him was very beautiful," murmured

his wife gently; "but there was something about her face that struck me as being very sad. I should like to know what relationship she bears to him."

"His granddaughter, I should imagine," said Miss Merridew, who was still watching the entrance to the next room as if she expected them to return.

"Nonsense!" cried the squire impatiently. "His great-granddaughter, you mean. I'll stake my reputation that the old fellow is as old as Methuselah. What say you, Forrester?"

I cannot now remember what answer I returned. I only know that we presently found ourselves on the pavement of Piccadilly, saying good-bye, and expressing our thanks in an aimless sort of fashion for the pleasure we had derived from each other's society.

Having seen them safely on their way towards Regent Street, I strolled along Piccadilly in the direction of my studio, thinking as I went of that terrible old man whose personality had twice given me such a shock, and also of the beautiful woman, his companion. The effect they had produced upon me must have been something out of the common, for I soon discovered that I could think of nothing else. It was in vain I looked in at my club and attempted to engage in conversation with friends, or that, when I reached home, I threw myself into an easy-chair and endeavoured to interest myself in a book. Out of the centre of every page peered that wicked old face, with its pallid, wrinkled skin, and lack-lustre eyes. For upwards of an hour I wrestled with the feeling, but without success. The man's image was not conducive to peace of mind, and I knew very well that unless I found some distraction I should be dream-

ing of him at night. Accordingly I rose from my chair
and crossed the room to a table on which stood a large
Satsuma bowl, in which it was my custom to place the
invitations I received. That evening fortune favoured
me. I had the choice of four houses. Two I rejected
without a second thought ; between the others I scarcely
knew how to decide. Though I was not aware of it, my
evil destiny, for the second time that day, was standing
at my elbow, egging me on to ruin. It appeared I had
the choice of a dance in the Cromwell Road, another in
Belgrave Square ; private theatricals in Queen's Gate,
and a musical " at home " in Eaton Square. I did not
feel equal to dances or private theatricals, and, thinking
music would soothe my troubled mind, I decided for
Eaton Square, and in so doing brought about the
misery and downfall of my life.

Nine o'clock that evening, accordingly, found me
ascending the staircase of Medenham House, greeting
my hostess in the anteroom, and passing thence into the
great drawing-room beyond. There is not a more con-
spicuous power within the range of her hobby than her
ladyship, and at her house one hears all that is newest
and most likely to be famous in the musical world. Many
now celebrated *artistes* owe much of what they have
since achieved to the helping hand she held out to
them when they were struggling up the rugged hill of
Fame.

On entering the room I looked about me in the hope
of finding some one I knew, but for some moments was
unsuccessful. Then I espied, seated in a corner, almost
hidden by a magnificent palm, a man with whom I
possessed some slight acquaintance. I strolled towards

him, and after a few moments' conversation took my place at his side. He had himself achieved considerable success as an amateur violinist, and was a distant relative of our hostess.

"I suppose, like the rest of us, you have come to hear Lady Medenham's latest prodigy?" he said, after the usual polite nothings had been said.

"I am ashamed to confess I have heard nothing at all about him," I answered.

"*Her*, my dear sir," he replied, with a little laugh. "Our hostess says she is marvellous."

"A pianist?"

"Indeed, no! A violinist, and with, I believe, the additional advantage of being a very beautiful woman. Lady Medenham met her in Munich, and has raved about her ever since. Needless to say, she invited her to visit her as soon as she reached London."

What the connection could have been it is impossible to say, but by some occult reasoning I instantly associated this new wonder with the magnificent creature I had seen at Burlington House that afternoon.

"You have already made her acquaintance, I presume?" I said in a tone of mild curiosity.

"No such luck," he answered. "I have not been permitted that pleasure. From all accounts, however, she is really very wonderful. All the people I have met who have heard her declare they have never known anything like her playing. And the funniest part of it is, she is accompanied everywhere by a man who is as physically repulsive as she is beautiful."

"A little old man with an extraordinary complexion,

deep-set, horrible eyes, who wears a fur coat and a peculiar cap in the height of the Season, and looks at least a hundred years old ? "

" From all accounts you describe him exactly. Where did you meet him ? "

" I saw them both at the Academy this afternoon," I answered. " She is, as you say, very beautiful ; but she scarcely struck me as being English."

" She is not. She is Hungarian, I believe, but she has travelled a great deal and speaks English perfectly."

" And her companion—what nation has the honour of claiming him as her son ? "

" Ah, that I cannot tell you ! He is a mystery, for no one seems to know anything about him. Nor is it at all certain what relationship he bears to the woman. But see, here is Lord Medenham. The performance is evidently about to commence."

As he spoke there was a general turning of heads in the direction of the anteroom, and almost simultaneously my hostess entered the room, accompanied by the exquisite creature I had seen emerging from the crowd before my picture that afternoon. If she had looked beautiful then, she was doubly so now. Dressed to perfection, as on the previous occasion, she towered head and shoulders above Lady Medenham, who is generally considered tall for her sex, and carried herself with a more imperial grace than is boasted by any empress I have ever seen.

A few paces behind her followed the man who had been her companion that afternoon. On this occasion also he disdained the orthodox style of dress, wore a

black velvet coat, closely buttoned beneath his chin,
and upon his head a skull cap of the same material.
As on the previous occasions, he walked with a stick,
leaning upon it heavily like an old man of ninety.
Reaching that portion of the room in which the piano
was situated, he dropped into a chair, without waiting
for his hostess to seat herself, and, laying his head back,
closed his eyes, as if the exertion of walking had been
too much for him. A servant, who had followed close
behind, wrapped a heavy rug about his knees, and then
withdrew.   Meanwhile his beautiful companion stood
for a moment looking down at him, and then, with a
little gesture, the significance of which I could not then
interpret, accepted her hostess's invitation and seated
herself beside her.

The first item on the programme was a nocturne,
rendered by the composer, a famous pianist who at the
time was delighting all London. He seated himself at
the piano and began to play. I am afraid, however, I
spared but small attention for his performance. My
interest was centred on that huddled-up figure under
the fur rug and the beautiful creature at his side. Then
a change came, and once more I experienced the same
sensation of revulsion that had overwhelmed me twice
before. Again I felt sick and giddy ; once more a
clammy sweat broke out upon my forehead, and at last,
unable any longer to control myself, I rose from my seat.

" What on earth is the matter ? " inquired my friend,
who had been watching me. " Are you ill ? "

" I believe I'm going to faint," I replied. " I must
get into the air. But there is no necessity for you to
come. I shall be all right alone."

So saying, I signed him back to his seat, and, slipping quietly from the corner, made my way through the anteroom into the marble corridor beyond. Once there, I leant against the balustrading of the staircase and endeavoured to pull myself together. A groom of the chambers, who was passing at the time, seeing there was something amiss, approached and inquired if he could be of service.

" I am feeling a little faint," I replied. " The heat of the drawing-room was too much for me. If you can get me a little brandy, I think I shall be quite well in a few moments."

The man departed, and presently came back with the spirit I had asked for. With the return of my self-possession I endeavoured to arrive at an understanding of what had occasioned the attack. I was not subject to fainting-fits, but was, in every respect, as strong as the majority of my fellow-creatures.

" It's all nonsense," I said to myself, " to ascribe it to that old fellow's presence. How could such a thing affect me? At any rate, I'll try the experiment once more."

So saying, I returned to the drawing-room.

I was only just in time, for, as I entered, the lady who had hitherto been seated by her hostess's side, rose from her chair and moved towards the piano, and, as no one else stirred, it was plain that she was going to dispense with the services of an accompanist. Taking her violin from a table, she drew her bow gently across the strings, and, when she had tuned it, stood looking straight before her down the room. How beautiful she was at that moment I cannot hope to make you under-

stand. Then she began to play. What the work was
I did not then know, but I have since discovered that
it was her own. It opened with a movement in the
minor—low and infinitely sad. There was a note of
unappeasable yearning in it, a cry that might well have
been wrung from a heart that was breaking beneath the
weight of a deadly sin ; a weird, unearthly supplication
for mercy from a soul that was beyond redemption or
the reach of hope. None but a great musician could
have imagined such a theme, and then only under the
influence of a supreme despair. While it lasted her
audience sat spell-bound. There was scarcely one
among them who was not a lover of music, and many
were world-famous for their talent. This, however, was
such playing as none of us had ever heard before, or,
indeed, had even dreamed of. Then, by imperceptible
gradations, the music reached its height, and died slowly
down, growing fainter and fainter, until it expired in a
long-drawn sob. Absolute silence greeted its termination. Not a hand was raised ; not a word was uttered.
If proof were wanting of the effect she had produced,
it was to be found in this. The violinist bowed, a trifle
disdainfully, I thought, and, having placed her instrument on the table once more, returned to Lady Medenham's side. Then a young German singer and his
accompanist crossed the room and took their places at
the piano. The famous pianist, who had first played,
followed the singer, and, when he had resumed his seat,
the violinist rose and once more took up her instrument.

This time there was no pause. With an abruptness
that was startling, she burst into a wild, barbaric dance.
The notes sprang and leapt upon each other in joyous

"Absolute silence greeted its termination."

Pharos the Egyptian.]
[*Page 41*

confusion, creating an enthusiasm that was as instanta-
neous as it was remarkable. It was a tarantella of the
wildest description—nay, I should rather say, a dance
of Satyrs. The player's eyes flashed above the instrument, her lithe, exquisite figure rocked and swayed
beneath the spell of the emotion she was conjuring up.
Faster and faster her bow swept across the strings, and,
as before, though now for a very different reason, her
audience sat fascinated before her. The first work had
been the outcome of despair, this was the music of
unqualified happiness, of the peculiar joy of living—nay,
of the very essence and existence of life itself. Then
it ceased as suddenly as it had begun, and once more
she bowed, put down her violin, and approached her
hostess. The programme was at an end, and the enthusiastic audience clustered round to congratulate her.
For my own part I was curiously ill at ease. In a
vague sort of fashion I had appropriated her music to
myself, and now I resented the praise the fashionable
mob was showering upon her. Accordingly I drew
back a little, and made up my mind to get through the
crowd and slip quietly away. By the time I was able
to emerge from my corner, however, there was a movement at the end of the room, and it became evident
that the player and her companion were also about to
take their departure. Accompanied by Lord and Lady
Medenham, they approached the spot where I was
standing, endeavouring to reach the door. Had it been
possible I would have taken shelter behind my palm
again in order that my presence might not have been
observed. But it was too late. Lady Medenham had
caught my eye, and now stopped to speak.

"Mr. Forrester," she said, "we have been permitted a great treat to-night, have we not? You must let me introduce you to the Fräulein Valere de Vocxqal."

I bowed, and, despite the fact that, regarded in the light of her genius, such a thing was little better than an insult, followed the example of my betters, and murmured a complimentary allusion to her playing and the pleasure she had given us. She thanked me, all the time watching me with grave, attentive eyes, into which there had suddenly flashed a light that was destined to puzzle me for a long time, and the reason of which I could not understand. Then came the crucial moment, when Lady Medenham turned to me again, and said—

"Mr. Forrester, Monsieur Pharos has expressed a desire to be introduced to you. I told him yesterday I thought you would be here to-night. May I have the pleasure of making you acquainted with each other?"

Those cold, dead eyes fixed themselves steadily on mine, and, under their influence, I felt as if my brain were freezing.

"I am indeed honoured, sir," he said, "and I trust I may be permitted to express a hope of enlarging our acquaintance. I understand you are the painter of that very wonderful picture I saw at the Academy this afternoon? Allow me to offer you my congratulations upon it. It interested me more deeply than I can say, and on some future date I shall be grateful if you will let me talk to you upon the subject. The knowledge it displayed of the country and the period is remarkable in these days. May I ask how it was acquired?"

"My father was a famous Egyptologist," I replied.

" All that I know I learned from him. Are you also familiar with the country ? "

" There are few things and fewer countries with which I am not familiar," he replied somewhat conceitedly, but still watching me and speaking with the same peculiar gravity. " Some day I shall hope to offer you conclusive evidence on that point. In the meantime, the hour grows late. I thank you, and bid you farewell."

Then, with a bow, he passed on, and a moment later I too had quitted the house and was making my way homeward, trying to collect my impressions of the evening as I went.

CHAPTER III

To infer that my introduction that evening to the beautiful violinist and her diabolical companion, Monsieur Pharos, produced no effect upon me, would be as idle as it would be misleading. On leaving Medenham House I was conscious of a variety of sensations, among which were attraction for the woman, repugnance for the man, and curiosity as to the history and relationship of both. What was perhaps still more perplexing, considering the small, but none the less genuine, antagonism that existed between us, by the time I reached my own abode I had lost my first intense hatred of the man, and was beginning to look forward, with a degree of interest which a few hours before would have surprised me, to that next meeting which he had prophesied would so soon come to pass. Lightly as I proposed to myself to treat it, his extraordinary individuality must have produced a deeper effect upon me than I imagined, for, as in the afternoon, I soon discovered that, try to divert my thoughts from it how I would, I could not dispel his sinister image from my mind. Every detail of the evening's entertainment was vividly photographed upon my brain. Without even the formality of shutting my eyes, I could see the crowded room, the beautiful violinist standing, instrument in hand, beside the piano, and in the chair at her

fect her strange companion, huddled up beneath his
heavy rug.

By the time I reached home it was considerably past
midnight ; but I was not in the least tired, so, exchang-
ing my dress coat for an old velvet painting jacket, for
which I entertained a lasting regard, I lit a cigar and
began to promenade the room. It had been a fancy of
mine when I first took the studio, which, you must
understand, was of more than the usual size, to have
it decorated in the Egyptian fashion, and, after my
meeting with Pharos, this seemed to have a singular
appropriateness. It was as if the quaint images of the
gods, which decorated the walls, were watching me with
almost human interest, and even the gilded face upon
the mummy case, in the alcove at the farther end, wore
an expression that I had never noticed on it before. It
might have been saying, "Ah, my nineteenth-century
friend, your father stole me from the land of my birth,
and from the resting-place the gods decreed for me ;
but beware, for retribution is pursuing you, and is even
now close upon your heels."

Cigar in hand, I stopped in my walk and looked at it,
thinking as I did so of the country from which it had
hailed, and of the changes that had taken place in the
world during the time it had lain in its Theban tomb,
whence it had emerged in the middle of the nineteenth
century, with colouring as fresh, and detail as perfect, as
on the day when the hieroglyphics had first left the
artist's hand. It was an unusually fine specimen—one
of the most perfect, indeed, of its kind ever brought to
England, and, under the influence of the interest it now
inspired in me, I went to an ancient cabinet on the

other side of the room, and, opening a small drawer,
took from it a bulky pocket-book, once the property of
my father. He it was, as I have already said, who
had discovered the mummy in question, and it was
from him, at his death, in company with many other
Egyptian treasures, that I received it.

As I turned the yellow, time-stained pages in search
of the information I wanted, the clock of St. Jude's, in
the street behind, struck one, solemnly and deliberately,
as though it were conscious of the part it played in
the passage of time. To my surprise the reference was
more difficult to find than I had anticipated. Entries
there were in hundreds ; records of distances travelled,
of measurements taken, evidence as to the supposed
whereabouts of tombs, translations of hieroglyphics,
paintings, and inscriptions, memoranda of amounts paid
to Arab sheiks, details of stores and equipments, but for
some time no trace of the information I required. At
last, however, it struck me to look in the pocket contained in the cover of the book. My diligence was
immediately rewarded, for there, carefully folded and
hidden away, was the small square of parchment upon
which my father had written the name once borne by
the dead man, also a complete translation of the record
upon the *cartonnage* itself. According to the statement
here set forth, the coffin contained the mortal remains
of a certain Ptahmes, Chief of the King's Magicians—
an individual who flourished during the reign of Merenptah (Amenepthes of the Greeks, but better known to
the nineteenth century as the Pharaoh of the Exodus).
For all I knew to the contrary, my silent property
might have been one of that band of conjurors who

pitted their wits against Moses, and by so doing caused Pharaoh's heart to be hardened so that he would not let the Children go. Once more I stood looking at the stolid representation of a face before me, wondering what the life's history of the man within could have been, whether his success in life had equalled his ambition, or was commensurate with his merits, and whether in that age, so long since dead, his heart had ever been thrilled by thoughts of love.

While wrapped in this brown study, my hearing, which on that particular occasion was for some reason abnormally acute, caught the sound of a soft footfall on the polished boards at the farther end of the room. I wheeled sharply round, and a moment later almost fell back against the mummy-case under the influence of my surprise. How he had got there I could not tell, for I was certain I had locked the door behind me when I entered the house. It is sufficient, however, that, standing before me, scarcely a dozen feet away, breathing rather heavily as though he had been running, and with what struck me as a frightened look in his eyes, was no less a person than Monsieur Pharos, the man I had met at the foot of Cleopatra's Needle some weeks before, at the Academy that afternoon, and at Medenham House only a couple of hours since. Upwards of a minute elapsed before I could find sufficient voice to question him as to the reason of his presence in my room.

"My dear Mr. Forrester," he said in a conciliatory tone, "while offering you ten thousand apologies for my intrusion, I must explain that it is quite by accident I am here. On reaching home this evening, I pined for a breath of fresh air. Accordingly I went for a stroll, lost my way, eventually found myself in this street, where, seeing an open door, I took the liberty of entering for the purpose of inquiring which turning I should follow to reach my hotel. It was not until you turned round that I realized my good fortune in having chanced upon a friend. It is plain, however, that my presence is not so welcome as I could have desired."

From the way he spoke, I gathered that for some purpose of his own he had taken, or was pretending to take, offence at my reception of him. Knowing, therefore, that if I desired to see anything further of his beautiful companion, an idea which I will confess had more than once occurred to me, I must exert myself to conciliate him, I hastened to apologise for the welcome I had given him, explaining that any momentary hesitation I might have shown was due more to my surprise than to any intended discourtesy towards himself.

"In that case let us say no more about it," he answered politely, but with the same expression of cunning malignity on his face to which I have referred elsewhere. "You were quite within your rights, for I should have remembered that in England an impromptu visit at one in the morning, on the part of an acquaintance of a few hours' standing, is scarcely likely to be well received."

"If you will carry your memory back a few weeks," I said, as I wheeled a chair up for him, "you will remember that our acquaintance is not of such a recent date."

"I am rejoiced to hear it," he replied, with a sharp

glance at me as he seated himself. "Nevertheless, I must confess that I fail for the moment to remember where I had the pleasure of meeting you on that occasion. It is not a complimentary admission, I will confess ; but, as you know, Age is proverbially forgetful, and my memory is far from being what it once was."

Could the man be pretending, or had the incident really escaped his memory? It was just possible, of course, that on that occasion my face had failed to impress itself upon his recollection ; but after the hard things I had said to him, I had to confess it seemed unlikely. Then the remembrance of the drowning man, his piteous cry for help, and the other's demoniacal conduct on the steps returned upon me, and I resolved to show no mercy.

"The occasion to which I refer, Monsieur Pharos," I said, standing opposite him and speaking with a sternness that in the light of all that has transpired since seems almost ludicrous, "was an evening towards the end of March—a cold, wet night when you stood upon the steps below Cleopatra's Needle, and not only refused help, but, in a most inhuman fashion, laughed at a drowning man."

I half expected that he would offer a vehement denial, or would at least put forward a plea of forgetfulness. To my surprise, however, he did neither.

"I remember the incident perfectly," he answered, with the most complete composure. "At the same time, I must say you wrong me when you declare I laughed—on my word, you do! Let us suppose, however, that I *did* do so ; and where would be the harm ?

The man desired death; his own action confessed it, otherwise how came he there? It was proved at the inquest that he had repeatedly declared himself weary of life. He was starving; he was without hope. Had he lived over that night, death, under any circumstances, would only have been a matter of a few days with him. Would you therefore have had me, knowing all this, prolong such an existence? In the name of that humanity to which you referred just now, I ask you the question. You say I laughed. Would you have had me weep?"

"A specious argument," I replied; "but I own to you frankly I considered the incident a detestable one."

"There I will meet you most willingly," he continued. "From your point of view it certainly *was*. From mine —well, as I said just now, I confess I view it differently. However, I give you my word that in this instance your pity is undeserved. The man was a contemptible scoundrel in every way. He came of respectable stock, was reared under the happiest auspices. Had he chosen, he might have been anything in his own rank of life; but he would not choose. At fifteen he robbed his father's till to indulge in debauchery, and had broken his parents' hearts before he was five-and-twenty. He married a girl as good as he was bad, and as a result starved not only himself but his wife and children. Though employment was offered him, he repeatedly refused it, not from any inability to work, but from sheer love of idleness and distaste of labour. He had not sufficient wit, courage, or energy to become a criminal; but throughout his life, wherever he went, and upon all with whom he came in contact, he brought misery and disgrace. Eventually he reached the end of his tether, and was cast off by every one. The result you know."

The fluency and gusto with which he related these sordid details amazed, while it disconcerted me. I inquired how, since by his own confession he had been such a short time in London, he had become cognizant of the man's history. He hesitated before replying.

"Have I not told you once before to-night," he said, "that there are very few things in this world hidden from my knowledge? I could tell you circumstances in your own life that you flatter yourself are known to no one. But do not let us talk of such things now. When I entered the room you were reading a paper. You hold it in your hand at this moment."

"It is a translation, by my father, of the inscription upon the mummy case over yonder," I replied, with an eagerness to change the subject for which I can scarcely account. "At his death many of his Egyptian treasures came into my possession, this among them. For some reason or another I had never read the translation until to-night. I suppose it must have been my meeting with you that put the idea into my head."

"I am interested in such matters, as you know. May I, therefore, be permitted to look at it?"

With a parade of indifference that I could easily see was assumed, Pharos had extended his withered old hand and taken it from me before I realized what he was doing. Having obtained it, he leaned back in his chair, staring at the paper as if he could not remove his eyes from it. For some moments not a word passed

his lips. Then, muttering something to himself in a
language I did not recognise, he sprang to his feet.
The quickness of the action was so different to his
usual enfeebled movements that I did not fail to notice it.

"The mummy!" he cried. "Show me the mummy!"

Before I could answer or comply with his request, he
had discovered it for himself, had crossed to it and was
devouring it with his eyes.

Upwards of three minutes must have elapsed before
he turned to me again. When he did so, I scarcely
recognised the man. So distorted was his countenance
that I instinctively recoiled from him in horror.

"Thy father, was it, wretched man," he cried, shaking
his skeleton fist at me, while his body trembled like a
leaf under the whirlwind of his passion, "who stole this
body from its resting-place? Thy father, was it, who
broke the seals the gods had placed upon the tombs of
those who were their servants? If that be so, then may
the punishment decreed against those guilty of the sin
of sacrilege be visited on thee and thine for evermore."
Then, turning to the mummy, he continued, as if to
himself, "Oh, mighty Egypt! hast thou fallen so far
from thy high estate that even the bodies of thy kings
and priests may no longer rest within their tombs, but
are ravished from thee to be gaped at in alien lands.
But, by Osiris, a time of punishment is coming. It is
decreed, and none shall stay the sword!"

If I had been surprised at the excitement he had
shown on reading the paper, it was nothing to the
astonishment I felt now. For the first time since I had
known him, a suspicion of his sanity crossed my mind,
and my first inclination was to draw away from him.

"I instinctively recoiled from him in horror."

Then the fit, as I deemed it, passed, and his expression changed entirely. He uttered a queer little laugh.

"Once more I must crave your forgiveness, Mr. Forrester," he said, as he sank exhausted into a chair. "Believe me, I had not the least intention of offending you. Your father was, I know, an ardent Egyptologist, one of that intrepid band who penetrated to every corner of our sacred land, digging, delving, and bringing to light such tombs, temples, and monuments as have for centuries lain hidden from the sight of man. For my own part, as you may have gathered from my tirade just now, my sympathies do not lie in that direction. I am one who reverences the past, and would fain have others do so."

"At the same time, I scarcely see that that justifies such language towards myself as you used a few moments since," I replied, with a fair amount of warmth, which I think it will be conceded I had every right to feel.

"It does not justify it in the least," he answered, with ready condescension. "The only way I can hope to do so is on the plea of the exuberance of my emotion. My dear Mr. Forrester, I beg you will not misunderstand me. I would not quarrel with you for the wealth of England. Though you are not aware of it, there is a bond between us that is stronger than chains of steel. You are required for a certain work, and for that reason alone I dare not offend you or excite your anger, even if I otherwise desired to do so. In this matter I am not my own master."

"A bond between us? A work for which I am required? I am afraid I do not understand you."

"And it is not in my power to enlighten you. Remain assured of this, however : when the time is ripe, you will be informed."

As he said this the same light that I have described before came into his eyes, causing them to shine as brightly as two stars. I did not like it. To use a fishing simile, it made me think of the gleam that comes into the eyes of a hungry pike as he darts towards his helpless prey. Taking this in conjunction with the extraordinary language he had used towards me, I felt more than ever convinced of his insanity. The thought was by no means a cheerful one. I had got myself into a nice position. Here I was, alone with a dangerous lunatic, in the middle of the night, and not a soul within call. How I was to rid myself of him I could not see. I felt, therefore, that I must humour him until I could hit upon a scheme. I accordingly tried to frame a conciliatory speech, but before I could do so he had turned to me again.

"Your thoughts are easily read," he began, with a repetition of that queer little laugh which I have described before ; and as he uttered it he leaned a little closer to me till I was sick and faint with the horror of his presence. "You think me mad, and it will take more than my assurance to make you believe that I am not. How slight is your knowledge of me ! But there, let us put that aside for to-night ! There is something of much greater importance to be arranged between us. In the first place, it is necessary, both for your sake—your safety, if you like—and for mine, that yonder mummy should pass into my possession."

"Impossible !" I answered. "I could not dream of

such a thing! It was one of my poor father's greatest treasures, and for that reason alone no consideration would induce me to part with it. Besides, despite your assertion that it is for our mutual safety, I cannot see by what right you ask such a favour of me."

" If you only knew how important it is," he repeated, "that that particular mummy should become my property, you would not know a single minute's peace until you had seen the last of it. You may not believe me when I say that I have been searching for it without intermission for nearly fifteen years, and it was only yesterday I learnt you were the owner of it."

If I had not had sufficient proof already, here was enough to convince me of his madness. Until that evening he had no notion of my identity, much less of the things I possessed. How, therefore, could he have become aware that I was the owner of the remains of Ptahmes, the King's Magician? Under the influence of the momentary irritation caused by his persistence, my intention of humouring him quite slipped my memory, and I answered sharply that it was no use his bothering me further about the matter, as I had made up my mind and was not to be moved from it.

He took my refusal with apparent coolness ; but the light which again came into his eyes warned me, before it was too late, not to rely too much upon this. I knew that in his heart he was raging against me, and that at any moment his passion might take active shape.

"You must excuse my saying so, Monsieur Pharos," I said, rising from my chair and moving towards the door, "but I think it would perhaps be better for both of us to terminate this most unpleasant interview. It

is getting late, and I am tired. With your permission, I
will open the door for you."

Seeing that I was determined he should go, and
realizing, I suppose, that it was no use his staying
longer, he also rose, and a more evil-looking figure than
he presented as he did so Victor Hugo himself could
scarcely have imagined. The light of the quaint old
Venetian hanging-lamp in the middle of the room fell
full and fair upon his face, showing me the deep-set
gleaming eyes, the wrinkled, nut-cracker face, and the
extraordinary development of shoulder to which I have
already directed attention. Old man as he was, a
braver man than myself might have been excused had
he declined the task of tackling him, and I had the
additional spur of knowing that if he got the better of
me he would show no mercy. For this reason alone I
watched his every movement.

"Come, come, my foolish young friend," he said at
length, "in spite of my warning, here we are at a dead-
lock again ! You really must not take things so
seriously. Had I had any idea that you were so
determined not to let me have the thing I want, I would
not have dreamed of asking for it. It was for your own
good as well as mine that I did so. Now, since you
desire to turn me out, I will not force my presence
upon you. But let us part friends."

As he said this he advanced towards me with extended hand, leaning heavily upon his stick, according
to his custom, and to all intents and purposes as
pathetic an example of senile decrepitude as a man
could wish to see. If he were going off like this, I
flattered myself, I was escaping from my horrible

predicament in an easier manner than I had expected. However, I was fully determined in my own heart, if I could but once get him on the other side of the street door, that no earthly consideration should induce me ever to admit him to my dwelling again. His hand was deathly cold—so cold, in fact, that even in my excitement I could not help noticing it. I had scarcely done so, however, before a tremor ran through his figure, and with a guttural noise that scarcely could be described as a cry, he dropped my hand and sprang forward at my throat.

If I live to the age of a hundred, I shall not forget the absolute, the unspeakable, the indescribable terror of that moment. Till then I had never regarded myself in the light of a coward ; on the contrary, I had on several occasions had good reason to congratulate myself upon what is popularly termed my "strength of nerve." Now, however, it was all different. Possibly the feeling of repulsion, I might almost say of fear, I had hitherto entertained for him had something to do with it. It may have been the mesmeric power, which I afterwards had good reason to know he possessed, that did it. At any rate, from the moment he pounced upon me I found myself incapable of resistance. It was as if all my will power were being slowly extracted from me by the contact of those skeleton fingers which, when they had once touched my flesh, seemed to lose their icy coldness, and to burn like bars of red-hot iron. In a dim and misty fashion, somewhat as one sees people across a street in a fog, I was conscious of the devilish ferocity of the face that was looking into mine. Then a strange feeling of numbness took possession of me, an entire lack of interest in everything, even in life itself. Gradually and easily I sank into the chair behind me, the room swam before my eyes, an intense craving for sleep overcame me, and little by little, still without any attempt at resistance, my head fell back and I lost consciousness.

CHAPTER IV

WHEN I came to myself again it was already morning. In the small square behind the studio the birds were discussing the prospects of breakfast, though as yet that earliest of all birds, the milkman, had not begun to make his presence known in the streets. Of all the hours of the day there is not one, to my thinking, so lonely and so full of dreariness as that which immediately precedes and ushers in the dawn; while, of all the experiences of our human life, there is, perhaps, not one more unpleasant than to awake from sleep at such an hour to find that one has passed the entire night in one's clothes and seated in a most uncomfortable armchair. That was my lot in this particular instance. On opening my eyes, I looked around me with a puzzled air. For the life of me I could not understand why I was not in my bed. It was the first time I had ever gone to sleep in my chair, and the idea disquieted me strangely. I studied the room, but, to all intents and purposes, everything there was just the same as when I had closed my eyes. I only was changed. My brain was as heavy as lead, and, though

I did my best to recall the events of the previous
evening, I found that, while I could recollect the "at
home" at Medenham House, and my return to my
studio afterwards, I could remember nothing that followed later. I was still pursuing this train of thought
when I became aware of a loud knocking at the street
door. I immediately hastened to it and drew the
bolts. My surprise may be imagined on discovering
an inspector of police standing upon the threshold, with
a constable behind him.

"Mr. Forrester, I believe?" he began; and as soon
as I had nodded an affirmative, continued, "You must
excuse my disturbing you, sir, at this early hour, but the
reason is imperative. I should be glad if you would
permit me the honour of five minutes' conversation with
you alone."

"With pleasure," I answered, and immediately invited
him to enter.

Having shut the door behind him, I led the way to
the studio, where I signed him to a chair, taking up a
position myself on the hearthrug before him. The constable remained in the passage outside.

"It is, as you say, rather an early hour for a call,"
I remarked, making a mental note as I spoke of the
man's character as I read it in his large, honest eyes,
well-shaped nose, and square, determined-looking chin.
"What can I do for you?"

"I believe you are in a position to furnish me with
some important information," he replied. "A diabolical
murder was committed at the old curiosity shop at the
corner of the next street, either late last night or during
the early hours of this morning, most probably between

midnight and one o'clock. It is altogether a most remarkable affair, and, from the evidence we have before
us, though no cries were heard, the struggle must have
been a desperate one. From the fact that the front
door was still locked and bolted when we forced our
way in, it is plain that the murderer must have effected
his escape by the back. Indeed, a man *was* seen entering the alley behind the house between one and two
o'clock, though this circumstance gave rise to no suspicion at the time. The witness who saw him reports
that he came along on this side of the street, in the
shadow, and, though he is not at all certain on this
point, believes that he entered one of the houses here-
abouts. That on your right is empty, and the doors
and windows are securely fastened. He could not,
therefore, have gone in there. That on the left is a
boarding-house. I have called upon the landlady, who
asserts most positively that her front door was not
opened to any one after ten o'clock last night. She
informs me, however, that a light was burning in your
studio all night, and I see for myself that you have not
been to bed. May I ask, therefore, if you saw anything
of such a man, or whether you can furnish me with
such particulars as will be likely to help us in our search
for him ? "

Like lightning, while he was talking, the memory of
all that had happened that morning, and the visit
Pharos had paid me, flashed into my mind. As it did
so, I glanced involuntarily towards that part of the room
where the mummy had hitherto stood. To my amazement—I might almost say to my consternation—it was
no longer there. What had become of it ? Could

Pharos, after disposing of me as he had done, have stolen it and transported it away? It seemed impossible, and yet I had the best of evidence before me that it was no longer there. And then another question : Had Pharos had any connection with the murder? The time at which it was supposed to have been committed, between midnight and one o'clock, was precisely that at which he had made his appearance before me. And yet what reason had I, but my own terrible suspicions, to lead me to the conclusion that he was the author of this fiendish bit of work? I saw, however, that my continued silence was impressing my companion unfavourably.

"Come, sir," he said, this time a little more sharply than before ; "I must remind you that my time is valuable. Am I to understand that you are in a position to help me, or not?"

God knows, if I had been my own master I should have loosed my tongue instantly and revealed all I knew. I should have told him under what terrible circumstances I had met Pharos on the Embankment that wet night towards the end of March, and have commented on his inhuman conduct on that occasion. I should have informed him of the appearance he had made in my studio early this morning, not only with a frightened look in his eyes, but breathing heavily as if he had been running, though such a thing would have seemed an impossibility in a man of his years. Then I should have gone on to tell how he had attempted to induce me to part with something upon which I placed considerable value, and, being disappointed, had hypnotised me and made off with the article in question. All this, as I say, I should have narrated had I been my own master. But God knows I was not. An irresistible force was at work within me, compelling me, even against my will, to screen him, and to tell the first deliberate lie to which I had ever given utterance in my life.

It was a poor excuse to offer, and I am aware that a world so censorious as our own will in all probability not believe this statement, but upon my hopes of forgiveness at the Last Great Day, at that dread moment when the sins of all men shall be judged and punishment awarded, I declare it to be true in every single particular : and, what is more, I further say that even if my life depended on it I could not have done otherwise.

Though it has taken some time to place these thoughts on paper, the interval that elapsed between the inspector's last question and my answer, which seemed to me so halting and suspicious, to the effect that I had neither seen nor heard anything of the man he wanted, was scarcely more than a few seconds.

Having received my assurance, the officer apologised for troubling me, and withdrew, and I was left alone with my thoughts. Deep down in my heart there was the desire to hasten after him and to tell him that not only had I lied to him, but that it was possible for me to make amends by putting him on the track of the man who, I felt morally certain, was the criminal. The wish, however, was scarcely born before it was dragged down and stifled by that same irresistible force I have described a few lines since. It seemed to me I was bound hand and foot, powerless to help myself, and incapable of aught save to carry out the will of the remorseless being into whose power I had fallen so completely. But had I really so fallen? Could it be possible that such power was permitted to a human being? No, no—a thousand times no! If he had that influence he must be an agent of the Evil One, whose mission it was to draw to perdition the souls of helpless men. Filled with shame, I sank into a chair and covered my face with my hands, as if by so doing I could shut out the horrible thoughts that filled my brain. Was it true, I asked myself, in the bitterest self-humiliation, that I, who had always regarded a liar as the most despicable of men, had sunk so low as to become one myself? God help me! God pity me! Of all the bitter hours my life has known, I think that moment was the worst.

For some time after the inspector had taken his departure I sat, as I have said, my face covered with my hands, trying to think coherently. Twenty-four hours before I had been one of the happiest men in England. Nothing had troubled me. I had lived *for* my art and *in* my art, and I believe I can confidently say that I had not an enemy in the world. Now, in a single hour, my whole life was changed. I had been drawn into the toils of a fiend in human shape, and I was paying the awful penalty.

Hour after hour went by. My servant arrived, and presently brought in my breakfast, but I put it aside; I had too much upon my mind to eat. It was in vain I tried to force myself. My food stuck in my throat and defied me. All the time I was oppressed by the diabolical picture of that murder. The shop in which it had occurred was one with which I was familiar. In my mind's eye I saw the whole scene as clearly as if I had been present at the time. I saw the shop, filled to overflowing with *bric-à-brac*, the light of the single gas lamp reflected in hundreds of varieties of brass and pottery work. At a desk in the corner sat the dealer himself, and before him, holding him in earnest conversation, the extraordinary figure of Pharos the Assassin. How he came to be there at such an hour I could not tell, but from what I knew of him I was convinced it was with no good purpose. I could imagine how off his guard and totally unprepared for attack the other would be; and, even if he had entertained any suspicions, it is extremely doubtful whether he would have credited this deformed atom with the possession, either of such malignity or of such giant strength. Then that same cruel light that had exercised such an influence upon me began to glisten in the murderer's eyes. Little by little he moved his right hand behind him, until it touched an Oriental dagger lying on a table beside which he stood. Then, with that cat-like spring which I had good reason to remember, he leapt upon his opponent and seized him by the throat, driving the blade deep in below the shoulder. His victim, paralysed with surprise, at first offered no resistance. Then, with the instinct of self-preservation, he began to struggle with his devilish opponent, only to discover the strength that seemingly attenuated form possessed. Little by little his power departed from him, and at last, with a crash, he fell back upon the floor. I pictured Pharos stooping over him, to see if he were dead, chuckling with delight at the success he had achieved. Having convinced himself on this head, he abstracted a key from the dead man's pocket, and approached a safe built into the wall. The handle turned, and the door swung open. A moment later he had taken a ring set with a scarabæus from a drawer and dropped it into his pocket. After that he paused while he considered in which direction it would be safest for him to make his escape. A policeman's step sounded on the pavement outside, and as he heard it he looked up, and his thin lips drew back, showing the wolfish teeth behind. His horrible cunning pointed out to him the danger he would incur in leaving by the front. Accordingly he made his way through the sitting-room behind the shop, and passed out by the gate in the yard beyond. A few seconds later he was in my presence, but whether by accident or design was more than I could say.

So vivid was the picture I had conjured up that I could not help believing it must be something more than mere conjecture on my part. If so, what course should I pursue? I had been robbed. I had given a murderer shelter at the very moment when he stood most in need of it, and when the law was close upon his heels I had pledged my word for his innocence and perjured myself to ensure his salvation. His presence had been repulsive to me ever since I had first set eyes on him. I hated the man as I had hitherto deemed it impossible I could hate any one. Yet, despite all this, by some power—how real I cannot expect any one to believe—he was compelling me to shield him and be-have towards him as if he had been my brother, or at least my dearest friend. I can feel the shame of that moment even now, the agonizing knowledge of the deep gulf that separated me from the man I was yesterday, or even an hour before.

I rose from the table, leaving my breakfast untouched, and stood at the window looking out upon the dismal square beyond. The sunshine of the earlier morning had given place to a cloudy sky, and, as I watched, a heavy shower began to fall. It was as if Nature were weeping tears of shame to see a Child of Man brought so low. I went to the place where, until a few hours before, the mummy had stood—that wretched mummy which had been the cause of all the trouble. As I had good reason to know, it weighed a considerable amount, more, indeed, than I should have imagined an old man like Pharos could have lifted, much less carried. I examined the floor to see if the case had been dragged over it, but highly polished as the boards were, I could detect no sign of such a thing. The wainscoting of the hall next received my attention, but with a similar result. And it was at this juncture that another curious point in the evening's story struck me. When I had admitted the inspector of police, I had unlocked and unchained the door. I was also the sole occupant of the building. How, therefore, had Pharos conveyed his burden outside, and locked, chained, and bolted the door behind him? Under the influence of this new discovery I returned with all speed to the studio. Perhaps he had not gone out by the front door at all, but had made his escape by the windows at the back. These I carefully examined, only to find them safely bolted as usual. The riddle was beyond me. I had to confess myself beaten. Was it possible I could have dreamed the whole thing? Had I fallen asleep in my chair and imagined a meeting with Pharos which had really never taken place? Oh, if only it could be true, what a difference it would make in my happiness! And yet, staring me in the face, was the damning evidence that the mummy was gone. When I rose from my chair my mind was made up. I would seek Pharos out, accuse him not only of the theft, but of the murder, and make him understand, with all the earnestness of which I was master, that justice should be done, and that I would no longer shield him from the consequences of his villainy. It was only then that I remembered that I had no knowledge of the man's whereabouts. I considered for a moment how I could best overcome this difficulty. Lady Medenham was, of course, the one person of all others to help me. Since she had invited the man to her house, it was almost certain that she could furnish me with his address. I would go to her without further waste of time. Accordingly I made the necessary changes in my toilet and left the studio. The rain had ceased, and the streets were once more full of sunshine. It was a pleasant morning for walking, but so urgent did my business seem that I felt I could not even spare the time for exercise. Hailing a hansom, I bade the man drive me with all possible speed to Eaton Square. To my delight Lady Medenham was at home, and I was shown forthwith to her boudoir. A few moments elapsed before she joined me there, and then her first remark was one of astonishment.

"Why, Mr. Forrester, what is the matter with you?" she cried. "I have never seen you look so ill."

"It is nothing," I answered, with a forced laugh. "I

have had some bad news this morning, and it has upset me. Lady Medenham, I have come to beg a favour at your hands."

" If it is within my power, you know it is already granted," she said kindly. " Won't you sit down and tell me what it is ? "

" I want you to furnish me with the address of that singular old gentleman who was at your ' at home ' last evening," I replied, as I seated myself opposite her.

" London would say that there were many singular old gentlemen at my ' at home,' " she answered with a smile ; " but my instinct tells me you mean Monsieur Pharos."

" That, I believe, is his name," I said ; and then, as if to excuse the question, I added, " He is, as I think you heard him say, an ardent Egyptologist."

" I do not know anything about his attainments in that direction," Lady Medenham replied, " but he is certainly a most extraordinary person. Were it not for his beautiful ward, whose case I must confess excites my pity, I should not care if I never saw him again."

" She is his ward, then ? " I said, with an eagerness that I could see was not lost upon my companion. " I had made up my mind she was his grand-daughter."

" Indeed, no," Lady Medenham replied. " The poor girl's story is a very strange and sad one. Her father was a Hungarian noble, a brilliant man in his way, I believe, but a confirmed spendthrift. Her mother died when she was but six years old. From a very early age she gave signs of possessing extraordinary musical talent, and this her father, perhaps with some strange prevision of the future, fostered with every care. When she was barely fifteen he was killed in a duel. It was then discovered that his money was exhausted, and that the home was mortgaged beyond all redemption to the Jews. Thus the daughter, now without relations or friends of any sort or description, was thrown upon the world to sink or swim just as Fate should decree. For any girl the position would have been sufficiently unhappy, but for her, who had seen nothing of life, and who was of an extremely sensitive disposition, it was well-nigh insupportable. What her existence must have been like for the next five years one scarcely likes to think. But it served its purpose. With a bravery that excites one's admiration she supported herself almost entirely by her music; gaining in breadth, power, and knowledge of technique with every year. Then—where, or in what manner I have never been able to discover, for she is peculiarly sensitive upon this point—she became acquainted with the old gentleman you saw last night, Monsieur Pharos. He was rich, eccentric, and perhaps what most attracted her, passionately fond of music. His extreme age obviated any scandal, even had there been any one to raise it, so that when he proposed to adopt the friendless but beautiful girl, and to enable her to perfect her musical education under the best masters, no one came forward to protest against it. She has, I believe, been with him upwards of seven years now."

I shuddered when I heard this. Knowing what I did of Pharos, I could not find it in my heart to credit him with the possession of so much kindly feeling. But if it were not so, what could be the bond between them?

"All you tell me is extremely interesting," I remarked, "and only adds to my desire to see the old gentleman once more. If you could let me have his address, I should be more grateful than I can say."

"I am very much afraid it is not in my power," she replied. "It is one of the least of Monsieur Pharos's many peculiarities, to take extraordinary precautions to prevent his whereabouts becoming known; but stay, I think I can tell you of some one who may be of more service to you. You know Sir George Legrath, do you not?"

"The Director of the Egyptian Museum?" I said. "Yes, I know him very well indeed. He was an old friend of my father's."

"To be sure he was," she answered. "Well then, go and see him. I think it is probable that he may be able to assist you. Monsieur Pharos is an acquaintance of his, and it was to Sir George's care that I sent the invitation to my 'at home' last night."

"I cannot thank you enough for your kindness, Lady Medenham," I replied, as I rose from my chair. "I will go and see Sir George at once."

"And I hope you may be successful. If I can help you in any other way, be sure I will do so. But before you go, Mr. Forrester, let me give you another piece of advice. You should really consult a doctor without delay. I do not like your appearance at all. We shall hear of your being seriously ill if you do not take more care of yourself."

I laughed uneasily. In my own heart I knew my ailment was not of the body but of the mind, and until my suspicions were set at rest, it was beyond the reach of any doctor's science to do me good. Once more I thanked Lady Medenham for her kindness, and then left her and made my way back to the cab.

"To the Egyptian Museum," I cried to the driver, as I took my seat in the vehicle, "and as quickly as you can go!"

The man whipped up his horse, and in less than ten minutes from the time the butler closed the front door upon me at Medenham House I was entering the stately portico of the world-famous Museum. For some years I had been a constant visitor there, and as a result my face was well known to the majority of the officials. I inquired from one, whom I met in the vestibule, whether I should find Sir George in his office.

"I am not quite certain, sir," the man replied. "It's only just gone half-past ten, and unless there is something important doing, we don't often see him much before a quarter to eleven. However, if you will be kind enough, sir, to step this way, I'll very soon find out whether he has come."

So saying, he led me along the corridor, past huge monuments and blocks of statuary, to a smaller passage on the extreme left of the building. At the farther end of this was a door, upon which he knocked. No answer rewarded him.

"I am very much afraid, sir, he has not arrived," remarked the man, "but perhaps you will be good enough to step inside and take a seat. I feel sure he won't be very long."

"In that case I think I will do so," I replied, and accordingly I was ushered into what is perhaps the most characteristic office in London. Having found the morning paper and with unconscious irony placed it before me, the man withdrew, closing the door behind him.

I have said that the room in which I was now seated was characteristic of the man who occupied it. Sir George Legrath is, as every one knows, the most competent authority the world possesses at the present day on the subject of Ancient Egypt. He had graduated under my own poor father, and, if only for this reason, we had always been the closest friends. It follows as a natural sequence that the walls of the room should be covered from ceiling to floor with paintings, engravings, specimens of papyrus, and the various odds and ends accumulated in an Egyptologist's career. He had also the reputation of being one of the best-dressed men in London, and was at all times careful to a degree of his appearance. This accounted for the velvet office-coat, a sleeve of which I could just see peeping out from behind a curtain in the corner. Kindly of heart and the possessor of a comfortable income, it is certain that but few of those in need who applied to him did so in vain; hence the pile of begging letters from charitable institutions and private individuals that invariably greeted his arrival at his office. I had not been waiting more than five minutes before I heard an active step upon the stone flagging of the passage outside. The handle of the door was sharply turned, and the man for whom I was waiting entered the room.

"My dear Cyril," he cried, advancing towards me with outstretched hand, "this is indeed a pleasure! It is now some weeks since I last saw you, but, on the other hand, I have heard of you. The fame of your picture is in every one's mouth."

"Every one is very kind," I replied, "but I am afraid in this instance the public says rather more than it means."

"Not a bit of it," answered my friend. "That reminds me, however, that there is one point in the picture about which I want to talk to you."

"At any other time I shall be delighted," I replied, "but to-day, Sir George, I have something else to say to you. I have come to you because I am very much worried."

"Now that I come to look at you I can see you are not very bright," he said. "But what is this worry? Tell me about it, for you know if I can help you I shall be only too glad to do so."

"I have come to seek your advice in a rather strange matter," I replied, "and before I begin I must ask that everything I say shall remain in the strictest confidence between us."

"I will give you that promise willingly," he said, "and I think you know me well enough to feel certain I shall keep it. Now let me hear your troubles."

"In the first place, I want you to tell me all you know of an extraordinary individual who has been seen a good deal in London society of late. I refer to a man named Pharos."

While I had been speaking, Sir George had seated himself in the chair before his writing-table. On hearing my question, however, he sprang to his feet with an exclamation that was as startling as it was unexpected. It did not exactly indicate surprise, nor did it express annoyance or curiosity ; yet it seemed to partake of all three. It was his face, however, which betrayed the greatest change. A moment before it had exhibited all the ruddiness of perfect health, now it was ashen pale.

"Pharos?" he cried. Then, recovering his composure a little, he added, "My dear Forrester, what can you possibly want with him?"

"I want to know all you can tell me about him," I replied gravely. "It is the greatest favour I have ever asked you, and I hope you will not disappoint me."

For some moments he paced the room as if in anxious thought. Then he returned to his seat at the writing-table. The long hand of the clock upon the mantelpiece had made a perceptible movement when he spoke again. So changed was his voice then that I scarcely recognised it.

"Cyril," he said, "you have asked me a question to which I can return you but one answer, and that is—may God help you if you have fallen into that man's power. What he has done or how he has treated you, I do not know, but I tell you this, that he is as cruel and as remorseless as Satan himself. You are my friend, and I tell you I would far rather see you dead than in his clutches. I do not fear many men, but Pharos the Egyptian is to me an incarnate terror."

"You say Pharos the Egyptian. What do you mean by that?"

"What I say. The man is an Egyptian, and claims, I believe, to be able to trace his descent back at least three thousand years."

"And you know no more of him?"

As I put this question I looked at Sir George's hand, which rested on his blotting-pad, and noticed that it was shaking as if with the palsy.

Once more a pause ensued.

"What I know must remain shut up in my own brain," he answered slowly, and as if he were weighing every word before he uttered it; "and it will go down to my grave with me. Dear lad, fond as I am of you, you must not ask any more of me, for I cannot satisfy your curiosity."

"But, Sir George, I assure you, with all the earnestness at my command, that this is a matter of life and death to me," I replied. "You can have no notion what it means. My honour, my good name—nay, my very existence itself depends upon it."

As if in answer to my importunity, my friend rose from his chair and picked up the newspaper which the attendant had placed on the table beside me. He opened it, and, after scanning the pages, discovered what he was looking for. Folding it carefully, he pointed to a certain column and handed it to me. I took it mechanically and glanced at the item in question. It was an account of the murder of the unfortunate curiosity dealer, but, so far as I could see, my name was not mentioned in it. I looked up at Sir George for an explanation.

"Well?" I said, but the word stuck in my throat.

"Though you will scarcely credit it, I think I understand everything," he replied. "The murdered man's shop was within a short distance of your abode. A witness states that he saw some one leave the victim's house about the time that the deed must have been committed, and that he made his way into your street. As I said, when you first asked me about him, may God help you, Cyril Forrester, if this is your trouble!"

" But what makes you connect Pharos with the murder described here ? " I asked, with an attempt to feign the surprise I was far from feeling.

" That I cannot tell you," he replied. " To do so would bring upon me——but no, my lips are sealed, hopelessly sealed."

" But surely you are in a position to give me the man's address. Lady Medenham told me you were ,aware of it."

" It is true I was, but I am afraid you have come too late."

" Too late ! What do you mean ? Oh, Sir George, for Heaven's sake do not trifle with me ! "

" I am not trifling with you, Forrester," he replied. " I mean that it is impossible for you to find him in London, for the simple reason that he left England with his companion early this morning."

On hearing this I must have looked so miserable that Sir George came over to where I sat and placed his hand upon my shoulder.

" Dear lad," he said, "you don't know how it pains me to be unable to help you. If it were possible, you have every reason to know that I would do so. In this case, however, I am powerless, how powerless you cannot imagine. But you must not give way like this. The man is gone, and in all human probability you will never see his face again. Try to forget him."

" It is impossible. I assure you, upon my word of honour, that I shall know neither peace nor happiness until I have seen him and spoken to him face to face. If I wish ever to be able to look upon myself as an honourable man, I *must* do it. Is there no way in which I can find him ? "

"I fear none ; but stay, now I come to think of it, there is a chance, but a very remote one. I will make inquiries and let you know within an hour."

"God bless you ! I will remain in my studio until I hear from you."

I bade him good-bye and left the museum. That he did not forget his promise was proved by the fact that within an hour a cab drove up to my door, and one of the attendants from the museum alighted. I took the note he brought from him at the door, and when I had returned to the studio, tore open the envelope and drew forth a plain visiting card. On it was written :

" Inquire for the man you seek from
CARLO ANGELOTTI,
Public Letter-Writer,
In the arches of the Theatre San Carlo,
Naples."

CHAPTER V

IF there is one place more than another for which I entertain a dislike that is akin to hatred, it is for Naples in the summer time—that wretched period when every one one knows is absent, all the large houses are closed, the roads are knee-deep in dust, and even the noise of the waves breaking upon the walls of the Castello del' Ovo seem unable to detract from the impression of heat and dryness which pervades everything. It is the season when the hotels, usually so cool—one might almost say frigid—have had time to grow hot throughout, and are in consequence well-nigh unbearable ; when the particular waiter who has attended to your wants during each preceding visit, and who has come to know your customs and to have survived his original impression that each successive act on your part is only a more glaring proof of your insular barbarity, is visiting his friends in the country, or whatever it is that waiters do during the dull season when the tourists have departed and their employers have no further use for them. It was at this miserable period of the year that I descended upon Naples in search of Monsieur Pharos.

Owing to a breakdown on the line between Spezia and Pisa, it was close upon midnight before I reached my destination, and almost one o'clock before I had transported my luggage from the railway station to my hotel. By this time, as will be readily understood by all those who have made the overland journey, I was in a condition bordering upon madness. Ever since I had called upon Sir George Legrath, and had obtained from him the address of the man from whom I hoped to learn the whereabouts of Pharos, I had been living in a kind of stupor. It took the form of a drowsiness that nothing would shake off, and yet, do what I would, I could not sleep. Times out of number during that long journey I had laid myself back in the railway carriage and closed my eyes in the hope of obtaining some rest ; but it was in vain. However artfully I might woo the drowsy god, sleep would not visit my eyelids. The mocking face of the man I had come to consider my evil angel was always before me, and in the dark-ness of the night, when the train was rolling its way towards the South, I could hear his voice in my ears telling me that this hastily conceived journey on my part had been all carefully thought out and arranged by him beforehand, and that in seeking him in Naples I was only advancing another step towards the fulfilment of my allotted destiny.

On reaching my hotel I went straight to bed. Every bone in my body ached with fatigue. Indeed, so weary was I that I could eat nothing and could scarcely think coherently. The proprietor of the hotel was an old friend, and for the reason that whenever I visited Naples I made it a rule to insist upon occupying the same room, I did not experience the same feeling of loneli-ness which usually assails one on retiring to rest in a strange place. In my own mind I was convinced that as soon as my head touched the pillow I should be asleep. But a bitter disappointment was in store for me. I laid myself down with a sigh of satisfaction and closed my eyes; but whether I missed the rocking of the train, or whether I was in reality overtired I cannot say—at any rate, I was soon convinced of one thing, and that was that the longer I lay there the more wakeful I became. I tried another position, but with the same result. I turned my pillow, only to make it the more uncomfortable. Every trick for the production of sleep that I had ever heard of I put into execution, but always with entire absence of success. At last, thoroughly awake and still more thoroughly exasperated, I rose from my couch, and dressing myself, opened the window of my room and stepped out on to the balcony. It was a glorious night, such a one as is seldom, if ever, seen in England; the air as soft and gentle as the first caress of love. Overhead the moon sailed in a cloudless sky, revealing with her exquisite light the city stretching away to right and left and the expanse of harbour lying directly before me, Vesuvius standing out black and awesome, and the dim outline of the hills towards Castellamare and Sorrento beyond. For some reason my thoughts no longer centred themselves on Pharos. I found the lovely face of his companion continually rising before my eyes. There was the same expression of hopelessness upon it that I remembered on the first occasion upon which I had seen her; but there was this difference, that in some vague, uncertain way she seemed now to be appealing to me to help her, to rescue her from the life she was leading

and from the man who had got her, as he had done
myself, so completely in his power. Her beauty affected
me as no other had ever done. I could still hear the
soft accents of her voice, and the echo of her wild,
weird music, as plainly as if I were still sitting listening
to her in Lady Medenham's drawing-room; and, strange
to relate, it soothed me to think that it was even possible we might be in the same town together.

For upwards of an hour I remained on the balcony
looking down at the moonlit city and thinking of the
change that had been brought about in my life by the
last few days. When I did return to my bedroom, and
once more sought my couch, scarcely five minutes
elapsed before I was wrapped in a heavy, dreamless
sleep, from which I did not wake until well-nigh nine
o'clock. Much refreshed, I dressed myself, and having
swallowed a hasty breakfast, to which I brought a better
appetite than I had known for some days past, I donned
my hat and left the hotel in search of Signor Angelotti,
who, as the card informed me, carried on his profession
of a public letter-writer under the arches of the San
Carlo Theatre.

In all the years which have elapsed since the illustrious
Don Pedro de Toledo laid the foundation of the magnificent thoroughfare which to-day bears his name, I
very much doubt if a man has made his way along it in
the prosecution of a more curious errand than I did that
day. To begin with, I had yet to discover what connection the illustrious Angelotti could have with
Monsieur Pharos, and then to find out how far it was in
his power to help me. Would he forsake his business
and lead me direct to the Egyptian's abode, or would he

deny any knowledge of the person in question and send me unenlightened away ? Upon these points I resolved to satisfy myself without delay.

Of all the characteristic spots of Naples, surely the point at which the Via Roma joins the Piazza San Ferdinando, in which is situated the theatre in question, is the most remarkable. Here one is permitted an opportunity of studying the life of the city under the most favourable auspices. My mind, however, on this occasion was too much occupied wondering what the upshot of my errand would be to have any time to spare to the busy scene around me. Reaching the theatre, I took the card from my pocket and once more examined it. It was plain and straightforward, like Sir George Legrath's own life, and, as I have already said, warned me that I must look for this mysterious Angelotti, who carried on the trade of a public letter-writer, and who was the custodian of the Egyptian's address, under the arches of the famous theatre. As I glanced at the words " Public Letter-writer " another scene rose before my mind's eye.

Several years before I had visited Naples with a number of friends, among whom was a young American lady whose vivacity and capacity for fun made her the life and soul of the party. On one occasion nothing would please her but to stop in the street and engage one of these public scribes to indite a letter for her to an acquaintance in New York. I can see the old man's amusement now, and the pretty, bright face of the girl as she endeavoured to make him understand, in broken Italian, what she desired him to say. That afternoon, I remember, we went to Capri and were late in reaching

home, for which we should in all probability have
received a wigging from the elder members of the party,
who had remained behind, but for the fact that two
important engagements, long hoped for, were announced
as resulting from the excursion. I could not help con-
trasting the enjoyment with which I had made a bet of
a pair of gloves with the young American, that she
would not employ the letter-writer as narrated above,
with my feelings as I searched for Angelotti now.
Approaching the first table, I inquired of the man
behind it whether he could inform me where I should
be most likely to find the individual I wanted.

"Angelotti, did you say, signore?" the fellow replied,
shaking his head. "I know no one of that name among
the writers here." Then, turning to a man seated a
little distance from him, he questioned him with the
same result.

It began to look as if Legrath must have made some
mistake, and that the individual in whose custody
reposed the secret of Pharos's address was as difficult to
find as his master himself. But, unsuccessful as my first
inquiry had been, I was not destined to be disappointed
in the end. A tall, swarthy youth, of the true Neapolitan loafer type, who had been leaning against a wall
close by, smoking a cigarette and taking a mild interest
in our conversation, now removed his back from its
resting-place and approached us.

"Ten thousand pardons, excellenza," he said, "but you
mentioned the name of one Angelotti, a public letter-
writer. I am acquainted with him, and with the
signor's permission will take him to that person."

"You are sure you know him?" I replied, turning

upon him sharply, for I had had to do with Neapolitan loafers before, and I did not altogether like the look of this fellow.

" Since he is my uncle, excellenza, it may be supposed that I do," he answered.

Having said this, he inhaled a considerable quantity of smoke and blew it slowly out again, watching me all the time. I do not know any being in the world who can be so servile, and at the same time so insolent at a moment's notice, as a youth of the Neapolitan lower classes. This fellow was an excellent specimen of his tribe.

" Since you know Angelotti, perhaps you will tell me his address ? " I said at last. " I have no doubt I shall then be able to find it for myself."

Seeing the advantage he held, and scenting employment of not too severe a kind, the young man made a gesture with his hands, as if to signify that while he was perfectly willing to oblige me in so small a matter, business was business, and he must profit by his opportunity. He would be perfectly willing, he said, to act as my guide ; but it must be remembered that it would occupy some considerable portion of his valuable time, and this would have to be paid for at a corresponding rate.

When I had agreed to his terms he bade me follow him, and leaving the precincts of the theatre struck out in the direction of the Strada di Chiaia. Whatever his other deficiencies may have been, he was certainly a good walker, and I very soon found that it took me all my time to keep up with him. Reaching the end of the street, he turned sharply to the right, crossed the road, and a few seconds later dived into an alley. Of all the filthy public places of Naples, that in which I now found myself was undoubtedly the dirtiest. As usual, the houses were many storeys high; but the road was so narrow, and the balconies projected so far from the windows, that an active man might easily have leapt from side to side with perfect safety. As a rule the houses consisted of small shops, though here and there the heavily-barred lower windows and carved doorways proclaimed them private residences. Halfway down this objectionable thoroughfare a still smaller and dirtier one led off to the right, and into this my guide turned, bidding me follow him. Just as I was beginning to wonder whether I should ever find my way out alive, the youth came to a standstill before a small shop in which a number of second-hand musical instruments were displayed for sale.

"This, excellenza, is the residence of the most illustrious Angelotti," he said, as he waved his hand towards the shop in question.

"But I understood that he was a letter-writer," I answered, believing for the moment that the youth had tricked me.

"And it was quite true," he replied. "Until a month ago the Signor Angelotti had his table at the theatre; but his cousin is dead, and now he sells the most beautiful violins in all Italy."

As he said this the young man lifted his hand and gently waved it in the air, as if it were impossible for him to find words sufficiently expressive to describe the excellence of the wares I should find within. It is probable he considered me an intending purchaser, and I do not doubt he had made up his mind, in the event of business ensuing, to return a little later in order to demand from his avuncular relative a commission upon the transaction. Rewarding him for the trouble he had taken, I bade him be off about his business and entered the shop. It was a dismal little place, and filthy to an indescribable degree. The walls were hung with musical instruments, the ceiling with rows of dried herbs, and in a corner, seated at a table busily engaged upon some literary composition, a little old man, with sharp, twinkling eyes and snow-white hair. On seeing me, he rose from his chair and came forward to greet me, pen in hand.

"I am looking for the Signor Angelotti," I said, by way of introducing myself, "whom I was told in England I should find among the public letter-writers at the Theatre San Carlo."

"Angelotti is my name," he answered, "and for many years I received my clients at the place you mention; but my cousin died, and though I would willingly have gone on writing my little letters—for I may tell you, excellenza, that writing letters for other people and seeing how the world goes on around one is a pleasurable employment—business is business, however, and here was this shop to be attended to. So away went letter-writing, and now, as you see, I sell violins and mandolins, of which I can show your excellency the very best assortment in all Naples."

As he said this he put his little sparrow-like head on one side and looked at me in such a comical fashion that I could scarcely refrain from laughing. I had no desire, however, to offend the little man, for I did not know how useful he might prove himself to me.

"Doubtless you miss your old employment," I said, "particularly as it seems to have afforded you so much interest. It was not in connection with your talents in that direction, however, that I called to see you. I have come all the way from England to ask you a question."

On hearing this he nodded his head even more vigorously.

"A great country," he answered with enthusiasm. "I have written many letters for my clients to relatives there. There is a place called Saffron Hill. Oh, excellenza, you would scarcely believe what stories I could tell you about the letters I have written to people there. But I am interrupting you, excellenza. I am an old man, and I have seen very many things, so it is only natural I should like to talk about them."

"Very natural, indeed," I answered; "but in this instance all I have come to ask of you is an address. I want to find a person who left England a few days since."

"And came to Naples? A countryman, perhaps?"

"No, he is no countryman of mine, nor do I even know that he came to Naples; but I was told by some one in England, from whom I made inquiries, that if I came here and asked for one Angelotti, a public letter-writer, I should, in all probability, be able to learn his whereabouts."

As if convinced of the importance of the part he was to play in the affair, the old man laid his pen carefully down upon the table, and then stood before me with his hands placed together, finger tip to finger tip.

"If his excellency would condescend to mention the individual's name," he said softly, "it is just possible I might be able to give him the information he seeks."

"The name of the person I want to find is Pharos,"
I replied. "He is sometimes called Pharos the
Egyptian."

Had I stated that I was in search of the Author of all
Evil, the placid Angelotti could scarcely have betrayed
more surprise. He took a step from me and for a
moment gazed at me in amazement that was not
unmixed with horror. Then the expression gradually
faded from his face, leaving it as devoid of emotion as
before.

"Pharos?" he repeated. "For the moment it does
not strike me, excellenza, that I know the individual."

I should have believed that he really had not the
power to help me had I not noticed the look that had
come into his face when I mentioned that fatal name.

"You do not know him?" I said. "Surely you
must be making some mistake. Think again, Signor
Angelotti. See, here is the card I spoke of. It has
your name and address upon it, and it was given me by
Sir George Legrath, the head of the Egyptian Museum
in London, of whom I think you must at least have
heard."

He shook his head after he had examined the card.

"It is my name, sure enough," he said, handing it
back to me, "but I cannot understand why you should
have supposed that I know anything of the person you
are seeking. However, if you will write your name and
address upon the card, and will leave it with me, I will
make inquiries, and, should I discover anything, will at
once communicate with you. I can do no more."

I saw then that my suppositions were correct, and
that the old fellow was not as ignorant as he desired me

to believe. I accordingly wrote my name, with that of the hotel at which I was staying, at the top of the card, and handed it to him, and then, seeing that there was nothing further to be done, bade him good-morning, and left the shop. Fortunately the road home was easier to find than I had expected it would be, and it was not very long before I was once more in the Piazza S. Ferdinando.

I was still thinking of the curious interview through which I had just passed when, as I crossed the road, I was suddenly recalled to the reality of the moment by a loud voice adjuring me, in scarcely complimentary terms, to get out of the way, unless I desired to be run over. I turned my head in time to see a handsome carriage, drawn by a pair of horses, coming swiftly towards me. With a spring I gained the pavement, and then turned to take stock of it. It was not, however, at the carriage I gazed, but upon its occupant. For, lying back upon her cushions, and looking even more beautiful than when I had seen her last, was Pharos's companion, the Fräulein Valerie de Vocxqal. That she saw and recognised me was evinced by the expression on her face and the way in which she threw up her right hand. I almost fancied I could hear the cry of amazement that escaped her lips. Then the carriage disappeared in the crowd of traffic, and she was gone again. For some moments I stood on the pavement looking after her as if rooted to the spot. It was only when I had recovered myself sufficiently to resume my walk that I could put two and two together and understand what significance this meeting had for me. If she were in Naples, it was well-nigh certain that Pharos must be there too ; and if he were there, then I hoped it would be in my power to find him and acquaint him with the determination at which I had arrived concerning him. That he desired to avoid me I could well understand, and the very fact that his companion showed so much astonishment at seeing me seemed to point to the same conclusion. Poor blind worm that I was, I hugged this conceit to my heart, and the more I did so the more resolved I became in my own mind that, when I *did* meet him, I would show no mercy. Debating with myself in this fashion, I made my way along the Strada S. Carlo, and so by a short cut to my hotel.

As I have already remarked, there is nothing drearier in the world than a foreign hotel out of the season. In this particular instance I seemed to have the entire building to myself. The long corridors were innocent of the step of a stranger foot, and when I sat down to lunch in the great dining-hall, I had not only the room, but the entire staff, or what was left of it, to wait upon me.

I had just finished my meal, and was wondering in what manner I could spend the afternoon, when a waiter approached and placed a note beside my plate. Had I never seen the writer, I should have been able to guess his profession by his penmanship. The caligraphy displayed upon the envelope was in every way too perfect not to be professional, and, as I looked at it, it seemed to me I could see the queer, sparrow-like head of the writer bending over it, and smell the odour of the dried herbs and the still drier violins hanging up in that quaint old shop to which I had paid a visit that morning. On the top was my name and address in my own writing, and below it the direction furnished to me by Sir George Legrath. Seeing that there was nothing new on that side, I took it to the window, and, turning it over, read as follows :—

"If Mr. Forrester desires to meet the person on whose account he is visiting Naples, he should be in the Temple of Mercury at Pompeii this afternoon at four o'clock. Provided he brings no one with him, he will be permitted the interview he seeks."

There was no signature, and nothing to show from whom it emanated, but that it was genuine I did not for a moment doubt. I looked at my watch, and finding that as yet it was scarcely half-past one, tried to make up my mind whether I should go by train or drive. The afternoon would be hot, I was very well aware, and so would be a long drive in an open carriage ; but the train would be hotter still. Eventually I decided for the road, and immediately despatched a waiter in search of a conveyance. Of the carriage and horses there is nothing to be said, and save the view, which is always beautiful, but little in favour of the drive. It was a quarter to four when I alighted at the entrance to the ruins, and by that time I was covered from head to foot with a coating of that indescribable dust so peculiar to Naples.

Informing the cabman that I should return to the city by train, I paid the admission fee, and, declining the services of a guide, entered the grounds, keeping my eyes wide open, as you may suppose, for any sign of the man I had come to meet. Entering the ruins proper by the Marine Gate, I made my way direct to the rendezvous named upon the card, and, surely, never in the history of that ancient place had a man done so with a stranger object in view. I need not have hurried, however, for on reaching the Forum, whence a full view of the Temple can be obtained, I found that I had the place to myself. Having satisfied myself on this point, I sat down on a block of stone and collected my thoughts in preparation for the coming interview. Times out of number I consulted my watch ; and when the hands pointed to four o'clock I felt as if the quarter of an hour I had spent there had in reality been an hour. It was a breathless afternoon ; beyond the city the blue hills appeared to float and quiver in mid-air. A lark was trilling in the sky above me, and so still was everything that the rumbling of a waggon on the white road half a mile or so away could be distinctly heard.

" My dear Mr. Forrester, allow me to wish you a very good afternoon ; I need scarcely say how delighted I am to meet you ! " said a voice behind me ; and, turning, I found myself face to face with Pharos.

CHAPTER VI

ANXIOUS as I was to see him, and eagerly as I had sought his presence, now that Pharos stood before me I was as frightened of him as I had been on the night I had first seen him at the foot of Cleopatra's Needle. I stood looking at his queer, ungainly figure for some thirty seconds, trying to make up my mind how I should enter upon what I had to say to him. That he was aware of my embarrassment I could see, and from the way his lips curled, I guessed that he was deriving considerable satisfaction from it. His face was as crafty and his eyes as wicked as ever I had seen them ; but I noticed that on this occasion he leant more heavily upon his stick than usual.

"I presume it is to my kind friend, Sir George Legrath, that I am indebted for the pleasure of this interview," he said, after the short pause that followed his introductory speech ; "for I need not flatter myself you will believe me when I say that I was fully aware, even before I met you in Lady Medenham's house the other day, that we should be talking together in this Temple within a week."

The palpable absurdity of this speech gave me just the opportunity for which I was waiting.

"Monsieur Pharos," I said, with as much sternness as I could manage to throw into my voice, " successful as you have hitherto been in deceiving me, it is not the least use your attempting to do so on the present occasion. I am quite willing to state that it was my friend, Sir George Legrath, who put me in the way of communicating with you. I called upon him on Tuesday morning, and obtained your address from him."

He nodded his head.

"You will pardon me, I hope, if I seat myself," he said. "It seems that this interview is likely to be a protracted one, and as I am no longer young, I doubt if I can go through it standing."

With this apology he seated himself on a block of stone at the foot of one of the graceful columns, which in bygone days had supported the entrance to the Temple, and, resting his chin on his hands, which again leant on the carved handle of his stick, he turned to me, and in a mocking voice said, "This air of mystery is no doubt very appropriate, my friend; but since you have taken such trouble to find me, perhaps you will be good enough to furnish me with your reason?"

I scratched in the dust with the point of my stick before I replied. Prepared as I was with what I had to say to him, and justified as I felt in pursuing the course I had determined to adopt, for the first time since I had arrived in Naples a doubt as to the probability, or even the sanity, of my case entered my head.

"I can quite understand your embarrassment, my dear Mr. Forrester," he said, with a little laugh, when he saw that I did not begin. "I am afraid you have formed a totally wrong impression of me. By some mischance a train of circumstances has arisen which has filled your mind with suspicion of me. As a result, instead of classing me among your warmest and most admiring friends, as I had hoped you would do, you distrust me and have nothing but unpleasant thoughts in your mind concerning me. Pray, let me hear the charges you bring against me, and I feel sure—nay, I am certain— I shall be able to refute them. The matter of what occurred at Cleopatra's Needle has already been disposed of, and I do not think we need refer to it again. What else have you to urge?"

His voice had entirely changed. It had lost its old sharpness, and was softer, more musical, and infinitely more agreeable than I had ever known it before. He rose from his seat and moved a step towards me. Placing his hand upon my arm, and looking me full and fair in the face, he said,—

"Mr. Forrester, I am an old man—how old you can have no idea—and it is too late in my life for me to begin making enemies. Fate, in one of her cruel moments, has cursed me with an unpleasing exterior. Nay, do not pretend that you think otherwise, for I know it to be true. Those whom I would fain conciliate are offended by it. You, however, I should have thought would have seen below the surface. Why should we quarrel? To quote your own Shakespeare, 'I would be friends with you and have your love.' I am rich, I have influence, I have seen a great deal of the world, and have studied mankind as few others have done. If, therefore, we joined forces, what is there we might not do together?"

Incredible as it may seem after all I had suffered on his account, such was the influence he exerted over me that I now began to find myself wishing it were not necessary for me to say the things I had come to say. But I had no intention of allowing him to suppose I could be moved as easily as he seemed to imagine.

"Before there can be any talk of friendship or even of association between us, Monsieur Pharos," I said, "it will be necessary for me to have a complete understanding with you. If I have wronged you, as, I confess, I sincerely hope I have done, I will apologise and endeavour to make amends for it. Are you aware that on the night of Lady Medenham's ' at home,' a diabolical murder was committed at the old curiosity shop at the corner of the street adjoining that in which my studio is situated ? "

" One could hardly read the English papers without being aware of it," he answered gravely ; " but I scarcely see in what way the matter affects me."

Here he stopped and gazed at me for a moment in silence, as if he were anxious to read what was passing in my mind. Then he began again :—

" Surely you do not mean to tell me, Mr. Forrester, that your dislike to me has carried you so far as to induce you to believe that I was the perpetrator of that ghastly deed ? "

" Since you are aware that a murder *was* committed," I said, " perhaps you also know that the deed was supposed to have been done between the hours of midnight and one o'clock. You may also have read that an individual was seen leaving the house by the back entrance almost on the stroke of one, and that he was believed to have taken refuge in my studio."

"Now that you recall the circumstance, I confess I did see something of the sort in the paper," he answered ; "and I remember reading also that you informed the inspector of police, who called upon you to make inquiries, that to the best of your knowledge no such man *had* entered your house. What then?"

"Well, Monsieur Pharos, it was a few moments after the hour mentioned that you made your appearance before me, breathing heavily as though you had been running. Upon my questioning you, you offered the paltry excuse that you had been for a walk after Lady Medenham's 'at home,' and that you had missed your way and come quite by chance to my studio."

"As I shall prove to your satisfaction when you have finished, that was exactly what happened."

"But you have not heard all," I replied. "While in my rooms you became desirous of possessing the mummy of the Egyptian magician Ptahmes. You expressed a wish that I should present it to you, and, when I declined to do so, you hypnotised me, and took it without either my leave or my license—a very questionable proceeding if viewed in the light of the friendship you profess to entertain for me. How the law of the land would regard it, doubtless you know as well as I do."

As I said this I watched his face closely, but if I hoped to find any expression of shame there I was destined to be disappointed.

"My dear Forrester," he said, "it is very plain indeed that you have developed an intense dislike to me. Otherwise you would scarcely be so ready to believe evil of me. How will you feel when I convince you

that all the ill you think of me is undeserved? Answer
me that!"

"If only you can do so," I cried, clutching eagerly at
the hope he held out. "If you can prove that I have
wronged you, I will only too gladly make you any
amends in my power. You cannot imagine what these
last few days have been to me. I have perjured myself
to save you. I have risked my good name, I have——"

"And I thank you," he answered. "I don't think
you will find me ungrateful. But before I accept your
services I must prove to you that I am not as bad as
you think me. Let us for a moment consider the
matter. We will deal with the case of the mummy first,
that being, as you will allow, of the least importance as
far as you, individually, are concerned. Before I un-
burden myself, however, I must make you understand
the disadvantage under which I am labouring. To
place my meaning more clearly before you, it would be
necessary for me to make an assertion which I have the
best of reasons for knowing you would not believe.
Perhaps I made a mistake on that particular evening
to which we are referring, when I induced you to believe
that it was by accident I visited your studio. I am prepared now to confess that it was not so. I was aware
that you had that mummy in your possession. I had
known it for some considerable time, but I had not been
able to get in touch with you. That night an opportunity offered, and I seized it with avidity. I could not
wait until the next day, but called upon you within a
few hours of meeting you at Lady Medenham's 'at
home.' I endeavoured to induce you to part with the
mummy, but in vain. My entreaties would not move

you. I exerted all my eloquence, argued and pleaded as I have seldom, if ever, done to a man before. Then, seeing that it was useless, I put into force a power of which I am possessed, and determined that, come what might, you should do as I desired. I do not deny that in so doing I was to blame, but I think, if the magnitude of the temptation were brought home to you, you would understand how difficult it would be not to fall. Let me make my meaning clearer to you, if possible."

" It would, perhaps, be as well," I answered, with a touch of sarcasm, " for at present I am far from being convinced."

"You have been informed already by our mutual friend, Sir George Legrath, if I remember rightly, that I am of Egyptian descent. Perhaps you do not under-stand that, while the ancient families of your country are proud of being able to trace their pedigrees back to the time of the Norman Conquest, a beggarly eight hundred years, or thereabouts, I, Pharos, can trace mine, with scarcely a break, back to the nineteenth dynasty of Egyptian history, a period, as your Baedeker will tell you, of over three thousand years. It was that very Ptahmes, the man whose mummy your father stole from its ancient resting-place, who was the founder of our house. For some strange reason, what I cannot tell, I have always entertained the belief that my existence upon this earth, and such success as I shall meet with hereon, depended upon my finding that mummy and returning it to the tomb from which sacrilegious hands had taken it. At first this was only a mere desire ; later it became a fixed determination, which grew in strength and intensity until it became more than a determination, a craving in which the happiness of my whole existence was involved. For many years, with a feverish longing which I cannot expect or hope to make you understand, I searched Europe from end to end, visiting all the great museums and private collections of Egyptian antiquities, but without success. Then, quite by chance, and in a most circuitous fashion, I discovered that it was your father who had found it, and that at his death it had passed on to you. I visited England immediately, obtained an introduction to you, and the rest you know."

"And where is the mummy now?" I inquired.

"In Naples," he replied. "To-morrow I start with it for Egypt, to return it to the place whence your father took it."

"But allow me to remark that it is not your property, Monsieur Pharos," I replied; "and even taking into consideration the circumstances you relate, you must see yourself that you have no right to act as you propose doing."

"And pray by what right did your father rifle the dead man's tomb?" said Pharos quietly. "And since you are such a stickler for what is equitable, perhaps you will show me his justification for carrying away the body from the country in which it had been laid to rest, and conveying it to England to be stared at in the light of a curiosity. No, Mr. Forrester, your argument is a poor one, and I should combat it to the last. I am prepared, however, to make a bargain with you."

"And what is that bargain?" I inquired.

"It is as follows," he replied. "Our interest in the dead man shall be equal. Since it was your father who stole the mummy from its resting-place, let it be the descendant of the dead Ptahmes who restores it. As you will yourself see, and as I think you must in common honesty admit, what I am doing in this matter can in no way advance my own personal interests. If I have taken from you a possession which you valued so highly, set your own figure upon it, and double what you ask I will pay. Can I say anything fairer?"

I did not know what to answer. If the man were what he said, the veritable descendant of the king's magician, then it was only natural he should be willing to sacrifice anything to obtain possession of the body of his three thousand years old ancestor. On my part the sentiment was undoubtedly a much weaker one. The mummy had been left me, among other items of his collection, by my father, and, when that has been said, my interest in the matter lapsed. There was, however, a weightier issue to be decided before I could do him the favour he asked.

"So much for the mummy incident," I said. "What you have to do now is to clear yourself of the more serious suspicion that exists against you. I refer to the murder of the curiosity dealer."

"But surely, Mr. Forrester," he said, "you cannot be serious when you say you believe I had anything to do with that dreadful affair?"

"You know very well what I do and what I do not believe," I answered. "I await your reply."

"Since you press me for it, I will give it," he continued. "But remember this, if I have to convince you of my innocence, your only chance will be gone, for I shall never feel the same towards you again."

As he said this, the old fierce light came into his eyes, and for a moment he looked as dangerous as on that evening in the studio.

"I repeat, I ask you for it," I said, as firmly as my voice could speak.

"Then you shall have it," he replied, and dived his hand into his coat pocket. When he produced it again it held a crumpled copy of a newspaper. He smoothed it out upon his knee, and handed it to me.

"If you look at the third column from the left, you will see a heading entitled, 'The mysterious murder in Bonwell Street.' Pray read it."

I took the paper and read as follows :—

"MYSTERIOUS MURDER IN BONWELL STREET.

"EXTRAORDINARY CONFESSION AND SUICIDE.

"Shortly before nine o'clock this morning, a tall, middle-aged man, giving the name of Johann Schmidt, a German, and evidently in a weak state of health, entered the precincts of Bow Street Police Station, and informed the officer in charge that he desired to give himself up to justice as the murderer of Herman Clausand, the curiosity dealer of Bonwell Street, the victim of the shocking tragedy announced in our issue of Tuesday last. Schmidt, who spoke with considerable earnestness, and seemed desirous of being believed, stated that several years before he had been in the deceased's employ, and since his dismissal had nursed feelings of revenge. On the day preceding the murder he had called at Bonwell Street, and, after informing Clausand that he was out of employment and starving, asked to be again taken into his service; the other, however, refused, whereupon Schmidt very reluctantly left the shop. For the remainder of the day he wandered about London, endeavouring to obtain work; but about midnight, having been unsuccessful, he returned to Bonwell Street and rang the bell. The door was opened by Clausand himself, who, as we stated in our first account of the murder, lived alone. Schmidt entered, and once more demanded employment, or at least money sufficient to enable him to find shelter for the night. Again Clausand refused, whereupon the man picked up a dagger from a stand near by, and stabbed him to the heart. Frightened at what he had done, he did not stay to rob the body, but made his way through the house and out by the back door. Passing into Murbrook Street, he saw a policeman coming towards him, but by stepping into a doorway he avoided him. Since that time, up to the moment of surrendering himself, he had been wandering about London, and it was only when he found starvation staring him in the face that he determined to give himself up. Having told his story, the man was about to be searched prior to being conducted to a cell, when he drew from his pocket a revolver and placed the muzzle to his forehead. Before the bystanders could stop him he had pulled the trigger; there was a loud report, and a moment later the wretched man fell dead at the officer's feet. The divisional surgeon was immediately summoned, but on his arrival found that life was extinct. Inquiries were at once made, with a view to ascertaining whether the story he had told had any foundation in fact. We have since learned that the description he gave of himself was a true one, that he had once been in Clausand's employ, and that on the day preceding the murder he had openly asserted in a public-house in the neighbourhood of Soho his intention of being revenged upon him.

"The coroner has been informed, and an inquest will be held to-morrow morning."

After I had read it, I stood for some moments looking at the paper in my hand. Then I turned to Pharos, who was still seated on the block of stone watching me intently. Since this miserable wretch had confessed to the crime, it was plain that I had wronged him in supposing he had committed it. A weight was undoubtedly lifted from my mind, but for some reason or another the satisfaction I derived from this was by no means as great as I had expected it would be. At the back of my mind there was still a vague impression that I was being deceived, and, do what I would, I could not rid myself of it.

"That, I think, should convince you, Mr. Forrester," said Pharos, rising and coming towards me, "how very unwise it is ever to permit one's feelings to outweigh one's judgment. You made up your mind that you disliked me, and for the simple reason that I had the misfortune to lose my way on that particular evening, and to reach your studio about the same time that that terrible murder was committed, you were ready at a moment's notice to believe me guilty of the crime."

"What you say is quite true," I answered humbly. "I acted very foolishly, I admit. I have done you a great wrong, and you have behaved very generously about it."

"In that case we will say no more about it," he replied. "It is an unpleasant subject ; let us forget it and never refer to it again. As I asked you to believe when last I saw you, my only desire is that you should think well of me and that we should be friends. As another proof of my kindly feeling towards yourself, I will go further than I originally intended, and say that I am willing to restore the mummy I took from you. It is here in Naples, but, if you wish, it shall be at once returned to your house in London."

This was more than I had expected from him, and it impressed me accordingly.

"I could not dream of such a thing," I replied. "Since you have been so generous, let me follow your example. I have wronged you, and, as some small return, I ask you to keep the king's magician, and do with him as you please."

"I accept your offer in the spirit in which it is made," he replied. "Now, perhaps, we had better be going. If you have nothing better to do this evening, I should be glad if you would dine with me. I think I can promise you a better dinner than you will get at your own hotel, and afterwards, I have no doubt, we shall be able to induce my ward to give us some music. You had better say 'Yes,' for, I assure you, we shall both be disappointed if you refuse."

"You are really very kind," I began, " but——"

"With your permission we will have no 'buts,'" he replied, with a wave of his hand. "The matter is settled, and I shall look forward to a pleasant evening. My carriage is at the gate, and if you will drive back with me I shall be doubly honoured."

If there had been any way of getting out of it, I think I should have taken advantage of it ; but as I could not discover one, I was perforce compelled to accept his invitation.

" I wonder if this city has the same fascination for you, Mr. Forrester, that it has for me ? " said Pharos after I had given my consent to the arrangement he proposed. "For my own part I confess I never come to Naples without paying it a visit ; but how very few are there of the numbers who visit it weekly that really understand it ! What tales I could tell you of it, if only they interested you ! How vividly I could bring back to you the life of the people who once spoke in this forum, bathed in yonder baths, applauded in the theatre nineteen hundred years ago ! Let us follow this street which leads towards the Temple of Isis, that temple in which the Egyptian goddess was worshipped by such as pretended to believe in her mysterious powers. I say *pretended*, because it was the fashion then to consult her oracles, a fashion as insulting as it was popular."

By this time we had passed out of the Temple of Mercury and were making our way along the time-worn pavement towards the building of which he spoke. The sun was sinking in the west, and already long shadows were drawing across the silent streets, intensifying the ghostliness of the long-deserted city. Reaching the Temple, we entered and looked about us.

" See how its grandeur has departed from it," said Pharos, with a note of sadness in his voice that made me turn and look at him in surprise. " Time was when this was the most beautiful temple in the city, when every day her courts were thronged with worshippers, when her oracles boasted a reputation that reached even to mighty Rome. On this spot stood the statue of the goddess herself. There that of her son, the god Horus. Here was the purgatorium, and there the bronze figure of the bull god Apis. Can you not picture the crowd of eager faces beyond the rails, the white-robed priests, and the sacrifice being offered up on yonder altar amid the perfumes of frankincense and myrrh? Where, Mr. Forrester, are these priests now? The crowd of worshippers, the statues? Gone—gone—dust and ashes, these nineteen hundred years. Come, we have lingered here long enough, let us go farther."

Leaving the Temple, we made our way into the Stabian Street, passed the Temple of Æsculapius, and did not stop until we had reached the house of Tullus Agrippa. Into this Pharos led me.

"O Tullus Agrippa!" he cried, as if apostrophising the dead man, "across the sea of time, I, Pharos the Egyptian, salute thee! Great was thy wealth and seemingly endless thy resources. Greedy of honour and praise wast thou, and this house was the apex of thy vanity. Here is that same triclinium where thy guests were wont to assemble when thou didst invite them to thy banquets. Here the room in which thou didst condemn thine only son to perpetual banishment. In those days, when the sun was warm and the table was spread, and friends crowded about thee and praised the beauty of thy frescoes, the excellence of thy wine, the cunning devices of thy cook, and the service of thy slaves, little didst thou dream that nineteen centuries later would find thy house roofless, dug up from the bowels of the earth, and thy cherished rooms a show

" ' I, Pharos the Egyptian, salute thee.' "

to be gaped at by all who cared to pay a miserable fee. Least of all didst thou think then that Pharos the Egyptian would be standing in the room where once thou didst rule so absolute, telling a man, of a race that in thy day was unknown, of thy faults and follies."

He stopped for a moment, and then, turning to me again, recommenced with fresh energy.

"The owner of this house, Tullus Agrippa, was avaricious, cruel, vain and sensual. He gave of his wealth only when he was assured of a large return. He was hated on every hand, and by his own family and dependants most of all. What did his wealth avail him on that last dread day, when the streets were filled with flying citizens, when all was confusion and none knew which way to turn for safety? The catastrophe found him tossing on a bed of sickness and scarcely able to stand alone. With the first shock of the earthquake he called imperiously for his favourite slave, but received no answer. He called again, this time almost with entreaty. Still no answer came. The walls of his house trembled and shook as he rose from his couch and staggered out into the fast darkening street. Like a blind man he groped his way to yonder corner, calling upon the names of his gods as he went, and offering every sestertia in his possession to the person who would conduct him to a place of safety. A man brushed against him. He looked up and recognised the gladiator, Tymon, the man he had encouraged and whose richest patron he was. Accordingly he seized him and clung to him, offering gifts innumerable if he would only carry him as far as the Marine Gate. But this was no time for helping others, with that terrible

shower of ashes pouring down upon them like rain.
The gladiator cast him off, but he was not to be denied.
He struggled to his knees and threw his arms around
the strong man's legs, but only for an instant. Roused
to a pitch of fury by his terror and the other's per-
sistency, Tymon struck him a blow on the temple with
the full strength of his ponderous fist. The old man
stumbled against the wall, clutched at it for support,
and at length fell senseless upon the ground. The
shower of ashes and scoria quickly covered him, and
nineteen hundred years later the workmen, excavating
the ruins, discovered his body at the base of yonder
wall. Such was the fate of the noble Tullus Agrippa,
citizen of Rome, and once the owner of this house."

Before I could reply or ask how he had become
familiar with these details, he had passed outside and
was in the road again. I followed him to the Street of
Fortune, passed the House of the Fawn, the Baths, and
the Villa of Glaucus. Of each he had some story to
tell—some anecdote to relate. From the graphic way
in which he described everything, the names and
characters he introduced, I might have been excused
had I even believed that he had known it in its prime
and been present on the day of its destruction. I said
as much to him, but he only shook his head.

" Think what you please," he said. " If I were to tell
you the truth, you would not believe me. For that
reason I prefer that you should credit me with the
possession of an exceedingly vivid imagination. If I
have succeeded in making the last hour pass pleasantly,
I am amply rewarded. But it grows late ; the guards
are coming in search of us ; let us return to the gate."

Accordingly we made our way back to the Porta
Marina, and down the path towards the entrance to the
ruins. My companion was evidently well known to the
officials, for they treated him with obsequious respect,
bowing before him and inquiring if he had seen certain
new excavations, as if the success of the latter depended
entirely on his good opinion of them. In the road
outside a carriage was standing, to which was attached
a magnificent pair of black horses. A coachman,
dressed in a neat but unpretentious black livery, sat
upon the box, while a footman stood beside the carriage
door. The whole turn-out was in excellent taste, and
would have made a creditable appearance in the Bois
de Boulogne or even in Hyde Park. Into this elegant
equipage Pharos invited me to step, and when I had
seated myself he took his place beside me. Hot though
the night was, a heavy fur rug was wrapped round his
knees, and he laid himself back upon the cushions with
a sigh of relief, as if the exertion of the afternoon had
been too much for him.

 " So much for Pompeii," he said, as the horses sprang
forward. "Now for Naples and the most beautiful
creature it contains at present, my ward, the Fräulein
Valerie De Vocxqal."

CHAPTER VII

IF any one had told me on the night that I first met
Pharos at the foot of Cleopatra's Needle that
within a very short space of time I should be driving
from Pompeii to Naples alone with him, I believe I
should have laughed that person to scorn. And what
is perhaps stranger, seeing how intense my dislike for
him had been less than two hours before, I was not only
paying attention to what he said to me, but was actually
deriving a certain measure of enjoyment from his society.
In my time I have met some of the cleverest talkers in
Europe, men whose conversational powers are above
the average, and to whom it is rightly enough considered
a privilege to listen. Pharos, however, equalled, if he
did not exceed them all. His range of topics was extraordinary and his language as easy and graceful as it was
free from the commonplace. Upon every conceivable
subject he had some information to impart, and in the
cases of events in the world's history, he did so with the
same peculiar suggestion of being able to speak from
the point of an eye-witness, or, at least, as one who had
lived in the same period, that I had noticed when he
conducted me through the ruins of Pompeii that afternoon. The topography of the country through which
we were passing, he also had at his fingers' ends. About

every portion of the landscape he had some remark of
interest to make, and when we had exhausted Italy and
proceeded to more distant countries, I found that he
was equally conversant with the cities they contained.
How long the drive lasted, I cannot say; but never in
my experience of the high road between Naples and
Pompeii had it seemed so short. Reaching the Castello
del Carmine we turned sharply to our right, passed up
the Corso Garibaldi for some considerable distance,
and eventually branched off to the left. After that, I
have no further knowledge of our route. We, traversed
street after street, some of them so narrow that there
was barely room for our carriage to pass along, until at
last we reached a thoroughfare that not only contained
better houses than the rest, but was considerably wider.
Before a large, old-fashioned residence the horses came
to a standstill; a pair of exquisitely wrought-iron gates
guarding a noble archway were thrown open, and through
them we passed into the courtyard beyond. Beautiful as
many of the courtyards are in Naples, I think this one
eclipsed them all. The house surrounded it on three
sides; on the fourth, and opposite that by which we
had entered, was the garden, with its fountains, vista of
palm trees, through which a peep of the waters of the
bay could be obtained, and its luxuriant orange groves.
In the soft light of evening a more picturesque picture
could not have been desired.

The footman, having descended from the box, opened
the door of the carriage, and when he had withdrawn
the rug from his master's knees, assisted him to alight.
I followed, and we proceeded up the steps into the
house. Prepared as I was by the fact that both Lady

Medenham and Sir George Legrath had informed me of
Pharos's wealth, I could scarcely contain my surprise
when the beauty of the house to which I was now introduced was revealed to me. The hall in which we
stood was filled from floor to ceiling with works of art,
carvings, paintings, statues, tapestry, the value of which
I could the better appreciate when I was permitted an
opportunity of examining them more closely.

"I make you welcome to my abode, Mr. Forrester,"
said Pharos, as I crossed the threshold. "You are not
the first English artist who has honoured me with a
visit, and I think, if you will glance round these walls,
you will admit that you are in good company. See,
here is a Fra Angelico, here a Botticelli, here a Perugino,
to your right a Giorgione—all your fellow-guests. At
the foot of the stairs is a Jan Steen, half-way up a
Madonna by Signorelli ; the monk above is, as doubtless
you can see for yourself, an Andra del Sarto, who has
found many admirers. But that is not all. If you will
follow me, I think I can show you something which will
have an equal interest for you, though perhaps in a
somewhat different way."

Feeling as if I were walking in a dream, I followed
him along the hall. Presently he stopped and pointed
to a large canvas.

"Do you recognise it ?" he inquired.

To my surprise it was neither more nor less than one
of my own earlier works which had appeared in the
Academy about three years before and represented a
fantastic subject. It had been purchased by a dealer,
and after it had left my possession I had lost sight of it
altogether. To find it here, in the home of the man

who had come to play such an extraordinary part in
my life, overwhelmed me with astonishment.

"You seem surprised at seeing it," said Pharos, as we
stood before it. "If you will allow me, I will relate to
you the circumstances under which it came into my
possession, and I think you will admit that they are
highly interesting. It is now two years since the event
occurred of which I am going to tell you. I was then
in Baden. It was the height of the season, and the city
was crowded, not only with interesting foreigners—if
you will permit the unintentional sarcasm—but with a
large proportion of your own English aristocracy.
Among the latter was a certain nobleman to whom I
was happily able to be of considerable service. He was
one of life's failures. In his earlier youth he had a
literary tendency which, had the Fates been propitious,
might possibly have brought him some degree of fame;
his accession to the title, however, and the wealth it
carried with it, completely destroyed him. When I
met him in Baden he was as near ruined as a man of
his position could be. He had with him one daughter,
a paralytic, to whom he was devotedly attached. Had
it not been for her, I am convinced he would have given
up the struggle and have done what he afterwards did
—namely, have made away with himself. In the hope
of retrieving his fortune and of distracting his mind, he
sought the assistance of the gaming-tables; but having
neither luck nor, what is equally necessary, sufficient
courage, eventually found himself face to face with ruin.
It was then that I appeared upon the scene, and managed to extricate him from his dilemma. As a token
of his gratitude he made me a present of this picture,

which up to that time had been one of his most treasured possessions."

"And the man himself—what became of him?"

Pharos smiled an evil smile.

"Well, he was always unfortunate. On the selfsame night that he made me the present to which I refer he experienced another run of ill luck."

"And the result?"

"Can you not guess? He returned to his lodgings to find that his daughter was dead, whereupon he wrote me a note, thanking me for the assistance I had rendered him, and blew his brains out at the back of the Kursaal."

On hearing this I recoiled a step from the picture. While it flattered my vanity to hear that the wretched man who had lost fame, fortune, and everything else, should still have retained my work, I could not repress a feeling of horror at the thought that in so doing he had, unconsciously, it is true, been bringing me into connection with the very man who I had not the least doubt had brought about his ruin. As may be supposed, however, I said nothing to Pharos on this score. For the time being we were flying a flag of truce, and having had one exhibition of his powers, I had no desire to experience a second. Whether he read what was passing in my mind or not, I cannot say. At any rate, he changed the subject abruptly and led me away from my own work to another at the farther end of the hall. From this we passed into an anteroom, which, like the hall, was hung with pictures. It was a magnificent apartment in every way, but, as I soon discovered, was eclipsed by the larger room into which it opened.

The latter could not have been less than eighty feet long by forty wide. The walls were decorated with exquisite pictures, and, if such a thing were possible, with still more exquisite china. All the appointments were in keeping. At the farther end was a grand piano, and seated near this, slowly fanning herself with a large ostrich-feather fan, was the woman I had seen first at the Academy, then at Medenham House, and earlier that very day in the Piazza S. Ferdinando. Upon our entrance she rose, and once more I thought I discovered a frightened look in her face. In a second, however, it had passed, and she had once more recovered her equanimity.

"Valerie," said Monsieur Pharos, "I have been fortunate enough to meet Mr. Forrester, who arrived in Naples last night, and to induce him to dine with us this evening."

While he was speaking, I had been watching the face of the beautiful woman whose affecting story Lady Medenham had told me, and had noticed how white it had suddenly become. The reason of this I have since discovered, but I know that at the time it puzzled me more than a little.

"I bid you welcome, sir," she said, in excellent English, but with no great degree of cordiality.

I made some suitable reply, and then Pharos departed from the room, leaving us together. My companion once more seated herself, and, making an effort, began a conversation that was doubtless of a very polite, but to me entirely unsatisfactory, nature. Presently she rose from her chair and went to the window, where she stood for some moments looking out into the fast-darkening street. Then she turned to me, as she did so making a little gesture with her hands that was more expressive than any words.

"Mr. Forrester," she said, speaking rapidly in a low voice, but with great earnestness, "have you taken leave of your senses that you come here? Are you tired of your life that you thrust your head into the lion's den in this foolish fashion?"

Her words were so startling, and her agitation so genuine, that I could make neither head nor tail of it. I accordingly hastened to ask for an explanation.

"I can tell you nothing," she said, "except that this place is fatal to you. Oh, if I could only make you understand how fatal!"

Her beauty and the agitation under which she was labouring exercised a most powerful effect upon me, which was increased rather than diminished when I reflected that it was being exerted on my behalf.

"I scarcely understand you," I stammered, for I was quite carried away by her vehemence. "From what you say, I gather that you believe me to be in a position of some danger, but I assure you such is not the case. I met Monsieur Pharos at Pompeii this afternoon, and he was kind enough to ask me to dine with him this evening. Surely there can be nothing dangerous in that. If, however, my presence is in any way distasteful to you, I can easily make an excuse and take my departure."

"You know it is not that," she answered quickly and with a little stamp of her foot. "It is for your own sake I am imploring you to go. If you knew as much of this house as I do, you would not remain in it another minute."

"My dear madame," I said, "if you would only be more explicit, I should be the better able to understand you."

"I cannot be more explicit," she answered; "such a thing is out of my power. But remember, if anything happens, I have warned you, and your fate will be upon your own head."

"But——" I cried, half rising from my seat.

"Hush!" she answered. "There is not time for more. He is coming."

A moment later Pharos entered the room. He had discarded his heavy fur coat, and was now dressed as I had seen him at Medenham House—that is to say, he wore a tight-fitting black velvet coat buttoned high up round his throat, and a skull cap of the same material. He had scarcely entered the room before dinner was announced.

"If you will take my ward," he said, "I will follow you."

I did as directed, and never while I live shall I forget the thrill that passed through me as I felt the pressure of her tiny hand upon my arm. Lovely as I had always thought her, I had never seen her look more beautiful than on this particular evening. As I watched her proud and graceful carriage, I could well believe, as Lady Medenham had said, that she traced her descent from one of the oldest families in Europe. There was something about her that I could not understand, though I tried repeatedly to analyse it—a vague, indescribable charm that made her different to all other women I had ever met.

The room in which we dined was a more sombre apartment than the others I had seen. The walls were hung with heavy tapestries, unrelieved by light or brilliant colour. The servants also struck me as remarkable. They were tall, elderly, dark-skinned, and, if the truth must be told, of somewhat saturnine appearance, and if I had been asked, I should have given my vote against their being Italians. They did their duty noiselessly and well, but their presence grated upon me, very much as Pharos's had done on the first three occasions that I had met him. Among other things, one singular circumstance arrested my attention. While the dinner was in every respect admirable, and would not have discredited the Maison Dorèe, or the Café de la Paix, Pharos did not partake of it. At the commencement of the meal a dish of fruit and a plate of small flat cakes were placed before him. He touched nothing else, save, when we had finished, to fill a wineglass with water and to pour into it a spoonful of some white powder, which he took from a small silver box standing before him. This he tossed off at one draught.

"You are evidently surprised," he said, turning towards me, "at the frugality of my fare, but I can assure you that in my case eating has been reduced almost to a vanishing point. Save a little fruit in the morning, and a glass of water in which I dissolve one of these powders, and a meal similar to that you now see me making in the evening, I take nothing else, and yet I am stronger than many men of half my age. If the matter interests you, I will some day give you proof of that."

To this speech I made some reply and then glanced

at the Fräulein Valerie. Her face was still deathly
pale, and I could see by the way her hands trembled
above her plate that the old fellow's words had in some
manner been the cause of it. Had I known as much
then as I do now, I should no doubt have trembled myself. For the moment, however, I thought she must be
ill, and should have said as much had my eyes not met
hers and found them imploring me to take no notice
of her agitation. I accordingly addressed myself to
Pharos on the subject of the journey from Paris to
Naples, and thus permitted her time to recover her self-
possession. The meal at an end, she rose and left the
room, not, however, before she had thrown another look
of entreaty at me, which, as I read it, seemed to say,
" For pity sake remember where you are, and be careful
what you say or do."

The door had scarcely closed behind her before another on the other side of the room opened, and a
servant entered carrying in his arms a monkey wrapped
in a small rug, from which its evil-looking little face
peered out at me as if it were wondering at my presence
there. Pharos noticed my surprise.

" Let me make you acquainted with my second self,"
he said, and then, turning to the monkey, continued,
" Pehtes, make your salutation."

The monkey, however, finding himself in his master's
arms, snuggled himself down and paid no more attention to me, whereupon Pharos pushed the decanters,
which the servant had placed before him, towards me
and invited me to fill my glass.

I thanked him, but declined.

" If you will permit me to say so, I think you are

foolish," he answered.   " I have been often complimented on that wine, particularly by your countrymen."

I wondered who the countrymen were who had sat
at this table, and what the reason could have been that
had induced them to accept his hospitality.   Could
Legrath have been among the number, and, if so, what
was the terrible connection between them ?   For terrible
I knew it must have been, otherwise it would scarcely
have made Sir George, usually the most self-contained
of men, betray such agitation when I inquired if he were
acquainted with the name of Pharos.

While these thoughts were passing through my
mind, I stole a glance at the old fellow as he sat at
the head of the table, propped up with cushions, and
with the monkey's evil countenance peeping out from
his hiding-place under the other's coat.   He was evidently in an expansive mood, and as anxious as possible to make himself agreeable.   The first horror of his
presence had by this time left me, and, as I said at the
commencement of this chapter, its place had been taken
by a peculiar interest for which I found it well-nigh impossible to account.

" If you will not take any wine, perhaps you will let
me offer you a cigarette," he said, after I had declined
his previous invitation.   "I am not a smoker myself,
but those who do enjoy the fragrant weed tell me the
brand is excellent.   It is grown on one of my own
estates in Turkey, and can be obtained nowhere else in
the world."

So saying, he produced a small silver case from his
pocket and handed it to me.   I took one of the cigar-

ettes it contained, lit it, and for the next two or three minutes sat back in my chair silently smoking. The tobacco was excellent. To have wasted a puff of that precious smoke in conversation would have been a sacrilege that I was determined not to commit. Having finished one, I was easily persuaded to take another, and was compelled to declare the flavour to be even better than the first.

"I am delighted to see that you enjoy them," said Pharos.

"I have never smoked any tobacco like it," I replied. "It seems hard that you should not enjoy it yourself."

"I could not enjoy it in a happier way," he answered, "than through my friends. I am amply compensated when I see the pleasure it gives them."

After this philanthropic contribution to the conversation of the evening, we were both silent again for some moments. My cigarette was half finished, but the case, still nearly full, lay upon the table for me to help myself when I felt inclined. Little by little the subtle intoxication of the weed was permeating my whole being; a gentle languor was stealing over me, and as a result my brain had never before seemed so bright or my capacity of enjoyment so keen as it did then.

"If you will not take wine, we might adjourn to the drawing-room," said Pharos at last. "It is possible we may be able to induce my ward to give us some music, and as she is partial to the aroma of these cigarettes, I think I may assure you beforehand that she will willingly give you permission to smoke in her presence."

Accordingly we sought the drawing-room, the same

in which the beautiful Hungarian had uttered her curious warning to me earlier in the evening. She was seated in the same chair as she had then occupied, and, on entering, Pharos, still carrying the monkey in his arms, crossed and patted her hand in a grandfatherly fashion. Kindly, however, as the action appeared to be, I noticed that she trembled beneath it.

"I have assured Mr. Forrester, my dear Valerie," he said, "that the odour of tobacco is not distasteful to you, and that you will permit him to smoke a cigarette in your presence. Was I not right?"

"Of course I will give permission," she answered, but never had I heard her voice so cold and monotonous. It was as if she were repeating something under compulsion. At any other time I should have declined to avail myself of what I could not help thinking was permission grudgingly given; but since Pharos insisted, and the Fräulein begged me to do so, I at length consented and made a further raid upon the case. As soon as he had seen the cigarette lighted and myself comfortably seated, Pharos installed himself in an armchair, while his ward wrapped the inevitable rug about his knees. Having done this, she took her violin from its case, and when she had tuned it, took up her position and commenced to play. I had still the same feeling, however, that she was doing it under compulsion; but how that force was being exerted, and for what reason, was more than I could tell. Once more the same gentle languor I had felt at the dinner-table began to steal over me, and again my senses became abnormally acute. Under the influence of the music, new ideas, new inspirations, new dreams of colour, crowded

"The violinist . . . fled from the room."

upon me thick and fast. In the humour in which I was then, I felt that there was nothing I could not do, no achievement of which I was not capable. What I had done in the past was as nothing compared with what I would do in the future. With this man's help I would probe the very heart of Wisdom and make myself conversant with her secrets. Through half-closed eyes I could see the violinist standing before me, and it was as if her white hands were beckoning me along the road of Fame. I turned from her to Pharos, and found him still seated in his chair, with his eyes fixed steadfastly upon me. Then the cigarette came to an end, the music ceased, and with a choking sob the violinist, unable to control herself any longer, fled from the room. I sprang to my feet and hastened to open the door for her, but was too late. She was gone.

" Mr. Forrester," said Pharos, after we had been alone together for a few moments, " I am going to make a proposition to you which I shall be very much honoured if you can see your way to accept."

" I shall be better able to tell you when I know what it is," I answered.

" It is eminently simple," he continued. " It is neither more nor less than this. I am the possessor of a steam-yacht—a comfortable craft, my friends tell me—and in her my ward and I start to-morrow for Port Said, *en route* for Cairo."

" For Cairo? " I cried, in amazement.

" For Cairo," he answered with a smile. " And why not? Cairo is a most delightful place, and I have important business in Egypt. Perhaps you can guess what that business is."

"The mummy?" I answered at a hazard.

"Exactly," he replied, nodding his head; "the mummy. It is my intention to restore it to the tomb from which your father sto— from which, shall we say, your father removed it."

"And your proposition?"

"Is that you accompany us. The opportunity is one you should not let slip. You will have a chance of seeing the Land of the Pharaohs under the most favourable auspices, and the hints you should derive for future work should be invaluable to you. What do you say?"

To tell the truth, I did not know what answer to give. I had all my life long had a craving to visit that mysterious country, and, as I have said elsewhere, I had quite made up my mind to do so at the end of the year. Now an opportunity was afforded me of carrying out my intentions, and in a most luxurious fashion. I remembered the extraordinary interest Pharos had lent to the ruins of Pompeii that afternoon, and I felt sure that in Egypt, since it was his native country, he would be able to do much more. But it was not the prospect of what I should learn from him so much as the knowledge that I should be for some weeks in the company of Valerie de Vocxqal that tempted me. The thought that I should be with her on board the yacht, and that I should be able to enjoy her society uninterruptedly in the mystic land which had played such an important part in my career, thrilled me to the centre of my being. That her life was a far from happy one I was quite convinced, and it was just possible, if I went with them, that I might be able to discover the seat of the trouble and perhaps be in a position to assist her.

"What have you to say to my plan?" inquired Pharos. "Does not the idea tempt you?"

"It tempts me exceedingly," I answered; "but the fact of the matter is, I had no intention of being absent so long from England."

"England will be still there when you get back," he continued with a laugh. "Come, let it be decided that you will join us. I think I can promise that you will enjoy the trip."

"I do not wish to appear discourteous," I said, "but would it not be better for me to take till to-morrow morning to think it over?"

"It would be the most foolish policy possible," he answered, "for in that case I feel convinced you would find some reason for not accepting my invitation, and by so doing would deprive yourself of a chance which, as I said just now, may never come again in your life. If Valerie were here, I feel sure she would add her voice to mine."

The mention of his ward's name decided me, and, with a recklessness that forces a sigh from me now, I gave my promise to accompany them.

"I am very glad to hear it," said Pharos. "I think you have decided wisely. We shall sail to-morrow evening at ten o'clock. My servants will call for your luggage and will convey it and you on board. You need not trouble yourself in any way."

I thanked him, and then, finding that it was close upon eleven o'clock, took leave of him. That I was disappointed in not being permitted an opportunity of

saying farewell to his ward, I will not deny.   I feared
that she was offended with me for not having taken
her advice earlier in the evening.   I did not mention
the matter, however, to Pharos, but bade him good-
night, and, declining his offer to send me home in his
carriage, made my way into the hall and presently left
the house.   Having crossed the courtyard, the ancient
gatekeeper passed me out through a small door beside
the gates.   The night was exceedingly warm, and as I
stepped into the street the moon was rising above the
opposite housetops.   Having made inquiries from
Pharos, I had no doubt of being able to make my way
back to my hotel.   Accordingly, as soon as I had rewarded the *concierge*, and the gate had closed behind
me, I set off down the pavement at a brisk pace.   I
had not gone very far, however, before a door opened
in a garden wall, and a black figure stole forth and
addressed me by my name.   It was the Fräulein
Valerie.

" Mr. Forrester," she said, " I have come at great risk
to meet you.   You would not listen to me this evening,
but I implore you to do so now.   If you do not heed
me and take my warning, it may be too late."

The moon shone full and fair upon her face, revealing her wonderful beauty and adding an ethereal charm
to it which I had never noticed it possessed before.

" Of what is it you would warn me, my dear lady ? "
I asked.

" I cannot tell you," she answered, " for I do not
know myself.   But of this I am certain : since he has
interested himself in you, and has declared his desire
for your friendship, it cannot be for your good.   You

do not know him as I do. You have no idea, it is impossible you should, of what he is. For your own sake, Mr. Forrester, draw back while you have time. Have no more to do with him. Shun his society, whatever it costs you. You smile! Ah, if you only knew! I tell you this—it would be better, far better for you to die than to fall into his power."

I was touched by the earnestness with which she spoke, but more by the sadness of her face.

"Fräulein," I said, "you speak as if you had done that yourself."

"I have," she answered. "I am in his power, and, as a result, I am lost, body and soul. It is for that reason I would save you. Take warning by what I have said and leave Naples to-night. Never mind where you go—go to Russia, to America, bury yourself in the wilds of Siberia or Kamtschatka—but get beyond his reach."

"It is too late," I answered. "The die is cast, for I have promised to sail with him to Egypt to-morrow."

On hearing this she uttered a little cry, and took a step away from me.

"You have promised to visit Egypt with him?" she cried, as if she could scarcely believe she heard aright. "Oh! Mr. Forrester, what can you be thinking of? I tell you it is fatal, suicidal. If you have any regard for your own safety, you will get away to-night, this very moment, and never return to Naples or see him again."

In her agitation she clutched at my arm and held it tightly. I could feel that she was trembling violently.

Her touch, however, instead of effecting the purpose she had in view, decided me on a contrary course.

"Fräulein," I said, in a voice I should not at any other time have recognised as my own, "you tell me that this man has you in his power. You warn me of the dangers I run by permitting myself to associate with him, and, having risked so much for me, you expect me to go away and leave you to his mercy. I fear you must have a very poor opinion of me."

"I am only trying to save you," she answered. "The first day I saw you I read disaster in your face, and from that moment I desired to prevent it."

"But if you are so unhappy, why do you not attempt to save yourself?" I asked. "Come, I will make a bargain with you. If I am to fly from this man, you must do so too. Let us set off this moment. You are beyond the walls now. Will you trust yourself to me? There is a steamer in the harbour sailing at midnight. Let us board her and sail for Genoa, thence anywhere you please. I have money, and I give you my word of honour, as a gentleman, that I will leave nothing undone to promote your safety and your happiness. Let us start at once, and in half an hour we shall be rid of him for ever."

As I said this, I took her arm and endeavoured to lead her down the pavement, but she would not move.

"No, no," she said in a frightened whisper. "You do not know what you are asking of me. Such a thing is impossible—hopelessly impossible. However much I may desire to do so, I cannot escape. I am chained to him for life by a bond that is stronger than fetters of steel. I cannot leave him. O God! I cannot leave him!"

She fell back against the wall and once more covered her face with her hands, while her slender frame shook with convulsive sobs.

"So be it then," I said ; and, as I did so, I took off my hat. "If you will not leave him, I swear before God I will not go alone. It is settled, and I sail with him for Egypt to-morrow."

She did not attempt to dissuade me further, but, making her way to the door in the wall through which she had entered the street, opened it and disappeared within. I heard the bolts pushed to, and then I was in the street alone.

"The die is cast," I said to myself. "Whether for good or evil, I accompany her to-morrow, and, once with her, I will not leave her until I am certain that she no longer requires my help."

Then I resumed my walk to my hotel.

CHAPTER VIII

THE clocks of the city had struck ten on the following evening when I left the carriage which Pharos had sent to convey me to the harbour, and, escorted by his servant, the same who had sat beside the coachman on the occasion of our drive home from Pompeii on the previous evening, made my way down the landing-stage and took my place in the boat which was waiting to carry me to the yacht.

Throughout the day I had seen nothing either of Pharos or his ward, nor had I heard anything from the former save a message to the effect that he had made arrangements for my getting on board. But if I had not seen them I had at least thought about them—so much so, indeed, that I had scarcely closed my eyes all night. And the more attention I bestowed upon them, the more difficult I found it to account for the curious warning I had received from the Fräulein Valerie. What the danger was which threatened me, it was beyond my power to tell. I endeavoured to puzzle it out, but in vain. Had it not been for that scene on the Embankment, and his treatment of me in my own studio, to say nothing of the suspicions I had erroneously entertained against him in respect of the murder of the curiosity dealer, I should in all probability have attributed it to a mere womanly superstition which,

although it appeared genuine enough to her, had no
sort of foundation in fact. Knowing, however, what I
did, I could see that it behoved me, if only for the sake
of my own safety, to be more than cautious; and when
I boarded the yacht, I did so with a full determination
to keep my eyes wide open, and to be prepared for
trouble whenever, or in whatever shape, it might come.

On gaining the deck, I was received by an elderly
individual whom I afterwards discovered to be the
captain. He informed me in French that both Monsieur Pharos and the Fräulein Valerie had already
arrived on board and had retired to their cabins. The
former had given instructions that everything possible
was to be done to promote my comfort, and, having
said this, the captain surrendered me to the charge of
the servant who had escorted me on board, and, bowing
reverentially to me, made some excuse about seeing the
yacht under way, and went forward. At the request of
the steward I passed along the deck to the after-com-
panion ladder, and thence to the saloon below. The
evidence of wealth I had had before me in the house
in Naples had prepared me in some measure for the
magnificent vessel in which I now found myself; nevertheless, I must confess to feeling astonished at the
luxury I saw displayed on every side. The saloon
must have been upwards of thirty feet long by eighteen
wide, and one glance round it showed me that the decorations, the carpet, and the furniture, were the best
that taste and money could procure. With noiseless
footfall the steward conducted me across the saloon,
and, opening a door on the port side, introduced me to
my cabin.

My luggage had preceded me, and, as it was now close upon eleven o'clock, I determined to turn in, and, if possible, get to sleep before the vessel started.

When I woke in the morning we were at sea. Brilliant sunshine streamed in through the port-hole and danced on the white and gold panelling of the cabin. Smart seas rattled against the hull and set the little craft rolling, till I began to think it was as well I was a good sailor, otherwise I should scarcely have looked forward with such interest to the breakfast I could hear preparing in the saloon outside.

As soon as I had dressed, I made my way to the deck. It was a lovely morning, a bright blue sky overhead, with a few snow-white clouds away to the southwest to afford relief and to add to the beauty of the picture. A smart sea was running, and more than once I had to make a bolt for the companion-ladder in order to escape the spray which came whistling over the bulwarks.

In the daylight the yacht looked bigger than she had done on the previous night. At a rough guess she scarcely could have been less than four hundred tons. Her captain, so I afterwards discovered, was a Greek, but of what nationality her crew were composed I was permitted no opportunity of judging. One thing is very certain—they were not English, nor did their behaviour realize my notion of the typical sailor. There was none of that good-humoured chaff or horseplay which is supposed to characterize the calling. These men, for the most part, were middle-aged, taciturn, and gloomy fellows, who did their work with automaton-like regularity, but without interest or apparent good-will. The officers, with the exception of the captain, I had not yet seen.

Punctually on the stroke of eight bells a steward emerged from the companion and came aft to inform me that breakfast was served. I inquired if my host and hostess were in the saloon, but was informed that Pharos made it a rule never to rise before midday, and that, on this occasion, the Fräulein Valerie intended taking the meal in her own cabin and begged me to excuse her. Accordingly I sat down alone, and when I had finished returned to the deck and lit a cigar. The sea by this time had moderated somewhat, and the vessel in consequence was making better progress. For upwards of half an hour I tramped the deck religiously, and then returned to my favourite position aft. Leaning my elbows on the rail, I stood gazing at the curdling wake, watching the beautiful blending of white and green created by the screw.

I was still occupied in this fashion when I heard my name spoken, and, turning, found the Fräulein Valerie standing before me. She was dressed in some dark material, which not only suited her complexion but displayed the exquisite outline of her figure to perfection.

"Good-morning, Mr. Forrester," she said, holding out her white hand to me. "I must apologise to you for my rudeness in not having joined you at breakfast; but I was tired, and did not feel equal to getting up so early."

There was a troubled look in her eyes which told me that while she had not forgotten our interview of two nights before, she was determined not to refer to it in any way, or even to permit me to suppose that she remembered it. I accordingly resolved to follow her example, though, if the truth must be confessed, there were certain questions I was more than desirous of putting to her.

"Since you are on deck the first morning out, I presume you are fond of the sea?" I said in a matter-of-fact voice, after we had been standing together for some moments.

"I love it," she answered fervently; "and the more so because I am a good sailor. In the old days, when my father was alive, I was never happier than when we were at sea, away from land and all its attendant troubles."

She paused, and I saw her eyes fill with tears. In a few moments, however, she recovered her composure, and began to talk of the various countries with which we were mutually acquainted. As it soon transpired, she had visited almost every capital in Europe since she had been with Pharos, but for what purpose I could not discover. The most eastern side of Russia and the most western counties of England were equally well known to her. In an unguarded moment I asked her which city she preferred.

"Is it possible I could have any preference?" she asked, almost reproachfully. "If you were condemned to imprisonment for life, do you think it would matter to you what colour your captors painted your cell, or of what material the wall was composed that you looked upon through your barred windows? Such is my case. My freedom is gone, and for that reason I take no sort of interest in the places to which my gaoler leads me."

To this speech I offered no reply, nor could I see that one was needed. We were standing upon dangerous ground, and I hastened to get off it as soon as possible. I fear, however, I must have gone clumsily to work, for she noticed my endeavour and smiled a little bitterly, I thought. Then, making some excuse, she left me and returned below.

It was well past midday before Pharos put in an appearance. Whether at sea or ashore he made no difference in his costume. He wore the same heavy coat and curious cap that I remembered seeing that night at Cleopatra's Needle.

"I fear, my dear Forrester," he said, "you will think me a discourteous host for not having remained on deck last night to receive you. My age, however, must be my excuse. I trust you have been made comfortable?"

"The greatest Sybarite could scarcely desire to be more comfortable," I answered. "I congratulate you upon your vessel and her appointments."

"Yes," he answered, looking along the deck, "she is a good little craft, and, as you may suppose, exceedingly useful to me at times."

As he said this, a curious expression came into his face. It was as if the memory of an occasion on which this vessel had carried him beyond the reach of pursuit had suddenly occurred to him. Exquisite, however, as the pleasure it afforded him seemed to be, I cannot say that it pleased me as much. It revived unpleasant memories, and just at the time when I was beginning to forget my first distrust of him.

After a few moments' further conversation he expressed a desire to show me the vessel, an invitation which, needless to say, I accepted with alacrity. We first visited the smoking-room on deck, then the bridge, after that the engine-room, and later on the men's quarters forward. Retracing our steps aft, we descended to the saloon, upon the beauty of which I warmly congratulated him.

"I am rejoiced that it meets with your approval," he said gravely. "It is usually admired. And now, having seen all this, perhaps it would interest you to inspect the quarters of the owner."

This was exactly what I desired to do, for from a man's sleeping quarters it is often possible to obtain some clue as to his real character.

Bidding me follow him, he led me along the saloon to a cabin at the farther end. With the remembrance of all I had seen in the other parts of the vessel still fresh in my mind, I was prepared to find the owner's berth replete with every luxury. My surprise may therefore be imagined when I discovered a tiny cabin, scarcely half the size of that occupied by myself, not only devoid of luxury, but lacking much of what is usually considered absolutely necessary. On the starboard side was the bunk, a plain wooden affair, in which were neatly folded several pairs of coarse woollen blankets. Against the bulwark was the wash-hand-stand, and under the port a settee covered with a fur rug, on which was curled up the monkey Pehtes. That was all. Nay, I am wrong—it was not all. For in a corner, carefully secured so that the movement of the vessel should not cause it to fall, was no less a thing than the mummy Pharos had stolen from me, and which was the first and foremost cause of my being where I was. From what he had told me of his errand, I had surmised it might be on board ; but I confess I scarcely expected to find it in the owner's cabin. With the sight of it the recollection of my studio rose before my eyes, and not only of the studio, but of that terrible night when the old man now standing beside me, had called upon me and had used such diabolical means to obtain possession of the thing he wanted. In reality it was scarcely a week since Lady Medenham's "at home"; but the gulf that separated the man I was then from the man I was now seemed one of centuries.

Accompanied by Pharos I returned to the deck, convinced that I was as far removed from an understanding of this strange individual's character as I had been since I had known him. Of the Fräulein Valerie I saw nothing until late in the afternoon. She was suffering from a severe headache, so the steward informed Pharos, and was not equal to leaving her cabin.

That this news was not palatable to my companion, I gathered from the way in which his face darkened. However, he pretended to feel only solicitude for her welfare, and, having instructed the steward to convey his sympathy to her, returned to his conversation with me. In this fashion, reading, talking, and perambulating the deck, the remainder of the day passed away, and it was not until we sat down to dinner at night that our party in the saloon was united. On board the yacht, as in his house in Naples, the cooking was perfection itself; but, as on that other occasion, Pharos did not partake of it. He dined as usual upon fruit and small wheaten cakes, finishing his meal by pouring the powder into the glass of water and drinking it off as before.

When we rose from the table, my host and hostess retired to their respective cabins, while I lit a cigar and went on deck. The sun was just disappearing below the horizon, and a wonderful hush had fallen upon the sea. Scarcely a ripple disturbed its glassy surface, while the track the vessel left behind her seemed to lead across the world into the very eye of the sinking sun beyond. There was something awe-inspiring in the beauty and stillness of the evening. It was like the hush that precedes a violent storm, and seeing the captain near the entrance to the smoking-room, I made my way along the deck and accosted him, inquiring what he thought of the weather.

"I scarcely know what to think of it, monsieur," he answered in French. "The glass has fallen considerably since morning. My own opinion is that it is working up for a storm."

I agreed with him, and after a few moments more conversation thanked him for his courtesy and returned aft.

Reaching the skylight, I seated myself upon it. The glasses were lifted, and through the open space I could see into the saloon below. The mellow light of the shaded electric lamps shone upon the rich decorations and the inlaid furniture, and was reflected in the mirrors on the walls. As far as I could see, no one was present. I was about to rise and move away when a sound came from the Fräulein Valerie's cabin that caused me to remain where I was. Some one was speaking, and that person was a woman. Knowing there was no other of her sex on board, this puzzled me more than I can say. The voice was harsh, monotonous, unmusical, and grated strangely upon the ear. There was a pause, then another, which I instantly recognised as belonging to Pharos, commenced.

I had no desire to play the eavesdropper, but for some reason which I cannot explain I could not choose but listen.

"Come," Pharos was saying in German, "thou canst not disobey me. Hold my hand so, open thine eyes, and tell me what thou seest!"

There was a pause for a space in which I could have counted fifty. Then the woman's voice answered as slowly and monotonously as before.

"I see a sandy plain, which stretches as far as the eye can reach in all directions save one. On that side it is bordered by a range of hills. I see a collection of tents, and in the one nearest me a man tossing on a bed of sickness."

"Is it he? The man thou knowest?"

There was another pause, and when she answered, the woman's voice was even harsher than before.

"It is he."

"What dost thou see now?"

"I am in the dark, and see nothing."

"Hold my hand and wait, thou wilt see more plainly anon. Now that thine eyes are accustomed to the darkness, describe to me the place in which thou standest."

There was another interval. Then she began again.

"I am in a dark and gloomy cavern. The roof is supported by heavy pillars, and they are carved in a style I have never seen before. On the ceilings and walls are paintings, and lying on a slab of stone—a dead man,"

Once more there was a long silence, until I began to think that I must have missed the next question and answer, and that this extraordinary catechism had terminated. Then the voice of Pharos recommenced.

"Place thine hand in mine and look once more."

This time the answer was even more bewildering than before.

"I see death," said the voice. "Death on every hand It continues night and day, and the world is full of wailing."

"It is well; I am satisfied," said Pharos. "Now lie down and sleep. In an hour thou wilt wake and wilt remember nought of what thou hast revealed to me."

Unable to make anything of what I had heard, I rose from the place where I had been sitting and began to pace the deck. The remembrance of the conversation to which I had listened irritated me beyond measure. Had I been permitted another insight into the devilry of Pharos, or what was the meaning of it? I was still thinking of this when I heard a step behind me, and, turning, found the man himself approaching me. In the dim light of the deck the appearance he presented was not prepossessing, but when he approached me I discovered he was in the best of humours,—in fact, in better spirits than I had ever yet seen him.

"I have been looking for you, Mr. Forrester," he said. "It is delightful on deck, and I am in just the humour for a chat."

I felt an inclination to tell him that I was not so ready, but before I could give him an answer he had noticed my preoccupation.

"You have something on your mind," he said. "I

" ' I see death,' said the voice, ' Death on every hand.' "

fear you are not as pleased with my hospitality as I could wish you to be. What is amiss? Is there anything I can do to help you?"

"Nothing, I thank you," I answered a little stiffly. "I have a slight headache, and am not much disposed for conversation this evening."

Though the excuse I made was virtually true, I did not tell him that I had only felt it since I had overheard his conversation a few moments before.

"You must let me cure you," he answered. "I am vain enough to flatter myself I have some knowledge of medicine."

I was beginning to wonder if there was anything of which he was ignorant. At the same time I was so suspicious of him that I had no desire to permit him to practise his arts on me. I accordingly thanked him, but declined his services on the pretext that my indisposition was too trifling to call for so much trouble.

"As you will," he answered carelessly. "If you are not anxious to be cured, you must, of course, continue to suffer."

So saying, he changed the subject, and for upwards of half an hour we wandered in the realm of art, discussing the methods of painters, past and present. Upon this subject, as upon every other, I was amazed at the extent and depth of his learning. His taste, I discovered, was cosmopolitan, but if he had any preference it was for the early Tuscan school. We were still debating this point when a dark figure emerged from the companion and came along the deck towards us. Seeing that it was the Fräulein Valerie, I rose from my chair.

"How hot the night is, Mr. Forrester!" she said, as she came up to us. "There is thunder in the air, I am sure, and, if I am not mistaken, we shall have a storm before morning."

"I think it more than likely," I answered. "It is extremely oppressive below."

"It is almost unbearable," she answered, as she took the seat I offered her. "Notwithstanding that fact, I believe I must have fallen asleep in my cabin, for I cannot remember what I have been doing since dinner."

Recalling the conversation I had overheard, and which had concluded with the instruction, "In an hour thou wilt wake and wilt remember nought of what thou hast revealed to me," I glanced at Pharos; but his face told me nothing.

"I fear you are not quite yourself, my dear," said the latter in a kindly tone, as he leant towards her and placed his skinny hand upon her arm. "As you say, it must be the thundery evening. Our friend Forrester here is complaining of a headache. Though he will not let me experiment upon him, I think I shall have to see what I can do for you. I will consult my medicine chest at once."

With this he rose from his seat, and, bidding us farewell, went below.

Presently the Fräulein rose, and, side by side, we walked aft to the taffrail. Though I did my best to rouse her from the lethargy into which she had fallen, I was unsuccessful. She stood with her slender hands clasping the rail before her, and her great, dark eyes staring out across the waste of water. Never had she

looked more beautiful, and certainly never more sad,
Her unhappiness touched me to the heart, and, under
the influence of my emotion, I approached a little
nearer to her.

"You are unhappy," I said. "Is there no way in
which I can help you?"

"Not one," she answered bitterly, still gazing steadfastly out to sea. "I am beyond the reach of help.
Can you realize what it means, Mr. Forrester, to be
beyond the reach of help?"

The greatest tragedienne the world has seen could
not have invested those terrible words with greater
or more awful meaning.

"No, no," I said; "I cannot believe that. You are
overwrought to-night. You are not yourself. You say
things you do not mean."

This time she turned on me almost fiercely.

"Mr. Forrester," she said, "you try to console me;
but, as I am beyond the reach of help, so I am also
beyond the reach of comfort. If you could have but
the slightest conception of what my life is, you would
not wonder that I am so wretched."

"Will you not tell me about it?" I answered. "I
think you know by this time that I may be trusted."
Then, sinking my voice a little, I added a sentence
that I could scarcely believe I had uttered when the
words had passed my lips. "Valerie, if you do not
already know it, let me tell you that, although we have
not known each other a fortnight, I would give my
life to serve you."

"And I believe you and thank you for it from the
bottom of my heart," she answered, with equal earnest-

ness; " but I can tell you nothing." Then, after an interval of silence that must have lasted for some minutes she declared her intention of going below.

I accompanied her as far as the saloon, where she once more gave me her hand and wished me good-night. As soon as her door had closed behind her, I went to my own cabin, scarcely able to realize that I had said what I had.

I do not know whether it was the heat, or whether it was the excitement under which I was labouring. At any rate, I soon discovered that I could not sleep. Valerie's beautiful, sad face haunted me continually. Hour after hour I lay awake, thinking of her and wondering what the mystery could be that surrounded her. The night was oppressively still. Save the throbbing of the screw, not a sound was to be heard. The yacht was upon an even keel, and scarcely a wavelet splashed against her side. At last I could bear the stifling cabin no longer, so, rising from my bunk, I dressed myself and sought the coolness of the deck. It was now close upon one o'clock, and when I emerged from the companion the moon was a hand's breadth above the sea line, rising like a ball of gold. I seemed to have the entire world to myself. Around me was the glassy sea, black as ink, save where the moon shone upon it. Treading softly, as if I feared my footsteps would wake the sleeping ship, I stepped out of the companion, and was about to make my way aft, when something I saw before me caused me to stop. Standing on the grating, which extended the whole width of the stern behind the after wheel, was a man whom I had no difficulty in recognising

as Pharos. His hands were lifted above his head, as
if he were invoking the assistance of the Goddess of
the Night. His head was thrown back, and from the
place where I stood I could distinctly see the expression upon it. Anything more fiendish could
scarcely be imagined. It was not the face of a
human being, but that of a ghoul, so repulsive and
yet so fascinating was it. Try how I would, I could
not withdraw my eyes ; and while I watched, he spread
his arms apart and cried something aloud in a language
I did not recognise. For upwards of a minute he
remained in this attitude, then, descending from the
grating, he made his way slowly along the deck, and
came towards the place where I stood.

Afraid of I know not what, I shrank back into the
shadow of the hatch. Had he discovered my presence,
I feel convinced, in the humour in which he then was,
he would have done his best to kill me. Fortunately,
however, my presence was unsuspected, and he went
below without seeing me. Then, wiping great beads
of sweat from my forehead, I stumbled to the nearest
skylight, and, seating myself upon it, endeavoured to
regain my composure. Once more I asked myself
the question, "Who and what was this man into
whose power I had fallen?"

CHAPTER IX

THE captain was not very far out in his reckoning when he prophesied that the unusual calm of the previous evening betokened the approach of a storm. Every one who has had experience of the Mediterranean is aware with what little warning gales spring up. At daybreak the weather may be all that can be desired, and in the evening your ship is fighting her way along in the teeth of a hurricane. In this particular instance, when I turned into my bunk after the fright Pharos had given me, as narrated in the preceding chapter, the sea was as smooth as glass and the sky innocent of a single cloud. When I opened my eyes on the morning following, the yacht was being pitched up and down and to and fro like a cork. A gale of wind was blowing overhead, while every timber sent forth an indignant protest against the barbarity to which it was being subjected. From the pantry, beyond the saloon companion-ladder, a clatter of breaking glass followed every roll, while I was able to estimate the magnitude of the seas the little vessel was encountering, by the number of times her propeller raced, as she hung suspended in mid-air. For upwards of an hour I remained in my bunk, thinking of the singular events of the night before, and telling myself that were it not for the Fräulein

Valerie, I could find it in my heart to wish myself
out of the yacht and back in my own comfortable
studio once more. By seven o'clock my curiosity was
so excited as to what was doing on deck, that I could
no longer remain inactive. I accordingly scrambled
out of bed and dressed myself, a proceeding which,
owing to the movement of the vessel, was attended
with no small amount of difficulty, and then, clutching
at everything that would permit of a grip, I passed out
of the saloon and made my way up the companion-
ladder. On glancing through the port-holes there,
a scene of indescribable tumult met my eye. In place
of the calm and almost monotonous stretch of blue
water, across which we had been sailing so peacefully
less than twenty-four hours before, I now saw a wild
and angry sea, upon which dark, leaden clouds looked
down. The gale was from the north-east, and beat
upon our port quarter with relentless fury.

My horizon being limited in the companion, I turned
the handle and prepared to step on to the deck outside.
It was only when I had done so that I realized how
strong the wind was ; it caught the door and dashed it
from my hand as if it had been made of paper, while
the cap I had upon my head was whisked off and
carried away into the swirl of grey water astern before I
had time to clap my hand to it. Undaunted, however,
by this mishap, I shut the door, and, hanging on to the
hand-rail, lest I too should be washed overboard, made
my way forward and eventually reached the ladder
leading to the bridge. By the time I put my foot upon
the first step I was quite exhausted, and had to pause in
order to recover my breath ; and yet, if it was so bad

below, how shall I describe the scene which greeted my eyes when I stood upon the bridge itself? From that dizzy height I was better able to estimate the magnitude of the waves and the capabilities of the little vessel for withstanding them.

The captain, sea-booted and clad in sou'-wester and oilskins, came forward and dragged me to a place of safety as soon as he became aware of my presence. I saw his lips move, but what with the shrieking of the wind in the shrouds and the pounding of the seas on the deck below, what he said was quite inaudible, Once in the corner to which he led me, I clung to the rails like a drowning man, and regarded the world above my canvas screen in silent consternation. And I had excellent reasons for being afraid, for the picture before me was one that might have appalled the stoutest heart. Violent as the sea had appeared from the port of the companion hatch, it looked doubly so now; and the higher the waves, the deeper the valleys in between. Tossed to and fro, her bows one moment in mid-air and the next pointing to the bottom of the ocean, it seemed impossible so frail a craft could long withstand the buffeting she was receiving. She rolled without ceasing, long, sickening movements followed on each occasion by a death-like pause that made the heart stand still, and forced the belief upon one that she could never right herself again. Times out of number, I searched the captain's face in the hope of deriving some sort of encouragement from it; but I found none. On the other hand, it was plain, from the glances he now and again threw back along the vessel, and from the strained expression that was never absent from his eyes, that he was as anxious as myself, and, since he was more conversant with her capabilities, with perhaps greater reason. Only the man at the wheel—a tall, gaunt individual, with bushy eyebrows and the largest hands I have ever seen on a human being—seemed undisturbed. Despite the fact that upon his handling of those frail spokes depended the lives of twenty human creatures, he was as undaunted by the war of the elements going on around him as if he were sitting by the fireside, smoking his pipe, ashore.

For upwards of half an hour I remained where the captain had placed me, drenched by the spray, listening to the dull thud of the seas as they broke upon the deck below, and watching with an interest that amounted almost to a pain the streams of water that sluiced backwards and forwards across the bridge every time she rolled. Then, summoning all my courage, for I can assure you it was needed, I staggered towards the ladder, and once more prepared to make my way below. I had not reached the deck, however, and fortunately my hands had not quitted the guide rails, when a wave larger than any I had yet seen mounted the bulwark and dashed aboard, carrying away a boat and twisting the davits, from which it had been suspended a moment before, like pieces of bent wire. Had I descended a moment earlier, nothing could have prevented me from being washed overboard. With a feeling of devout thankfulness in my heart for my escape, I remained where I was, clinging to the ladder long after the sea had passed and disappeared through the scuppers. Then I descended, and, holding on to the rails as before, eventually reached the saloon entrance in safety.

To be inside, in that still, warm atmosphere, out of the pressure of the wind, was a relief beyond all telling, though what sort of object I must have looked, with my hair blown in all directions by the wind, and my clothes soaked through and through by the spray that had dashed upon me on the bridge, is more than I can say. Thinking it advisable I should change as soon as possible, I made my way to my own cabin, but, before I reached it, the door of that occupied by the Fräulein Valerie opened, and she came out. That something unusual was the matter I saw at a glance.

"Mr. Forrester," she said, with a scorn in her voice that cut like a knife, " come here. I have something curious to show you."

I did as she wished, and forthwith she led me to her cabin. I was not prepared, however, for what I found there. Crouching in a corner, almost beside himself with fear, and with the frightened face of the monkey, Pehtes, peering out from beneath his coat, was no less a person than Pharos, the man I had hitherto supposed insensible to such an emotion. In the presence of that death, however, which we all believed to be so imminent, he showed himself a coward passed all believing. Terror incarnate stared from his eyes and rendered him unconscious of our scorn. At every roll the vessel gave he shrank farther into his corner, glaring at us meanwhile with a ferocity that was not very far removed from madness.

At any other time and in any other person such an exhibition might have been conducive of pity ; in his case, however, it only added to the loathing I already felt for him. One thing was very certain : in his present

condition he was no fit companion for the woman who
stood clinging to the door behind me. I accordingly
determined to get him either to his own cabin or to
mine without delay.

"Come, come, Monsieur Pharos," I said, "you must
not give way like this. I have been on deck, and I can
assure you there is no immediate danger."

As I said this, I stooped and placed my hand upon
his shoulder. He threw it off with a snarl and a snap
of his teeth that was more like the action of a mad
dog than that of a man.

"You lie, you lie!" he cried in a paroxysm of rage
and fear. "I am cursed, and I shall never see land
again. But I will not die—I will not die. There must
be some way of keeping the yacht afloat. The captain
must find one. If any one is to be saved, it must be
me. Do you hear what I say? It must be me."

For the abominable selfishness of this remark I could
have struck him.

"Are you a man that you can talk like this in the
presence of a woman?" I cried. "For shame, sir, for
shame. Get up, and let me conduct you to your own
cabin."

With this I lifted him to his feet, and, whether he
liked it or not, half led and half dragged him along the
saloon to his own quarters. Once there, I placed him
on his settee, but the next roll of the vessel brought him
to the floor and left him crouching in the corner, still
clutching the monkey, his knees almost level with his
shoulders, and his awful face looking up at me between
them. The whole affair was so detestable that my
gorge rose at it, and when I left him I returned to the

saloon with a greater detestation of him in my heart than I had felt before. I found the Fräulein Valerie seated at the table.

"Fräulein," I said, seating myself beside her, "I am afraid you have been needlessly alarmed. As I said in there, I give you my word there is no immediate danger."

"I *am* frightened," she answered. "See how my hands are trembling. But it is not death I fear."

"You fear that man," I said, nodding my head in the direction of the cabin I had just left ; "but I assure you, you need not do so, for to-day, at least, he is harmless."

"Ah! you do not know him as I do," she replied. "I have seen him like this before. As soon as the storm abates he will be himself again, and then he will hate us both the more for having been witnesses of his cowardice." Then, sinking her voice a little, she added, "I often wonder, Mr. Forrester, whether he can be human. If so, he must be the only one of his kind in the world, for Nature surely could not permit two such men to live."

CHAPTER X

I T was almost dark when the yacht entered the harbour of Port Said, though the sky at the back of the town still retained the last lingering colours of the sunset, which had been more beautiful that evening than I ever remembered to have seen it before. Well acquainted as I was with the northern shores of the Mediterranean, this was the first time I had been brought into contact with the southern, and, what was more important, it was also the first occasion on which I had joined hands with the Immemorial East. In the old days I had repeatedly heard it said by travellers that Port Said was a place not only devoid of interest, but entirely lacking in artistic colour. I take the liberty of disagreeing with my informants *in toto*. Port Said greeted me with the freshness of a new life. The colouring and quaint architecture of the houses, the vociferous boatmen, the monotonous chant of the Arab coalers, the string of camels I could just make out turning the corner of a distant street, the donkey boys, the Soudanese soldiers at the barriers, and last, but by no means least, the crowd of shipping in the harbour, constituted a picture that was as full of interest as it was of new impressions.

As soon as we were at anchor, and the necessary formalities of the port had been complied with, Pharos's

servant, the man who had accompanied us from Pompeii
and who had brought me on board in Naples, made his
way ashore, whence he returned in something less than
an hour to inform us that he had arranged for a special
train to convey us to our destination.   We accordingly
bade farewell to the yacht and were driven to the rail-
way-station, a primitive building on the outskirts of the
town.   Here an engine and a single carriage awaited
us.   We took our places, and five minutes later were
steaming across the flat, sandy plain that borders the
Canal and separates it from the Bitter Lakes.

Ever since the storm, and the unpleasant insight it
had afforded me into Pharos's character, our relations
had been somewhat strained.   As the Fräulein Valerie
had predicted, as soon as he recovered his self-possession
he hated me the more for having been a witness of his
cowardice.   For the remainder of the voyage he scarcely
put in an appearance on deck, but spent the greater
portion of his time in his own cabin, though in what
manner he occupied himself there I could not imagine.

Now that we were in our railway-carriage, *en route*
to Cairo, looking out upon that dreary landscape, with
its dull expanse of water on one side, and the high bank
of the Canal, with, occasionally, glimpses of the passing
stations, on the other, we were brought into actual contact, and, in consequence, things improved somewhat.
But even then we could scarcely have been described as
a happy party.   The Fräulein Valerie sat for the most
part silent and preoccupied, facing the engine in the
right-hand corner; Pharos, wrapped in his heavy fur
coat and rug, and with his inevitable companion cuddled
up beside him, had taken his place opposite her.   I sat

in the farther corner, watching them both, and dimly wondering at the strangeness of my position. At Ismailya another train awaited us, and when we and our luggage had been transhipped to it we continued our journey, entering now on the region of the desert proper. The heat was almost unbearable, and to make matters worse, as soon as darkness fell and the lamps were lighted, swarms of mosquitoes emerged from their hiding-places and descended upon us. The train rolled and jolted its way over the sandy plain, passed the battlefields of Tel-el-Kebir and Kassassin, and still Pharos and the woman opposite him remained seated in the same position, he with his head thrown back, and the same deathlike expression upon his face, and she, staring out of the window, but, I am certain, seeing nothing of the country through which we were passing. It was long after midnight when we reached the capital. Once more the same obsequious servant was in attendance. A carriage, he informed us, awaited our arrival at the station door, and in it we were whirled off to the hotel, at which rooms had been engaged for us. However disagreeable Pharos might make himself, it was at least certain that to travel with him was to do so in luxury.

Of all the impressions I received that day, none struck me with greater force than the drive from the station to the hotel. I had expected to find a typical Eastern city; in place of it I was confronted with one that was almost Parisian, as far as its handsome houses and broad, tree-shaded streets were concerned. Nor was our hotel behind it in point of interest. It proved to be a gigantic affair, elaborately decorated in the Egyptian fashion, and replete, as the advertisements say, with every modern convenience. The owner himself met us at the entrance, and from the fact that he informed Pharos, with the greatest possible respect, that his old suite of rooms had been retained for him, I gathered that they were not strangers to each other.

"At last we are in Cairo, Mr. Forrester," said the latter with an ugly sneer, when we had reached our sitting-room, in which a meal had been prepared for us, "and the dream of your life is realized. I hasten to offer you my congratulations."

In my own mind I had a doubt as to whether it was a matter of congratulation to me to be there in his company. I, however, made an appropriate reply, and then assisted the Fräulein Valerie to divest herself of her travelling cloak. When she had done so, we sat down to our meal. The long railway journey had made us hungry; but, though I happened to know that he had tasted nothing for more than eight hours, Pharos would not join us. As soon as we had finished, we bade each other good-night and retired to our various apartments.

On reaching my room, I threw open my window and looked out. I could scarcely believe that I was in the place in which my father had taken such delight, and where he had spent so many of the happiest hours of his life.

When I woke, my first thought was to study the city from my bedroom window. It was an exquisite morning, and the scene before me more than equalled it in beauty. From where I stood I looked away across the flat roofs of houses, over the crests of palm trees, into the blue distance beyond, where, to my delight, I could just discern the Pyramids peering up above the Nile. In the street below, stalwart Arabs, donkey boys, and almost every variety of beggar could be seen; and while I watched, emblematical of the change in the administration of the country, a guard of Highlanders, with a piper playing at their head, marched by, *en route* to the headquarters of the Army of Occupation.

As usual, Pharos did not put in an appearance when breakfast was served. Accordingly, the Fräulein and I sat down to it alone. When we had finished, we made our way to the cool stone verandah, where we seated ourselves, and I obtained permission to smoke a cigarette. That my companion had something upon her mind, I was morally convinced. She appeared nervous and ill at ease, and I noticed that more than once, when I addressed some remark to her, she glanced eagerly at my face, as if she hoped to obtain an opening for what she wanted to say, and then, finding that I was only commenting on the stateliness of some Arab passer-by, the beautiful peep of blue sky permitted us between two white buildings opposite, or the graceful foliage of a palm overhanging a neighbouring wall, she would heave a sigh and turn impatiently from me again.

"Mr. Forrester," she said at last, when she could bear it no longer, "I intended to have spoken to you yesterday, but I was not vouchsafed an opportunity. You told me on board the yacht that there was nothing you would not do to help me. I have a favour to ask of you now. Will you grant it?"

Guessing from her earnestness what was coming, I hesitated before I replied.

"Would it not be better to leave it to my honour to do or not to do so after you have told me what it is?" I asked.

"No; you must give me your promise first," she replied. "Believe me, I mean it when I say that your compliance with my request will make me a happier woman than I have been for some time past." Here she blushed a rosy red, as though she thought she had said too much. "But it is possible my happiness does not weigh with you."

"It weighs very heavily," I replied. "It is on that account I cannot give my promise blindfold."

On hearing this, she seemed somewhat disappointed.

"I did not think you would refuse me," she said, "since what I am going to ask of you is only for your own good. Mr. Forrester, you have seen something on board the yacht of the risk you run while you are associated with Pharos. You are now on land again, and your own master. If you desire to please me, you will take the opportunity and go away. Every hour that you remain here only adds to your danger. The crisis will soon come, and then you will find that you have neglected my warning too long."

"Forgive me," I answered, this time as seriously as even she could desire, "if I say that I have not neglected your warning. Since you have so often pointed it out to me, and judging from what I have already seen of the character of the old gentleman in question, I can quite believe that he is capable of any villainy; but, if you will pardon my reminding you of it, I think you have heard my decision before. I am willing, nay, even eager to go away, provided you will do the same.

If, however, you decline, then I remain. More than that I will not, and less than that I cannot, promise."

"What you ask is impossible; it is out of the question," she continued. "As I have told you so often before, Mr. Forrester, I am bound to him for ever, and by chains that no human power can break. What is more, even if I were to do as you wish, it would be useless. The instant he wanted me, if he were thousands of miles away and only breathed my name, I should forget your kindness, my freedom, his old cruelty—everything, in fact—and go back to him. Have you not seen enough of us to know that where he is concerned, I have no will of my own? Besides —but there, I cannot tell you any more! Let it suffice that I cannot do as you ask."

Remembering the interview I had overheard that night on board the yacht, I did not know what to say. That Pharos had her under his influence, I had, as she had said, seen enough to be convinced. And yet, regarded in the light of our sober, every-day life, how impossible it all seemed! I looked at the beautiful, fashionably-dressed woman seated by my side, playing with the silver handle of her Parisian parasol, and wondered if I could be dreaming, and whether I should presently waken to find myself in bed in my comfortable rooms in London once more, and my servant entering with my shaving water.

"I think you are very cruel!" she said, when I returned no answer. "Surely you must be aware how much it adds to my unhappiness to know that another is being drawn into his toils, and yet you refuse to do the one and only thing which can make my mind easier."

"Fräulein," I said, rising and standing before her, "the first time I saw you I knew that you were unhappy. I could see that the canker of some great sorrow was eating into your heart. I wished that I could help you, and Fate accordingly willed that I should make your acquaintance. Afterwards, by a terrible series of coincidences, I was brought into personal contact with your life. I found that my first impression was a correct one. You were miserable, as, thank God! few human beings are. On the night that I dined with you in Naples you warned me of the risk I was running in associating with Pharos, and implored me to save myself. When I knew that you were bound hand and foot to him, can you wonder that I declined? Since then I have been permitted further opportunities of seeing what your life with him is like. Once more you ask me to save myself, and once more I make you this answer. If you will accompany me, I will go; and if you do so, I swear to God that I will protect and shield you to the best of my ability. I have many influential friends who will count it an honour to take you into their families until something can be arranged, and with whom you will be safe. On the other hand, if you will not go, I pledge you my word that so long as you remain in this man's company I will do so too. No argument will shake my determination, and no entreaty move me from the position I have taken up."

I searched her face for some sign of acquiescence, but could find none. It was bloodless in its pallor, and yet so beautiful, that at any other time and in any other place I should have been compelled by the love I felt for her—a love that I now knew to be stronger than life itself—to take her in my arms and tell her that she was the only woman in the wide world for me, that I would protect her, not only against Pharos, but against his master, Apollyon himself. Now, however, such a confession was impossible. Situated as we were, hemmed in by dangers on every side, to speak of love to her would have been little better than an insult.

"What answer do you give me?" I said, seeing that she did not speak.

"Only that you are cruel," she replied. "You know my misery, and yet you add to it. Have I not told you that I should be a happier woman if you went?"

"You must forgive me for saying so, but I do not believe it," I said, with a boldness and a vanity that surprised even myself. "No, Fräulein, do not let us play at cross purposes. It is evident you are afraid of this man, and that you believe yourself to be in his power. I feel convinced it is not as bad as you say. Look at it in a matter-of-fact light and tell me how it can be so? Supposing you leave him now, and we fly, shall we say, to London. You are your own mistress and quite at liberty to go. At any rate, you are not his property to do with as he likes, so if he follows you and persists in annoying you, there are many ways of inducing him to refrain from doing so."

She shook her head.

"Once more, I say, how little you know him, Mr. Forrester, and how poorly you estimate his powers! Since you have forced me to it, let me tell you that I have twice tried to do what you propose. Once in St.

Petersburg and once in Norway. He had terrified me, and I swore that I would rather die than see his face again. Almost starving, supporting myself as best I could by my music, I made my way to Moscow, thence to Kiev and Lemburg and across the Carpathians to Buda-Pesth. Some old friends of my father's, to whom I was ultimately forced to appeal, took me in. I remained with them a month, and during that time heard nothing either of or from Monsieur Pharos. Then, one night, when I sat alone in my bedroom, after my friends had retired to rest, a strange feeling that I was not alone in the room came over me—a feeling that something, I do not know what, was standing behind me, urging me to leave the house and to go out into the wood which adjoined it to meet the man whom I feared more than poverty, more than starvation, more even than death itself. Unable to refuse, or even to argue with myself, I rose, drew a cloak about my shoulders, and, descending the stairs, unbarred a door and went swiftly down the path towards the dark wood to which I have just referred. Incredible as it may seem, I had not been deceived. Pharos was there, seated on a fallen tree, waiting for me."

"And the result?"

"The result was that I never returned to the house, nor have I any recollection of what happened at our interview. The next thing I remember was finding myself in Paris. Months afterwards I learnt that my friends had searched high and low for me in vain, and had at last come to the conclusion that my melancholy had induced me to make away with myself. I wrote to them to say that I was safe, and to ask their forgiveness, but my letter has never been answered. The next time was in Norway. While we were there, a young Norwegian pianist came under the spell of Pharos's influence. But the load of misery he was called upon to bear was too much for him, and he killed himself. In one of his cruel moments Pharos congratulated me on the success with which I had acted as his decoy. Realizing the part I had unconsciously played, and knowing that escape in any other direction was impossible, I resolved to follow the wretched lad's example. I arranged everything as carefully as a desperate woman could do. We were staying at the time near one of the deepest fjords, and if I could only reach the place unseen, I was prepared to throw myself over into the water five hundred feet below. Every preparation was made, and when I thought Pharos was asleep, I crept from the house and made my way along the rough mountain path to the spot where I was going to say farewell to my wretched life for good and all. For days past I had been nerving myself for the deed. Reaching the spot, I stood upon the brink, gazing down into the depths below, thinking of my poor father, whom I expected soon to join, and wondering when my mangled body would be found. Then, lifting my arms above my head, I was about to let myself go, when a voice behind me ordered me to stop. I recognised it, and though I knew that before he could approach me it was possible for me to effect my purpose, and place myself beyond even his power for ever, I was unable to do as I desired.

"'Come here,' he said,—and since you know him you can imagine how he would say it,—'this is the second

time you have endeavoured to outwit me.   First you
sought refuge in flight, but I brought you back.   Now
you have tried suicide, but once more I have defeated
you.   Learn this, that as in life so even in death you
are mine to do with as I will.'   After that he led me
back to the hotel, and from that time I have been convinced that nothing can release me from the chains that
bind me."

Once more I thought of the conversation I had overheard through the saloon skylight on board the yacht.
What comfort to give her, or what answer to make, I
did not know.   I was still debating this in my mind
when she rose, and, offering some excuse, left me and
went into the house.   When she had gone, I seated
myself in my chair again and tried to think out what
she had told me.   It seemed impossible that her story
could be true, and yet I knew her well enough by this
time to feel sure that she would not lie to me.   But for
such a man as Pharos to exist in this prosaic nineteenth
century, and stranger still, for me, Cyril Forrester, who
had always prided myself on my clearness of head, to
believe in him, was absurd.   That I was beginning to
do so was, in a certain sense, only too true.   I was
resolved, however, that, happen what might in the
future, I would keep my wits about me and endeavour
to outwit him, not only for my own sake, but for that of
the woman I loved, whom I could not induce to seek
refuge in flight while she had the opportunity.

During the afternoon I saw nothing of Pharos.   He
kept himself closely shut up in his own apartment, and
was seen only by that same impassive manservant I
have elsewhere described.   The day, however, was not

destined to go by without my coming in contact with
him. The Fräulein Valerie and I had spent the evening in the cool hall of the hotel, but being tired she had
bidden me good-night and gone to her room at an early
hour. Scarcely knowing what to do with myself, I was
making my way upstairs to my room, when the door of
Pharos's apartment opened, and to my surprise the old
man emerged. He was dressed for going out—that is
to say, he wore his long fur coat and curious cap. On
seeing him, I stepped back into the shadow of the doorway, and was fortunate enough to be able to do so
before he became aware of my presence. As soon as
he had passed, I went to the balustrading and watched
him go down the stairs, wondering, as I did so, what was
taking him from home at such a late hour. The more
I thought of it the more inquisitive I became. A great
temptation seized me to follow him and find out.
Being unable to resist it, I went to my room, found my
hat, slipped a revolver into my pocket, in case I might
want it, and set off after him.

On reaching the great hall, I was just in time to see
him step into a carriage, which had evidently been
ordered for him beforehand. The driver cracked his
whip, the horses started off, and, by the time I stood
in the porch, the carriage was a good distance down
the street.

"Has my friend gone?" I cried to the porter, as if I
had hastened downstairs in the hope of seeing him
before he left. "I had changed my mind and intended
accompanying him. Call me a cab as quickly as you
can."

One of the neat little victorias which ply in the

streets of Cairo was immediately forthcoming, and into it I sprang.

"Tell the man to follow the other carriage," I said to the porter, " as fast as he can go."

The porter said something in Arabic to the driver, and a moment later we were off in pursuit.

It was a beautiful night, and, after the heat of the day, the rush through the cool air was infinitely refreshing. It was not until we had gone upwards of a mile, and the first excitement of the chase had a little abated, that the folly of what I was doing came home to me, but even then it did not induce me to turn back. Connected with Pharos as I was, I was determined, if possible, to find out something more about him and his doings before I permitted him to get a firmer hold upon me. If I could only discover his business on this particular night, it struck me, I might know how to deal with him. I accordingly pocketed my scruples, and slipping my hand into my pocket to make sure that my revolver was there, I permitted my driver to proceed upon his way unhindered. By this time we had passed the Kasr en-nil Barracks, and were rattling over the great Nile Bridge. It was plain from this that, whatever the errand might be that was taking him abroad, it at least had no connection with old Cairo.

Crossing the Island of Bulak, and leaving the caravan depôt on our left, we headed away under the avenue of beautiful Lebbek trees along the road to Gizeh. At first I thought it must be the museum he was aiming for, but this idea was dispelled when we passed the great gates and turned sharp to the right hand. Hold-

ing my watch to the carriage-lamp, I discovered that it
wanted only a few minutes to eleven o'clock.

Although still shaded with Lebbek trees, the road no
longer ran between human habitations, but far away on
the right and left a few twinkling lights proclaimed the
existence of Fellahin villages. Of foot-passengers we
saw none, and save the occasional note of a night-bird,
the howling of a dog in the far distance, and the rattle
of our own wheels, scarcely a sound was to be heard.
Gradually the road, which was raised several feet above
the surrounding country, showed a tendency to ascend,
and just as I was beginning to wonder what sort of a
will-o'-the-wisp chase it was upon which I was being
led, and what the upshot of it would be, it came to an
abrupt standstill, and, towering into the starlight above
me, I saw two things which swept away all my doubts,
and told me, as plainly as any words could speak, that
we were at the end of our journey. *We had reached the
Pyramids of Gizeh.* As soon as I understood this, I
signed to my driver to pull up, and, making him understand as best I could that he was to await my return,
descended and made my way towards the Pyramids on
foot.

Keeping my eye on Pharos, whom I could see ahead of
me, and taking care not to allow him to become aware
that he was being followed, I began the long pull up to
the plateau on which the largest of these giant monuments is situated. Fortunately for me the sand not
only prevented any sound from reaching him, while its
colour enabled me to keep him well in sight. The road
from the Mena House Hotel to the Great Pyramid is
not a long one, but what it lacks in length it makes up in

steepness.   Never losing sight of Pharos for an instant,
I ascended it.   On arriving at the top, I noticed that he
went straight forward to the base of the huge mass, and
when he was sixty feet or so from it, called something
in a loud voice.   He had scarcely done so before a
figure emerged from the shadow and approached him.
Fearing they might see me, I laid myself down on the
sands behind a large block of stone, whence I could
watch them, remaining myself unseen.

As far as I could tell, the new-comer was undoubtedly an Arab, and, from the way in which he
towered above Pharos, must have been a man of
gigantic stature.   For some minutes they remained in
earnest conversation.   Then, leaving the place where they
had met, they went forward towards the great building,
the side of which they presently commenced to climb.
After a little they disappeared, and, feeling certain they
had entered the Pyramid itself, I rose to my feet and
determined to follow.

The Great Pyramid, as all the world knows, is
composed of enormous blocks of granite, each about
three feet high, and arranged after the fashion of enormous steps.   The entrance to the passage which leads
to the interior is on the thirteenth tier, and nearly fifty
feet from the ground.   With a feeling of awe which
may be very well understood, when I reached it I
paused before entering.   I did not know on the threshold of what discovery I might be standing.   And what
was more, I reflected that if Pharos found me following
him, my life would in all probability pay the forfeit.   My
curiosity, however, was greater than my judgment, and
being determined, since I had come so far, not to go

back without learning all there was to know, I hardened my heart, and, stooping down, entered the passage. When I say that it is less than four feet in height, and of but little more than the same width, and that for the first portion of the way the path slopes downwards at an angle of twenty-six degrees, some vague idea may be obtained of the unpleasant place it is. But if I go on to add that the journey had to be undertaken in total darkness, without any sort of knowledge of what lay before me, or whether I should ever be able to find my way out again, the foolhardiness of the undertaking will be even more apparent. Step by step, and with a caution which I can scarcely exaggerate, I made my way down the incline, trying every inch before I put my weight upon it, and feeling the walls carefully with either hand in order to make sure that no other passages branched off to right or left. After I had been advancing for what seemed an interminable period, but could not in reality have been more than five minutes, I found myself brought to a standstill by a solid wall of stone. For a moment I was at a loss how to proceed. Then I found that there was a turn in the passage, and the path, instead of continuing to descend, was beginning to work upwards, whereupon, still feeling my way as before, I continued my journey of exploration. The heat was stifling, and more than once foul things, that only could have been bats, flapped against my face and hands and sent a cold shudder flying over me. Had I dared for a moment to think of the immense quantity of stone that towered above me, or what my fate would be had a stone fallen from its place and blocked the path behind me, I believe I should have been lost for good and all. But, frightened as I was, a greater terror was in store for me.

After I had been proceeding for some time along the passage, I found that it was growing gradually higher. The air was cooler, and raising my head cautiously in order not to bump it against the ceiling, I discovered that I was able to stand upright. I lifted my hand, first a few inches, and then to the full extent of my arm ; but the roof was still beyond my reach. I moved a little to my right in order to ascertain if I could touch the wall, and then to the left. But once more only air rewarded me. It was evident that I had left the passage and was standing in some large apartment ; but, since I knew nothing of the interior of the Pyramid, I could not understand what it was or where it could be situated. Feeling convinced in my own mind that I had missed my way, since I had neither heard nor seen anything of Pharos, I turned round and set off in what I considered must be the direction of the wall ; but though I walked step by step, once more feeling every inch of the way with my foot before I put it down, I seemed to have covered fifty yards before my knuckles came in contact with it. Having located it, I fumbled my way along it in the hope that I might discover the doorway through which I had entered ; but though I tried for some considerable time, no sort of success rewarded me. I paused and tried to remember which way I had been facing when I made the discovery that I was no longer in the passage. In the dark, however, one way seemed like another, and I had turned myself about so many times that it was impossible to tell which was the original direction. Oh, how bitterly I repented having ever left the hotel! For all I knew to the contrary, I might have wandered into some subterranean chamber never visited by the Bedouins or tourists, whence my feeble cries for help would not be heard, and in which I might remain until death took pity on me and released me from my sufferings.

Fighting down the terror that had risen in my heart and threatened to annihilate me, I once more commenced my circuit of the walls, but again without success. I counted my steps backwards and forwards in the hope of locating my position. I went straight ahead on the chance of striking the doorway haphazard, but it was always with the same unsatisfactory result. Against my better judgment I endeavoured to convince myself that I was really in no danger, but it was useless. At last my fortitude gave way, a clammy sweat broke out upon my forehead, and remembering that Pharos was in the building, I shouted aloud to him for help. My voice rang and echoed in that ghastly chamber till the reiteration of it well-nigh drove me mad. I listened, but no answer came. Once more I called, but with the same result. At last, thoroughly beside myself with terror, I began to run aimlessly about the room in the dark, beating myself against the walls and all the time shouting at the top of my voice for assistance. Only when I had no longer strength to move, or voice to continue my appeals, did I cease, and falling upon the ground rocked myself to and fro in silent agony. Times out of number I cursed myself and my senseless stupidity in having left the hotel to follow Pharos. I had sworn to protect the woman I loved, and yet on the first opportunity I had ruined everything by behaving in this thoughtless fashion.

Once more I sprang to my feet, and once more I set off on my interminable search. This time I went more quietly to work, feeling my way carefully, and making a mental note of every indentation in the walls. Being unsuccessful, I commenced again, and once more scored a failure. Then the horrible silence, the death-like atmosphere, the flapping of the bats in the darkness, and the thought of the history and age of the place in which I was imprisoned, must have affected my brain, and for a space I believe I went mad. At any rate, I have a confused recollection of running round and round that loathsome place, and of at last falling exhausted upon the ground, firmly believing my last hour had come. Then my senses left me, and I became unconscious.

How long I remained in the condition I have just described, I cannot say. All I know is that, when I opened my eyes, I found the chamber bright with the light of torches, and no less a person than Pharos kneeling beside me. Behind him, but at a respectful distance, were a number of Arabs, and among them a man whose height could scarcely have been less than seven feet. This was evidently the individual who had met Pharos at the entrance to the Pyramid.

"Rise," said Pharos, addressing me, "and let this be a warning to you never to attempt to spy on me again. Think not that I was unaware that you were following me, or that the mistake on your part in taking the wrong turning in the passage was not ordained. The time has now gone by for me to speak to you in riddles; our comedy is at an end, and for the future you are my property, to do with as I please. You will have no will but my pleasure, no thought but to act as I shall tell you. Rise and follow me."

Having said this, he made a sign to the torch-bearers, who immediately led the way towards the door, which was now easy enough to find. Pharos followed them, and, more dead than alive, I came next, while the tall man I have mentioned brought up the rear. In this order we groped our way down the narrow passage. Then it was that I discovered the mistake I had made in entering. Whether by accident, or by the exercise of Pharos's will, as he had desired me to believe, it was plain I had taken the wrong turning, and, instead of going on to the King's Hall, where no doubt I should have found the man I was following, I had turned to the left, and had entered the apartment popularly, but erroneously, called the Queen's Chamber.

It would have been difficult to estimate the thankfulness I felt on reaching the open air once more. How sweet the cool night wind seemed after the close and suffocating atmosphere of the Pyramid, I cannot hope to make you understand. And yet, if I had only known, it would have been better for me, far better, had I never been found, and my life come to an end when I fell senseless upon the floor.

When we had left the passage and had clambered down to the sands once more, Pharos bade me follow him, and, leading the way round the base of the Pyramid, conducted me down the hill towards the Sphinx.

For fully thirty years I had looked forward to the moment when I should stand before this stupendous monument and try to read its riddle ; but in my wildest dreams I had never thought to do so in such company. Looking down at me in the starlight, across the gulf of untold centuries, it seemed to smile disdainfully at my small woes.

"To-night," said Pharos, in that same extraordinary voice he had used a quarter of an hour before, when he bade me follow him, "you enter upon a new phase of your existence. Here, under the eyes of the Watcher of Harmachis, you shall learn something of the wisdom of the ancients."

At a signal, the tall man whom he had met at the foot of the Pyramid sprang forward and seized me by the arms from behind with a grip of iron. Then Pharos produced from his pocket a small case containing a bottle. From the latter he poured a few spoonfuls of some fluid into a silver cup, which he placed to my mouth.

"Drink," he said.

At any other time I should have refused to have complied with such a request; but on this occasion so completely had I fallen under his influence that I was powerless to disobey.

The opiate, or whatever it was, must have been a powerful one, for I had scarcely swallowed it before an attack of giddiness seized me. The outline of the Sphinx and the black bulk of the Great Pyramid beyond was merged in the general darkness. I could hear the wind of the desert singing in my ears, and the voice of Pharos muttering something in an

" ' Drink,' he said."

unknown tongue beside me. After that I sank down on the sand, and presently became oblivious of everything.

How long I remained asleep I have no idea. All I know is, that with a suddenness that was almost startling, I found myself awake and standing in a crowded street. The sun shone brilliantly, and the air was soft and warm. Magnificent buildings, of an architecture that my studies had long since made me familiar with, lined it on either hand, while in the roadway were many chariots and gorgeously furnished litters, before and beside which ran slaves, crying aloud in their masters' names for room.

From the position of the sun in the sky, I gathered that it must be close upon mid-day. The crowd was momentarily increasing, and as I walked, marvelling at the beauty of the buildings, I was jostled to and fro, and oftentimes called upon to stand aside. That something unusual had happened to account for this excitement was easily seen, but what it was, being a stranger, I had no idea. Sounds of wailing greeted me on every side, and in all the faces upon which I looked signs of overwhelming sorrow were to be seen.

Suddenly a murmur of astonishment and anger ran through the crowd, which separated hurriedly to right and left. A moment later a man came through the lane thus formed. He was short and curiously misshapen, and, as he walked, he covered his face with the sleeve of his robe, as though he were stricken with grief or shame.

Turning to a man who stood beside me, and who

seemed even more excited than his neighbours, I
inquired who the new-comer might be.

"Who art thou, stranger?" he answered, turning
sharply on me. "And whence comest thou that thou
knowest not Ptahmes, Chief of the King's Magicians?
Learn, then, that he hath fallen from his high estate,
inasmuch as he made oath before Pharaoh that the
firstborn of the King should take no hurt from the
spell this Israelitish sorcerer, Moses, hath cast upon
the land. Now the child and all the firstborn of
Egypt are dead, and the heart of Pharaoh being
hardened against his servant, he hath shamed him,
and driven him from before his face."

As he finished speaking, the disgraced man withdrew his robe from his face, and I realized the
astounding fact *that Ptahmes the Magician and Pharos
the Egyptian were not ancestor and descendant, but one
and the same person.*

CHAPTER XI

O F the circumstances under which my senses returned to me after the remarkable vision—for that is the only name I can assign to it—which I have described in the preceding chapter, not the vaguest recollection remains to me.

When Pharos bade me drink the stuff he had poured out, we were standing before the Sphinx at Gizeh; now, when I opened my eyes, I was back once more in my bedroom at the hotel in Cairo. Brilliant sunshine was streaming in through the jalousies, and I could hear the sound of footsteps in the corridor outside. At first I felt inclined to treat the whole as a dream,—not a very pleasant one, it is true,—but the marks upon my hands, made when I had beaten them on the rough walls of that terrible chamber in the Pyramid, soon showed me the futility of so doing. I remembered how I had run round and round that dreadful place in search of a way out, and the horror of the recollection was sufficient to bring a cold sweat out once more upon my forehead. Strange to say, I mean strange in the light of all that has transpired since, the memory of the threat Pharos had used to me caused me no uneasiness, and yet, permeating my whole being, there was a loathing for him and a haunting fear that was beyond description in words.

Indeed, I cannot hope to make you understand the light in which this man figured to me. In other and more ordinary phases of life the hatred one entertains for a man is usually of a less passive nature. One either shuns his society outright, or, if compelled to associate with him, makes a point of letting him see that unless he changes his behaviour and withdraws the cause of offence, it will, in all likelihood, lead him into trouble. With Pharos, however, the case was different. The dislike I felt for him was the outcome, not so much of a physical animosity, if I may so designate it, as of a peculiar description of supernatural fear. Reason with myself as I would, I could not get rid of the belief that the man was more than he pretended to be, that there was some link between him and the Unseen World which it was impossible for me to understand, and arguing with myself in this way, I was the more disposed to believe in the vision of the preceding night.

On consulting my watch, I was amazed to find that it wanted only a few minutes of ten o'clock. I sprang from my bed, and a moment later came within an ace of measuring my length upon the floor. What occasioned this weakness I could not tell, but the fact remains that I was as feeble as if I had been confined to my bed for six months. The room spun round and round, until I became so giddy that I was compelled to clutch at a table for support. What was stranger, as soon as I stood upon my feet, I was conscious of a sharp pricking sensation on my left arm, a little above the elbow ; indeed, so sharp was it, that it could be felt, not only on the tips of my fingers, but for some distance down my side. To examine the place was the work of a moment. On the fleshy part of the arm, three inches or so above the elbow, was a small spot, such as might have been made by some sharp-pointed instrument—a hypodermic syringe, for instance—and which was fast changing from a pale pink to a purple hue. Seating myself on my bed, I examined it carefully. My wonderment was increased when I discovered that the spot itself, and the flesh surrounding it for a distance of more than an inch, was to all intents and purposes incapable of sensation. I puzzled my brains in vain to account for its presence there. I did not remember scratching myself with anything in my room, nor could I discover that the coat I had worn on the preceding evening showed any signs of a puncture.

After a few moments the feeling of weakness which had seized me when I first left my bed wore off. I accordingly dressed myself with as much despatch as I could put into the operation, and my toilet being completed, left my room and went in search of the Fräulein Valerie. To my disappointment, she was not visible. I, however, discovered Pharos seated in the verandah, in the full glare of the morning sun, with the monkey, Pehtes, on his knee. For once he was in the very best of tempers. Indeed, since I had first made his acquaintance, I had never known him so merry. At a sign, I seated myself beside him.

"My friend," he began, "permit me to inform you that you had a narrow escape last night. However, since you are up and about this morning, I presume you are feeling none the worse for it."

I described the fit of vertigo that had overtaken

me when I rose from my bed, and went on to question him as to what had happened after I had become unconscious on the preceding night.

"I can assure you, you came very near being a lost man," he answered. "As good luck had it, I had not left the Pyramid, and so heard you cry for help, otherwise you might be in the Queen's Hall at this minute. You were quite unconscious when we found you, and you had not recovered by the time we reached home again."

"Not recovered?" I cried in amazement. "But I walked out of the Pyramid unassisted, and accompanied you across the sands to the Sphinx, where you gave me something to drink and made me see a vision."

Pharos gazed incredulously at me.

"My dear fellow, you must have dreamt it," he said. "After all you had gone through, it is scarcely likely I should have permitted you to walk, while as for the vision you speak of—well, I must leave that to your own common sense. If necessary, my servants will testify to the difficulty we experienced in getting you out of the Pyramid, while the very fact that you yourself have no recollection of the homeward journey would help to corroborate what I say."

This was all very plausible; at the same time I was far from being convinced. I knew my man too well by this time to believe that because he denied any knowledge of the circumstance in question he was really as innocent as he was anxious I should think him. The impression the vision—for, as I have said, I shall always call it by that name—had made upon me was still clear and distinct in my mind. I closed my eyes and once more saw the street filled with that strangely-dressed crowd, which drew back on either hand to make a way for the disgraced Magician to pass through. It was all so real, and yet, as I was compelled to confess, so improbable, that I scarcely knew what to think. Before I could come to any satisfactory decision, Pharos turned to me again.

"Whatever your condition last night may have been," he said, "it is plain you are better this morning, and I am rejoiced to see it, for the reason I have made arrangements to complete the business which has brought us here. Had you not been well enough to travel, I should have been compelled to leave you behind."

I searched his face for an explanation.

"The mummy?" I asked.

"Exactly," he replied. "The mummy. We leave Cairo this afternoon for Luxor. I have made the necessary arrangements, and we join the steamer at mid-day,—that is to say, in about two hours' time."

Possibly it was this preparation to complete the work he had come to do, by replacing the mummy of the King's Magician in the tomb in which it had lain for so many thousand years, and from which my father had taken it, that had put him in such a good humour. At any rate, never since I had known him had I found him so amiable as on this particular occasion. I inquired after the Fräulein Valerie, whom I had not yet seen, whereupon Pharos informed me that she had gone to her room to prepare for the excursion up the Nile.

" And now, Mr. Forrester," he said, rising from his chair and returning the monkey to his place of shelter in the breast of his coat, " if I were you, I should follow her example. It will be necessary for us to start as punctually as possible."

Sharp on the stroke of twelve a carriage made its appearance at the door of the hotel. The Fräulein Valerie, Pharos, and myself took our places in it, the gigantic Arab whom I had seen at the Pyramid on the preceding night, and who I was quite certain had held my arms when Pharos compelled me to drink the potion before the Sphinx, took his place beside the driver, and we set off along the road to Bulak *en route* to the Embabeh. Having reached this, one of the most characteristic spots in Cairo, we made our way along the bank towards a landing-stage, beside which a handsome steamer was moored. If anything had been wanting in my mind to convince me of the respect felt for Pharos by such Arabs as he was brought in contact with, I should have found it in the behaviour of the crew of this vessel. Had he been imbued with the powers of life and death, they could scarcely have stood in greater awe of him.

Our party being on board, there was no occasion for any further delay ; consequently, as soon as we had reached the upper deck, the ropes were cast off, and with prodigious fuss the steamer made her way out into mid-stream, and began the voyage which was destined to end in such a strange fashion, not for one alone, but indeed for all our party.

Full as my life had been of extraordinary circumstances during the last few weeks, I am not certain that my feelings as I stood upon the deck of the steamer, while she made her way up stream, past the Khedive's Palace, the Kasr-en-Nil barracks, Kasr-el-Ain, the Island of Rodah, and Gizeh, did not eclipse them. Our vessel was in every way a luxurious one, and to charter her must have cost Pharos a pretty penny. Immediately we got under weigh, the latter departed to his cabin, while the Fräulein Valerie and I stood side by side under the awning, watching the fast-changing landscape, but scarcely speaking. The day was hot, with scarcely a breath of wind to cool the air. Ever since the first week in June the Nile had been slowly rising, and was now running, a swift and muddy river, only a few feet below the level of her banks. I looked at my companion, and, as I did so, thought of all that we had been through together in the short time we had known each other. Less than a month before, Pharos and I had to all intents and purposes been strangers, and Valerie and I had not met at all. Then I had travelled with them to Egypt, and was now embarking on a voyage up the Nile in their company, and for what purpose? To restore the body of Merenptah's Chief Magician to the tomb from which it had been taken by my own father nearly twenty years before. Could anything have seemed more unlikely, and yet could anything have been more true? Amiable as were my relations with my host at present, there was a feeling deep down in my heart that troublous times lay ahead of us. The explanation Pharos had given me of what had occurred on the preceding night had been plausible enough, as I have said, and yet I was far from being convinced

by it. There were only two things open to me to
believe. Either he had stood over me saying, " For
the future you are mine to do with as I please. You
will have no will but my pleasure, no thought but to
act as I shall tell you," or I had dreamt it. When I
had taxed him with it some hours before, he had
laughed at me, and had told me to attribute it all to
the excited condition of my brain. But the feeling
of reality with which it had inspired me was, I felt
sure, too strong for it to have been imaginary ; and
yet, do what I would, I could not throw off the unpleasant belief that, however much I might attempt to
delude myself to the contrary, I was in reality more
deeply in his power than I fancied myself to be.

One thing struck me most forcibly, and that was
the fact that, now we were away from Cairo, the
Fräulein Valerie was in better spirits than I had yet
seen her. Glad as I was, however, to find her happier,
the knowledge of her cheerfulness, for some reason or
another, chilled and even disappointed me. Yet,
Heaven knows, had I been asked, I must have confessed that I should have been even more miserable
had she been unhappy. When I joined them at lunch,
I was convinced that I was a discordant note. I was
thoroughly out of humour, not only with myself, but
with the world in general, and the fit had not left me
when I made my way up to the deck again.

Downcast as I was, however, I could not repress an
exclamation of pleasure at the scene I saw before me
when I reached it. In the afternoon light the view,
usually so uninviting, was picturesque in the extreme.
Palm groves decorated either bank, with here and

there an Arab village peering from among them ; while, as if to afford a fitting background, in the distance could be seen the faint outline of the Libyan Hills. At any other time I should have been unable to contain myself until I had made a sketch of it ; now, however, while it impressed me with its beauty, it only served to remind me of the association in which I found myself. The centre of the promenade deck, immediately abaft the funnel, was arranged somewhat in the fashion of a sitting-room, with a carpet, easy-chairs, a sofa, and corresponding luxuries. I seated myself in one of the chairs, and was still idly watching the country through which we were passing, when Pharos made his appearance from below, carrying the monkey, Pehtes, in his arms, and seated himself beside me. It was plain that he was still in a contented frame of mind, and his opening speech, when he addressed me, showed that he had no intention of permitting me to be in anything else.

"My dear Forrester," he said in what was intended to be a conciliatory tone, " I feel sure you have something upon your mind that is worrying you. Is it possible you are still brooding over what you said to me this morning? Remember you are my guest, therefore I am responsible for your happiness. I cannot permit you to wear such an expression of melancholy. Pray tell me your trouble, and if I can help you in any way, rest assured I shall be only too glad to do so."

"I am afraid, after the explanation you gave me this morning, that it is impossible for you to help me," I answered. "To tell you the truth, I have been worrying over what happened last night, and the more I think of it, the less able I am to understand it."

"What is it you find difficult to understand?" he inquired. "I thought we were agreed on the subject when we spoke of it this morning."

"Not as far as I am concerned," I replied. "And if you consider for a moment, I fancy you will understand why. As I told you then, I have the best possible recollection of all that befell me in the Pyramid, and of the fright I sustained in that terrible room. I remember your coming to my assistance, and I am as convinced that, when my senses returned to me, I followed you down the passage, out into the open air, and across the sands to a spot before the Sphinx, where you gave me some concoction to drink, as I am that I am now sitting on this deck beside you."

"And I assure you with equal sincerity that it is all a delusion," the old man replied. "You must have dreamt the whole thing. Now I come to think of it, I *do* remember that you said something about a vision which I enabled you to see. Perhaps, as your memory is so keen on the subject, you may be able to give me some idea of its nature."

I accordingly described what I had seen. From the way he hung upon my words, it was evident that the subject interested him more than he cared to confess. Indeed, when I had finished, he gave a little gasp that was plainly one of relief, though why he should have been so I could not understand.

"And the man you saw coming through the crowd, this Ptahmes, what was he like? Did you recognise him? Should you know his face again?"

"I scarcely know how to tell you," I answered diffi-
dently, a doubt as to whether I had really seen the
vision I had described coming over me for the first
time, now that I was brought face to face with the
assertion I was about to make. "It seems so impossible, and I am weak enough to feel that I should not
like you to think I am jesting. The truth of the
matter is, the face of the disgraced Magician was
none other than your own. You were Ptahmes, the
man who walked with his face covered with his mantle,
and before whom the crowd drew back as if they
feared him, and yet hated him the more because they
did so."

"The slaves, the craven curs," muttered Pharos fiercely
to himself, oblivious of my presence, his sunken eyes
looking out across the water, but I am convinced seeing
nothing. "So long as he was successful they sang his
praises through the city, but when he failed and was
cast out from before Pharaoh, there were only six in all
the country brave enough to declare themselves his
friends."

Then, recollecting himself, he turned to me, and with
one of his peculiar laughs, to which I had by this time
grown accustomed, he continued, "But there, if I talk
like this, you will begin to imagine that I really have
some association with my long-deceased relative, the
man of whom we are speaking, and whose mummy is
in the cabin yonder. Your account of the vision, if by
that name you still persist in calling it, is extremely interesting, and goes another step towards proving how
liable the human brain is, under stress of great excitement, to seize upon the most unlikely stories, and even

to invest them with the necessary *mise-en-scène.* Now I'll be bound you could reproduce the whole picture, were such a thing necessary — the buildings, the chariots, the dresses, nay, even the very faces of the crowd."

" I am quite sure I could," I answered, filled with a sudden excitement at the idea, "and what is more, I will do so. So vivid was the impression it made upon my mind that not a detail has escaped my memory. Indeed, I really believe it will be found that a large proportion of the things I saw then I had never seen or heard of before. This, I think, should go some way towards proving whether or not my story is the fallacy you suppose."

"You mistake me, my dear Forrester," he hastened to reply. " I do not go so far as to declare it to be altogether a fallacy ; I simply say that what you think you saw must have been the effect of the fright you received in the Pyramid. But your idea of painting the picture is distinctly a good one, and I shall look forward with pleasure to giving you my opinion upon it when it is finished. As you are well aware, I am a fair Egyptologist, and I have no doubt I shall be able to detect any error in the composition, should one exist."

" I will obtain my materials from my cabin, and set to work at once," I said, rising from my chair, "and when I have finished you shall certainly give me your opinion on it."

As on a similar occasion already described, under the influence of my enthusiasm the feeling of animosity I usually entertained towards him left me entirely. I went to my cabin, found the things I wanted, and re-

turned with them to the deck. When I reached it, I
found the Fräulein Valerie there. She was dressed in
white from head to foot, and was slowly fanning herself
with the same large ostrich feather fan which I remembered to have seen her using on that eventful night when
I had dined with Pharos in Naples. Her left hand
was hanging by her side, and as I greeted her and re-
seated myself in my chair, I could not help noticing
its whiteness and exquisite proportions.

"Mr. Forrester was fortunate enough to be honoured
by a somewhat extraordinary dream last night," said
Pharos by way of accounting for my sketching
materials. "The subject was Egyptian, and I have
induced him to try and make a picture of the scene
for my especial benefit."

"Do you feel equal to the task?" Valerie inquired,
with unusual interest as I thought. "Surely it must
be very difficult. As a rule, even the most vivid
dreams are so hard to remember in detail."

"This was something more than a dream," I answered confidently, "as I shall presently demonstrate
to Monsieur Pharos. Before I begin, however, I am
going to make one stipulation."

"And what is that?" asked Pharos.

"That while I am at work you tell us, as far as
you know it, the history of Ptahmes, the King's
Magician. Not only does it bear upon the subject of
my picture, but it is fit and proper, since we have his
mummy on board, that we should know more than
we do at present of our illustrious fellow-traveller."

Pharos glanced sharply at me, as if he were desirous
of discovering whether any covert allusion was con-

tained in my speech. I flatter myself, however, that my face told him nothing.

"What could be fairer?" he said, after a slight pause. "While you paint I will tell you all I know, and since he is my ancestor, and I have made his life my especial study, it may be supposed I am acquainted with as much of his history as research has been able to bring to light. Ptahmes, or, as his name signifies, the man beloved of Ptah, was the son of Netruhôtep, a Priest of the High Temple of Ammon, and a favourite of Rameses II. From the moment of his birth great things were expected of him, for, by the favour of the gods, he was curiously misshapen, and it is well known that those whom the mighty ones punish in one way usually have it made up to them in another. It is just possible that it may be from him I inherit my own unpleasing exterior. However, to return to Ptahmes, whose life, I can assure you, forms an interesting study. At an early age the boy showed an extraordinary partiality for the mystic, and it was doubtless this circumstance that induced his father to entrust him to the care of the Chief Magician, Haper, a wise man, by whom the lad was brought up. Proud of his calling, and imbued with a love for the sacred rites, it is small wonder that he soon outdistanced those with whom he was brought in contact. So rapid, indeed, were the strides he made that the news of his attainments at length came to the ears of Pharaoh. He was summoned to the royal presence, and commanded to give an exhibition of his powers. So pleased was the King at the result that he ordered him to remain at Court, and to be constantly in attendance upon his person.

From this point the youth's career was assured. Year by year, and step by step, he made his way up the ladder of fame till he became a mighty man in the land, a councillor, Prophet of the North and South, and Chief of the King's Magicians. Then, out of the land of Midian rose the star that, as it had been written, should cross his path and bring about his downfall. This was the Israelite Moses, who came into Egypt and set himself up against Pharaoh, using magic, the like of which had never before been seen. But that portion of the story is too well known to bear repetition. Let it suffice that Pharaoh called together his councillors, the principal of whom was Ptahmes, now a man of mature years, and consulted with them. Ptahmes, scenting a rival in this Hebrew, and foreseeing the inevitable result, was for acceding to the request he made, and letting the Israelites depart in peace from the kingdom. To this course, however, Pharaoh would not agree, and at the same time he allowed his favourite to understand that, not only was such advice the reverse of palatable, but that a repetition of it would in all probability deprive him of the royal favour. Once more the Hebrews appeared before Pharaoh and gave evidence of their powers, speaking openly to the King and using threats of vengeance in the event of their demands not being acceded to. But Pharaoh was stiff-necked and refused to listen, and in consequence evil days descended upon Egypt. By the magic of Moses the fish died, and the waters of the Nile were polluted so that the people could not drink ; frogs, in such numbers as had never been seen before, made their appearance and covered the whole face of the land. Then

Pharaoh called upon Ptahmes and his Magicians, and bade them imitate all that the others had done. And the Magicians did so, and by their arts frogs came up out of the land, even as Moses had made them do. Seeing this, Pharaoh laughed the Israelites to scorn, and once more refused to consider their request. Whereupon plagues of lice, flies, and boils, which broke out upon man and beast, mighty storms, and a great darkness in which no man could see another's face, fell upon the Egyptians. Once more Pharaoh, whose heart was still hardened against Moses, called Ptahmes to his presence, and bade him advise him as to the course he should pursue. Being already at war with his neighbours, he had no desire to permit this horde to cross his borders only to take sides with his enemies against him. And yet to keep them and to risk further punishment was equally dangerous. Moses was a stern man, and, as the King had had already good reason to know, was not one to be trifled with. Only that morning he had demanded an audience, and had threatened Pharaoh with a pestilence that should cause the death of every first-born son throughout the land if he still persisted in his refusal.

" Now Ptahmes, who, as I have said, was an astute man, and who had already been allowed to see the consequences of giving advice that did not tally with his master's humour, found himself in a position, not only of difficulty, but also of some danger. Either he must declare himself openly in favour of letting the Hebrews go, and once more run the risk of Pharaoh's anger and possible loss of favour, or he must side with his master, and, having done so, put forth every effort to prevent the punishment Moses had decreed. After hours of suspense and overwhelming anxiety, he adopted the latter course. Having taken counsel with his fellow Magicians, he assured Pharaoh, on the honour of the gods, that what the Israelite had predicted could never come to pass. Fortified with this promise, Pharaoh once more refused to permit the strangers to leave the land. As a result, the first-born son of the King, the child whom he loved better even than his kingdom, sickened of a mysterious disease and died that night, as did the first-born of all the Egyptians, rich and poor alike. In the words of your own Bible, ' There was a great cry in Egypt; for there was not a house where there was not one dead.' Then Pharaoh's hatred was bitter against his advisers, and he determined that Ptahmes in particular should die. He sought him with the intention of killing him, but the Magician had received timely warning and had escaped into the mountains, where he hid himself for many months. Little by little the strain upon his health gave way, he grew gradually weaker, and in the fiftieth year of his life Osiris claimed him for his own. It was said at the time that for the sin he had caused Pharaoh to do, and the misery he had brought upon the land of Egypt, and swearing falsely in the name of the gods, he had been cursed with perpetual life. This, however, could not have been so, seeing that he died in the mountains and that his mummy was buried in the tomb whence your father took it. Such is the story of Ptahmes, the beloved of Ptah, son of Netruhôtep, Chief of the Magicians and Prophet of the North and South."

CHAPTER XII

STRANGE as it may seem, when all the circumstances attending it are taken into consideration, I
am compelled to confess, in looking back upon it now,
that that voyage up the Nile was one of the most en-
joyable I have ever undertaken. It is true, the weather
was somewhat warmer than was altogether agreeable ;
but if you visit Egypt at midsummer, you must be
prepared for a little discomfort in that respect. From
the moment of rising until it was time to retire to rest
at night, our time was spent under the awning on deck,
reading, conversing, and watching the scenery on either
bank, and on my part in putting the finishing touches
to the picture I had commenced the afternoon we left
Cairo.

When it was completed to my satisfaction, which was
on the seventh day of our voyage, and that upon which
we expected to reach Luxor, I showed it to Pharos.
He examined it carefully, and it was some time before
he offered an opinion upon it.

" I will pay you the compliment of saying I consider
it a striking example of your art," he said, when he did
speak. " At the same time, I must confess it puzzles
me. I do not understand whence you drew your in-
spiration. There are things in this picture, important

details in the dress and architecture, that I feel certain
have never been seen or dreamt of by this century.
How, therefore, you could have known them passes my
comprehension."

" I have already told you that that picture represents
what I saw in my vision," I answered.

" So you still believe you saw a vision ? " he asked,
with a return to his old sneering habit, as he picked the
monkey up and began to stroke his ears.

" I shall always do so," I answered. " Nothing will
ever shake my belief in that."

At this moment the Fräulein Valerie joined us,
whereupon Pharos handed her the picture and asked
for her opinion upon it. She looked at it steadfastly,
while I waited with some anxiety for her criticism.

" It is very clever," she said, still looking at it, " and
beautifully painted ; but, if you will let me say so, I do
not know that I altogether like it. There is something
about it that I do not understand. And see, you have
given the central figure Monsieur Pharos's face."

She looked up from the picture at me as if to inquire
the reason of this likeness, after which we both glanced
at Pharos, who was seated before us, wrapped as usual
in his heavy rug, with the monkey, Pehtes, looking out
from his invariable hiding-place beneath his master's
coat. For the moment I did not know what answer to
return. To have told her in the broad light of day,
with the prosaic mud banks of the Nile on either hand,
and the Egyptian sailors washing paint-work at the
farther end of the deck, that in my vision I had been
convinced that Pharos and Ptahmes were one and the
same person, would have been too absurd. Pharos,

however, relieved me of the necessity of my saying anything by replying for me.

"Mr. Forrester has done me great honour, my dear,"
he said gaily, "in choosing my features for the central
figure. I had no idea before that my unfortunate
person was capable of such dramatic effect. But now
to more serious business. If at any time, Forrester, you
should desire to dispose of that picture, I shall be delighted to take it off your hands."

"You may have it now," I answered. "If you think
it worthy of your acceptance, I will gladly give it you.
To tell the truth, I myself, like the Fräulein here, am a
little frightened of it, though why I should be, seeing
that it is my own work, Heaven only knows."

"As you say, Heaven only knows," returned Pharos
solemnly, and then making the excuse that he would
put the picture in a place of safety, he left us and went
to his cabin, Pehtes hopping along the deck behind
him.

For some time after he had left us the Fräulein and I
sat silent. The afternoon was breathless, and even our
progress through the water raised no breeze. At the
time we were passing the town of Keneh, a miserable
collection of buildings of the usual Nile type, and famous
only as being a rallying place for Mecca pilgrims, and
for the Kulal and Ballas (water bottles), which bear its
name.

While her eyes were fixed upon it, I was permitted an
opportunity of studying my companion's countenance.
I noted the proud poise of her head, the beauty of her
face, and the luxuriance of the hair coiled so gracefully
above it. She was a queen among women, as I had so

often told myself ; one whom any man might be proud to love, and then I added, as another thought struck me, one for whom the man she loved would willingly lay down his life to save. That I loved her with a sincerity and devotion greater than I had ever felt for any other human being, I was fully aware by this time. If the truth must be told, I believe I had loved her from the moment I first saw her face. But was it possible that she could love me? That was for time to show.

"I have noticed that you are very thoughtful to-day, Fräulein," I said, as the steamer dropped the town behind her and continued her journey up stream in a more westerly direction.

"Have I not good reason to be?" she answered. "You must remember I have made this journey before."

"But why should that fact produce such an effect upon you?" I asked. "To me it is a pleasure that has not yet begun to pall, and as you will, I am sure, admit, Pharos has proved a most thoughtful and charming host."

I said this with intention, for I wanted to see what reply she would make.

"I have not noticed his behaviour," she answered wearily. "It is always the same to me. But I *do* know this, that after each visit to the place for which we are now bound, great trouble has resulted for some one. Heaven grant it may not be so on this occasion."

"I do not see what trouble *can* result," I said. "Pharos is simply going to replace the mummy in the tomb from which it was taken, and after that I presume we shall return to Cairo, and probably to Europe."

" And then ? "

" After that—— "

But I could get no farther. The knowledge that in all likelihood as soon as we reached Europe I should have to bid her good-bye and return to London was too much for me, and for this reason I came within an ace of blurting out the words that were in my heart. Fortunately, however, I was able to summon up my presence of mind in time to avert such a catastrophe, otherwise I cannot say what the result would have been. Had I revealed my love to her and asked her to be my wife and she had refused me, our position, boxed up together as we were on board the steamer, and with no immediate prospect of release, would have been uncomfortable in the extreme. So I crammed the words back into my heart, and waited for another and more favourable opportunity.

The sun was sinking behind the Arabian hills, in a wealth of gold and crimson colouring, as we obtained our first glimpse of the mighty ruins we had come so far to see. Out of a dark green sea of palms to the left rose the giant pylons of the Temple of Ammon at Karnak. A few minutes later Luxor itself was visible, and within a quarter of an hour our destination was reached, and the steamer was at a standstill.

We had scarcely come to an anchor before the vessel was surrounded by small boats, the occupants of which clambered aboard, despite the efforts of the officers and crew to prevent them. As usual, they brought with them spurious relics of every possible sort and description, not one of which, however, our party could be induced to buy. The Fräulein Valerie and I were still

"Pushing, struggling, even jumping headlong into the water."

protesting when Pharos emerged from his cabin and approached us. Never shall I forget the change that came over the scene. From the expressions upon the rascals' faces as they recognised him, I gathered that he was well known to them; at any rate, within five seconds of his appearance, not one of our previous persecutors remained aboard the vessel. Pushing, struggling, even jumping headlong into the water, they made their way over the side.

"They seem to know you," I said to Pharos, with a laugh, as the last of the gang took a header from the rail into the water.

"They do," he answered grimly. "I think I can safely promise you that, after this, not a man in Luxor will willingly set foot upon this vessel, not for all the wealth of Egypt. Would you care to try the experiment?"

"Very much," I said, and taking an Egyptian pound piece from my pocket, I stepped to the side and invited the rabble to come aboard and claim it. But the respect they entertained for Pharos was evidently greater than their love of gold, at any rate not a man seemed inclined to venture.

"A fair test," said Pharos. "You may rest assured that, unless you throw it over to them, your money will remain in your own pocket. But see, some one of importance is coming off to us. I am expecting a messenger, and in all probability it is he."

A somewhat better boat than those clustered around us was putting off from the bank, and seated in her was an Arab, clad in white bernouse and wearing a black turban upon his head.

"Yes, it is he," said Pharos, as with a few strokes of their oars the boatmen brought their craft alongside.

Before I could inquire who the person might be whom he was expecting, the man I have just described had reached the deck, and, after looking about him, had approached the spot where Pharos was standing. Accustomed as I was to the deference shown by the Arabs towards their superiors, of whose rank they were aware, I was far from expecting the exhibition of servility I now beheld. So overpowered was the new-comer by the reverence he felt for Pharos, that he could scarcely stand upright.

"I expected thee, Salem Awad," said Pharos, in Arabic. "What tidings dost thou bring?"

"It was to tell thee," the man replied, "that he whom thou didst order to be here has heard of thy coming, and will await thee at the place of which thou hast spoken."

"It is well," continued Pharos, "and I am pleased. Has all that I wrote to thee of been prepared?"

"All has been prepared and awaits thy coming."

"Return, then, and tell him who sent thee to me that I will be with him before he sleeps to-night."

The man bowed once more and made his way to his boat, in which he departed for the bank.

When he had gone, Pharos turned to me.

"We are expected," he said, "and, as you heard him say, preparations have been made to enable us to carry out the work we have come to do. After all his journeying, Ptahmes has at last returned to the city of his birth and death. It is a strange thought, is it not? Look about you, Mr. Forrester, and remember that you are among the mightiest ruins the world has known. Yonder is the Temple of Luxor, away to the north you can see the remains of the Temple of Ammon at Karnak, both of which, five thousand years ago, were connected by a mighty road. On the west bank is the Necropolis of Thebes, with the tombs that once contained the mortal remains of the mighty ones of Egypt. Where are those mighty ones now? Scattered to the uttermost parts of the earth, stolen from their resting-places to adorn glass cases in European museums, and to be sold by auction by Jew salesmen at so much per head, according to their dates and state of preservation. But there! time is too short to talk of such indignity. The gods will avenge it in their own good time. Let it suffice that to-night we shall fulfil our errand. Am I right in presuming that you desire to accompany me?"

"I should be sincerely disappointed if I could not do so," I answered. "But if you would prefer to go alone, I will not force my presence upon you."

"I shall only be too glad of your company," he answered. "Besides, you have a right to be present, since it is through you I am permitted an opportunity of replacing my venerable ancestor in his tomb. In that case, perhaps you will be good enough to hold yourself in readiness to start about eleven o'clock? Owing to the publicity now given to anything that happens in the ruins of this ancient city, the mere fact that we are returning a mummy to its tomb, of the existence of which the world has no knowledge, would be sufficient to attract a concourse of people, whose presence would be in the highest degree objectionable to me."

"You must excuse my interrupting you," I said, thinking I had caught him tripping, "but you have just said that you are going to open a tomb of the existence of which the world has no knowledge. Surely my father opened it many years ago, otherwise how did he become possessed of the mummy?"

"Your father discovered it, it is true, but he stumbled upon it quite by chance, and it was reburied within a few hours of his extracting the mummy. If he were alive now, I would defy him to find the place again."

"And you are going to open it to-night?"

"That is my intention. And when I have done so, it will once more be carefully hidden, and may woe light upon the head of the man who shall again disturb it!"

I do not know whether this speech was intended to have any special significance for me, but, as he said it, he looked hard at me, and never since I have known him had I seen a more diabolical expression upon his countenance. I could scarcely have believed that the human face was capable of such an exhibition of malignity. He recovered himself as quickly, however, and then once more bidding me prepare for the excursion of the evening, took himself off to his cabin, and left me to ponder over all he had said.

It was well after eleven o'clock that night when the tall Arab, my acquaintance of the Pyramids, came along the deck in search of me. I was sitting with the Fräulein Valerie at the time, but as soon as he told me that Pharos was waiting and that it was time for us to start, I made haste to rise. On hearing our errand, my companion became uneasy.

" I do not like it," she said. " Why could he not do
it in the daytime? This going off under cover of the
night savours too much of the conspirator, and I beg
you to be careful of what you do. Have you a
revolver ? "

I answered in the affirmative, whereupon she earnestly
advised me to carry it with me—a course which I
resolved to adopt. Then bidding her good-bye, I left
her and went to my cabin, little dreaming that upwards
of a week would elapse before I should see her again.

When I joined Pharos on deck, I discovered that he
had made no difference in his attire, but was dressed
just as I had always seen him, even to the extent of
his heavy coat, which he wore despite the heat of the
night.

" If you are ready," he said, " let us lose no time in
starting." Then turning to the tall Arab, who stood
by his side, he bade him call the boat up, and as soon
as it was at the ladder we descended into it and took
our places in the stern. A few strokes of the oars
brought us to the bank. Here we found two camels
awaiting us. On closer inspection I discovered that
the individual in charge of them was none other than
the man who had boarded the steamer that afternoon,
and whom I have particularized as having shown such
obsequious respect to Pharos.

At a sign from the latter, one of the camels was
brought to his knees, and I was invited to take my
place in the saddle. I had never in my life ridden one
of these ungainly brutes, and it was necessary for the
driver to instruct me in the art. Pharos, however,
seemed quite at home, and as soon as he had mounted,

and the camels had raised themselves to their feet once more, we set off.

If my drive to the Pyramids, a week before, had been a singular experience, this camel ride among the ruins of ancient Thebes at midnight was much more so. On every side were relics of that long-departed age when the city, through the remains of which we were now making our way, had been the centre of the civilized world. Leaving the river on our left, and skirting the modern town, we set off in a northerly direction along what might very well once have been a properly built road.

After the heat of the day the coolness of the night was most refreshing. Overhead the stars shone more brilliantly than I had ever seen them, while from the desert a little lonely wind came up and sighed over the desolation of the place. Nothing could have been in better keeping with the impressiveness of the occasion. One thing, however, puzzled me, for so far I had seen nothing of the chief, and indeed the only, reason of the expedition ; namely, the mummy of the dead Magician. I questioned Pharos on the subject, who answered briefly that it had been sent on ahead to await our coming at the tomb, and, having given this explanation, lapsed into silence once more.

It must have been upwards of half an hour later when the tall Arab, who had all the way walked in front of the camel upon which Pharos was seated, stopped and held up his hand. The animals immediately came to a standstill. Peering into the darkness ahead, I found that we were standing before a gigantic building, which measured at least a hundred feet from

end to end, and towered into the starlight to a height
of possibly a hundred and fifty feet. This proved to
be the main pylon of the great Temple of Ammon, the
most stupendous example of human architecture ever
erected on the surface of our globe. On either side
of the open space upon which we stood rows of kriosphinxes showed where a noble road had once led from
the temple to the river.

At a signal from Pharos the man who had come
aboard the steamer that afternoon left us and entered
the building, while we remained outside.

Fully five minutes must have elapsed before he returned, and said something to Pharos in a low voice,
who immediately descended from his camel and signed
to me to do the same. Then we, in our turn, approached the gigantic pylon, at the entrance of which
we were met by a man carrying a lighted torch.
Viewed by this dim and uncertain light, the place appeared indescribably mysterious. Overhead the walls
towered up and up until I lost sight of them in the
general darkness. Presently we entered a large court,
so large indeed that even with the assistance of the
guide's torch we could not see the farther end of it.
Then passing through a doorway formed of enormous
blocks of stone, the architrave of which could scarcely
have been less than a hundred feet from the ground,
we found ourselves standing in another and even greater
hall. Here we paused, while Pharos went forward
into the darkness alone, leaving me in the charge of
the tall Arab and the man who bore the torch. Where
he had gone, and his reason for thus leaving me, I
could not imagine, and my common-sense told me it

would only be waste of time on my part to inquire.
Minutes went by until perhaps half an hour had elapsed,
and still he did not return. I was about to make some
remark upon this, when I noticed that the man holding
the torch, who had hitherto been leaning against a
pillar, suddenly drew himself up and looked towards
another side of the great hall. I followed the direction
of his eyes, and saw approaching me an old man, clad
in white from head to foot, and with a long white beard
descending to within a few inches of his waist. As
soon as he was certain that I saw him, he signed to
me with his hand to follow him, and then turning, led
me across the hall in the direction he had come. I
followed close at his heels, threaded my way among the
mighty pillars carved all over with hieroglyphics, and
so passed into yet another court. Here it was all black
darkness, and so lonely that I found my spirits sinking lower and lower with every step I took. Reaching
the centre of the court, my guide stopped and bade me
pause. I did so, whereupon he also departed, but in
what direction he went I could not tell.

Had it been possible, I think at this stage of the
proceedings I should have left Pharos to his own
devices, and have made my way out of the ruins and
back to the steamer without further ado. Under the
circumstances I have narrated, however, I had no option
but to remain where I was, and in any case I doubt
whether I should have had time to make my escape, for
the old man presently returned, this time with a torch,
and once more bade me follow him. I accordingly
accompanied him across the court, and among more
pillars, to a small temple, which must have been situated

at some considerable distance from the main pylon through which we had entered the ruins.

Approaching the farther corner of this temple, he stooped and, when he had brushed away an amount of sand with his hand, either touched some hidden spring or lifted a ring, for I distinctly heard the jar of iron on stone. Then a large block of masonry wheeled round on its own length and disappeared into the earth, revealing a cavity possibly four feet square at our feet. As soon as my eyes became accustomed to the darkness, I was able to detect a flight of steps leading down into a dark vault below. These the old man descended, and, feeling certain that I was intended to accompany him, I followed his example. The steps were longer than I expected them to be, and were possibly some fifty in number. Reaching the bottom, I found myself standing in a subterranean hall, which perhaps describes it more fully than the word *vault* would do. The roof or ceiling was supported by a number of elegantly sculptured *papyrus-bud* columns, while the walls were covered with paintings, every one of which was in a perfect state of preservation. For what purpose the hall had been used in bygone days I could not, of course, tell, but that it had some connection with the mysterious rites of the god Ammon was shown, not only by the frescoes, but by the trouble which had been taken to conceal the entrance to the place.

When we had reached the centre of the hall, the old man turned and addressed me.

"Stranger," he said, in a voice as deep and resonant as the tolling of a bell, " by reason of the share that has been allotted thee in the vengeance of the gods, it has been decreed that thou shalt witness a portion of the mysteries of this holy place, the like of which not one of thy race or people has ever yet beheld. Fear not that evil will befall thee ; thou art in the hands of the mighty ones of Egypt. They will protect thee. Follow me."

CHAPTER XIII

IN describing what occurred after the curious admonition addressed to me by the old man who had conducted me to the subterranean chamber mentioned in the last chapter, I am oppressed by the fear that my narrative may seem too extraordinary to carry with it any semblance of reality. The whole affair, from the moment when we had left the steamer until I stood where I now was, had been so mysterious, so unbelievable, I might almost say, that I had passed from stage to stage of bewilderment, scarcely conscious of anything but what was occurring at the moment. In a vague fashion I wondered how it was that these rooms had never been discovered by the hundreds of Egyptologists who, since the time of Napoleon, had explored the temple. That it had not been so brought to light I felt convinced, otherwise the necessity would scarcely have existed for such secrecy as had been shown when I was conducted to it. Besides, I had studied my guide-books carefully on our voyage up the river, and was quite convinced that no mention of such places had been made in any one of them.

Having finished the speech with which I closed the preceding chapter, the old man led me towards a doorway at the farther end of the room. The posts which supported it, and which must have been something like ten feet in width, were covered with hieroglyphics, as were the neighbouring walls. On either side of the doorway stood two enormous kriosphinxes, similar to those which had once lined the avenue between the Temples of Karnak and Luxor. These had the bodies of lions and heads of rams, and were as perfect as on the day when they had left the sculptor's hands, who knew how many thousand years ago. Entering the archway,—for archway I should prefer to call it rather than door,—I found myself standing between two rows of life-sized statues, all excelling in workmanship, and in the most perfect state of preservation. Though I was not sufficiently learned in Egyptian history to be able to assign names to them, I was nevertheless quite capable of appreciating their immense value, and could well imagine the find they would prove to any Egypt-ologist who, in days to come, might discover the secret of the stone and penetrate into this mysterious place.

From what I remember, and speaking at a guess, the passage could scarcely have been less than a hundred feet in length, and must have contained at least a dozen statues. At the farther end it opened into a smaller chamber or catacomb, in the walls of which were a number of niches, each one containing a mummy. The place was intolerably close, and was filled with an over-powering odour of dried herbs. In the centre, and side by side, were two alabaster slabs, each about seven feet long by three in width. A stone pillar was at the head of each, but for what purpose the blocks were originally intended I have no idea.

At a signal from my conductor, two beings—I cannot

call them men,—who from their faces I should have judged to be as old as Pharos himself,—made their appearance, bringing with them certain vestments and a number of curiously shaped bottles. The robes, which were of some white material, were embroidered with hieroglyphics. These they placed about my shoulders, and, when they had done so, the old fellow who had conducted me to the place bade me stretch myself upon one of the slabs I have just mentioned.

Under other circumstances I should have protested most vigorously, but I was in such a position now that I came to the conclusion that it would not only be useless but most impolitic on my part to put myself in opposition against him thus early in the day. I accordingly did as I was ordered. The two attendants, who were small, thin, and wizened almost beyond belief, immediately began to anoint my face and hands with some sweet-smelling essences taken from the bottles they had brought with them. The perfume of these unguents was indescribably soothing, and gradually I found myself losing the feeling of excitement and distrust which had hitherto possessed me. The cigarettes Pharos had given me on the occasion that I had dined with him in Naples must have contained something of a like nature, for the effect was similar in more than one essential. I refer in particular to the sharpening of the wits, to the feeling of peculiar physical enjoyment, and to the dulling of every sense of fear.

It was just as well, perhaps, that I was in this frame of mind ; for though I did not know it, I was about to be put to a test that surpassed in severity anything of which I could have dreamed.

Little by little a feeling of extreme lassitude was overtaking me ; I lost all care for my safety, and my only desire was to be allowed to continue in the state of exquisite semi-consciousness to which I had now been reduced. The figures of the men who continued to sprinkle the essences upon me, and of the old man who stood at my feet, his arms stretched above his head as if he were invoking the blessing of the gods upon the sacrifice he was offering to them, faded farther and farther into the rose-coloured mist before my eyes. How long an interval elapsed before I heard the old man's voice addressing me again, I cannot say. It may have been a few seconds, it may have been hours ; I only know that, as soon as I heard it, I opened my eyes and looked about me. The attendants had departed, and we were alone together. He was still standing before me, gazing intently down at my face.

" Rise, son of an alien race," he said, " rise purified for the time of thy earthly self, and fit to enter and stand in the presence of Ammon-Ra ! "

In response to his command, I rose from the stone upon which I had been lying. Strangely enough, however, I did so without perceptible exertion. In my new state my body was as light as air, my brain without a cloud, while the senses of hearing, of sight, of smell, and of touch were each abnormally acute.

Taking me by the hand, the old man led me from the room in which the ceremony of anointing had taken place along another passage, on either side of which, as in the apartment we had just left, were a number of shelves, each containing a mummy case. Reaching the end of this passage, he paused and extinguished the

" I lost all care for my safety."

Pharos the Egyptian.]   [Page 218

torch he carried, and then, still leading me by the hand, entered another hall which was in total darkness. In my new state, however, I experienced no sort of fear, nor was I conscious of feeling any alarm as to my ultimate safety.

Having brought me to the place for which he was making, he dropped my hand, and, from the shuffling of his feet upon the stone pavement, I knew that he was moving away from me.

"Wait here and watch," he said, and his voice echoed and re-echoed in that gloomy place. "For it was ordained from the first that this night thou shouldst see the mysteries of the gods. Fear not, thou art in the hands of the watcher of the world, the ever-mighty Harmachis, who sleepeth not day or night, nor hath rested since time began."

With this he departed, and I remained standing where he had put me, watching and waiting for what should follow. To attempt to make you understand the silence that prevailed would be a waste of time, nor can I tell you how long it lasted. Under the influence of the mysterious preparation to which I had been subjected, such things as time, fear, and curiosity had been eliminated from my being.

Suddenly, in the far distance, so small as to make it uncertain whether it was only my fancy or not, a pinpoint of light attracted my attention. It moved slowly to and fro with the regular and evenly-balanced swing of a pendulum, and as it did so it grew larger and more brilliant. Such was the fascination it possessed for me that I could not take my eyes off it, and as I watched it everything grew bright as noonday. How I had been

moved, I know not, but to my amazement I discovered
that I was no longer in that subterranean room below
the temple, but was in the open air in broad daylight,
and standing on the same spot before the main pylon
where Pharos and I had waited while the man who had
conducted us to the temple went off to give notice of
our arrival. There was, however, this difference : the
temple which I had seen then was nothing more than
a mass of ruins, now it was restored to its pristine
grandeur, and exceeded in beauty anything I could
have imagined. High into the cloudless sky above me
rose the mighty pylons, the walls of which were no
longer bare and weather-worn, but adorned with brilliant
coloured paintings. Before me, not covered with sand
as at present, but carefully tended and arranged with a
view to enhancing the already superb effect, was a broad
and well-planned terrace from which led a road lined on
either side with the same stately kriosphinxes that to-
day lie headless and neglected on the sands. From this
terrace the waters of the Nile could be distinctly seen,
with the steps, at which the avenue I have just described
terminated, leading down to them. Away to the south-
west rose the smaller Temple of Khunsi, and from it the
avenue of sphinxes which connected it with the Temple
of Ammon two miles away at Luxor. From the crowds
that congregated round these mighty edifices, and from
the excitement which prevailed on every hand, it was
plain that some great festival was about to be celebrated.
While I watched, the commencement of the procession
made its appearance on the farther side of the river,
where state barges ornamented with much gold and
many brilliant colours were waiting to carry it across.

On reaching the steps it continued its march towards
the temple. It was preceded by a hundred dancing
girls clad in white, and carrying timbrels in their hands.
Behind them was a priest bearing the two books of
Hermes, one containing hymns in honour of the gods,
and the other precepts relating to the life of the King.
Next came the Royal Astrologer bearing the measure
of Time, the hour-glass and the Phœnix. Then the
King's Scribe, carrying the materials of his craft.
Following him were more women playing on single and
double pipes, harps, and flutes, and after the musicians
the Stolistes, with the sign of Justice and the cup of
Libation. Next walked twelve servants of the temple,
headed by the Chief Priest, clad in his robes of leopard
skins, after whom marched a troop of soldiers with the
sun glittering on their armour and accoutrements.
Behind, the runners were carrying white staves in their
hand, and after them fifty singing girls, strewing flowers
of all colours upon the path. Then, escorted by his
bodyguard, the Royal Arms bearers, and seated upon
his throne of state, which again was borne upon the
shoulders of the chief eight nobles of the land, and had
above it a magnificent canopy, was Pharaoh himself,
dressed in his robes of state and carrying his sceptre
and the flagellum of Osiris in either hand. Behind him
were his fan-bearers, and by his side a man whom, in
spite of his rich dress, I recognised as soon as my eyes
fell upon him. He was none other than the servant
whom Pharaoh delighted to honour, his favourite,
Ptahmes, son of Netruhôtep, Chief of the Magicians, and
Lord of the North and South. Deformed as he was, he
walked with a proud step, carrying himself like one who

knows that his position is assured. Following Pharaoh
were his favourite generals, then another detachment of
soldiers, still more priests, musicians, and dancing girls,
and last of all a choir robed in white, and numbering
several hundred voices. If you can picture the blue sky
overhead, the sunshine, the mighty pylons and temples,
the palm trees, the glittering procession, the gorgeous
uniforms, the avenues of kriosphinxes, and the waters of
the Nile showing in the background, you will have some
notion of the scene I have attempted to portray.

Reaching the main pylon of the temple, the dancing
girls, musicians and soldiers drew back on either side,
and Pharaoh, still borne upon the shoulders of his
courtiers, and accompanied by his favourite magician,
entered the sacred building and was lost to view.

He had no sooner disappeared than the whole scene
vanished, and once more I found myself standing in the
darkness. It was only for a few moments, however.
Then the globule of light which had first attracted my
attention reappeared. Again it swung before my eyes,
and again I suddenly found myself in the open air.
Now, however, it was night time. As on the previous
occasion, I stood before the main pylon of the temple.
This time, however, there was no crowd, no brilliant
procession, no joyous music. Heavy clouds covered the
sky, and at intervals the sound of sullen thunder came
across the sands from the west. A cold wind sighed
round the corners of the temple and added to the pre-
vailing dreariness. It was close upon midnight, and I
could not help feeling that something terrible was about
to happen. Nor was I disappointed. Even as I waited,
a small procession crossed the Nile and made its way,

just as the other had done, up the avenue of kriosphinxes. Unlike the first, however, this consisted of
but four men, or, to be exact, of five, since one was being
carried on a bier. Making no more noise than was
necessary, they conveyed their burden up the same well-
kept roadway and approached the temple. From where
I stood I was able to catch a glimpse of the dead man,
for dead he certainly was. To my surprise he was none
other than Ptahmes. Not, however, the Ptahmes of the
last vision. Now he was old and poorly clad, and a
very different creature from the man who had walked so
confidently beside Pharaoh's litter on the occasion of the
last procession.

Knowing as I did the history of his downfall, I was
easily able to put two and two together and to ascribe a
reason for what I saw. He had been in hiding to escape
the wrath of Pharaoh, and now he was dead, and his
friends among the priests of Ammon were bringing him
by stealth to the temple to prepare his body for the
tomb. Once more the scene vanished and I stood in
darkness. Then, as before, the light reappeared, and
with it still another picture.

On this occasion also it was night, and we were in the
desert. The same small party I had seen carrying the
dead man before was now making its way towards a
range of hills. High up on a rocky spur a tomb had
been prepared, and to it the body of the man, once so
powerful and now fallen so low, was being conveyed.
Unseen by the bearers, I followed, and entered the
chamber of death. In front was the Chief Priest, a
venerable man, but to my surprise without his leopard-
skin dress. The mummy was placed in position without

ceremony of any kind. Even the most simple funerary
rites were omitted. No sorrowing relatives made an
oblation before it, no scroll of his life was read. Cut off
from the world, buried by stealth, he was left to take the
long rest in an unhallowed tomb from which my own
father, three thousand years later, was destined to remove his body. Then, like the others, this scene also
vanished, and once more I found myself standing in the
dark hall.

"Thou hast seen the splendour and the degradation
of the man Ptahmes," said the deep voice of the old man
who had warned me not to be afraid. "How he rose
and how he fell. Thou hast seen how the mortal body
of him who was once so mighty that he stood before
Pharaoh unafraid, was buried by night, having been
forbidden to cross the sacred Lake of the Dead. For
more than three thousand years, by thy calculation, that
body has rested in an unconsecrated tomb, it has been
carried to a far country, and throughout that time his
soul has known no peace. But the gods are not venge-
ful for ever, and it is decreed that by thy hand, inasmuch
as thou art not of his country or of his blood, he shall
find rest at last. Follow me, for there is much for thee
to see."

Leading the way across the large hall, he conducted
me down another flight of steps into yet another hall,
larger than any I had yet seen, the walls of which were
covered with frescoes, in every case having some connection with the services rendered to the dead. On a
stone slab in the centre of this great place was the
mummy case which had for so many years stood in the
alcove of my studio, and which was undoubtedly the

cause of my being where I now was. I looked again, and could scarcely believe my eyes, for there, seated at its head, gazing from the old man to myself, was the monkey, Pehtes, with an expression of terror upon his wizened little face.

I must leave you to imagine what sort of effect the solemnity of this great hall, the solitary mummy case lying in the centre, and the frightened little monkey seated at its head had upon me.

At a signal from my companion, the men who had anointed me on my arrival in this ghostly place made their appearance, but whence I could not discover. Lifting the lid of the case, despite the monkey's almost human protests, they withdrew the body, swaddled up as it was, and laid it upon the table. One by one the cloths were removed until the naked flesh (if flesh it could be called) lay exposed to view. To the best of my belief it had never seen the light, certainly not in my time, since the day, so many thousand years before, when it had been prepared for the tomb. The effect it had upon me was almost overwhelming. My guide, however, permitted no sign of emotion to escape him. When everything had been removed, the men who had done the work withdrew as silently as they had come, and we three were left alone together.

"Draw near," said the old man solemnly, "and if thou wouldst lose conceit in thy strength, and learn how feeble a thing is man, gaze upon the form of him who lies before you. Here on this stone is all that is left of Ptahmes, the son of Netruhôtep, Magician to Pharaoh, and chief of the Prophets of the North and South."

I drew near and looked upon the mummified remains. Dried up and brown as they were, the face was still distinctly recognisable, and as I gazed I sprang back with a cry of horror and astonishment. Believe it or not as you please, but what I saw there was none other than the face of Pharos. The likeness was unmistakable. There could be no sort of doubt about it. I brushed my hand across my eyes to find out if I were dreaming. But no, when I looked again the body was still there. And yet it seemed so utterly impossible, so unheard of, that the man stretched out before me could be he whom I had first seen at the foot of Cleopatra's Needle, at the Academy, in Lady Medenham's drawing-room, and with whom I had dined at Naples after our interview at Pompeii. And as I looked, as if any further proof were wanting, the monkey, with a little cry, sprang upon the dead man and snuggled himself down beside him.

Approaching the foot of the slab, the old man addressed the recumbent figure.

"Open thine eyes, Ptahmes, son of Netruhôtep," he said, "and listen to the words that I shall speak to thee. In the day of thy power, when yet thou didst walk upon the earth, thou didst sin against Ra and against the mighty ones, the thirty-seven gods. Know now that it is given thee for thy salvation to do the work which has been decreed against the peoples upon whom their wrath has fallen. Be strong, O Ptahmes! for the means are given thee, and if thou dost obey thou shalt rest in peace. Wanderer of the centuries, who cometh out of the dusk, and whose birth is from the house of death, thou wast old and art born again.

Through all the time that has been thou hast waited for this day. In the name, therefore, of the great gods Osiris and Nephthys, I bid thee rise from thy long rest and go out into the world ; but be it ever remembered by thee that if thou usest this power to thy own advantage, or failest even by as much as one single particular in the trust reposed in thee, then thou art lost, not for to-day, not for to-morrow, but for all time. In the tomb from whence it was stolen thy body shall remain until the work which is appointed thee is done. Then shalt thou return and be at peace for ever. Rise, Ptahmes, rise and depart!"

As he said this, the monkey sprang up from the dead man's side with a little cry and beat wildly in the air with his hands. Then it was as if something snapped, my body became deadly cold, and with a great shiver I awoke (if, as I can scarcely believe, I had been sleeping before) to find myself sitting on the same block of stone in the great Hypostile Hall where Pharos had left me many hours before. The first pale light of dawn could be seen through the broken columns to the east. The air was bitterly cold, and my body ached all over as if, which was very likely, I had caught a chill. Only a few paces distant, seated on the ground, their faces hidden in their folded arms, were the two Arabs who had accompanied us from Luxor. I rose to my feet and stamped upon the ground in the hope of imparting a little warmth to my stiffened limbs. Could I have fallen asleep while I waited for Pharos, and if so, had I dreamed all the strange things that I have described in this chapter? I discarded the notion as impossible, and yet what other explanation had I to offer? I thought of the secret passage beneath the stone, and which led to the vaults below. Remembering as I did the direction in which the old man had proceeded in order to reach it, I determined to search for it. If only I could find the place, I should be able to set all doubt on the subject at rest for good and all. I accordingly crossed the great hall, which was now as light as day, and searched the place which I considered most likely to contain the stone in question. But though I gave it the most minute scrutiny for upwards of a quarter of an hour, no sign could I discover. All the time I was becoming more and more convinced of one thing, and that was the fact that I was unmistakably ill. My head and bones ached, while my left arm, which had never yet lost the small purple mark which I had noticed the morning after my adventure at the Pyramids, seemed to be swelling perceptibly and throbbed from shoulder to wrist. Unable to find the stone, and still more unable to make head or tail of all that had happened in the night, I returned to my former seat. One of the Arabs, the man who had boarded the steamer on our arrival the previous afternoon, rose to his feet and looked about him, yawning heavily as he did so. He, at least, I thought, would be able to tell me if I had slept all night in the same place. I put the question to him, only to receive his solemn assurance that I had not left their side ever since I had entered the ruins. The man's demeanour was so sincere, that I had no reason to suppose that he was not telling the truth. I accordingly seated myself again, and devoutly wished I were back with Valerie on board the steamer.

A nice trick Pharos had played me in bringing me out to spend the night catching cold in these ruins. I resolved to let him know my opinion of his conduct at the earliest opportunity. But if I had gone to sleep on the stone, where had he been all night, and why had he not permitted me to assist in the burial of Ptahmes according to agreement? What was more important still, when did he intend putting in an appearance again? I had half made up mind to set off for Luxor on my own account, in the hope of being able to discover an English doctor, from whom I could obtain some medicine and find out the nature of the ailment from which I was suffering. I was, however, spared the trouble of doing this; for just as my patience was becoming exhausted, a noise behind me made me turn round, and I saw Pharos coming towards me. It struck me that his step was more active than I had yet seen it, and I noticed the pathetic little face of the monkey, Pehtes, peeping out from the shelter of his heavy coat.

"Come," he said briskly, "let us be going. You look cold, my dear Forrester, and if I am not mistaken, you are not feeling very well. Give me your hand."

I did as he ordered me. If, however, my hand was cold, his was like ice.

"I thought as much," he said; "you are suffering from a mild attack of Egyptian fever. Fortunately, however, that can soon be set right."

I followed him through the main pylon to the place where we had dismounted from our camels the night before. The patient beasts were still there just as we had left them.

"Mount," said Pharos, "and let us return with all speed to the steamer."

I did as he desired, and we accordingly set off. I noticed, however, that on the return journey we did not follow the same route as that which had brought us to the temple. By this time, however, I was feeling too ill to protest or to care very much where we went.

"We are nearly there," said Pharos. "Keep up your heart. In less than ten minutes you will be in bed and on the high-road to recovery."

"But this is not the way to Luxor," I said feebly, clinging to the pommel of my saddle as I spoke and looking with aching eyes across the dreary stretch of sand.

"We are not going to Luxor," Pharos replied. "I am taking you to a place where I can look after you myself, and where there will be no chance of any meddlesome European doctors interfering with my course of treatment."

The ten minutes he had predicted seemed like centuries, and, had I been asked, I should have declared that at least two hours elapsed between our leaving the Temple of Ammon and our arrival at our destination. During that time my agony was well-nigh unbearable. My throat was swelling, and I felt as if I were suffocating. My limbs quivered as though they had been stricken with the palsy, and the entire landscape was blotted out by a red mist as thick as blood.

More dead than alive, I accommodated myself to the shuffling tread of the camel as best I could, and when at last I heard Pharos say in Arabic, "It is here; bid the beast lie down," my last ounce of strength departed, and I lost consciousness.

How long I remained in this state, I had no idea at the time; but when I recovered my senses again, I found myself lying in an Arab tent, upon a rough bed made up upon the sand. I was as weak as a kitten, and when I looked at my hand as it lay upon the rough blanket, I scarcely recognised it, so white and emaciated was it. Not being able to understand the reason of my present location, I raised myself on my elbow and looked out under the flap of the tent. All I could see there, however, was desert sand, a half-starved dog prowling about in the foreground in search of something to eat, and a group of palm trees upon the far horizon. While I was thus investigating my surroundings, the same Arab who had assured me that I had slept all night on the block of stone in the temple, made his appearance with a bowl of broth which he gave to me, putting his arm round me and assisting me to sit up while I drank it. I questioned him as to where I was, and how long I had been there; but he only shook his head, saying that he could tell me nothing. The broth, however, did me good, more good than any information could have done, and, after he had left me, I laid myself down and in a few moments was asleep again. When I woke, it was late in the afternoon, and the sun was sinking behind the palm trees to which I referred just now. As it disappeared, Pharos entered the tent and expressed his delight at finding me conscious once more. I put the same questions to him that I had asked the Arab, and found that he was inclined to be somewhat more communicative.

"You have now been ill three days," he said, "so ill, indeed, that I dared not move you. Now, however, that you have got your senses back, you will make rapid progress. I can assure you I shall not be sorry, for events have occurred which necessitate my immediate return to Europe. You on your part, I presume, will not regret saying farewell to Egypt?"

"I would leave to-day, if such a thing were possible," I answered. "Weak as I am, I think I could find strength enough for that. Indeed, I feel stronger already, and, as a proof of it, my appetite is returning. Where is the Arab who brought me my broth this morning?"

"Dead," said Pharos laconically. "He held you in his arms and died two hours afterwards. They've no stamina, these Arabs—the least thing kills them. But you need have no fear. You have passed the critical point, and your recovery is certain."

But I scarcely heard him. "Dead! dead!" I was saying over and over again to myself as if I did not understand it. "Surely the man cannot be dead?" He had died through helping me. What, then, was this terrible disease of which I had been the victim?

CHAPTER XIV

I N travelling either with Pharos or in search of him, it
was necessary to accustom one's self to rapid movement. I was in London on June 7th, and had found
him in Naples three days later; had reached Cairo in
his company on the 18th of the same month, and was
four hundred and fifty miles up the Nile by the 27th.
I had explored the mysteries of the great Temple of
Ammon as no other Englishman, I feel convinced, had
ever done; had been taken seriously ill, recovered, returned to Cairo, travelled thence to rejoin the yacht
at Port Said; had crossed in her to Constantinople,
journeyed by the Orient Express to Vienna, and on the
morning of July 15th stood at the entrance to the Teyn
Kirche in the wonderful old Bohemian city of Prague.

From this itinerary it will be seen that the grass
was not allowed to grow under our feet. Indeed, we
had scarcely arrived in any one place before our remorseless leader hurried us away again. His anxiety
to return to Europe was as great as it had been to
reach Egypt. On land the trains could not travel fast
enough; on board the yacht his one cry was, " Push on,
push on ! " What this meant to a man like myself, who
had lately come so perilously near death, I must leave
you to imagine. Indeed, looking back upon it now, I

wonder that I emerged from it alive. Looked at from another light, I believe I could not have done so but for Pharos. Callous as he had been to my sufferings hitherto, he could scarcely do enough for me now. His first inquiry in the morning was as to how I felt, and his last injunction at night was to the effect that, if I felt any return of fever, I was to communicate with him immediately. From this show of consideration on his part it would probably be argued that I should at least have felt some gratitude towards himself. The contrary, however, was the case. Ever since he had announced the death of the Arab to me, my fear and dislike of him had been intensified rather than diminished. I was afraid of him very much in the same way as a man is afraid of a loathsome snake, and yet with that fear there was a peculiar fascination which I was powerless to resist.

We had reached Constantinople early on Thursday morning, and had left for Vienna at four o'clock in the afternoon. In the latter place we had remained only a few hours, had caught the next available train, and reached Prague the following morning. What our next move would be I had not the least idea, nor did Pharos enlighten me upon the subject. Times out of number I made up my mind that I would speak to him about it, and let him see that I was tired of so much travelling, and desired to return to England forthwith. But I could not leave Valerie, and whenever I began to broach the subject my courage deserted me, and it did not require much self-persuasion to make me put the matter off for a more convenient opportunity.

Of the Fräulein Valerie, up to the time of our arrival

in the city, there is little to tell. She had evidently been informed of my illness at Karnak, for when I returned to the steamer she had arranged that everything should be in readiness for my reception. By the time we reached Cairo again I was so far recovered as to be able to join her on deck, but by this time a curious change had come over her : she was more silent and much more reserved than heretofore, and, when we reached the yacht, spent most of her days in her own cabin, where I could hear her playing to herself such wild, sad music that to listen to it made me feel miserable for hours afterwards. With Pharos, however, it was entirely different. He, who had once been so morose, now was all smiles ; while his inseparable companion, the monkey, Pehtes, for whom I had conceived a dislike that was only second to that I entertained for his master, equalled, if he did not excel him, in the boisterousness of his humour.

At the commencement of this chapter I have said that on this particular morning, our first in Prague, I was standing before the doors of the Teyn Kirche, beneath the story of the Crucifixion as it is told there in stone. My reason for being there will be apparent directly. Let it suffice that, when I entered the sacred building, I paused, thinking how beautiful it was, with the sunshine straggling in through those wonderful windows, which, in bygone days, had looked down on the burial of Tycho Brahe, and had in all probability seen John of Nepomuc standing in the pulpit. Their light illumined the grotesque old organ with its multitude of time-stained pipes and dingy, faded ornaments, and contrasted strangely with that of the lamps and candles

burning before the various altars and shrines. Of all
the churches of Europe there is not one that affects me
so deeply as this famous old Hussite building. With
the exception, however, of myself and a kneeling figure
near the entrance to the Marian Capelle, no worshippers
were in the church. I stood for a moment looking
round the building. Its vague suggestion of sadness
harmonized with my own feelings, and I wondered if,
among all those who had worshipped inside its walls
since the days when the German merchants had first
erected it, there had ever been one who had so strange
a story to tell as myself. At last, having screwed my
courage to the sticking point, I made my way down the
nave between the carved, worm-eaten pews, and approached the figure I have referred to above. Though
I could not see her face, I knew that it was Valerie.
Her head was bent upon her hands and her shoulders
shook with emotion. She must have heard my step
upon the stones, for she suddenly looked up, and, seeing
me before her, rose from her knees and prepared to
leave the pew. The sight of her unhappiness affected
me keenly, and when she reached the spot where I was
standing, I could control myself no longer. For the
last few weeks I had been hard put to it to keep my
love within bounds, and now, under the influence of her
grief, it got the better of me altogether. She must
have known what was coming, for she stood before
me with a troubled expression in her eyes.

" Mr. Forrester," she began, " I did not expect to see
you. How did you know that I was here ? "

" Because I followed you," I answered unblushingly.

" You followed me ? " she said

"Yes, and I am not ashamed to own it," I replied. "Surely you can understand why?"

"I am afraid I do not," she answered, and, as she did so, she took a step away from me, as if she were afraid of what she was going to hear.

"In that case there is nothing left but for me to tell you," I said, and, approaching her, I took possession of the slender hand which rested upon the back of the pew behind her. "I followed you, Valerie, because I love you, and because I wished to guard you. Unhappily, we have both of us the best of reasons for knowing that we are in the power of a man who would stop at nothing to achieve any end he might have in view. Did you hear me say, Valerie, that I love you?"

From her beautiful face every speck of colour had vanished by this time; her bosom heaved tumultuously under the intensity of her emotion. No word, however, passed her lips. I still held her hand in mine, and it gave me courage to continue when I saw that she did not attempt to withdraw it.

"Have you no answer for me?" I inquired, after the long pause which had followed my last speech. "I have told you that I love you. If it is not enough, I will do so again. What better place could be found for such a confession than this beautiful old church, which has seen so many lovers and has held the secrets of so many lives? Valerie, I believe I have loved you since the afternoon I first saw you. But since I have known you and have learnt your goodness, that love has become doubly strong."

"I cannot hear you!" she cried, almost with a sob; "indeed, I cannot. You do not know what you are saying. You have no idea of the pain you are causing me."

"God knows I would not give you pain for anything," I answered. "But now you *must* hear me. Why should you not? You are a good woman, and I am, I trust, an honest man. Why, therefore, should I not love you? Tell me that."

"Because it is madness," she answered in despair. "Situated as we are, we should be the last to think of such a thing. Oh, Mr. Forrester, if only you had taken my advice, and had gone away from Naples when I implored you to do so, this would not have happened."

"If I have anything to be thankful for, it is that," I replied fervently. "I told you then that I would not leave you. Nor shall I ever do so until I know that your life is safe. Come, Valerie, you have heard my confession ; will you not be equally candid with me? You have always proved yourself my friend. Is it possible you have nothing more than friendship to offer me?"

I knew the woman I was dealing with. Her beautiful, straightforward nature was incapable of dissimulation.

"Mr. Forrester, even if what you hope is impossible, it would be unfair on my part to deceive you," she said. "I love you, as you are worthy to be loved, but having said that I can say no more. You must go away and endeavour to forget that you ever saw so unhappy a person as myself."

"Never," I answered, and then dropping on one knee and pressing her hand to my lips, I continued : "You have confessed, Valerie, that you love me, and nothing can ever separate us now. Come what may, I will not leave you. Here, in this old church, by the cross on yonder altar, I swear it. As we are together in trouble, so will we be together in love, and may God's blessing rest upon us both."

"Amen," she answered solemnly.

She seated herself in a pew, and I took my place beside her.

"Valerie," I said, "I followed you this morning for two reasons. The first was to tell you of my love, and the second was to let you know that I have made up my mind on a certain course of action. At any risk we must escape from Pharos, and since you have confessed that you love me, we will go together."

"It is useless," she answered sorrowfully, "quite useless."

"Hush!" I said, as three people entered the church. "We cannot talk here. Let us find another place."

With this we rose and left the building. Proceeding into the street, I hailed a cab, and as soon as we had taken our places in it, bade the man drive us to the Baumgarten. Some of my pleasantest recollections of Prague in days gone by were clustered round this park, but they were as nothing compared with the happiness I now enjoyed in visiting it in the company of the woman I loved. When we had found a seat in a secluded spot, we resumed the conversation that had been interrupted in the church.

"You say that it is useless our thinking of making our escape from this man?" I said. "I tell you that it is not useless, and that at any hazard we must do so. We know now that we love each other. I know, at

least, how much you are to me. Is it possible, therefore, that you can believe I should allow you to remain
in his power an instant longer than I can help? In my
life I have not feared many men, but I confess that I
fear Pharos as I do the devil.   Since I have known him,
I have had several opportunities of testing his power.
I have seen things, or he has *made* me believe I have
seen things, which, under any other circumstances, would
seem incredible, and, if it is likely to have any weight
with you, I do not mind owning that his power over
me is growing greater every day.   And that reminds me
there is a question I have often desired to ask you.   Do
you remember one night on board the yacht, when we
were crossing from Naples to Port Said, telling Pharos
that you could see a cave in which a mummy had once
stood ? "

She shook her head.

" I remember nothing of it," she said.   " But why do
you ask me such strange questions ? "

I took her hand before I answered.   I could feel that
she was trembling violently.

" Because I want to prove to you the diabolical power
the man possesses. You described a tomb from which
the mummy had been taken. I have seen that tomb. It
was the burial-place of the Magician, Ptahmes, whose
mummy once stood in my studio in London, which
Pharos stole from me, and which was the primary cause
of my becoming associated with him. You described a
subterranean hall with carved pillars and paintings on
the walls, and a mummy lying upon a block of stone.
I have seen that hall, those pillars, those carvings and
paintings, and the mummy of Ptahmes lying stretched

out as you portrayed it. You mentioned a tent in the desert and a sick man lying on a bed inside it. I was that sick man, and it was to that tent that Pharos conveyed me after I had spent the night in the ruins of the Temple of Ammon. The last incident has yet to take place; but, please God, if you will help me in my plan, we shall have done with him long before then."

"You say you saw all the things I described. Please do not think me stupid, but I do not understand how you could have done so."

Thereupon I told her all that had befallen me at the ruins of Karnak. She listened with feverish interest.

"How is it that Providence allows this man to live?" she cried when I had finished. "Who is he and what is the terrible power he possesses? And what is to be the end of all his evil ways?"

"That is a problem which only the future can solve," I answered. "For ourselves it is sufficient that we must get away from him and at once. Nothing could be easier. He exercises no control over our movements. He does not attempt to detain us. We go in and out as we please, therefore all we have to do is to get into a train and be hundreds of miles away before he is even aware that we are outside the doors of the hotel. You are not afraid, Valerie, to trust yourself and your happiness to me?"

"I would trust myself with you anywhere," she answered; and as she said it she pressed my hand and looked into my face with her brave, sweet eyes. "And for your sake I would do and bear anything."

Brave as her words were, however, a little sigh escaped her lips before she could prevent it.

"Why do you sigh?" I asked. "Have you any doubt as to the safety of our plan? If so, tell me, and I will change it."

"I have no doubt as to the plan," she answered. "All I fear is that it may be useless. I have already told you how I have twice tried to escape him, and how on each occasion he has brought me back."

"He shall not do so this time," I said with determination. "We will lay our plans with the greatest care, behave towards him as if we contemplated remaining for ever in his company, and then to-morrow morning we will catch the train for Berlin, be in Hamburg next day, and in London three days later. Once there, I have a hundred friends who, when I tell them that you are hiding from a man who has treated you most cruelly, and that you are about to become my wife, will be only too proud to take you in. Then we will be married as quickly as can be arranged, and as man and wife defy Pharos to do his worst."

She did her best to appear delighted with my plan, but I could see that she had no real faith in it. Nor, if the truth must be told, was I in my own heart any too sanguine of success. I could not but remember the threat the man had held over me that night in the Pyramid at Gizeh: "For the future you are my property, to do with as I please. You will have no will but my pleasure, no thought but to act as I shall tell you." However, we could but do our best, and I was determined it should not be my fault if our enterprise did not meet with success. Not once but a hundred times we overhauled our plan, tried its weak spots, arranged our behaviour before Pharos, and endeavoured to convince each other as far as possible that it could not fail. And if we did manage to outwit him, how proud I should be to parade this glorious creature in London as my wife; and as I thought of the happiness the future might have in store for us, and remembered that it all depended on that diabolical individual Pharos, I felt sick and giddy with anxiety to see the last of him.

Not being anxious to arouse any suspicion in our ogre's mind by a prolonged absence, we at last agreed that it was time for us to think of returning. Accordingly, we left the park and, finding the cab which had been ordered to wait for us at the gates, drove back to the city. On reaching the hotel, we discovered Pharos in the hall, holding in his hand a letter which he had just finished reading as we entered. On seeing us, his wrinkled old face lit up with a smile.

"My dear," he said to Valerie, placing his hand upon her arm in an affectionate manner, "a very great honour has been paid you. His Majesty, the Emperor King, as you are perhaps aware, arrived in the city yesterday, and to-night a state concert is to be given at the palace. Invitations have been sent to us, and I have been approached in order to discover whether you will consent to play. Not being able to find you, I answered that I felt sure you would accept his Majesty's command. Was I right in so doing?"

Doubtless, remembering the contract we had entered into together that morning to humour Pharos as far as possible, Valerie willingly gave her consent. Though

I did not let him see it, I for my part was not so pleased. He should have waited and have allowed her to accept or decline for herself, I thought. However, I held my peace, trusting that on the morrow we should be able to make our escape and so be done with him for good and all.

For the remainder of the day Pharos exhibited the most complete good-humour. He was plainly looking forward to the evening. He had met Franz Josef on more than one occasion, he informed me, and remembered with gusto the compliments that had been paid him the last time about his ward's playing.

" I am sure we shall both rejoice in her success, shall we not, my dear Forrester ? " he said ; and as he did so he glanced slyly at me out of the corner of his eye. " As you can see for yourself, I have discovered your secret."

I looked nervously at him. What did he mean by this ? Was it possible that by that same adroit reasoning he had discovered our plan for escaping on the following day ?

"I am afraid I do not quite understand," I replied, with as much nonchalance as I could manage to throw into my voice. " Pray, what secret have you discovered ? "

" That you love my ward," he answered. " But why look so concerned ? It does not require very great perceptive powers to see that her beauty has exercised considerable effect upon you. Why should it not have done so ? And where would be the harm ? She is a most fascinating woman, and you, if you will permit me to tell you so to your face, are—what shall we say ?—well, far from being an unprepossessing man.

Like a foolish guardian, I have permitted you to be a good deal, perhaps too much, together, and the result even a child might have foreseen. You have learnt to love each other. No; do not be offended. I assure you there is no reason for it. I like you, and I promise you, if you continue to please me, I shall raise no objection. Now what have you to say to me ? "

" I do not know what to say," I said, and it was the truth. " I had no idea you suspected anything of the kind."

" I fear you do not give me the credit of being very sharp," he replied. " And perhaps it is not to be wondered at. An old man's wits cannot hope to be as quick as those of the young. But there, we have talked enough on this subject ; let us postpone consideration of it until another day."

" With all my heart," I answered. " But there is one question I had better ask you while I have the opportunity. I should be glad if you could tell me how long you are thinking of remaining in Prague. When I left England, I had no intention of being away from London more than a fortnight, and I have now trespassed on your hospitality for upwards of two months. If you are going west within the next week or so, and will let me travel with you, I shall be only too glad to do so, otherwise I fear I shall be compelled to bid you good-bye and return to England alone."

" You must not think of such a thing," he answered, this time throwing a sharp glance at me from his sunken eyes. " Neither Valerie nor I could get on without you. Besides, there is no need for you to worry.

Now that this rumour is afloat, I have no intention of remaining here any longer than I can help."

" To what rumour do you refer ? " I inquired. " I have heard nothing."

" That is what it is to be in love," he replied. " You have not heard, then, that one of the most disastrous and terrible plagues of the last five hundred years has broken out on the shores of the Bosphorus, and is spreading with alarming rapidity through Turkey and the Balkan States."

" I have not heard a word about it," I said, and as I did so I was conscious of a vague feeling of terror in my heart, that fear for a woman's safety which comes some time or another to every man who loves. " Is it only newspaper talk, or is it really as serious as your words imply ? "

" It is very serious," he answered. " See, here is a man with the evening paper. I will purchase one and read you the latest news."

He did so, and searched the columns for what he wanted. Though I was able to speak German, I was unable to read it ; Pharos accordingly translated for me.

" The outbreak of the plague which has caused so much alarm in Turkey," he read, " is, we regret having to inform our readers, increasing instead of diminishing, and to-day fresh cases to the number of seven hundred and thirty-three have been notified. For the twenty-four hours ending at noon the death-rate has equalled 80 per cent. of those attacked. The malady has now penetrated into Russia, and three deaths were registered as resulting from it in Moscow, two in Odessa, and one in Kiev yesterday. The medical experts are still unable to assign a definite name to it, but incline to the belief that it is of Asiatic origin, and will disappear with the break up of the present phenomenally hot weather."

" I do not like the look of it at all," he said, when he had finished reading. " I have seen several of these outbreaks in my time, and I shall be very careful to keep well out of this one's reach."

" I agree with you," I answered, and then bade him good-bye and went upstairs to my room, more than ever convinced that it behoved me to get the woman I loved out of the place without loss of time.

The concert at the palace that night was a brilliant success in every way, and never in her career had Valerie looked more beautiful or played so exquisitely as on that occasion. Of the many handsome women present that evening she was undoubtedly the queen. And when, after her performance, she was led up and presented to the Emperor by Count de Schelyani, an old friend of her father's, a murmur of such admiration ran through the room as those walls had seldom heard before. I, also, had the honour of being presented by the same nobleman, whereupon his Majesty was kind enough to express his appreciation of my work. It was not until a late hour that we reached our hotel again. When we did, Pharos, whom the admiration Valerie had excited seemed to have placed in a thoroughly good humour, congratulated us both upon our success, and then, to my delight, bade us good-night and took himself off to his bed. As soon as I heard the door of his room close behind him, and not until then, I took Valerie's hand.

" I have made all the arrangements for our escape to-morrow," I whispered, "or rather I should say to-day, since it is after midnight. The train for Berlin, *viâ* Dresden, I have discovered, leaves here at a quarter past six. Do you think you can manage to be ready so early?"

"Of course I can," she answered confidently. "You have only to tell me what you want, and I will do it."

"I have come to the conclusion," I said, "that it will not do for us to leave by the city station. Accordingly, I have arranged that a cab shall be waiting for us in the Platz. We will enter it and drive down the line, board the train, and bid farewell to Pharos for good and all."

Ten minutes later I had said good-night to her and had retired to my room. The clocks of the city were striking two as I entered it. In four hours we should be leaving the house to catch the train which we hoped would bring us freedom. Were we destined to succeed or not?

CHAPTER XV

SO anxious was I not to run any risk of being asleep at the time we had arranged to make our escape that I did not go to bed at all, but seated myself in an armchair and endeavoured to interest myself in a book until the fateful hour arrived. Then, leaving a note upon my dressing-table, in which was contained a sufficient sum to reimburse the landlord for my stay with him, I slipped into one pocket the few articles I had resolved to carry with me, and taking care that my money was safely stowed away in another, I said good-bye to my room and went softly down the stairs to the large hall. Fortune favoured me, for only one servant was at work there, an elderly man with a stolid, good-humoured countenance, who glanced up at me, and being satisfied as to my respectability, continued his work once more. Of Valerie I could see no sign, and since I did not know where her room was situated, I occupied myself, while I waited, wondering what I should do if she had overslept herself and did not put in an appearance until too late. In order to excuse my presence downstairs at such an early hour, I asked the man in which direction the cathedral lay, and whether he could inform me at what time early mass was celebrated.

He had scarcely instructed me on the former point, and declared his ignorance of the latter, before Valerie appeared at the head of the stairs and descended to meet me, carrying her violin case in her hand. I greeted her in English, and after I had slipped a couple of florins into the servant's hand, we left the hotel together and made our way in the direction of the Platz, where to my delight I found the cab I had ordered the previous afternoon already waiting for us. We took our places, and I gave the driver his instructions. In less than a quarter of an hour he had brought us to the station I wanted to reach. I had taken the tickets, and the train was carrying us away from Prague and the man whom we devoutly hoped we should never see again as long as we lived. Throughout the drive we had scarcely spoken a couple of dozen words to each other, having been far too much occupied with the affairs of the moment to think of anything but our flight. Knowing Pharos as we did, it seemed more than probable that he might even now be aware of our escape, and be taking measures to ensure our return. But when we found ourselves safely in the train, our anxiety lessened somewhat, and with every mile we threw behind us our spirits returned. By the time we reached Dresden we were as happy a couple as any in Europe, and when some hours later we stepped out of the carriage on to the platform at Berlin, we were as unlike the pair who had left the hotel at Prague as the proverbial chalk is like cheese. Even then, however, we were determined to run no risk. Every mile that separated us from Pharos meant greater security, and it was for this reason I had made up my mind to reach

the German capital, if possible, instead of remaining at
Dresden, as had been our original intention.

When our train reached its destination, it was a few
minutes after six o'clock, and for the first time in my
life I stood in the capital of the German empire.
Though we had been travelling for more than ten hours,
Valerie had so far shown no sign of fatigue.

"What do you propose doing now?" she inquired, as
we stood together on the platform.

"Obtain some dinner," I answered, with a promptness
and directness worthy of the famous Mr. Dick.

"You must leave that to me," she said, with one of
her own bright smiles, which had been so rare of late.
"Remember I am an old traveller, and probably know
Europe as well as you know Piccadilly."

"I will leave it to you, then," I answered, "and
surely man had never a fairer pilot."

"On any other occasion I should warn you to beware of compliments," she replied, patting me gaily
on the arm with her hand, "but I feel so happy now
that I am compelled to excuse you. To-night, for
the last time, I am going to play the part of your
hostess. After that it will be your duty to entertain
me. Let us leave by this door."

So saying, she led me from the station into the
street outside, along which we passed for some considerable distance. Eventually we reached a restaurant,
before which Valerie paused.

"The proprietor is an old friend of mine," she said,
"who, though he is acquainted with Pharos, will not,
I am quite sure, tell him he has seen us."

We entered, and when the majordomo came forward

to conduct us to a table, Valerie inquired whether his master were visible. The man stated that he would find out, and departed on his errand.

While we waited I could not help noticing the admiring glances that were thrown at my companion by the patrons of the restaurant, among whom were several officers in uniform. Just, however, as I was thinking that some of the latter would be none the worse for a little lesson in manners, the shuffling of feet was heard, and presently, from a doorway on the right, the fattest man I have ever seen in my life made his appearance. He wore carpet slippers on his feet, and a red cap upon his head, and carried in his hand a long German pipe with a china bowl. His face was clean shaven, and a succession of chins fell one below another, so that not an inch of his neck was visible. Having entered the room, he paused, and when the waiter had pointed us out to him as the lady and gentleman who had asked to see him, he approached and affected a contortion of his anatomy which was evidently intended to be a bow.

"I am afraid, Herr Schuncke, that you do not remember me," said Valerie, after the short pause which followed.

The man looked at her rather more closely, and a moment later was bowing even more profusely and inelegantly than before.

"My dear young lady," he said, "I beg your pardon ten thousand times. For the moment, I confess, I did not recognise you. Had I done so, I should not have kept you standing here so long."

Then, looking round, with rather a frightened air,

he added, "But I do not see Monsieur Pharos? Perhaps he is with you, and will be here presently?"

"I sincerely hope not," Valerie replied. "That is the main reason of my coming to you." Then, sinking her voice to a whisper, she added, as she saw the man's puzzled expression, "I know I can trust you, Herr Schuncke. The truth is, I have run away from him."

"Herr Gott!" said the old fellow. "So you have run away from him. Well, I do not wonder at it, but you must not tell him I said so. How you could have put up with him so long, I do not know; but that is no business of mine. But I am an old fool; while I am talking so much, I should be finding out how I can be of assistance to you."

"You will not find that very difficult," she replied. "All we are going to trouble you for is some dinner, and your promise to say nothing, should Monsieur Pharos come here in search of us."

"I will do both with the utmost pleasure," he answered. "You may be sure I will say nothing, and you shall have the very best dinner old Ludwig can cook. What is more, you shall have it in my own private sitting-room, where you will be undisturbed. Oh, I can assure you, Fräulein, it is very good to see your face again."

"It is very kind of you to say so," said Valerie, "and also to take so much trouble. I thank you."

"You must not thank me at all," the old fellow replied. "But some day, perhaps, you will let me hear you play again." Then, pointing to the violin-case, which I carried in my hand, he continued, "I see you have brought the beautiful instrument with you. Ah, Gott! what recollections it conjures up for me. I can see old—but there, there, come with me, or I shall be talking half the night!"

We accordingly followed him through the door by which he had entered, and along a short passage to a room at the rear of the building. Here he bade us make ourselves at home, while he departed to see about the dinner. Before he did so, however, Valerie stopped him.

"Herr Schuncke," she said, "before you leave us, I want your congratulations. Let me introduce you to Mr. Forrester, the gentleman to whom I am about to be married."

The old fellow turned to me, and gave another of his grotesque bows.

"Sir," he said, "I congratulate you with all my heart. To hear her play always, ah! what good fortune for a man! You will have a treasure in your house that no money could buy. Be sure that you treat her as such."

When I had promised to do so, the warm-hearted old fellow departed on his errand.

I must leave you to imagine the happiness of that dinner. Even now it sends a thrill through me to think of it. I can recall the quaint little room, so undeniably German in its furniture and decorations; the table laden with the good things the landlord had provided for us—even to the extent of a bottle of his own particular wine, which only saw the light on most important occasions; the military-looking waiter, with his close-cropped hair and heavy eyes; and Valerie seated opposite, looking so beautiful and so happy that I could scarcely believe she was the same woman I had seen rising from her knees in the Teyn Kirche only the day before.

"I hope all this travelling has not tired you, dearest?" I said, when the waiter had handed us our coffee, and had left the room.

"You forget that I am an old traveller," she said, "and not likely to be fatigued by such a short journey. You have some reason, however, for asking the question. What is it?"

"I will tell you," I answered. "I have been thinking that it would not be altogether safe for us to remain in Berlin. It is quite certain that, as soon as he discovers that we are gone, Pharos will make inquiries, and find out what trains left Prague in the early morning. He will then put two and two together, after his own diabolical fashion, and as likely as not, he will be here in search of us to-morrow morning, if not sooner."

"In that case, what do you propose doing?" she asked.

"I propose, if you are not too tired, to leave here by the express at half-past seven," I replied, "and travel as far as Wittenberge, which place we should reach by half-past ten. We can manage it very easily. I will telegraph for rooms, and to-morrow morning early we can continue our journey to Hamburg, where we shall have no difficulty in obtaining a steamer for London. Pharos would never think of looking for us in a small place like Wittenberge, and we should be on board the steamer and *en route* to England by this time to-morrow evening."

"I can be ready as soon as you like," she answered

bravely, " but before we start you must give me time to reward Herr Schuncke for his kindness to us."

A few moments later, our host entered the room. I was about to pay for our meal, when Valerie stopped me.

"You must do nothing of the kind," she said ; "remember, you are my guest. Surely you would not deprive me of one of the greatest pleasures I have had for a long time?"

"You shall pay with all my heart," I answered, "but not with Pharos' money."

"I never thought of that," she replied, and her beautiful face flushed crimson. "No, no, you are quite right. I could not entertain you with his money. But what am I to do? I have no other."

"In that case you must permit me to be your banker," I answered, and with that I pulled from my pocket a handful of German coins.

Herr Schuncke at first refused to take anything, but when Valerie declared that if he did not do so she would not play to him, he reluctantly consented, vowing at the same time that he would not accept it himself, but would bestow it upon Ludwig. Then Valerie went to the violin-case, which I had placed upon a side table, and taking her precious instrument from it —the only legacy she had received from her father— tuned it, and stood up to play. As Valerie informed me later, the old man, though one would scarcely have imagined it from his commonplace exterior, was a passionate devotee of the beautiful art, and now he stood, leaning against the wall, his fat hands clasped before him, and his upturned face expressive of the most celestial enjoyment. Nor had Valerie, to my thinking, ever done herself greater justice. She had escaped from a life of misery that had been to her a living death, and her whole being was in consequence radiant with happiness; this was reflected in her playing. Nor was the effect she produced limited to Herr Schuncke. Under the influence of her music, I found myself building castles in the air, and upon such firm foundations, too, that for the moment it seemed no wind would ever be strong enough to blow them down. When she ceased, Schuncke uttered a long sigh, as much as to say, "It will be many years before I shall hear anything like that again," and then it was time to go. The landlord accompanied us into the street and called a cab. As it pulled up beside the pavement, a cripple passed, making his way slowly along with the assistance of a pair of crutches. Valerie stopped him.

"My poor fellow," she said, handing him the purse containing the money with which, ten minutes before, she had thought of paying for our dinner, "there is a little present which I hope may bring you more happiness than it has done me. Take it."

The man did so, scarcely able to contain his surprise, and when he had examined the contents, burst into a flood of thanks.

"Hush!" she said; "you must not thank me. You do not know what you are saying." Then turning to Schuncke, she held out her hand. "Good-bye," she said, "and thank you for your kindness. I know that you will say nothing about having seen us."

"You need have no fear on that score," he said.

"Pharos shall hear nothing from me, I can promise you that. Farewell, Fräulein, and may your life be a happy one."

I said good-bye to him, and then took my place in the vehicle beside Valerie. A quarter of an hour later we were on our way to Wittenberge, and Berlin, like Prague, was only a memory. Before leaving the station I had purchased an armful of papers, illustrated and otherwise, for Valerie's amusement. Though she professed to have no desire to read them, but to prefer sitting by my side, holding my hand, and talking of the happy days we hoped and trusted were before us, she found time, as the journey progressed, to skim their contents. Seeing her do this brought the previous evening to my remembrance, and I inquired what further news there was of the terrible pestilence which Pharos had declared to be raging in eastern Europe.

"I am afraid it is growing worse instead of better," she answered, when she had consulted the paper. "The latest telegram declares that there have been upwards of a thousand fresh cases in Turkey alone within the past twenty-four hours, that it has spread along the Black Sea as far as Odessa, and north as far as Kiev. Five cases are reported from Vienna; and, stay, here is a still later telegram in which it says"—she paused, and a look of horror came into her face—"Can this be true?—it says that the pestilence has broken out in Prague, and that the Count de Schelyani, who, you remember, was so kind and attentive to us last night at the palace, was seized this morning, and at the time this telegram was despatched, was lying in a critical condition."

"That is bad news indeed," I said. "Not only for Austria, but also for us."

"How for us?" she asked.

"Because it will make Pharos move out of Prague," I replied. "When he spoke to me yesterday of the way in which this disease was gaining ground in Europe, he seemed visibly frightened, and stated that as soon as it came too near he should at once leave the city. We have had one exhibition of his cowardice, and you may be sure he will be off now, as fast as trains can take him. It must be our business to take care that his direction and ours are not the same."

"But how are we to tell in which direction he will travel?" asked Valerie, whose face had suddenly grown bloodless in its pallor.

"We must take our chance of that," I answered. "My principal hope is that knowing, as he does, the whereabouts of the yacht, he will make for her, board her, and depart for mid-ocean, to wait there until all danger is passed. For my own part, I am willing to own that I do not like the look of things at all. I shall not feel safe until I have got you safely into England, and that little silver streak of sea is between us and the Continent."

"You *do* love me, Cyril, do you not?" she inquired, slipping her little hand into mine, and looking into my face with those eyes that seemed to grow more beautiful with every day I looked into them. "I could not live without your love now."

"God grant you may never be asked to do so," I answered; "I love you, dearest, as I believe man never loved woman before, and, come what may, nothing shall separate us. Surely even death itself could not be so cruel. But why do you talk in this dismal strain? The miles are slipping behind us; Pharos, let us hope, is banished from our lives for ever; we are together, and as soon as we reach London, we shall be man and wife. No, no, you must not be afraid, Valerie."

"I am afraid of nothing," she answered, "when I am with you. But ever since we left Berlin I seem to have been overtaken by a fit of melancholy which I cannot throw off. I have reasoned with myself in vain. Why I should feel like this, I cannot think. It is only transitory, I am sure; so you must bear with me; to-morrow I shall be quite myself again."

"Bear with you, do you say?" I answered. "You know that I will do so. You have been so brave till now, that I cannot let you give way just at the moment when happiness is within your reach. Try and keep your spirits up, my darling, for both our sakes. To-morrow you will be on the blue sea, with the ship's head pointing for old England. And after that—well, I told you just now what would happen then."

In spite of her promises, however, I found that in the morning my hopes were not destined to be realized. Though she tried hard to make me believe that the gloom had passed, it needed very little discernment upon my part to see that the cheerfulness she affected was all assumed, and, what made it doubly hard to bear, that it was for my sake.

Our stay at Wittenberge was not a long one. As soon as we had finished our breakfast, we caught the

8.30 express and resumed our journey to Hamburg, arriving there a little before midday. Throughout the journey, Valerie had caused me considerable anxiety. Not only had her spirits reached a lower level than they had yet attained, but her face, during the last few hours, had grown singularly pale and drawn ; and when I at last drove her to it, she broke down completely, and confessed to feeling far from well.

"But it cannot be anything serious !" she cried. " I am sure it cannot. It only means that I am not such a good traveller as I thought. Remember, we have covered a good many hundred miles in the last week, and we have had more than our share of anxiety. As soon as we reach our hotel in Hamburg, I will go to my room and lie down. After I have had some sleep, I have no doubt I shall be myself again."

I devoutly hoped so ; but in spite of her assurance, my anxiety was in no way diminished. Obtaining a cab, we drove at once to the Hôtel Continental, at which I had determined to stay. Here I engaged rooms as usual for Mr. and Miss Clifford, for it was as brother and sister we had decided to pass until we should reach England and be made man and wife. It was just luncheon-time when we arrived there ; but Valerie was so utterly prostrated that I could not induce her to partake of anything. She preferred, she declared, to retire to her room at once, and believing that this would be the wisest course for her to pursue, I was only too glad that she should do so. Accordingly, when she had left me, I partook of lunch alone, but with no zest, as may be supposed, and having despatched it, put on my hat and made my way to the premises of the Steamboat Company in order to inquire about a boat for England.

On arrival at the office in question, it was easily seen that something unusual had occurred. In place of the business-like hurry to which I was accustomed, I found the clerks lolling listlessly at their desks. So far as I could see, they had no business wherewith to occupy themselves. Approaching the counter, I inquired when their next packet would sail for the United Kingdom, and in return received a staggering reply.

"I am afraid, sir," said the man, "you will find considerable difficulty in getting into England just now."

"Difficulty in getting into England?" I cried in astonishment; "and why so, pray?"

"Surely you must have heard?" he replied, and looking me up and down as if I were a stranger but lately arrived from the moon. The other clerks smiled incredulously.

"I have heard nothing," I replied, a little nettled at the fellow's behaviour. "Pray be kind enough to inform me what you mean. I am most desirous of reaching London at once, and will thank you to be good enough to tell me when, and at what hour, your next boat leaves?"

"We have no boat leaving," the clerk answered, this time rather more respectfully than before. "Surely, sir, you must have heard that there have been two cases of the plague notified in this city to-day, and more than a hundred in Berlin; consequently, the British Government have closed their ports to German vessels, and, as it is rumoured that the disease has made its appearance in France, it is doubtful whether you will get into a French port either."

"But I must reach England," I answered desperately. "My business is most important. I do not know what I shall do if I am prevented. I must sail to-day, or to-morrow at latest."

"In that case, sir, I am afraid it is out of my power to help you," said the man. "We have received a cablegram from our London office this morning advising us to despatch no more boats until we receive further orders."

"Are you sure there is no other way in which you can help me?" I asked. "I shall be glad to pay anything in reason for the accommodation."

"It is just possible—though I must tell you, sir, I do not think it is probable—that you might be able to induce the owner of some small craft to run the risk of putting you across; but, as far as we are concerned, it is out of the question. Why, sir, I can tell you this, if we had a boat running this afternoon, I could fill every berth thrice over, and in less than half an hour. What's more, sir, I'd be one of the passengers myself. We've been deluged with applications all day. It looks as if everybody is being scared off the Continent by the news of the plague. I only wish I were safe back in England myself. I was a fool ever to have left it."

While the man was talking, I had been casting about me for some way out of my difficulty, and the news that this awful pestilence had made its appearance in the very city in which we now were filled me with so great a fear that, under the influence of it, I very nearly broke down. Pulling myself together, however, I thanked the

man for his information, and made my way into the
street once more.   There I paused, and considered what
I should do.   To delay was impossible.   Even now
Pharos might be close behind me.   A few hours more,
and it was just possible he might have tracked us to
our hiding-place.   But I soon discovered that even
my dread of Pharos was not as great as my fear of the
plague, and, as I have said before, I did not fear that
for myself.   It was of Valerie I thought—of the woman
I loved more than all the world ; whose existence was
so much to me that without her I should not have
cared to go on living.   The recollection of her illness
brought a thought into my mind that was so terrible,
so overpowering, that I staggered on the pavement,
and had to clutch at a tree for support.

"My God," I said to myself, "what should I do if
this illness proved to be the plague ? "

The very thought of such a thing was more than
I could bear.   It choked, it suffocated me, taking all
the pluck out of me, and making me weaker than a
little child.   But it could not be true, I said ; happen
what might, I would not believe it.   Fate, which had
brought so much evil upon me already, could not be
so cruel as to frustrate all my hopes just when I thought
I had turned the corner and was in sight of peace once
more.

What the passers-by must have thought, I do not
know, nor do I care.   The dreadful thought that filled
my mind was more to me than any one else's good
opinion could possibly be.   When I recovered myself,
I resumed my walk to the hotel, breathing in gasps
as the thought returned upon me, and my whole body

alternately flushing with hope and then numbed with
terror. More dead than alive, I entered the building
and climbed the stairs to the sitting-room I had engaged. I had half hoped that, on opening the door,
I should find Valerie awaiting me there, but I was
disappointed. Unable to contain my anxiety any
longer, I went along the passage and knocked at the
door of her room.

"Who is there?" a voice that I scarcely recognised
asked in German.

"It is I," I replied. " Are you feeling better?"

"Yes, better," she answered, still in the same hard
tone ; " but I think I would prefer to lie here a little
longer. Do not be anxious about me ; I shall be quite
myself again by dinner-time."

I asked if there was anything I could procure for
her, and, on being informed to the contrary, left her
and went down to the manager's office in the hope
that I might be able to discover from him some way
in which we might escape to our own country.

" You have reached Hamburg at a most unfortunate
time," he answered. " As you are doubtless aware, the
plague has broken out here, and Heaven alone knows
what we shall do if it continues. I have seen one of
the councillors within the last hour, and he tells me
that three fresh cases have been notified since midday. The evening telegrams report that more than
five thousand deaths have already occurred in Turkey
and Russia alone. It is raging in Vienna, and indeed
through the whole of Austria. In Dresden and Berlin
it has also commenced its dreadful work, while three
cases have been certified in France. So far England

is free ; but how long she will continue to be so, it is impossible to say. That they are growing anxious there is evident from the stringency of the quarantine regulations they are passing. No vessel from any in- fected country—they do not limit it even to ports—is allowed to land either passengers or cargo until after three weeks' quarantine, so that communication with the Continent is practically cut off. The situation is growing extremely critical, and every twenty-four hours promises to make it more so."

" In that case I do not know what I shall do," I said, feeling as if my heart would break under the load it was compelled to carry.

" I am extremely sorry for you, sir," the manager answered ; " but what is bad for you is even worse for us. You simply want to get back to your home. We have home, nay, even life itself at stake."

" It is bad for every one alike," I answered, and then, with a heart even heavier than it was before, I thanked him for his courtesy and made my way up- stairs to our sitting-room once more. I opened the door and walked in, and then uttered a cry of delight, for Valerie was at the farther end of the room, standing before the window. My pleasure, however, was short- lived, for on hearing my step she turned, and I was able to see her face. What I saw there almost brought my heart into my mouth.

" Valerie ! " I cried, " what has happened ? Are you worse that you look at me like that ? "

" Hush ! " she whispered ; " do not speak so loud. Cannot you see that Pharos is coming ? "

Her beautiful eyes were open to their widest extent,

"It was Pharos."

and there was an air about her that spoke of an impend·
ing tragedy.

"Pharos is coming," she said again, this time very
slowly and deliberately. "It is too late for us to
escape. He is driving down the street."

There was a long pause, during which I felt as if
I were being slowly turned to stone.

"He has entered the hotel."

There was another pause.

"He is here." And as she spoke the handle of the
door was turned.

As the person, whoever he might be, entered, Valerie
uttered a little cry and fell senseless into my arms.
I held her tightly, and then wheeled round to see who
the intruder might be.

It was Pharos!

CHAPTER XVI

FOR more than a minute neither of us moved. Valerie lay in my arms just as she had fallen, Pharos stood a foot or so inside the door, while I stood looking first at her and then at him, without being able to utter a word. As far as my own feelings were concerned, the end of the world had come, for I had made up my mind that Valerie was dying. If that were so, Pharos might do his worst.

"My friends, it would seem as if I have come only just in time," he said with sarcastic sweetness. "My dear Forrester, I must offer you my congratulations upon the neat manner in which you effected your escape. Unfortunately, I was aware of it all along. Knowing what was in your heart, I laid my plans accordingly, and here I am. And pray, may I ask, what good have you done yourself by your impetuosity? You chase across Europe at express speed, hoping to get to England before I can catch you, only to find on arrival here that the plague has headed you off, and that it is impossible for you to reach your destination."

"Are you going to stand talking all day?" I said, forgetting caution and the need that existed for humouring him,—everything, in fact, in my anxiety.

"Cannot you see that she is ill? Good heavens, man, she may be dying!"

"What do you mean?" he asked quickly, with a change of voice as he crossed the room and came over to where I was standing. "Let me see her instantly!"

With a deftness, and at the same time a tenderness I had never noticed in him before, he took her from me and placed her upon a sofa. Having done so, he stooped over her and commenced his examination. Thirty seconds had not elapsed before he turned fiercely on me again.

"You fool!" he cried, "are you mad? Lock that door this instant. This is more serious than I imagined. Do you know what it is?"

"How should I?" I answered in agony. "Tell me, tell me; cannot you see how much I am suffering?"

I clutched him by the arm so tightly that he winced under it, and had to exert his strength to throw me off.

"It is the plague," he answered, "and but for your folly in running away from me she would never have caught it. If she dies, the blame will rest entirely with you."

But I scarcely heard him. The knowledge that my darling was the victim of the scourge that was ravaging all Europe drove me back against the wall faint and speechless with terror. "If she dies," he had said, and the words rang in my ears like a funeral knell. But she should not die. If any power in the world could save her, it should be found.

"What can I do?" I whispered hoarsely. "For pity's sake, let me help in some way. She must not die, she shall not die!"

" In that case you had better bestir yourself," he said.
" There is but one remedy, and that we must employ.
Had it not been for your folly, I should have it with me
now. As it is, you must go out and search the town for
it. Give me writing materials."

These were on a neighbouring table, and when I had
put them before him he seized the pen and scrawled
something upon a sheet of notepaper, then folding it, he
handed it to me.

" Take that with all speed to a chemist," he said.
" Tell him to be particularly careful that the drugs are
fresh, and bring it back with you as soon as you can.
In all probability you will have a difficulty in procuring
it, but you must do so somewhere. Rest assured of this,
that if she does not receive it within an hour nothing
can possibly save her."

" I will be back in less than half that time," I answered, and hastened from the room.

From a man in the street I inquired the address of
the nearest chemist, and, as soon as he had directed me
hastened thither as fast as my legs could carry me.
Entering the shop, I threw the prescription upon the
counter, and in my impatience could have struck the
man for his slowness in picking it up. If his life had
depended upon his deciphering it properly, he could not
have taken longer to read it. Before he had got to the
end of it, my impatience had reached boiling heat.

" Come, come," I said, " are you going to make it up
or not ? It is for an urgent case, and I have wasted ten
minutes already."

The man glanced at the paper again, smoothed it
out between his fat fingers, and shook his head until

I thought his glasses would have dropped from his nose.

"I cannot do it," he said at length. "Two of the drugs I do not keep in stock. Indeed, I do not know that I ever saw another prescription like it."

"Why did you not say so at once?" I cried angrily, and, snatching the paper from his hand, I dashed madly out and along the pavement. At the end of the street was another shop, which I entered. On the door it was set forth that English, French, and German were spoken there. I was not going to risk a waste of time on either of the first two, however, but opened upon the man in his own language. He was very small, with an unwholesome complexion, and was the possessor of a nose large enough to have entitled him to the warmest esteem of the great Napoleon. He took the prescription, read it through in a quarter of the time taken by the other man, and then retired behind his screen. Scarcely able to contain my delight at having at last been successful, I curbed my impatience as well as I could, examined all the articles displayed in the glass case upon the counter, fidgeted nervously with the indiarubber change mat, and when, at the end of several minutes, he had not made it up, was only prevented from going in search of him by his appearance before me once more.

"I am exceedingly sorry to say," he began, and directly he opened his mouth I knew that some fresh misfortune was in store for me, "that I cannot make up the prescription for you at all. Of one of the drugs I remember once reading, but of the other I have never even heard. However, if——"

But before he could utter another word I had seized the paper and was out of the shop. This was the second time I had been fooled, and upwards of half an hour, thirty precious minutes, had been wasted. Even then Valerie might be dying, and I was powerless to save her. Never in my life before had time seemed so precious. I stopped a passer-by and inquired the direction of the nearest chemist. He referred me to the shop I had just left; I stopped another, but he confessed himself a stranger in the city. At last, at my wits' end to know what to do, finding myself before the office of the steamship company I had visited that afternoon, I determined to go inside and make inquiries.

To my surprise, in place of the half-dozen clerks who had stared at me only a few hours before, I found but one man, and before he had opened his lips I realized that he was drunk.

" Ha, ha ! " he said, with a burst of tipsy laughter, " so you have come back again, my friend ? Want to get a boat to take you to England, I suppose. Oh, of course you do. We know all about that. We're not as blind, I mean as blind drunk, as you suppose."

With that he lurched against the desk, and cannoned off it on to me. Then, having reached that stage of inebriation when music becomes a necessity, he leant against the wall and burst into song :—

> " Drink to me only with thine eyes,
> And I will pledge with mine,
> Or leave a kiss within . . ."

He had got no farther when I took him by the collar, and, pushing him back against the wall, bumped his head against it until it is a wonder I did not fracture his skull.

"Hold your tongue, you drunken fool !" I said, feeling as if I could kill him where he stood, "and tell me where the man is who attended to me this afternoon."

The energy with which I had administered the punishment must have somewhat sobered the fellow, for he pulled himself together, and rubbing the back of his head with his hand asked me if I had heard the news.

"I have heard nothing," I cried. "What news do you mean ? "

"Why, that the man you spoke to this afternoon is dead. He died of the plague within an hour after you were here, rolling on the floor, and making an awful mess of things. Then all the other fellows ran away. They didn't know there was a bottle and a half of brandy in the cupboard in the manager's room ; but, bless your heart, I did, and now I'm not afraid of the plague. Don't you believe it ? "

"Dead !" I cried, for I could scarcely credit that what he told me could be true. The man had seemed so well when I had seen him only a few hours before. However, I had no time to think of him.

"I want a chemist," I cried. "I must find one at once. Can you give me the address of one ? "

"The first turning to the left," he cried, "and the third shop on the right ; Dittmer is the name. But, I say, you're looking precious white about the gills. Though you did treat me badly just now, I don't bear any malice, so you can have a drop of this if you like. There's enough here for two of us. You won't ? Well,

then, I will.   A short life and a merry one's my motto,
and here's to you, my buck."

Before he could have half filled his glass, I had passed
out of the office and was in the street he had mentioned.
Drunk as he was, his information proved correct, and a
chemist's shop, with the name of Dittmer over the door,
was the third house on the right-hand side.   I entered
and handed the prescription to the venerable-looking
man I found behind the counter.

" I am afraid you will have some difficulty in getting
this made up," he said after he had read it.   " Two of
the drugs are not in common use, and personally I do
not keep them.   Is the case an urgent one ? "

" It's a matter of life and death," I answered.
" All my happiness in life depends upon it.   If you
cannot help me, can you direct me to any one who
will ?   I assure you there is not a moment to be
lost."

Evidently the man was touched by my anxiety.   At
any rate he went out of his way to do a kindly action,
for which no amount of gratitude on my part will ever
be able to repay him.

" I do not know anything about the merits of the
prescription," he said, "but if these two drugs are
necessary, I don't mind telling you that I think I know
where I can procure them.   I have an old friend, a
quack, so the other chemists call him, who is always
trying experiments.   It is within the bounds of possi-
bility he may have them.   If you will wait here for a
few minutes, I'll run up to his house and see.   It is only
a few doors from here, and he is always at home at this
hour."

" I will wait only too willingly," I answered earnestly. " Heaven grant you may be successful ! "

He said no more, but ran out of the shop. While he was gone, I paced up and down in a fever of impatience. Every minute seemed an hour, and as I looked at my watch and realized that, if I wished to get back to the hotel within the time specified by Pharos, I had only ten minutes in which to do it, I felt as if my heart would stop beating. In reality the man was not gone five minutes, and when he burst into the shop again he waved two bottles triumphantly above his head.

" There's not another man in Hamburg could have got them ! " he cried with justifiable pride. " Now I can make it up for you."

Five minutes later he handed the prescription to me.

" I shall never be able to thank you sufficiently for your kindness," I said as I took it. " If I can get back with it in time, you will have saved a life that I love more than my own. I do not know how to reward you, but if you will accept this and wear it as a souvenir of the service you have rendered me, I hope you will do so."

So saying, I took from my pocket my gold watch and chain and handed them across the counter to him. Then, without waiting for an expression of his gratitude, I passed into the street and, hailing a cab, bade the man drive me as fast as his horse could go to my hotel.

Reaching it, I paid him with the first coin I took from my pocket and ran upstairs. What my feelings were as I approached the room where I had left Pharos and Valerie together, I must leave you to imagine. With a heart beating like a sledge-hammer, I softly turned the handle of the door and stole in, scarcely daring to look in the direction of the sofa. However, I might have spared myself the pain, for neither Pharos nor Valerie was there; but just as I was wondering what could have become of them, the former entered the room.

"Have you got it?" he inquired eagerly, his voice trembling with emotion.

"I have," I answered, and handed him the medicine. "Here it is. At one time I began to think I should have to come back without it."

"Another ten minutes and I can promise you you would have been too late," he answered. "I have carried her to her room and placed her upon her bed. You must remain here and endeavour to prevent any one suspecting what is the matter. If your medicine proves what I hope, she should be sleeping quietly in an hour's time, and on the high-road to recovery in two. But remember this, if the people in this house receive any hint of what she is suffering from, they will remove her to the hospital at once, and in that case, I pledge you my word, she will be dead before morning."

"You need have no fear on that score," I answered. "They shall hear nothing from me."

Thereupon he took his departure, and for the next hour I remained where I was, deriving what satisfaction I could from the assurance he had given me.

It was quite dark by the time Pharos returned.

"What news do you bring?" I inquired anxiously,

" Why do you not tell me at once how she is? Can you not see how I am suffering?"

" The crisis is past," he replied, " and she will do now. But it was a very narrow escape. If I had not followed you by the next train, in what sort of position would you be at this minute?"

" I should not be alive," I answered. " If her life had been taken, it would have killed me."

" You are very easily killed, I have no doubt," was his sneering rejoinder. " At the same time, take my advice and let this be a lesson to you not to try escaping from me again. You have been pretty severely punished. On another occasion your fate may be even worse."

I gazed at him in pretended surprise.

" I do not understand your meaning when you say that I escaped from you," I said, with an air of innocence that would not have deceived any one. " Why should I desire to do so? If you refer to my leaving Prague so suddenly, please remember that I warned you the night before that it would be necessary for me to leave at once for England. I presume I am at liberty to act as I please?"

" I am not in the humour just now to argue the question with you," he answered, " but if you will be advised by me, my dear Forrester, you will, for the future, consult me with regard to your movements. My ward has given you her experiences, and has told you with what result she, on two occasions, attempted to leave me. At your instigation she has tried a third time, and you see how that attempt has turned out. You little thought that when you were dining so comfortably in Herr Schuncke's restaurant in Berlin, last night, that I was watching your repast."

"I do not believe it," I answered angrily. "It is impossible that you could have been there, if only for the reason that there was no train to bring you."

He smiled pityingly upon me.

"I am beginning to think, my friend," he said, "that you are not so clever as I at first supposed you. I wonder what you would say if I were to tell you that, while Valerie was playing for Schuncke's entertainment, I, who was travelling along between Prague and Dresden, was an interested spectator of the whole scene. Shall I describe to you the arrangement of the room? Shall I tell you how Schuncke leant against the wall near the door, his hands folded before him, and his great head nodding? How you sat at the table near the fireplace, building castles in the air, upon which, by the way, I offer you my felicitations? while Valerie, standing on the other side of the room, made music for you all? It is strange that I should know all that, particularly as I did not do myself the honour of calling at the restaurant, is it not?"

I made no answer. To tell the truth, I did not know what to say. Pharos chuckled as he observed my embarrassment.

"You will learn wisdom before I have done with you," he continued. "However, that is enough on the subject just now. Let us talk about something else. There is much to be done to-night, and I shall require your assistance."

The variety of emotions to which I had been subjected that day had exercised such an effect upon me that, by this time, I was scarcely capable of even a show of resistance. In my own mind I felt morally certain that, when he said there was much to do, he meant the accomplishment of some new villainy, but what form it was destined to take I neither knew nor cared. He had got me so completely under his influence by this time that he could make me do exactly as he required.

" What is it you are going to do?" I inquired, more because I saw that he expected me to say something than for any other reason.

" I am going to get us all out of this place and back to England without loss of time," he answered, in a tone of triumph.

"To England?" I replied, and the hideous mockery of his speech made me laugh aloud,—as bitter a laugh surely as was ever uttered by mortal man. "You accused me just now of not being as clever as you had at first supposed me. I return the compliment. You have evidently not heard that every route into England is blocked."

" No route is ever blocked to me," he answered. " I leave for London at midnight to-night, and Valerie accompanies me."

" You must be mad to think of such a thing!" I cried, Valerie's name producing a sudden change in my behaviour towards him. " How can she possibly do so? Remember how ill she is. It would be little short of murder to move her."

" It will be nothing of the kind," he replied. " When I want her, she will rise from her bed and walk downstairs and go wherever I bid her, looking to all appearances as well and strong as any other woman in this town."

"By all means let us go to England, then," I said, clutching eagerly at the hope he held out. "Though how you are going to manage it, I do not know."

"You shall see," he said. "Remember, you have never known me fail. If you would bear that fact in mind a little oftener, you would come nearer a better appreciation of my character than that to which you have so far attained. However, while we are wasting time talking, it is getting late and you have not dined yet. I suppose it is necessary for you to eat, otherwise you will be incapable of anything?"

"I could not touch a thing," I answered in reply to his gibe. "You will not therefore be hindered by me. But how can we go out and leave Valerie behind in her present condition?"

"I shall give her an opiate," he said, "which will keep her sleeping quietly for the next three or four hours. When she wakes, she will be capable of anything."

He thereupon left the room, and upwards of a quarter of an hour elapsed before he rejoined me. When he did, I noticed that he was dressed for going out. I immediately picked up my hat and stick and followed him downstairs. Once in the street, Pharos started off at a smart pace, and as soon as he reached the corner, near the first chemist's shop I had visited that afternoon, turned sharply to his left, crossed the road, and entered a by-lane. The remainder of the journey was of too tortuous a description for me to hope to give you any detailed account of it. Up one back street and

down another, over innumerable canals, we made our
way, until at last we reached a quarter of the town
totally distinct from that in which our hotel was
situated. During the walk Pharos scarcely spoke, but
times out of number he threw angry glances at me over
his shoulder when I dropped a little behind. Indeed, he
walked at such a pace, old man though he was, that at
times I found it extremely difficult to keep up with
him. At last, entering a dirtier street than any we had
so far encountered, he stopped short before a tall,
austere building, which from a variety of evidences had
seen better days, and might a couple of centuries or so
before have been the residence of some well-to-do
merchant. Mounting the steps, he rapped sharply
upon the door with his stick. A sound of laughter and
the voice of a man singing reached us from within,
and when Pharos knocked a second time the rapidity
of the blows and the strength with which they were
administered bore witness to his impatience. At last,
however, the door was opened a few inches by a
man, who looked out and inquired with an oath what
we wanted.

"I have come in search of Captain Wisemann," my
companion answered. "If he is at home, tell him that
if he does not receive Monsieur Pharos at once, he
knows the penalty. Carry him that message, and be
quick about it. I have waited at this door quite long
enough."

With an unintelligible grunt the man departed on
his errand, and it was plain that the news he brought
had a sobering effect upon the company within, for a
sudden silence prevailed, and a few moments later he

returned and begged us with comparative civility to
enter. We did so, and followed our guide along a filthy
passage to a room at the back of the dwelling, a
magnificent chamber, panelled with old oak, every inch
of which spoke of an age and an art long since dead.
The dirt of the place, however, passes description.
Under the *régime* of the present owner, it seemed
doubtful whether any attempt had ever been made to
clean it. The ceiling was begrimed with smoke and
dirt, cobwebs not only decorated the cornices and the
carved figures on the chimneypiece, but much of the
panelling on the walls themselves was cracked and
broken. On the table in the centre of the room was
all that remained of a repast, and at this Pharos sniffed
disdainfully.

"A pig he was when I first met him, and a pig he
will remain to the day of his death," said Pharos, by
way of introducing the man upon whom we were
calling. "However, a pig is at all times a useful animal, and so is Wisemann."

At this moment the man of whom he had spoken in
these scarcely complimentary terms entered the room.

I have elsewhere described the Arab who met Pharos
at the Pyramids, on the occasion of my momentous
visit, as being the biggest man I had ever beheld in my
life, and so he was, for at that time I had not the
pleasure of Herman Wisemann's acquaintance. Since
I have seen him, however, the Arab has, as the Ameri-
cans say, been compelled to take a back place. Wisemann must have stood six foot nine if an inch, and in
addition to his height his frame was correspondingly
large. Though I am not short myself, he towered

above me by fully a head. To add to the strangeness of his appearance, he was the possessor of a pair of enormous ears that stood out at right angles to his head. That he was afraid of Pharos was shown by the sheepish fashion in which he entered the room.

"Three years ago I called upon you," said Pharos, "and was kept waiting while you fuddled yourself with your country's abominable liquor. To-night I have been favoured with a repetition of that offence. On the third occasion I shall deal with you more summarily. Remember that! Now to business."

"If Herr Pharos will condescend to tell me what it is he requires of me," said the giant, "he may be sure I will do my best to please him."

"You had better not do otherwise, my friend," snapped Pharos with his usual acidity. "Perhaps you remember that on one occasion you made a mistake. Don't do so again. Now listen to me. I am anxious to be in London on Friday morning next. You will, therefore, find me a fast vessel, and she must leave to-night at midnight."

"But it is impossible to get into England," replied the man. "Since the outbreak of the plague the quarantine laws have been stricter even than they were before. Heinrich Clausen tried last week and had to return unsuccessful."

"How does Heinrich Clausen's failure affect me?" asked Pharos. "I shall not fail, whatever any one else may do. Your friend Clausen should have known better than to go to London. Land me on the coast of Norfolk, and that will do."

"But it is eight o'clock now," the man replied, "and

you say you wish to start at midnight. How am I to
arrange it before then ? "

"*How* you are to do it does not concern me," said
Pharos. " All I know is that you must do it. Otherwise, well then, the punishment will be the same as
before, only on this occasion a little more severe. You
can send me word in an hour's time, how, and where,
we are to board her. I am staying at the Continental,
and my number is eighty-three."

The man had evidently abandoned all thought of
refusing.

" And the remuneration ? " he inquired. " The risk
will have to be taken into account."

" The price will be the same as on the last occasion,
provided he lands us safely at the place which I shall
name to him as soon as we are on board. But only
half that amount, if, by any carelessness on his part, the
scheme is unsuccessful. I shall expect to hear from you
within an hour. Be careful, however, that your messenger does not arouse any suspicions at the hotel. We
do not want the English authorities put upon their guard."

Wisemann accompanied us to the door, and bowed us
out. After that we returned as quickly as possible to
our hotel. My delight may be imagined on hearing
from Pharos, who visited her as soon as he returned,
that, throughout the time we had been absent, Valerie
had been sleeping peacefully, and was now making as
good progress towards recovery as he could desire.

At nine o'clock, almost punctual to the minute, a note
was brought to Pharos. He opened it, and having read
it, informed the man that there was no answer.

" Wisemann has arranged everything," he said. "The

steamer *Margrave of Brandenburg* will be ready to pick us up in the river at the hour appointed, and in fifty hours from the first revolution of her screw we should be in England."

" And what would happen then ? " I asked myself.

CHAPTER XVII

WHEN the sun rose on the following morning, nothing but green seas surrounded us, and the *Margrave of Brandenburg* was doing her best to live up to the reputation I soon discovered she possessed— namely, of being the worst roller in the North Sea trade. She was by no means a large craft, nor, as I soon remarked, was she particularly well found; she belonged to a firm of Altona Jews, and, as the captain was wont to say pathetically, "The only thing they did not grudge him was the right to do as much work on the smallest amount of pay on which it was possible for a man to keep body and soul together." The captain's nationality was more difficult to determine than that of his employers. He called himself an Englishman, but, unfortunately for this assertion, his accent belied him. In addition to English, he spoke German like a Frenchman, and French like a German, was equally at home in Russian—which, to say the least of it, is not a language for the amateur—Italian also, while in a moment of confidence he found occasion to inform me that he had served for three years on board a Spanish troopship, an assertion which would lead one to suppose that he was conversant with that language also. In point of fact, he was one of that curious class of sailor commonly met with outside the British mercantile marine, who, if you asked them, would find it difficult to tell you where they were born, and who have been so long at sea that one country has become like another to them, provided the liquor is good and they can scrape together a sufficient living out of it; and one flag is equal to another, provided, of course, it is not Chinese, which, as every one knows, is no use to any one, not even to themselves.

For the week, and more particularly for the forty-eight hours preceding our departure from Hamburg, I had been living in such a state of nervous tension that, as soon as we were once clear of the land, the reaction that set in was almost more than I could bear. The prophecy Pharos had given utterance to regarding Valerie had been verified to the letter. At the hour appointed for leaving, she had descended from her room, looking at first glance as healthy and strong as I had ever seen her. It was only when I came close up to her and could catch a glimpse of her eyes that I saw how dilated the pupils were and how unnatural was the light they contained. From the moment she appeared upon the stairs, throughout the drive through the city, and until we reached the steamer, not a word crossed her lips, and it was only when we were in the saloon and Pharos bade her retire to her cabin, that she found her voice and spoke to me.

"Good-night," she said very slowly, as if it hurt her even to speak the words, and then added with infinite sadness, "You have been very good and patient with me, Cyril." Having said this, she disappeared into her cabin, and I saw no more of her that night.

As I remarked at the commencement of this chapter, the sun when it rose next morning found us in open water. Not a trace of the land was to be seen, and you may be sure I was not sorry to be away from it. Taking one thing with another, I had not spent a pleasant night. I had tried sleeping in my bunk, but without success. It was filthy in the extreme, and so small that I found it quite impossible to stretch myself out at full length. Accordingly, I had tumbled and tossed in it, tried every position, and had at last vacated it in favour of the settee in the saloon, where I had remained until the first signs of day showed themselves. Then I went on deck to find a beautiful pearl-grey dawn, in which the steamer seemed a speck on the immensity of sea. I tried to promenade the deck, only to find that the vessel's rolling rendered it extremely difficult, if not well-nigh impossible. I accordingly made my way to a sheltered spot, just abaft the saloon entrance, and, seating myself on the skylight, endeavoured to collect my thoughts. It was a more difficult matter than would at first be supposed, for the reason that the side issues involved were so many, and also so important, and I found myself being continually drawn from the main point at issue, which was the question as to what was to become of Valerie and myself since we found it impossible to escape from Pharos. How the latter had become possessed of the secret of our intention to escape from him, I could not imagine, nor could I understand how he had been able to pursue and capture us with such accuracy and dispatch. As it had turned out, it was just as well that he did follow us, and I shivered again as I thought of what Valerie's fate might have been had he not come upon the scene so opportunely. Of one thing I was quite convinced, in spite of the threats he had used, and that was that, as soon as we reached England, I would find some way—how I was to do so I did not for the moment quite realize—of getting the woman I loved out of his clutches, this time for good and all.

I breakfasted that morning alone, Valerie being still too ill to leave her bunk, while Pharos, as usual, did not put in appearance until close upon midday. By the time he did so the sea had lost much of its former violence, and the vessel was, in consequence, making better progress. How I longed to be in England, no one can have any idea. The events of the last few months, if they had done nothing else, had at least deprived me of my taste for travel ; and as for the land of Egypt, the liking I had once entertained for that country had given place to a hatred that was as vigorous as I had deemed the other sincere.

I have already said that it was midday before Pharos made his appearance on deck ; but when he did, so far as his amiability was concerned, he would have been very much better below. Being accustomed by this time to note the changes in his manner, it did not take me very long to see that this was one of his bad days. For this reason I resolved to keep out of his way as far as possible, but in my attempt I was only partly successful.

"In thirty-eight hours, my friend," he said, when he had found me out, "you will be in England once more, and the desire of your heart will be gratified. You should be grateful to me, for had I not followed you to

Hamburg, it is quite certain *you* would still be in that plague-ridden city, and where would Valerie be? Well, Valerie would be—— But there, we will have no more of those little escapades, if you please, so remember that. The next time you attempt to play me false, I shall know how to deal with you. All things considered, it was a good day for me when you fell in love with Valerie."

"What do you mean?" I asked, for I neither liked the look on his face nor the way he spoke.

"I mean what I say," he answered. "You love Valerie, and she loves you; but—— Well, to put it mildly, she does what I tell her, and for the future so must you! It would be as well, perhaps, if you would bear that fact in mind."

I rose from the skylight upon which I had been sitting and faced him.

"Monsieur Pharos," I said, holding up my hand in protest, "you have gone quite far enough. Let me advise you to think twice before you make use of such threats to me. I do not understand by what right you speak to me in this fashion."

"There are many things you do not understand, and at present it is not my intention to enlighten you," he answered, with consummate coolness. "Only remember this—while you act in accordance with my wishes, you are safe, but if at any time you attempt to thwart me, I give you fair warning, I will crush you like a worm."

So saying, he darted another glance at me full of intense malignity, and then took his departure. When he had gone, I seated myself again and endeavoured to solve the riddle of his behaviour. What his purpose could be in keeping me with him, and why he was always threatening me with punishment if I did not act in accordance with his wishes, were two questions I tried to answer, but in vain. That there was something behind it all which boded ill for myself, I felt morally certain; but what that something was, I had yet to discover. If I had known all, I wonder what course of action I should have pursued.

For the remainder of the day I saw nothing of Pharos. He had shut himself up in his cabin, with only the monkey for company. Towards the end of the afternoon, however, he sent for the captain, and they remained closeted together for a quarter of an hour. When the latter appeared again, it was with an unusually white face. He passed me on the companion-ladder, and from the light I saw in his eyes I surmised that Pharos had been treating him to a sample of his ill-humour, and that he had come out of it considerably scared. Once more I partook of the evening meal alone, and, as I was by this time not only thoroughly tired of my own company, but worn out with anxiety and continual brooding upon one subject, I sought my couch at an early hour. My dreams that night were far from good. It may have been my quarrel with Pharos that occasioned it; at any rate, I found myself reviewing every detail of my life during the past two months. I recalled my first meeting with this terrible man on the Thames Embankment; the visit he had paid me at my studio on the night of the murder of the curiosity dealer; our interview in Pompeii, and our voyage across the Mediterranean in the yacht. Then followed my terrible adventure in the Queen's Hall at the Pyramid, and the vision of the disgraced Magician I had afterwards seen. I went through the ordeal in the Temple of Ammon, and once more heard the old man, who had conducted me to the vaults below, bid the dead Ptahmes rise and go out into the world again, when, by carrying out the work the gods had decreed, he might win for himself the rest which, for more than three thousand years, had been denied him. I saw myself tossing on my bed of sickness in the Arab tent; I recalled the incidents connected with our journey across Europe and our flight from Pharos at Prague. The recollection of that terrible afternoon in Hamburg, when Valerie had been taken ill, and Pharos had so unexpectedly appeared in time to save her, was sufficient to wake me up in a cold sweat of fear. When I had somewhat recovered, I became aware that some one was knocking on my cabin door. To my surprise, it proved to be the captain.

"What is the matter?" I inquired, as he entered. "What brings you here?"

"I have come to you for your advice," he said nervously, as he fidgeted with his cap. "I can tell you we're in a bad way aboard this ship."

"Why, what has happened?" I inquired, sitting up and staring at his white face. "Have we met with an accident?"

"We have," he answered, "and a bad one. A worse could scarcely have befallen us." Then, sinking his voice to a whisper, he added, "*The plague has broken out aboard!*"

"The plague!" I cried, in consternation. "Do you

mean it? For Heaven's sake, man, be sure you are not making a mistake before you say such a thing!"

"I only wish I were not," he replied. "Unfortunately, there is no getting away from the fact. The plague's upon us, sure enough, and, what's worse, I'm afraid it's come to stay."

"How many cases are there?" I asked, "and when did you discover it? Tell me everything."

"We found it out early this morning," the captain replied. "There are two cases, the steward aft here and the cook for'ard. The steward is dead; we pitched him overboard just before I came down to you. The cook is very nearly as bad. I can tell you, I wish I was anywhere but where I am. I've got a wife and youngsters depending on me at home. The thing spreads like fire, they say, and poor Reimann was as well as you are a couple of hours ago. He brought me a cup of coffee and a biscuit up on to the bridge at eight bells, and now to think he's overboard!"

The captain concluded his speech with a groan, and then stood watching me and waiting for me to speak.

"But I can't understand what brings you to me," I said. "I don't see how I can help you."

"I came to you because I wanted to find out what I had better do," he returned. "I thought most probably you would be able to advise me, and I didn't want to go to him." Here he nodded his head in the direction of Pharos's cabin. "If you could only have heard the way he bullyragged me yesterday, you would understand why. If I'd been a dog in the street he couldn't have treated me worse, and all because I was unable to make the boat travel twice as fast as her engines would let her go."

" But I don't see how I'm to help you in this matter," I said, and then added, with what could only have been poor comfort, " We don't know who may be the next case."

" That's the worst part of it," he answered. " For all we can tell, it may be you, and it might be me. I suppose you're as much afraid of it as I am."

I had to confess that I was, and then inquired what means he proposed to adopt for stamping it out.

" I don't know what to do," he answered, and the words were scarcely out of his mouth before another rap sounded on the cabin door. He opened it to find a deck hand standing outside. A muttered conversation ensued between them, after which the captain, with a still more scared look upon his face, returned to me.

" It's getting worse," he said. " The chief engineer's down now, and the bosun has sent word to say he don't feel well. God help us if this sort of thing is going to continue. Every mother's son aboard this ship will make sure he's got it, and then who's to do the work? We may as well go to the bottom right off."

Trouble was indeed pursuing us. It seemed as if I were destined to get safely out of one difficulty only to fall into another. If this terrible scourge continued we should indeed be in straits ; for the Continent was barred to us on one hand, and England on the other, while to turn her head and put back to Hamburg was a course we could not dream of adopting. One thing was plain to me : to avoid any trouble later, we must inform Pharos. So, advising the captain to separate those who had contracted the disease from those who were still well, I left my cabin and crossed to the further side of the saloon. To my surprise, Pharos received the news with greater equanimity than I had expected he would show.

" I doubted whether we should escape unscathed," he said ; " but the captain deserves to die of it himself for not having informed me as soon as the first man was taken ill. However, let us hope it is not too late to put a stop to it. I must go and see the men, and do what I can to pull them round. It would not do to have a breakdown out here for the want of sufficient men to work the boat."

So saying, he bade me leave him while he dressed, and when this operation was completed, departed on his errand, while I returned to the saloon. I had not been there many minutes before the door of Valerie's cabin opened, and my sweetheart emerged. I sprang to my feet with a cry of surprise, and then ran forward to greet her. Short though her illness had been, it had effected a great change in her appearance ; but since she was able to leave her cabin, I trusted that the sea air would soon restore her accustomed health to her. After a few preliminary remarks, which would scarcely prove of interest even if recorded, she inquired when we expected to reach England.

"About midnight to-night, I believe," I replied ; "that is, if all goes well."

There was a short silence, and then she placed her hand in mine and looked anxiously into my face.

" I want you to tell me, dear," she said, "all that

happened the night before last. In my own heart I felt quite certain from the first that we should not get safely away. Did I not say that Pharos would never permit it? I must have been very ill, for though I remember standing in the sitting-room at the hotel, waiting for you to return from the steamship office, I cannot recall anything else. Tell me everything; I am quite strong enough to bear it."

Thus entreated, I described how she had foretold Pharos's arrival in Hamburg, and how she had warned me that he had entered the hotel.

"I can remember nothing of what you tell me," she said sadly, when I had finished. Then, still holding my hand in hers, she continued in an undertone, "We were to have been so happy together."

"Not '*were to have been*,'" I said, with a show of confidence I was far from feeling, "but '*are to be*.' Believe me, darling, all will come right yet. We have been through so much together, that surely we must be happy in the end. We love each other, and nothing can destroy that."

"Nothing," she answered, with a little catch of her breath; "but there is one thing I must say to you while I have time—something that I fear may possibly give you pain. You told me in Hamburg that up to the present no case of the plague had been notified in England. If that is so, darling, what right have we to introduce it? Surely none! Think of the misery its coming must inevitably cause to others! For aught we know to the contrary, we may carry the infection from Hamburg with us, and thousands of innocent people will suffer in consequence. I have been thinking

over it all night, and it seems to me that if we did
this thing, we should be little better than murderers."

I had thought of this myself, but lest I should
appear to be taking credit for more than I deserve,
I must confess that the true consequences of the action
to which she referred had never struck me. Not having
any desire to frighten her, I did not tell her that the
disease had already made its appearance on board the
very vessel in which we were travelling.

"You are bargaining without Pharos, however," I
replied. "If he has made up his mind to go, how are
we to gainsay him? Our last attempt could scarcely
be considered a success."

"At any cost to ourselves we must not go," she said
firmly and decidedly. "The lives of loving parents, of
women and little children, the happiness of an entire
nation depends upon our action. What is our safety,
great as it seems to us, compared with theirs?"

"Valerie, you are my good angel," I said. "Whatever you wish, I will do."

"We must tell Pharos that we have both determined
on no account to land with him," she continued. "If
the pestilence had already shown itself there, it would
be a different matter; but as it is, we have no choice
left us but to do our duty."

"But where are we to go if we do not visit England?
And what are we to do?" I asked, for I could plainly
see the difficulties ahead.

"I do not know," she answered simply. "Never
fear; we will find some place. You may be certain
of this, dear—if we wish God to bless our love, we must
act as I propose."

"So it shall be," I answered, lifting her hand to my lips. "You have decided for me. Whatever it may mean to ourselves, we will not do anything that will imperil the lives of the people you spoke of just now."

A few moments later I heard a footstep on the companion-ladder. It was Pharos returning from his examination of the plague-stricken men. In the dim light of the hatchway he looked more like a demon than a man, and as I thought of the subject I had to broach to him, and the storm it would probably bring down upon us, I am not ashamed to confess that my heart sank into my shoes.

It was not until he was fairly in the saloon that he became aware of Valerie's presence.

"I offer you my compliments upon your improved appearance," he said politely. "I am glad of it, for it will make matters the easier when we get ashore."

I had already risen from my seat, though I still held Valerie's hand.

"Your pardon, Monsieur Pharos," I said, trying to speak calmly, "but on that subject it is necessary that I should have a few words with you."

"Indeed!" he answered, looking at me with the customary sneer upon his face. "In that case, say on, for, as you see, I am all attention. I must beg, however, that you will be quick about it, for matters are progressing so capitally on board this ship that, if things go on as they are doing at present, we may every one of us expect to be down with the plague before midday."

"The plague!" Valerie repeated, with a note of fear in her voice. "Do you mean to say that it has broken out on board this steamer?" Then, turning to me, she added reproachfully, "You did not tell me that."

"Very probably not, my dear," Pharos answered for me. "Had he done so, you would scarcely have propounded the ingenious theory you were discussing shortly before I entered."

Overwhelming as was Valerie's surprise at the dreadful news Pharos had disclosed to her, and unenviable as our present position was, we could not contain our astonishment at finding that Pharos had become acquainted with the decision we had arrived at a few moments before. Instinctively I glanced up at the skylight overhead, thinking it might have been through that he had overheard our conversation. But it was securely closed. By what means, therefore, he had acquired his information I could not imagine.

"You were prepared to tell me when I entered," he said, "that you would refuse to enter England, on what I cannot help considering most absurd grounds. You must really forgive me if I do not agree with your views. Apart from the idea of your thwarting me, your decision is ludicrous in the extreme. However, now that you find you are no safer on board this ship than you would be ashore—in point of fact, not so safe—you will doubtless change your minds. By way of emphasizing my point, I might tell you that out of the twelve men constituting her crew, no less than four are victims of the pestilence, while one is dead and thrown overboard."

"Four!" I cried, scarcely able to believe that what he said could be true. "There were only two half an hour ago."

"I do not combat that assertion," he said; "but you forget that the disease travels fast—faster even than you do when you run away from me, my dear Forrester. However, I don't know that that fact matters very much. What we have to deal with is your obliging offer to refuse to land in England. Perhaps you will be good enough to tell me, in the event of your not doing so there, where you will condescend to go ashore? The *Margrave of Brandenburg* is only a small vessel, after all, and with the best intention she cannot remain at sea for ever."

"What we mean to tell you is," I answered, "that we have decided not to be the means of introducing this terrible scourge into a country that so far is free from it."

"A very philanthropic decision on your part," he answered sarcastically. "Unfortunately, however, I am in a position to be able to inform you that your charity is not required. Though the authorities are not aware of it, the plague has already broken out in England. For this reason you will not be responsible for such deaths as may occur."

He paused, and looked first at Valerie and then at myself. The old light I remembered having seen in his eyes the night he had hypnotised me in my studio was shining there now. Very soon the storm which had been gathering broke, and its violence was the greater for having been so long suppressed.

"I have warned you several times already," he cried,

shaking his fist at me, "but you take no notice. You will try to thwart me again, and then nothing can save you. You fool! cannot you see how thin the crust is upon which you stand? Hatch but one more plot, and I will punish you in a fashion of which you do not dream. As with this woman here, I have but to raise my hand, and you are powerless to help yourself. Sight, hearing, power of speech, may be all taken from you in a second, and for as long a time as I please." Then, turning to Valerie, he continued : " To your cabin with you, madame. Let me hear no more of such talk as this, or 'twill be time for me to give you another exhibition of my power."

Valerie departed to her cabin without a word, and Pharos, with another glance at me, entered his, while I remained standing in the centre of the saloon, not knowing what to do nor what to say.

It was not until late that evening that I saw him again, and then I was on deck. The sea was much smoother than in the morning, but the night wind blew cold. I had not left the companion-ladder very long before I was aware of a man coming slowly along the deck towards me, lurching from side to side as he walked. To my astonishment it proved to be the captain, and it was plain that something serious was the matter with him. When he came closer, I found that he was talking to himself.

"What is the matter, captain?" I inquired, with a foreboding in my heart. "Are you not feeling well?"

He shook off the hand I had placed upon his arm.

"It is no good, I will not do it!" he cried fiercely.

"I have done enough for you already, and you won't get me to do any more."

"Come, come," I said, "you mustn't be wandering about the deck like this! Let me help you to your cabin." So saying, I took him by the arm and was about to lead him along the deck in the direction of his own quarters, when, with a shout of rage, he turned and threw himself upon me. The onslaught was so sudden that I was taken completely off my guard, and before I could defend myself he had dragged me to within a few inches of the rails. Then began a struggle such as I had never known in my life before. The man was undoubtedly mad, and I soon found that I had to put out all my strength to hold my own against him. It is a matter for conjecture, indeed, whether I should have got the better of him at all had not assistance come to me from an unexpected quarter.

While we were still wrestling, Pharos made his appearance from below. He took in the situation at a glance, and as we swayed towards him threw himself upon the captain, twining his long, thin fingers about the other's throat and clinging to him with the tenacity of a bulldog. The result may be easily foreseen. Overmatched as he was, the wretched man fell like a log upon the deck, and I with him. The force with which his head struck the planks must have stunned him, for he lay, without moving, just where he had fallen. The light of the lamp in the companion fell full upon his face and enabled me to see a large swelling on the right side of the throat, a little below the ear.

"Another victim," said Pharos, and I could have sworn a chuckle escaped him. "You had better leave him to me. There is no hope for him. That swelling is an infallible sign. He is unconscious now ; in half an hour he will be dead."

Unhappily his prophecy proved to be correct, for though we bore him to his cabin and did all that was possible, in something under the time Pharos had mentioned death had overtaken him.

Our position was even less amiable now than before. We had only the second mate to fall back upon, and if anything happened to him I did not see how it would be possible for us to reach our destination. As it turned out, however, I need not have worried myself, for we were closer to the English coast than I imagined.

Owing to the stringency of the quarantine laws, and to the fact that the coastguards all round the British Isles were continually on the look-out for vessels attempting to land passengers, orders had been given that no lights should be shown ; the skylights and portholes were accordingly covered with tarpaulins.

It wanted a quarter of an hour to midnight when Pharos came along the deck and, standing by my side, pointed away over our bow.

" The black smudge you can distinguish on the horizon is England," he said abruptly, and then was silent, in order, I suppose, that I might have time to digest the thoughts his information conjured up.

CHAPTER XVIII

LITTLE by little we drew closer to the shore. First came a headland, then a range of cliff, afterwards a deeply indented bay, and presently a tiny fishing village. As I said at the conclusion of the previous chapter, we showed no lights, consequently it would have required a keen eye to have detected our presence on the water.

Pharos and I stood leaning against the bulwarks, gazing at the land. For my part I must confess that there was a feeling in my heart that was not unlike that of a disgraced son who enters his home by stealth after a long absence. And yet it would be impossible to tell you how my heart warmed to it. Times out of number I had thought of my return to England, and had pictured Valerie standing by my side upon the deck of the steamer, watching the land loom up, and thinking of the happiness that was to be our portion in the days to come. Now Valerie and I were certainly nearing England together; Pharos, however, was with us, and while we were in his power happiness was, to all intents and purposes, unknown to us.

"What do you propose doing when you get ashore?" I inquired of my companion, more for the sake of breaking the silence than for any desire I had for the information.

"That will very much depend upon circumstances," he replied, still without looking at me. "Our main object must be to reach London as quickly as possible." Then, changing his tone, he turned to me. "Forrester, my dear fellow," he said, almost sorrowfully, "you cannot think how I regret our little disagreement of this morning. I am afraid, while I am touchy, you are headstrong ; and, in consequence, we misunderstand each other. I cannot, of course, tell what you think of me in your heart, but I venture to believe that if you knew everything, you would be the first to own that you have wronged me. Bad as I may be, I am not quite what you would make me out. If I were, do you think, knowing your antagonism as I do, I should have kept you so long with me ? You have doubted me from the beginning ; in fact, as you will remember, you once went so far as to accuse me of the crime of murder. You afterwards acknowledged your mistake —in handsome terms, I will own ; but to counterbalance such frankness, you later on accused me of drugging you in Cairo. This was another fallacy, as you your- self will, I am sure, admit. In Prague you ran away from me, taking my ward with you, a very curious pro- ceeding, regarded in whatever light you choose to look at it. What was your object? Why, to reach Eng- land. Well, as soon as I knew that, I again showed my desire to help you. As a proof of that, are we not on board this ship, and is not that the coast of Eng- land over yonder ? "

I admitted that it was. But I was not at all prepared to subscribe to his generous suggestion that he had only undertaken the voyage for my sake.

" That, however, is not all," he continued, still in the same tone. " As I think I told you in Prague, I am aware that you entertain a sincere affection for my ward. Many men in my position would doubtless have refused their consent to your betrothal, if for no other reason, because of your behaviour to myself. I am, however, cast in a different mould. If you will only play fair by me, you will find that I will do so to you. I like you, as I have so often said, and, though I am doubtless a little hasty in my temper, there is nothing I would not do to help you, either in your heart, your ambition, or your love. And I can assure you my help is not to be despised. If it is fame you seek, you have surely seen enough of me to know that I can give it to you. If it is domestic happiness, who can do so much for you as I ? "

" I hope, Monsieur Pharos," I answered, in as dignified a manner as I could assume, " that I appreciate your very kind remarks at their proper value, and also the generous manner in which you have offered to forget and forgive such offences as I have committed against yourself. You must, however, pardon me if I fail to realize the drift of your remarks. There have been times during the last six weeks when you have uttered the most extraordinary threats against myself. Naturally, I have no desire to quarrel with you ; but, remembering what has passed between us, I am compelled to show myself a little sceptical of your promises."

He glanced sharply at me, but was wise enough to

say nothing. A moment later, making the excuse that he must discover where the mate intended to bring up, he left me and went forward to the bridge. We were gradually closing upon the land, and in less than an hour's time, if all went well, we should be off the plague-stricken vessel and ashore in old England once more. A very different home-coming to that to which I had looked forward.

I was still thinking of my conversation with Pharos, and considering whether I had been wise in letting him see my cards, when a little hand stole into mine, and I found Valerie beside me.

"I could not remain below," she said, "when we were nearing England. I knew the effect the land would have upon you, and I wanted to be with you, not only to share that feeling, but to tell you how bitterly I have been reproaching myself, dear, for the cowardice I betrayed this morning."

"Cowardice!" I said. "Pray in what way did you show yourself a coward?"

Before she answered, she looked round her as if she were afraid that Pharos might be within hearing distance.

"He laughed at the idea of our refusing to enter England," she said, "and hinted that I would rather allow you to do that and carry the infection with us, than permit you to run the risk of remaining on board this fever-stricken vessel."

"Well," I asked, "and what of that? He is welcome to his own opinions."

"Yes," she answered; "but—but, oh, dearest, it hurts me the more because it is true! I did not know, when

I said it, that the pestilence had broken out upon this boat, and that you might any moment catch the infection. Directly I did hear it, however, nothing else mattered. I remembered only that you were the man I loved, and I wanted you ashore and out of reach of danger. You see I am a coward, after all."

I slipped my arm around her waist and pressed her closer to me.

"If you are a coward, I will love you all the better for it," I said. "The truth is, we are in the hands of a remorseless fate, and are being dragged along by it, powerless to help ourselves. But, as I said this morning, we have one consolation of which nothing can deprive us—we are together, and we love each other."

"There is always that to be remembered," she answered, with a gentle pressure of my arm.

I then gave her an account of the interview I had had with Pharos, and of all he had said to me and I to him. She listened attentively enough; but I could see that she was far from being impressed.

"Do not trust him," she said. "Surely you know him well enough by this time not to do so? You may be very sure he has some reason for saying this, otherwise he would not trouble himself to speak about it."

"I shall not trust him," I replied. "You need have no fear of that. My experience of him has taught me that it is in such moments as these that he is most dangerous. When he is in one of his bad humours, one is on the alert and prepared for anything he may do or say; but when he repents and appears so anxious to be friendly, one scarcely knows how to take him. Suspicion is lulled to sleep for the moment, there is a feeling of security, and it is then the mischief is accomplished."

"We will watch him together," she continued; "but, whether he is friendly or otherwise, we will not trust him even for a moment."

So close were we by this time to the shore, and so still was the night, that we could even hear the wavelets breaking upon the beach. Then the screw of the steamer ceased to revolve, and when it was quite still, Pharos and the second mate descended from the bridge and joined us.

"This has been a bad business—a very bad business," the mate was saying. "The skipper, the chief engineer, the steward, and three of the hands all dead, and no port to put into for assistance. I wish I was going ashore like you."

Callous as it may appear to say so, none of us paid very much attention to his lamentations, for the reason that we were watching the hands lowering a boat. When it was safely in the water, and the accommodation ladder had been rigged, the mate turned to Pharos.

"If you are ready, sir," he said, "you had better not waste any more time than you can help in getting ashore. There's no knowing who may not have seen us from the cliffs yonder. The coastguards are uncommon sharp just about here, and the sooner you're off and the boat is back, the sooner I can get away again."

We shook hands with him in turn, and then descended the ladder to the boat alongside. The thought of the mate's position on board that plague-stricken vessel may possibly have accounted for the silence in which we pushed off and headed for the shore; at any rate, not a word was spoken. The sea was as calm as a mill-pond, and for the reason that the night was dark, and we were all dressed in sombre colours, while the boat chosen for the work of landing us was painted a deep black, it was scarcely likely our presence would be detected. Be that as it may, no coastguard greeted us on our arrival. Therefore, as soon as the boat was aground, we made our way into the bows, and with the assistance of the sailors reached the beach. Once more I stood on English soil; but what a different being to the Forrester who had left it! Pharos rewarded the men, and remained standing beside the water until he had seen them safely embarked on their return journey to the steamer. Then, without a word to us, he turned himself about, crossed the beach, and carrying his beloved monkey in his arms, began slowly to ascend the steep path which led to the high land on which the village was situated. We did not, however, venture to approach the place itself. Had we been gaol-breakers of the most desperate description, we could scarcely have shown more anxiety not to let our presence be discovered. We walked in silence, as we had come ashore, and once when a hare, startled by our approach, rose from her form and sped away into the darkness, you might have supposed, from the way we stopped and shrank back into the bushes, that we had come near being caught red-handed in the committal of a deed of the most determined atrocity.

The remembrance of that strange night often returns to me now. In my mind's eye I can see the squat figure of Pharos tramping on ahead, Valerie following a few steps behind him, and myself bringing up the rear, and all this with the brilliant stars overhead, the lights of the village showing dimly across the sandhills to our right, and the continuous murmur of the sea behind us. For the time of year the night was bitterly cold, and the spirits of two of us at least were at their lowest. In the same order we reached the top of the cliff, crossed the strip of moorland, dotted here and there with tufts of rushes and coarse grass, and finally struck the high-road at a point where it branched off a mile or so above the village. Here we paused for a few minutes beside a stile, while Pharos, still without speaking, made up his mind in which direction we should next proceed. To this day I have no notion whether he was acquainted with the country, or whether he was merely trusting to chance and his own peculiar instinct to bring him out at a railway station. At last, however, he came to a decision, and we accordingly set off along that road which turned to the left. From the dust that lay upon it, it was evident they had had no rain in these parts for some time past; and as we trudged along, I wondered in a vague sort of fashion what sort of appearance we should present by the time we found a train and reached our destination.

For upwards of an hour we tramped on in this fashion, and in that time scarcely covered a distance of four miles. Had it occurred at the commencement of our acquaintance, I should not have been able to understand how Pharos, considering his age and infirm appearance, could have accomplished even so much. Since then, however, I had been permitted so many opportunities of noting the enormous strength and vitality contained in his meagre frame that I was past any feeling of wonderment. Valerie it was who caused me most anxiety. Only two days before she had been stricken by the plague; yesterday she was still confined to her cabin. Now here she was, subjected to intense excitement and no small amount of physical exertion. Pharos must have had the same thought in his mind, for more than once he stopped and inquired if she felt capable of proceeding, and on one occasion he poured out for her from a flask he carried in his pocket a small cupful of some fluid he had doubtless brought with him for that purpose. At last the welcome sight of a railway line came into view. It crossed the road, and as soon as we saw it we stopped and took counsel together. The question for us to consider was whether it would be wiser to continue our walk along the high-road, on the chance of its bringing us to a station, or whether we should clamber up the embankment to the railway line itself, and follow that along in the hope of achieving the same result. On the one side there was the likelihood of our having to go a long way round, and on the other the suspicion that might possibly be aroused in the minds of the railway officials should we make an appearance at the station in such an unorthodox fashion. Eventually, however, we decided for the railway line. Accordingly we mounted the stile beside the arch, and having clambered up the embankment to the footpath beside the permanent way, resumed our march, one behind the other as before. We had not, however, as it turned out, very much farther to go, for on emerging from the cutting, which began at a short distance from the arch just referred to, we saw before us a glimmering light, emanating, so we discovered later, from the signal-box on the farther side of the station. I could not help wondering how Pharos would explain our presence at such an hour; but I knew him well enough by this time to feel sure that he would be able to do so, not to his own, but to everybody else's satisfaction. The place itself proved to be a primitive roadside affair, with a small galvanized shelter for passengers, and a cottage at the farther end, which we set down rightly enough as the residence of the station-master. The only lights to be seen were an oil-lamp above the cottage door, and another in the waiting-room. No sign of any official could be discovered.

"We must now find out," said Pharos, "at what time the next train leaves for civilization. Even in such a hole as this they must surely have a time-table."

So saying, he went into the shelter before described and turned up the lamp. His guess proved to be correct, for a number of notices were pasted upon the wall.

"Did you happen to see the name of the station as you came along the platform?" he inquired of me, as he knelt upon the seat and ran his eye along the printed sheets.

"I did not," I replied; "but I will very soon find out."

Leaving them, I made my way along the platform towards the cottage. Here on a board suspended upon the fence was the name "Tebworth" in large letters. I returned and informed Pharos, who immediately placed his skinny finger upon the placard before him.

"Tebworth," he said. "Here it is. The next train for Norwich leaves at 2.48. What is the time now?"

I consulted my watch.

"Ten minutes to two," I replied. "Roughly speaking, we have an hour to wait."

"We are lucky in not having longer," Pharos replied. "It is a piece of good fortune to get a train at all at such an early hour."

With that he seated himself in a corner and closed his eyes, as if preparatory to slumber. A more curious picture than that meagre little waiting-room presented ten minutes later could scarcely have been discovered. In the right-hand corner was Pharos, his always ugly countenance looking in sleep even more diabolical than usual, with the pathetic little face of the monkey, Pehtes, gazing out at us from beneath his master's coat. In the centre Valerie was seated, a woman whose beauty and music was famous from St. Petersburg to Dublin. I occupied the corner on her left again. Ptahmes, the king's magician, Valerie de Vocxqal, the finest violinist in Europe, and Cyril Forrester, an Associate of the Royal Academy. And here we all were, at two in the morning, sitting in semi-darkness in a roadside station of the very name of which we had been ignorant until a very few moments before.   I suppose I must have dozed off after a while, for I have no remembrance of anything further until I was awakened by hearing the steps of a man on the platform outside, and his voice calling to a certain Joel, whoever he might be, to know if there was any news of the train for which we were waiting.

Before the other had time to answer, Pharos had risen

and gone out. The exclamation of surprise, to say nothing of the look of astonishment upon the station-master's face,—for the badge upon his cap told me it was he,—when he found Pharos standing before him, was comical in the extreme.

"Good-evening," said the latter in his most urbane manner, "or rather, since it is getting on for three o'clock, I suppose I should say 'Good-morning.' Is your train likely to be late, do you think?"

"I don't fancy so, sir," the man replied. "She always runs up to time."

Then, unable to contain the curiosity our presence on his platform at such an hour occasioned him, he continued: "No offence, I hope, sir, but we don't have many passengers of your kind by it as a general rule. It's full early for ladies and gentlemen Tebworth way to be travelling about the country."

"Very likely," said Pharos, with more than his usual sweetness; "but you see, my friend, our case is peculiar. We have a poor lady with us whom we are anxious to get up to London as quickly as possible. The excitement of travelling by day would be too much for her, so we choose the quiet of the early morning. Of course you understand."

Pharos tapped his forehead in a significant manner, and his intelligence being thus complimented, the man glanced into the shelter, and seeing Valerie seated there with a sad expression upon her face, turned to Pharos and said :—

"Poor young thing! And such a sweet-looking lady, too. Well, well, we none of us know what's in store for us, do we, sir? My wife's sister now was the same way

a year or so back. Melancholy, the doctor called it,
which is not to be wondered at, seeing that her young
man went and drowned himself, being in liquor at the
time. That being so, I can understand your wanting to
travel by night. I am sure I should do the same me-
self, I make no doubt. When the train comes in, sir,
you leave it to me, and I'll see if I can't find you a
carriage which you can have to yourselves right through.
You'll be in Norwich at three-twenty."

We followed him along the platform to the booking-
office, and Pharos had scarcely taken the tickets before
the whistle of the train, sounding as it entered the cutting by which we had reached the station, warned us to
prepare for departure.

"Ah, here she is, running well up to time!" said the
station-master. "Now, sir, you come with me."

Pharos beckoned us to follow ; the other opened the
door of a first-class coach. We all got in. Pharos
slipped a sovereign into the man's hand ; the train
started, and a minute later we were safely out of Tebworth and on the road once more. Our arrival in
Norwich was punctual almost to the moment, and
within twenty minutes of our arrival there we had
changed trains and were speeding towards London at a
rate of fifty miles an hour.

From Norwich, as from Tebworth, we were fortunate
enough to have a carriage to ourselves, and during the
journey I found occasion to discuss with Pharos the
question as to what he thought of doing when we
reached town. In my own mind I had made sure that as
soon as we got there he would take Valerie away to the
house he had occupied on the occasion of his last visit,

while I should return to my own studio. This, however, I discovered was by no means what he intended.

"I could not hear of it, my dear Forrester," he said emphatically. "Is it possible that you can imagine, after all we have been through together, I should permit you to leave me? No! no! Such a thing is not to be thought of for an instant. I appreciate your company, even though you told me so plainly last evening that you do not believe it. You are also about to become the husband of my ward, and for that reason alone I have no desire to lose sight of you in the short time that is left me. I arranged with my agents before I left London in June, and I heard from them in Cairo that they had found a suitable residence for me in a fashionable locality. Valerie and I do not require very much room, and if you will take up your abode with us —that is to say, of course, until you are married—I assure you we shall both be delighted. What do you say, my dear?"

I saw Valerie's face brighten on hearing that we were not destined to be separated, and that decided me. However, for the reason that I did not for an instant believe in his expressions of friendship, I was not going to appear too anxious to accept his proposal. There was something behind it all that I did not know, and before I pledged myself I desired to find out what that something was.

"I do not know what to say," I answered, as soon as I had come to the conclusion that for the moment it would be better to appear to have forgotten and forgiven the past. "I have trespassed too much upon your hospitality already."

" You have not trespassed upon it at all," he answered.
" I have derived great pleasure from your society, and I
shall be still more pleased if you can see your way to
fall in with my plan."

Thereupon I withdrew my refusal, and promised to
take up my residence with him at least until the arrangements should be made for our wedding.

As it turned out, my astonishment on hearing that he
had taken a London house was not the only surprise in
store for me, for on reaching Liverpool Street, who
should come forward to meet us but the same peculiar
footman who had ridden beside the coachman on that
memorable return journey from Pompeii. He was
dressed in the same dark and unpretentious livery he
had worn then, and, while he greeted his master,
mistress, and myself with the most obsequious respect,
did not betray the least sign of either pleasure or
astonishment. Having ascertained that we had brought
no luggage with us, he led us from the platform to the
yard outside, where we found a fine landau awaiting us,
drawn by a pair of jet-black horses, and driven by the
same coachman I had seen in Naples on the occasion
referred to above. Having helped Valerie to enter, and
as soon as I had installed myself with my back to the
horses, Pharos said something in an undertone to the
footman, and then took his place opposite me. The
door was immediately closed, and we drove out of the
yard.

I cannot tell you how the first glimpse of the streets
affected me. In bygone days I had often said that I
would rather live anywhere than in the Metropolis
Now, however, after all I had been through in the last

few months, I was firmly convinced that there was no other place like London in the world. In Naples, Cairo, Prague, Berlin, and Hamburg, I had been a stranger in strange lands ; now I was in my own birth-place once more, and I derived an indescribable sense of security from the crowded streets, and even from the stalwart policemen on duty at the crossings. Under the influence of this feeling, it seemed to me as if I could have listened to the roar and rattle of the traffic, and have watched the hurrying figures on the pavements, the crowd of 'buses and other vehicles drawn up opposite the Mansion House, for hours without growing weary. And when we left the City and reached the West End, Pharos's reference to my marriage, the knowledge of my darling's love, and the feeling that I was back once more in my own land, all combined to make me one of the happiest men alive. The past, if not forgotten, was, at least, consigned to oblivion for the time being.

Leaving the Embankment, the carriage proceeded along Victoria Street, and so by way of Grosvenor Place to Park Lane, where it drew up before a house at which, in the days when it had been the residence of the famous Lord Tollingtower, I had been a constant visitor.

" I presume, since we have stopped here, that this must be the place," said Pharos, gazing up at it.

"Do you mean that this is the house you have taken?" I asked in astonishment, for it was one of the finest residences in London.

" I mean that this is the house that my agents have taken for me," Pharos replied. " Personally I know nothing whatsoever about it."

" But surely you do not take a place without making some inquiries about it ? " I continued.

"Why not ? " he inquired. " I have servants whom I can trust, and they know that it is more than their lives are worth to deceive me. Strangely enough, however, it is recalled to my mind that this house and I do happen to be acquainted. The late owner was a personal friend. As a matter of fact, I stayed with him throughout his last illness and was with him when he died."

You may be sure I pricked up my ears on hearing this, for, as every one knew, the late Lord Tollingtower had reached the end of his extraordinary career under circumstances that had created rather a sensation at the time. Something, however, warned me to ask no questions.

" Let us alight," said Pharos, and when the footman had opened the door we accordingly did so.

On entering the house, I was surprised to find that considerable architectural changes had been made in it. Nor was my wonderment destined to cease there, for when I was shown to the bedroom which had been prepared for me, there, awaiting me at the foot of the bed, was the luggage I had left at the hotel in Prague, and which I had made up my mind I had lost sight of for ever. Here, at least, was evidence to prove that Pharos had never intended that I should leave him.

CHAPTER XIX

AFTER the excitement of the past few days, and her terrible experience in Hamburg, to say nothing of the fact that she had landed from a steamer under peculiar circumstances, and had been tramping the country half the night, it is not to be wondered at that, by the time we reached Park Lane, Valerie was completely knocked up. Pharos had accordingly insisted that she should at once retire to her room and endeavour to obtain the rest of which she stood so much in need.

"For the next few weeks,—that is to say, until the end of the season,—I intend that you shall both enjoy yourselves," he said with the utmost affability, when we were alone together, "to the top of your bent. And that reminds me of something, Forrester. Your betrothal must be announced as speedily as possible. It is due to Valerie that this should be done. I presume you do not wish the engagement to be a long one ? "

"Indeed, I do not," I answered, not, however, without a slight feeling of surprise that he should speak so openly and so soon upon the subject. "As you may suppose, it cannot be too short to please me. And our marriage ? "

"Your marriage can take place as soon after the season as you please," he continued with the same extraordinary geniality. "You will not find me placing any obstacles in your way."

"But you have never asked me as to my means, or my power to support her," I said, putting his last remark aside as if I had not heard it.

"I have not," he answered. "There is no need for me to do so. Your means are well known to me; besides, it has always been my intention to make provision for Valerie myself. Provided you behave yourselves, and do not play me any more tricks such as I had to complain of in Hamburg, you will find that she will bring you a handsome little nest-egg that will make it quite unnecessary for you ever to feel any anxiety on the score of money. But we will discuss all that more fully later on. See, here are a number of invitations that have arrived for us. It looks as if we are not likely to be dull during our stay in London."

So saying, he placed upwards of fifty envelopes before me, many of which I was surprised to find were addressed to myself. These I opened with the first feeling of a return to my old social life that I had experienced since I had re-entered London. The invitations hailed, for the most part, from old friends. Some were for dinners, others for musical "At homes," while at least a dozen were for dances, one of the last-named being from the Duchess of Amersham.

"I have taken the liberty of accepting that on your behalf," said Pharos, picking the card up. "The Duchess of Amersham and I are old friends, and I think it will brighten Valerie and yourself up a little if we look in at her ball an hour or so to-night."

"But surely," I said, "we have only just reached London, and——" Here I paused, not knowing quite how to proceed.

"What objection have you to raise?" he asked, with a sudden flash of the old angry look in his eyes.

"My only objection was that I thought it a little dangerous," I said. "On your own confession, it was the plague from which Valerie was suffering in Hamburg."

Pharos laughed a short, harsh laugh, that grated upon the ear.

"You must really forgive me, Forrester, for having deceived you," he said, "but I had to do it. It was necessary for me to use any means I could think of for getting you to England. As you have reason to know, Valerie is possessed of a peculiarly sensitive temperament. She is easily influenced, particularly by myself, and the effect can be achieved at any distance. If I were in London and she in Vienna, I could, by merely exercising my will, not only induce her to do anything I might wish, but could make her bodily health exactly what I pleased. You will therefore see that it would be an easy task for me to cause her to be taken ill in Hamburg. Her second self— that portion of her mind which is so susceptible to my influence, as you saw for yourself—witnessed my arrival in Prague and at the hotel. As soon as I entered the room in which she was waiting for me, the attraction culminated in a species of fainting fit.

I despatched you post haste to a chemist with a prescription which I thought would be extremely difficult,
if not impossible, for you to get made up. At any
rate, it would, I knew, serve my purpose if it kept
you some time away."

"Then you mean that while I was hurrying from
place to place like a madman, suffering untold agonies
of fear, and believing that Valerie's life depended upon
my speed, you were in reality deceiving me?"

"If I am to be truthful, I must confess that I was,"
he replied; "but I give you my word the motive was
a good one. Had I not done so, who knows what
would have happened? The plague was raging on
the Continent, and you were both bent on getting
away from me again on the first opportunity. What
was the result? Working on your fears for her, I
managed to overcome the difficulties, and got you
safely into England. Valerie has not been as ill as
you supposed. I have sanctioned your engagement,
and, as I said just now, if you will let me, will provide
for you both for life, and will assist in lifting you to
the highest pinnacle of fame. After this explanation,
surely you are not going to be ungenerous enough to
still feel vindictive against me?"

"It was a cruel trick to play me," I answered; "but
since the result has not been as serious as I supposed,
and you desire me to believe you did it all with a
good object, I will endeavour to think no more about
it."

"You have decided sensibly," he said. "And now
let us arrange what we shall do this evening. My
proposal is that we rest this afternoon, that you dine

with me at my club, the Antiquarian, in the evening,
and that afterwards I show you London as I see it
in my character of Pharos the Egyptian. I think
you will find the programme both interesting and
instructive. Shortly before midnight we might return
here, pick Valerie up, and go on to the Duchess of
Amersham's ball. Does that meet with your approval ? "

I was so relieved at finding that Valerie had not
really been attacked by the plague, that however much
I should have liked to spend the evening alone with
her, I could see no reason for declining Pharos's invitation. I accordingly stated that I should be very glad
to do as he wished.

We followed out his plan to the letter. After lunch
we retired to our respective apartments and rested
until it was time to prepare for the evening. At the
hour appointed, I descended to the drawing-room, where
I found Pharos awaiting me. He was dressed as I
had seen him at Lady Medenham's well-remembered
" At home "—that is to say, he wore his velvet jacket
and black skull cap, and, as usual, carried his gold-
topped walking-stick in his hand.

" The carriage is at the door, I think," he said as
I entered, " so if you are ready we will set off."

I signified my assent, and we accordingly proceeded
into the hall, where one of the menservants who had
waited upon us in Naples and on board the yacht
assisted Pharos into his great-coat, and then performed
the same operation for me, while another opened the
door.

A neat brougham was drawn up beside the pave-

ment, we took our places in it, and ten minutes later
had reached the Antiquarian Club, of all the establish-
ments of the kind in London perhaps the most magnificent. How Pharos became a member of it, I do
not know; but there, as at Pompeii, Cairo, Luxor,
Prague, and, indeed, every other European city, he
seemed to be not only quite at home, but equally
well known. The dignified servants having removed
our coats, we ascended the marble staircase and passed
through the ante-room, decorated with the portraits
of many distinguished members past and present, to
the dining-room itself. A more beautiful room could
scarcely be imagined. Wide and lofty, and yet boast-
ing the most harmonious proportions, the dining-room
at the Antiquarian Club always remains in my mind
the most stately of the many stately banqueting halls
in London. Pharos's preference, I found, was for a
table in one of the large windows overlooking the
Embankment and the river, and this had accordingly
been prepared for him.

"If you will sit there," said Pharos, motioning with
his hand to a chair on the right, "I will take this one
opposite you."

I accordingly seated myself in the place he indicated.

"Though my fare is necessarily simplicity itself,"
he said, as we unfolded our serviettes, "I have come
to the conclusion that there are only four places at
which to dine in Europe. The first is the Vladimir
Club in St. Petersburg, overlooking the Neusky Prospect, where they have secured the services of the
inimitable Benitot; the next is the Metternich Res-

taurant in the Ring Strasse in Vienna; the third is
the Café de Parnassus in Paris; while the last is this
club in London. Doubtless you have dined here
many times before?"

"Once or twice," I answered; "but that is sufficient
to enable me to endorse all you say concerning it."

And, indeed, the encomium I had passed upon it
was well deserved. The dinner was perfect in every
respect. My host himself, however, dined after his
own fashion, in the manner I have elsewhere described.
Nevertheless, he did the honours of the table with
the most perfect grace, and had any stranger been
watching us, he would have found it difficult to believe
that the relationship existing between us was not of
the most cordial nature possible.

By eight o'clock the room was crowded, and with
as fine a collection of well-born, well-dressed, and well-
mannered men as could be found in London. The
decorations, the portraits upon the walls, the liveried
servants, the snowy drapery and sparkling silver, all
helped to make up a picture that, after the sordidness
of the *Margrave of Brandenburg*, was like a glimpse
of a new life.

"This is the first side of that London life I am
desirous of presenting to you," said Pharos in his
capacity of showman, after I had finished my dessert,
and had enjoyed a couple of glasses of the famous
Antiquarian port—"one side of that luxury and ex-
travagance which is fast drawing this great city to
its doom. It would interest you, I am sure, to know
the histories of the people now dining in this room.
Many of them are known to me, and at more I can

give a very shrewd guess. Do you see that tall, well-bred-looking man, with the grey hair and the hawk-like nose, sitting in the window yonder?"

I answered in the affirmative. He was an individual I had often seen before, but with whose name I was not familiar.

"His history alone would be worth writing," continued Pharos. "Though the world is not aware of it, he has, on more than one occasion, been invited to leave Russia at a few hours' notice. Some day he will not leave at all. Two or three times in the year you will find him at Dover, and when the boat comes in you will see him meet some curious-looking individual, speak a few words to him, and then return to London in the same train, but in a different carriage. If you were to speak to him now, you would find him a quiet, unassuming man. Some day, however, he will suddenly disappear, and this club will know him no more. The little stout fellow with the bald head, at the next table, has been a member for a number of years, and though by no means handsome himself, he boasts one of the most beautiful and popular wives in England. They keep an excellent establishment, a yacht at Cowes, a hunting-box near Leicester, and a villa on the Riviera, yet it is proverbial that neither of them possesses, nor has ever been known to possess, a single penny piece. The tall, thin man with the big moustache next him is the younger son of a peer, whose name is as old as that of England itself. He earns his livelihood pigeon-shooting and billiard-playing, and is little more than a titled blackleg. The tall, stout man with the uncomfortable expression,

dining with the prematurely old man at the table
under the big portrait, has made his fortune in South
Africa, and is desirous of entering the world of fashion.
To that end he has been taken up by his present
companion, of whom you can see he is so proud—the
notoriously impecunious Earl of Smatterdale. The
latter's wife ran away from him last year with an
American millionaire, and ever since that time he
has been existing on the damages the Court awarded
him, which were not as big as they would otherwise
have been, for the simple reason that he had to pay
half away as commission to her. So I could continue
from end to end of the room. They make an interesting study, do they not? but scarcely edifying from a
humanitarian point of view. Now, if you have quite
finished, we might move on. We have a good deal
of work to get through, and very little time in which
to do it."

I acquiesced, and we accordingly descended to the
hall and donned our coats.

" If you would care to smoke, permit me to offer
you one of the same brand of cigarettes of which you
expressed your approval in Naples," said Pharos, producing from his pocket a silver case, which he handed
to me. I took one of the delicacies it contained and
lit it. Then we passed out of the hall to Pharos's
own carriage, which was waiting in the street for us.

As on the previous occasion that I had smoked his
cigarettes, I was compelled to admit the excellence
of the tobacco. And also, as before, it had a wonder-
fully soothing effect upon me, while it caused me to
feel better disposed towards my companion than I had

done for some time past. When that one was finished,
I willingly accepted another, and by the time that
was too hot to hold we had reached our destination,
the Renaissance Theatre. Knowing how crowded this
place of entertainment usually is in the season, I had
been wondering whether we should experience any
difficulty in obtaining seats. But as soon as we entered
the vestibule an attendant came forward, and, bowing
to my companion, informed him that by the manager's
orders a box had been placed at his disposal. We
accordingly followed him down a few steps and along
a narrow passage towards a box on the prompt side
of the stage. The orchestra were playing, but the
curtain had not yet risen. The dress-circle, pit, and
gallery were filled to overflowing, while the stalls—the
fashionable portion of the house—contained scarcely
an occupant.

"Here you have an opportunity of studying one of
the most curious phases of London Society," he said,
as he pulled his chair forward and looked down on
the place to which I have just referred. "It does not
matter how interesting the play about to be performed
may be, it is quite certain that a large proportion of
the stalls will not put in an appearance until the curtain has risen, when they will interrupt the action of
the play and disturb the comfort of the house, with
that superb disregard for other people's feelings which
is so characteristic of the fashionable world. During
the progress of the piece they will discuss their own
affairs with each other in voices so audible that those
about them who are anxious to hear the play can
scarcely do so."

Bitter as his words were, I had to confess that in a measure they were true. In this particular instance the latter portion of the indictment would have been a distinct advantage, for the play itself was a nauseating one in every way, and ten years before would have been impossible. I glanced at Pharos to see what he thought of it, and found him sitting back in the box with an expression of fiendish rage upon his face, as if, were such a thing possible, he would willingly destroy every man and woman within the building.

"What think you of the authors of such a play and of the men who bring their wives and daughters to listen to it, and, while admitting its indecency, excuse themselves by saying that the lesson it teaches is a salutary one? I beg you to observe the faces of the young girls. On my word, it is a curious age that can permit such things, and a still more curious age that can enjoy them. And these are the people who rifle the tombs of the dead kings and queens of Egypt, and write and talk patronizingly about the civilization of the Ancients. But it will not last. A time, however, is coming, and is even now at hand, when—— But, see, the curtain is falling; we have heard enough. Let us proceed to our next place of amusement."

Leaving our box, we made our way to the front of the theatre once more, where we entered the carriage which was still waiting for us, and drove off in the direction of Charing Cross. Throughout the drive I sat back in my corner watching the lamp-lit streets, the cabs dashing past me, and the crowds upon the pavements, with that curious sense of being with them,

and yet not of them, which I always experienced in
Pharos's company.   At last we drew up before the
illuminated portals of the Occidental Music Hall.

"Let us enter," said Pharos, "and see what we can
discover here."

We did so, and as soon as we had paid for our admission, mounted a carpeted staircase and passed into
the theatre itself.   Many and curious were the glances
thrown at my companion by the people about us as we
entered, and I noticed, with a satisfaction for which I
could scarcely account at the time, the expressions of
fear and undisguised abhorrence his unique personality
inspired in them.   To attempt to describe the building
itself, since it is so well known, would be waste of time.
It is only necessary for me to say that on the stage a
brilliant ballet was proceeding, though it might have
been performed a thousand miles away for all the attention the men and women about me bestowed upon
it.   The entire house was impregnated with tobacco
smoke, in the stalls powdered footmen passed hither and
thither with salvers of refreshments, crowds of young
old men and old young men clustered round the bars,
the orchestra played as if each individual member were
determined to execute a certain number of notes in
an allotted time, the couple of dozen scantily clothed
females upon the stage kicked and pirouetted with a
vigour that compensated for their lack of grace, while
in the promenade itself, where Pharos and I had taken
up our position, the scene, though of a different kind,
was scarcely less animated.

"Here you have yet another phase of English life,"
said my companion, after we had been watching it for

some minutes without speaking ; and then he added,
" I will leave you to draw your own conclusions from
it."

For upwards of ten minutes we remained silent
spectators of all that was going on. Then Pharos
made a sign to me and moved towards the door. I
followed close at his heels, and when we were in the
street once more took my place in the cab beside him.
This time we drove to Westminster and entered the
House of Commons. A pass had been previously obtained, and with it we ascended to the Members'
Gallery. The House was crowded, for the business
then before Parliament dealt with the plague, and was
exceedingly important.

As usual, Pharos had his own opinions concerning
the Chamber to express, and as usual they were equally
far from being complimentary to the people he described. As at the Occidental, as soon as he had
pointed out to me the sordid side of their lives and
characters, and the pettiness of their ambition, the
show of party feeling they exhibited even in the face
of a grave national peril, he led me away again, saying
as he did so,—

" We will now return to pick up Valerie, after which
we will drive to Amersham House, where I have no
doubt we shall meet many of those whom we have seen
here to-night."

We found Valerie awaiting us in the drawing-room.
She was dressed for the ball, and, superb as I thought
she looked on the evening she had been presented to
the Emperor in Prague, I had to confess to myself that
she was even more beautiful now. Her face was flushed

with excitement, and her lovely eyes sparkled like twin stars. I hastened to congratulate her on her altered appearance, and had scarcely done so before the butler announced that the carriage was at the door. Whereupon we departed for Carlton House Terrace.

On the subject of the ball itself it is not my intention to say very much ; let it suffice that, possibly by reason of what followed later, it is talked of to this day. The arrangements were of the most sumptuous and extravagant description, princes of the blood and their wives were present, Cabinet Ministers jostled burly country squires upon the staircase, fair but haughty aristocrats rubbed shoulders with the daughters of American millionaires, whose money had been made goodness knows where or how ; half the celebrities of England nodded to the other half ; but in all that distinguished company there was no woman to eclipse Valerie in beauty, and, as another side of the picture, no man who could equal Pharos in ugliness. Much to my astonishment, the latter seemed to have no lack of acquaintances, and I noticed also that every one with whom he talked, though they paid a most servile attention to his remarks while he was with them, invariably heaved a sigh of relief when he took his departure. To me the evening was one of qualified enjoyment. Needless to say, I derived pleasure from Valerie's society, and found an exquisite delight in presenting her to my friends as my affianced wife ; but mixed up with it was a presentiment of coming danger that, do what I would, I could neither explain nor dispel. Times out of number Valerie rallied me upon my quietness, but it was in vain. Do what I would, I could not shake it off. The pictures I had seen that evening in Pharos's company rose before my eyes continually ; and when later in the evening he came to my side and, with the same look upon his face that I had seen at the Renaissance, pointed out to me the hollowness of this ball also, and showed me the scheming mothers, the false wives and husbands, and the inner lives of many for whom up to that time I had entertained the greatest reverence, my cup was full—I could bear no more.

At two o'clock Valerie was tired, and we accordingly decided to leave. But I soon found that it was not to return home. Having placed my darling in her carriage, Pharos directed the coachman to drive to Park Lane, declaring that we preferred to walk.

It was a beautiful night, cool and fresh, with a few clouds in the south-west, but brilliant starlight overhead. Leaving Carlton House Terrace, we passed into Waterloo Place, ascended it as far as Piccadilly, and then hailed a cab.

"Our evening is not completed yet," said Pharos. "I have still some places to show you. It is necessary that you should see them in order that you may appreciate what is to follow. The first will be a fancy dress ball at Covent Garden, where yet another side of London life is to be found."

If such a thing could possibly have had any effect, I should have objected ; but so completely did his will dominate mine, that I had no option but to consent to anything he proposed. We accordingly stepped into the cab and were driven off to the place indicated. From the sounds which issued from the great building as we entered it, it was plain that the ball was proceeding with its accustomed vigour, a surmise on our part which proved to be correct when we reached the box Pharos had bespoken. A floor had been laid over the stalls and pit, and upon this upwards of fifteen hundred dancers, in every style of fancy dress the ingenuity of man could contrive, were slowly revolving to the music of a military band. It was a curious sight, and at any other time would have caused me considerable amusement. Now, however, with the fiendish face of Pharos continually at my elbow, and his carping criticisms sounding without ceasing in my ear, mocking at the people below us, finding evil in everything, and hinting always at the doom which was hanging over London, it reminded me more of Dante's Inferno than anything else to which I could liken it. For upwards of an hour we remained spectators of it. Then, with a final sneer, Pharos gave the signal for departure.

"We have seen the finest club in Europe," he said, as we emerged into the cool air of Bow Street, "London's most artistic theatre, the House of Commons, the most fashionable social event of the season, and a fancy dress ball at Covent Garden. We must now descend a grade lower, and, if you have no objection, we will go on in search of it on foot."

I had nothing to urge against this suggestion, so, turning into Long Acre, we passed through a number of squalid streets, with all of which Pharos seemed to be as intimately acquainted as he was in the West End, and finally approached the region of Seven Dials—that delectable neighbourhood bordered on the one side by Shaftesbury Avenue, and on the other by Drury Lane

Here, though it was by this time close upon three o'clock, no one seemed to have begun to think of bed. In one narrow alley through which we were compelled to pass at least thirty people were assembled, more than half of which number were intoxicated. A woman was screaming for assistance from a house across the way, and a couple of men were fighting at the farther end of an adjoining court. In this particular locality the police seemed as extinct as the dodo. At any other time, and in any other company, I should have felt some doubt as to the wisdom of being in such a place at such an hour. But with my present companion beside me I felt no fear.

We had walked some distance before we reached the house Pharos desired to visit. From its outward appearance it might have been a small drinking-shop in the daytime; now, however, every window was closely shuttered, and not a ray of light showed through chink or cranny. Approaching the door, he knocked four times upon it, whereupon it was opened on a chain for a few inches. A face looked through the aperture thus created, and Pharos, moving a little closer, said something in a whisper to it.

"Beg pardon, sir," said the woman, for a woman I soon discovered it was. "I didn't know as it was you. I'll undo the chain. Is the gentleman with you safe?"

"Quite safe," Pharos replied. "You need have no fear of him. He is my friend."

"In you come, then," said the woman to me, my character being thus vouched for, and accordingly in I stepped.

The passage was in total darkness, and when the

door was shut behind us, and the bolts and bars had been replaced in the positions they had occupied before our entrance, I began to wonder into what sort of place my guide had led me.

Dirty as were the streets outside, the house in which we now stood more than equalled them. The home of Captain Wisemann in Hamburg, which I had up to that time thought the filthiest I had ever seen, was nothing to it. Taking the candle in her hand, the old woman led us along the passage towards another door. Before this she paused and rang a bell, the handle of which was cleverly concealed in the wood-work. Almost instantly it was opened, and we entered a room the like of which I had never seen or dreamt of before. Its length was fully thirty feet, its width possibly fifteen. On the wall above the fireplace was a gas bracket, from the burner of which a large flame was issuing with a hissing noise. In the centre of the room was a table, and seated round it were at least twenty men and women, who, at the moment of our entering, were engaged upon a game the elements of which I did not understand. On seeing us the players sprang to their feet with one accord, and a scramble ensued for the money upon the table. A scene of general excitement followed, which might very well have ended in the gas being turned out and our finding ourselves upon the floor with knives between our ribs, had not the old woman who had introduced us called out that there was no need for alarm, and added, with an oath, what might in Pharos's case possibly have been true, but in mine was certainly not, that we had been there hundreds of times before, and were proper sort o' gents. Thereupon

"The players sprang to their feet."

Pharos contributed a sovereign to be spent in liquid re-freshment, and when our healths had been drunk with a variety of toasts intended to be complimentary, our presence was forgotten, and the game once more pro-ceeded. One thing was self-evident: there was no lack of money among those present, and when a member of the company had not the wherewithal to continue the gamble, he in most cases produced a gold watch, a ring, or some other valuable from his pocket, and handed it to a burly ruffian at the head of the table, who advanced him an amount upon it which nine cases out of ten failed to meet with his approval.

"Seeing you have not been here before," said Pharos, " I might explain that this is the most typical thieves' gambling hell in London. There is not a man or woman in this room at the present moment who is not a hardened criminal in every sense of the word. The fellow at the end narrowly escaped the gallows, the man on his right has but lately emerged from seven years' penal servitude for burglary, while the girl with the somewhat more refined face next him is his mistress. She obtains admittance to houses by making love to butlers and footmen, and in that way discovering where the valuables are kept, and how it will be possible for her paramour to enter later on. The three sitting to-gether next the banker are at the present moment badly wanted by the police, while the old woman who admitted us, and who was once not only a celebrated variety actress, but an exceedingly beautiful woman, is the mother of that sickly youth drinking gin beside the fireplace, who assisted in the murder of an old man in Shaftesbury Avenue a fortnight or so ago, and will certainly be captured and brought within measurable distance of the gallows before many more weeks have passed over his head."

" But how do you know all this ? " I inquired, for the extent of his knowledge astonished me.

" Did I not tell you when I first made your acquaintance, three months ago, that there are very few things with which I have not some sort of an acquaintance ? " he replied. " Have you seen enough of this to satisfy you ? "

" More than enough," I answered truthfully.

" Then let us leave. It will soon be daylight, and there are still many places for us to visit before we return home."

We accordingly bade the occupants of the room good-night, and when we had been escorted to the door by the old woman who had admitted us left the house.

From the neighbourhood of Seven Dials Pharos carried me off to other equally sad and disreputable quarters of the city. We visited Salvation Army Shelters, the cheapest of cheap lodging-houses, doss-houses in comparison to which a workhouse would be a palace ; dark railway arches, where we found homeless men, women, and children endeavouring to snatch intervals of rest between the visits of patrolling policemen ; the public parks, where the grass was dotted with recumbent forms, and every seat was occupied ; and then, turning homewards, reached Park Lane just as the clocks were striking seven, as far as I was concerned sick to the heart, not only of the sorrow and the sin of London, but of the callous indifference to it displayed by Pharos.

CHAPTER XX

WHEN I woke next morning, the feeling I had had in my heart the evening before that something terrible was about to happen had not left me. With a shudder of intense disgust, I recalled the events of the previous night. Never, since I had known him, with the exception of that one occasion on the Embankment, had Pharos appeared so loathsome to me. I remembered the mocking voice in which he had pointed out to me the follies and frailties of our great city, the cruel look in his eyes as he watched those about him in the different places we had visited. For the life of me I could not comprehend what his object had been in taking me to them. While I dressed I debated the subject with myself, but though I had a very shrewd suspicion that the vengeance to which he alluded, and which he had declared to be so imminent, was the plague, yet I could not see how he was able to speak with such authority upon the subject. On the other hand, I had to remember that I had never yet known him fail, either in what he had predicted, or anything he had set himself to do. Having got so far in my calculations, I stopped, as another thought occurred to me, and with my brushes still in either hand stared at the wall before me. From the fact that he had informed me of the existence of the plague in

London, it was certain that he knew of it, though the authorities did not. Could it be possible, therefore, that he had simply crossed from the Continent to London in order to be able to gloat over the misery that was to come?

The diabolical nature of the man, and his love of witnessing the sufferings of others, tallied exactly with the conclusion I had arrived at; and if my reasoning were correct, this would account for the expression of triumph I had seen upon his face. When I descended to the breakfast-room, I found Valerie awaiting me there. She was looking quite her own self again by this time, and greeted me with a pretty exhibition of shyness upon her face, which I could understand when she handed me a number of letters she had received, congratulating her upon our engagement.

"You were late last night," she said. "Hour after hour I lay awake listening for your step, and it was broad daylight when I heard you ascend the stairs. I cannot tell you how frightened I was while you were away. I knew you were with him, and I imagined you exposed to a hundred dangers."

I told her where and with whom I had been.

"But why did he take you with him?" she inquired, when I had finished. "I cannot understand that."

"I must confess that it has puzzled me also," I replied.

"The whole thing is very strange," she continued, "and I do not like the look of it. We have reason to know that he does nothing without a motive. But what can the motive have been in this particular instance?"

"That is more than I can say," I answered, and with that we changed the subject, and interested ourselves in our own and more particular concerns. So engrossing were they, and so pleasant were the thoughts they conjured up, that when breakfast was finished I remained on in the dining-room, and did not open any of the morning papers which were lying in a heap upon the library table. At half-past ten I said good-bye to Valerie, who was practising in the drawing-room—Pharos I had not yet seen—and, putting on my hat, left the house. It was the first opportunity I had had, since my return to London, of visiting my studio, and I was exceedingly anxious to discover how things had been progressing there during my absence. It was a lovely morning for walking, the sky being without a cloud, and the streets in consequence filled with sunshine. In the Row a considerable number of men and women were enjoying their morning canter, and nursemaids in white dresses were to be counted by the dozen in the streets leading to the Park. At the corner of Hamilton Place a voice I recognised called to me to stop, and, on turning round, I found my old friend, Sir George Legrath, hastening after me.

"My dear Cyril," he said, as he shook hands with me, "I am indeed glad to see you. I had no idea you had returned."

"I reached London yesterday morning," I answered, but in such a constrained voice that he must have been dense indeed if he did not see that something was amiss. "How did you know I had been away?"

"Why, my dear fellow," he answered, "have you forgotten that I sent you a certain address in Naples? And then I called at your studio the following morning, when your man told me you were abroad. But somehow you don't look well. I hope nothing is the matter?"

"Nothing, nothing," I replied, almost sharply, and for the first time in my life his presence was almost distasteful to me, though if I had been asked the reason I should have found it difficult to say why. "Sir George, when I called on you at the Museum that morning, you told me you would rather see me in my grave than connected in any way with Pharos."

"Well?" he inquired, looking up at me with a face that had suddenly lost its usual ruddy hue. "What makes you remind me of that now?"

"Because," I answered, "if it were not for one person's sake, I could wish that that opportunity had been vouchsafed you. I have been two months with Pharos."

"Well?" he said again.

"What more do you expect me to say?" I continued. Then, sinking my voice a little, as if I were afraid Pharos might be within hearing distance, I added, "Sir George, if I were to tell you all I know about that man——"

"You must tell me nothing!" he cried hastily. "I know too much already."

We walked for some distance in silence, and it was not until we were opposite Devonshire House that we spoke again.

Then Sir George said abruptly, and with a desire to change the subject that could not be disguised,

"Of course you have heard the terrible news this morning?"

Following the direction of his eyes, I saw what had put the notion into his head. A news-seller was standing in the gutter on the other side of the street, holding in his hand the usual placard setting forth the contents of the papers he had for sale. On this was printed in large letters :—

TERRIBLE OUTBREAK OF THE PLAGUE IN LONDON.

"You refer to the plague, I presume?" I said, with an assumed calmness I was far from feeling. "From that headline it would seem to have made its appearance in London after all."

"It has, indeed," said Sir George, with a gloominess that was far from usual with him. "Can it be possible you have not seen the papers?"

"I have scarcely seen a paper since I left London," I replied. "I have been far too busy. Tell me about it. Is it so very bad?"

"It has come upon us like a thunderclap," he answered. "Two days ago it was not known. Yesterday there was but one case, and that in the country. This morning there are no less than three hundred and seventy-five, and among them some of our most intimate friends. God help us if it gets worse! The authorities assure us they can stamp it out with ease, but it is my opinion this is destined to prove a grave crisis in England's history. However, it does not do to look on the black side of things, so I'll not turn prophet. Our ways part here, do they not? In that case, good-bye. I am very glad to have seen you. If you should be passing the Museum, I hope you will drop in. You know my hours, I think?"

"I shall be very glad to do so," I answered, and thereupon we parted with the first shadow of a cloud between us that our lives had seen. On reviewing our conversation afterwards, I could recall nothing that should have occasioned it; nevertheless, there it was, "that little rift within the lute," as Tennyson says, "which by-and-by would make the music mute."

After we had parted, I crossed the road and walked by way of Dover Street to my studio. Scarcely two months had elapsed since that fatal day when I had left it to go in search of Pharos, and yet those eight weeks seemed like years. So long did I seem to have been away that I almost expected to find a change in the houses of the street, and when I passed the curiosity shop at the corner where the murder had taken place, that terrible tragedy which had been the primary cause of my falling into Pharos's power, it was with a sensible feeling of surprise I found the windows still decorated with the same specimens of china, and the shop still carrying on its trade under the name of Clausand. I turned the corner and crossed the road. Instinctively my hand went into my pocket and produced the latchkey. I tapped it twice against the right-hand pillar of the door, just as I had been in the habit of doing for years, and inserted it in the lock. A few seconds later I had let myself in and was standing amongst my own *lares* and *penates* once more. Everything was just as I had left it; the clock was ticking on the mantelpiece, not a speck of dirt or dust was upon chair or china; indeed, the only thing

that served to remind me that I had been away at all
was the pile of letters which had been neatly arranged
upon my writing-table. These I opened, destroyed
what were of no importance, and placed the rest in
my pocket to be answered at a more convenient opportunity. Then leaving a note upon my table to inform
my servant that I had returned, and would call again
on the following morning, I let myself out, locked the
door, and returned to Piccadilly *en route* to Park Lane.

A great writer has mentioned somewhere that the
gravest issues are often determined by the most insig-
nificant trifles. As I have just remarked, I had, in
this instance, made up my mind to return to Park
Lane, in the hope that I might be able to induce
Valerie to take a stroll with me in the Park, and had
left Bond Street in order to turn westward, when,
emerging from a shop on the other side of the road,
I espied the writer of one of the most important of
the many letters I had found awaiting me at the studio.
He was a member of my own club, and thinking I had
better apologise to him while I had the chance for not
having answered his letter sooner, I hastened after him.
He, however, seemed to be in a hurry; and as soon as
it came to a race between us, it was evident that he
had the advantage of me on a point of speed. I
chased him until I saw that he was bound for the club,
whereupon, knowing I should be certain to catch him
there, I slackened my pace and strolled leisurely along.
In other days I had often been twitted in a jocular
fashion by my friends about my membership of this
particular club. The reputation it possessed was excellent in every way, but it certainly must be confessed

that what it gained in respectability it lacked in liveliness. For the most part the men who made use of it were middle-aged ; in point of fact I believe there were but two younger than myself, consequently the atmosphere of the house, while being always dignified, was sometimes cold almost to the borders of iciness.

On this particular day there was an additional air of gloom about it that rather puzzled me. When, however, I had finished my conversation with the man I had been following, and sought the smoking-room, the reason of it soon became apparent. That terrible fear which was destined within a few hours to paralyse all London was already beginning to make its presence felt, and as a result the room, usually so crowded, now contained but four men. These greeted me civilly enough, but without any show of interest. They were gathered round one of their number who was seated at a table with a pencil in his hand and a map of Europe spread out before him. From the way in which he was laying down the law, I gathered that he was demonstrating some theory upon which he pinned considerable faith.

" I have worked the whole thing out," he was saying as I entered, "and you can see it here for yourselves. On this sheet of paper I have pasted every telegram that has reached London from the time the disease first made its appearance in Constantinople. As each country became affected I coloured it upon the map in red, while these spots of a darker shade represent the towns from which the first cases were notified. At a glance, therefore, you can see the way in which the malady has travelled across Europe."

On hearing this, you may be sure I drew closer to the table, and looked over the shoulders of the men at the map below.

" As you see," said the lecturer, with renewed interest, as he observed this addition to his audience, " it started in Constantinople, made its appearance next in Southern Russia and the Balkan States. Two days later a case was notified from Vienna and another in Prague. Berlin was the next city visited, then Wittenberg, then Hamburg. France did not become infected until some days later, and then the individual who brought it was proved to have arrived the day before from Berlin. Yesterday, according to the official returns, there were twelve hundred cases in France, eighteen thousand in Austria, sixteen thousand in Germany—of which Hamburg alone contributes five thousand three hundred and fifty—while in Italy there have been three thousand four hundred, in Spain and Portugal only two hundred and thirty, while Turkey and Russia have forty-five thousand, and thirty-seven thousand three hundred and eighty, respectively. Greece returns seventeen thousand six hundred and twenty, Holland seven thousand two hundred and sixty-four, Belgium nine thousand five hundred and twenty-three, while Denmark completes the total of Europe with four thousand two hundred and twenty-one. The inferences to be drawn from these figures are apparent. The total number of deaths upon the Continent up to midnight last night was one hundred and fifty-nine thousand eight hundred and thirty-eight. The nations most seriously affected are Turkey and the countries immediately surrounding her, namely, Greece, Russia, and Austria. Germany follows next, though why Hamburg should contribute such a large proportion as five thousand three hundred and fifty I must admit it is difficult to see. England hitherto has stood aloof; now, however, it has broken out in London, and three hundred and seventy-five cases have been notified up to eight o'clock this morning."

On hearing this, the men standing round him turned pale and shuffled uneasily upon their feet. As for myself, I might have been changed to stone, so cold and so incapable of moving was I. It was as if a bandage had suddenly been removed from my eyes, enabling me to see everything plainly and in its proper light.

"The returns for our own country," continued this indefatigable statistician, without noticing my condition, "are as interesting as those from the Continent. I have filed everything already published, and have applied the result to this map of London. The two cases that occurred in Norfolk—the porter in Norwich, and the stationmaster at Tebworth Junction—I omit, for the reason that they tell us nothing. Of the cases notified in this city, careful inquiries on the part of the authorities have elicited the information that sixty-eight were present at the Renaissance Theatre last night, twenty-five spent the evening at the Antiquarian Club last night, eighty-five have been traced to the Occidental Music Hall, seventy-one to the Fancy Dress Ball at Covent Garden, twenty-six to the House of Commons, while, strangely enough, no less than thirty-seven can be proved to have been among the guests of the Duchess of Amersham at her ball in Carlton House

Terrace. The others are more difficult to account for, being made up of costermongers, homeless vagrants, street-hawkers, and others of the same class."

I could bear no more, but stumbled from the room like a drunken man out into the hall beyond. A servant, thinking I was ill, hastened to inquire if he could be of any assistance to me.

"Get me a cab," I faltered huskily.

The man ran into the street and blew his whistle. A hansom drove up, and I made my way into the street and scrambled into it, scarcely knowing how I managed it, and then fell back upon the cushions as if I were in a fit. The cab sped along the streets, threaded its way in and out of the traffic with a dexterity and a solicitude for my safety that was a more biting sarcasm than any lips could utter. What was my safety to me now? Knowing what I knew, I had better, far better, be dead.

The dreadful secret was out. In less than five minutes the mystery of two months had been solved. Now I knew the meaning of the spot I had discovered upon my arm on the morning following my terrible adventure in the Pyramid; now I could understand my illness in the desert, and the sudden death of the poor Arab who had nursed me. In the light of this terrible truth, everything was as clear as daylight, and all I wanted was to get back to Park Lane and find myself face to face with Pharos, in order that I might tax him with it, and afterwards go forth and publish his infamy to the world. Fast as the man was driving, he could not make his horse go fast enough for me. Though at first my blood had been as cold as ice, it

now raced through my veins like liquid fire. A feverish
nervousness had seized me, and for the time being I
was little better than a madman. Regardless of the
passers-by, conscious only of the vile part I had been
induced to play—unwittingly, it is true—in his unbelievable wickedness, I urged the driver to greater
speed. At last, after what seemed an eternity, we
reached our destination. I alighted, and, as I had
done in Hamburg, paid the cabman with the first
money I took from my pocket, and then went up the
steps and entered the house. By this time the all-
consuming fire of impatience which had succeeded the
icy coldness of the first discovery had left me, and was
succeeded by a strange, unnatural calm, in which I
seemed to be myself, and yet to be standing at a distance, watching myself. In a voice that I scarcely
recognised, I inquired from the butler where I could
find his master. He informed me that he was in the
drawing-room, and I accordingly went thither in search
of him. I had not the least notion of what I was going
to say to him when I found him, or how I should say
it, but I had to relieve my mind of the weight it was
carrying, and then—— Why, after that, nothing would
matter. I opened the door and entered the room. The
sunshine was streaming in through the windows at the
farther end, falling upon the elegant furniture, the em-
broideries and draperies, the china, and the hundred-
and-one knick-knacks that go to make up a fashionable
drawing-room. Of Pharos, however, there was no sign.
In place of him Valerie rose from a chair by the
window and greeted me with a little exclamation of
delight. Then, seeing the look upon my face, and the

deadly pallor of my complexion, she must have realized that something serious had happened to me, for she ran forward and took my hands in hers.

"My darling!" she cried, with a look of terror upon her face, "what has happened? Tell me, for pity's sake, for your face terrifies me!"

The pressure of her hands and the sight of those beautiful frightened eyes gazing up into mine cut me to the heart. Overwhelmed with sorrow as I was, she alone of all the world could soothe me and alleviate the agony I was suffering. It was not possible, however, that I could avail myself of her sympathy. I was dishonoured enough already, without seeking to dishonour her. Here our love must end. For the future I should be an outcast, a social leper, carrying with me to my grave the knowledge of the curse I had brought upon my fellow-men. I tried to put her from me, but she would not be denied.

"Oh, what can have happened that you treat me like this?" she cried. "Your silence breaks my heart."

"You must not come near me, Valerie," I muttered hoarsely. "Leave me. You have no notion what I am."

"You are the man I love," she answered. "That is enough for me. Whatever it may be, I have the right to share your sorrow with you."

"No, no!" I cried. "You must have no more to do with me. Drive me away from you. I tell you I am viler than you can believe, lower than the common murderer, for he kills but one, while, God help me, I have killed thousands."

She must have thought me mad, for she uttered a

little choking sob and sank down upon the floor, the very picture and embodiment of despair.   Then the door opened, and Pharos entered.

Seeing me standing in the centre of the room with a wild look upon my face, and Valerie crouching at my feet, he paused and gazed from one to the other of us in surprise.

"I am afraid I am *de trop*," he said, with the old nasty sneer upon his face.   "If it is not putting you to too much trouble, perhaps one of you will be good enough to tell me what it means."

Neither of us answered for upwards of a minute; then I broke the spell that bound us and turned to Pharos.   How feeble the words seemed, when compared with the violence of my emotions and the unbelievable nature of the charge I was bringing against him, I must leave you to imagine.

"It means, Monsieur Pharos," I said, "that I have discovered everything."

I could say no more, for a lump was rising in my throat which threatened to choke me.   It soon appeared, however, that I had said enough, for Pharos must either have read my thoughts and have understood that denial would be useless, or, since I was no longer necessary to him, he did not care whether he confessed to me or not.   At any rate, he advanced into the room, his cruel eyes watching me intently the while.

"So you have discovered everything, have you, my friend?" he said.   "And pray what is this knowledge that you have accumulated?"

"How can I tell you?" I cried, scarcely knowing how to enter upon my terrible indictment.   "How can

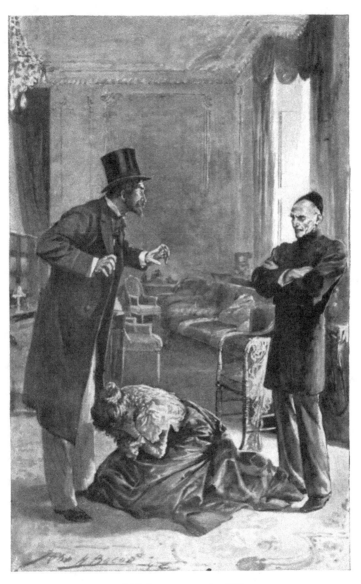

"'Inhuman monster!'"

I make you understand your wickedness? I have discovered that it is you who are responsible for the misery
from which Europe is now suffering. I know that it
was I, through you, who introduced the plague and
carried it from Constantinople to London. Inhuman
monster!" I continued, having by this time worked myself to a white heat. "I was in your power and you
made me your tool. But you shall not escape. It
is not too late even now to punish you. Within an
hour the world shall know everything, and you will
be dead, if devils can die. I have been your tool, but,
since I know your wickedness, I will not be your ac-
complice. Oh, my God! is it possible that a man
breathing the pure air of heaven can be so vile?"

All the time I had been thus denouncing him, I had
been standing just as I was when he entered the room,
with Valerie still crouching at my feet. The dangerous
light I remembered so well of old had returned to his
eyes, making him look indescribably fiendish.

"Are you mad that you dare to talk to me in this
fashion?" he said at last, but with a calmness the meaning of which there was no mistaking. "Since it is plain
that you do not remember the hold I have upon you,
nor what your fate will be if you anger me, I must
enlighten you. You bring these accusations against
me and you threaten to betray me to the world—me,
Pharos the Egyptian, and to your pitiful world which
I spurn beneath my feet. Once more I ask you, are
you mad? But since there is no further need for con-
cealment, and you desire the truth, you shall hear it."
He paused, and when he spoke again it was noticeable
that he had dropped his former conversational tone

and had adopted a manner more in keeping with the
solemnity of what he had to say. " Know, then, that
what thou sawest in the vision before the Sphinx and
in the Temple of Ammon was the truth, and not a
dream, as I desired thee to believe. I, whom thou hast
known as Pharos, am none other than Ptahmes, son of
Netruhôtep, Prophet of the North and South, the same
whom Pharaoh sought to kill, and who died in hiding
and was buried by his faithful priests under cover of
night more than three thousand years ago. Cursed by
the gods, and denied the right of burial by order of the
King, I have inhabited this shape since then. Darest
thou, knowing this, pit thyself against the servant of
the mighty ones? For I tell thee assuredly that the
plague which is now destroying Europe was decreed
by the gods of Egypt against such nations as have
committed the sin of sacrilege."

He paused, and for a moment I thought he would
have sprung upon me as he had done that night in my
studio. But he controlled himself with an effort, and
a moment later his voice was as soft and conciliatory
and yet as full of malice as before. I also noticed that
he had returned to his ordinary and more colloquial
tone.

" Are you anxious to hear more? If you are determined to proclaim my doings to the world, it is only
fit you should know everything. I will willingly confess. Why should I not do so? You are mine to do
with as I please. Without my leave you are powerless
to hurt me, and who would believe you if you were to
tell? No one! They would call you mad, as you
undoubtedly are, and say that fear of the plague had

turned your brain. In Naples you accused me of the murder of Clausand, the curiosity dealer. I denied it because the time was not then ripe for me to acquaint you with the truth. Now I confess it. I stabbed him because he would not give me a certain scarabeus, and to divert suspicion willed that the half-crazy German, Schmidt, whom the other had cast out of his service, should declare that he did the deed. In obedience to my desire you followed me to Italy and accompanied me thence to Egypt. I it was who drew you to the Pyramid and decreed that you should lose your way inside, in order that when fear had deprived you of your senses I might inoculate you with the plague. Seven days later you were stricken with it in the desert. As soon as you recovered, I carried you off to Europe to begin the work required of you. In Constantinople, Vienna, Prague, Berlin, Hamburg, wherever you went you left the fatal germs of the disease as a legacy behind you. You infected this woman here, and but for me she would have died. To-day the last portion of that vengeance which has been decreed commences, and when all is finished I go to that rest in ancient Thebes which has been denied me these long three thousand years. Hark! Even now the sound of wailing is to be heard in London. Hour by hour the virulence of the pestilence increases, and the strong men and weak women, youths and maidens, children and babes, go down before it like corn before the reaper. On every hand the voices of mourners rise into the summer air, and it is I, Ptahmes, the servant of the gods, the prophet of the king, the man whom thou hast said thou wilt proclaim to the world, who has brought it about."

Then, lifting his right hand, he pointed it at me.

"Fool—fool!" he cried, with withering scorn. "Frail atom in the path of life, who art thou that thou shouldst deem thyself strong enough to cope with me? Learn, then, that the time is not yet ripe. I have further need of thee. Sleep again, and in that sleep do all I shall require of thee."

As he said this his diminutive form seemed to grow larger and more terrible, until it appeared to have attained twice its ordinary size. His eyes shone in his head like living coals, and seemed to burn into my brain. I saw Valerie rise from the place where she had hitherto been crouching, and snatch an Oriental dagger from a table. Then, swift as a panther, she sprang upon him, only to be hurled back against the wall as if struck by an invisible hand. Then, obedient as a little child, I closed my eyes and slept.

CHAPTER XXI

FOR no less a period than five days and six nights Pharos kept me in the same hypnotic condition, and, incredible though it may seem, I have not the slightest recollection of any one single circumstance that occurred during the whole of that time. Valerie has since informed me that I moved about the house very much as usual, that I went in and out with Pharos, but that I never spoke to her, and while I seemed conscious of my actions and well enough in my bodily health, I did everything with that peculiar listless air that one notices in a man while walking in his sleep. I also gather from the same source that Pharos's behaviour during that terrible period was equally extraordinary. Never for one instant did he allow her to remain alone with me. The greater portion of his time was spent out of the house with myself, though in what pursuit he was engaged she could not discover. He would take me away with him early in the morning and not return until late at night, when he would conduct me to my room and then retire himself. At times he would scarcely speak a word, then a fit of loquacity would come over him, and he would openly boast to her of the misery he had caused, and find a diabolical delight in every bulletin that proclaimed the increasing virulence of the plague. To this day the picture of that impish creature perambulating the death-stricken streets and alleys to the accompaniment of tolling bells, watching with ghoulish satisfaction the futile efforts of the authorities to cope with the disease, haunts me like a nightmare. Every day fresh tidings were pouring in of the spread of the infection into other cities and towns, until the entire kingdom was riddled like a honeycomb.

How long Pharos would have kept me under his influence, had he possessed the power, I cannot say. I only know that on the morning of the sixth day I woke with a strange and confused feeling in my head. Though my eyes were open and I was to all outward appearances wide awake, I was like a man hovering on the borderland of sleep. My senses were gradually coming back to me; the strength of my brain was reasserting itself, and by some strange process, how arrived at it is impossible for me to say, the hold Pharos had obtained upon me was slowly weakening. Then it was as if I suddenly awoke to find myself standing fully dressed in my own room. My bed had been slept in, and one glance out of my window showed me that it was early morning. And yet I had not the least recollection of having been in bed or of having made my toilet. Then the scene with Pharos, and the awful knowledge it had given rise to, came back to me, and I remembered how he had pointed his hand at me, and how I had fallen asleep before him. Here was the logical explanation of the whole thing. It was plain that after I had become unconscious, Pharos had caused me to be carried to my room and put to bed. This then, I argued, must be the morning following. Now that the effect he had produced had worn off, there was still time for me to do what I had originally intended. Having arrived at this decision, I opened my door and went downstairs. A curious silence prevailed, not only in the house, but outside. I stopped on the first landing and looked out of the window. So far as I could see, there were no cabs or carriages in the street, no riders in the Row, no children with their nurses upon the pavements, and yet the old Chippendale timepiece in the hall told me that the hour was considerably past nine o'clock. A curious feeling of drowsiness still possessed me, but it was fast leaving me, and, what was more, leaving me filled with but one purpose in life, which was to seek out the authorities and proclaim to them the devilry of Pharos, and the part I had myself played in his abominable wickedness. After that I would wait for Fate to say what should become of me.

Putting on my hat, I opened the front door and stepped out into the street. At any cost I would endeavour to reach the Home Office, and tell my story there, before Pharos could prevent me. With this end in view I hurried towards Piccadilly, intending to take a cab there and so save time. But when I set out I had not the least notion of the misery that had befallen London, nor of anything that had happened since Pharos had pointed his finger at me. In my wildest dreams I had never imagined such a picture of desolation as that which was now presented to me. It seemed impossible that so terrible a change should have come over a city in so short a time (I must

remind you here that I still believed that only twenty
hours had elapsed since I had had my fatal interview
with Pharos). In all Park Lane not a house, save
that occupied by Pharos, showed any sign of being
inhabited. Without exception the blinds were down,
and in most cases the shutters had been put up, while
in numerous instances broad lines of red paint had
been drawn across the pavement opposite them, but
for what purpose, or their indication, I had not the
remotest idea. In Piccadilly, from Apsley House to
Berkeley Street, it was the same, though here a few
solitary foot-passengers were to be seen. Thinking I
must have mistaken the hour, and that it was earlier
than I supposed, I looked at my watch, but it said
a quarter to ten. In vain I searched for a cab of any
sort. In the road, usually so crowded at that hour
with vehicles of all descriptions, omnibuses, hansoms,
private carriages, vans, and even costermongers' bar-
rows, two dogs were fighting over a piece of food.
But the silence was the worst part of it all. Not a
sound, save the chirruping of the sparrows in the trees
of the park, was to be heard. Realizing that it was
useless waiting for a cab, I crossed the road and entered
the Green Park, intending to make my way to St.
James's Park, and thence to the Home Office. With
feverish haste I pushed on, walking as if every life in
England depended on my speed. Here also the desolation was most marked. At any other time the turf
would have been dotted with human forms; now I
could only distinguish two or three at most. I passed
within a few yards of one. He was lying upon his
back, his arms stretched out, and when I looked at

him I found to my horror that he was dead. So awful was the face, indeed, in its terrible disfiguration that I recoiled from it in terror. I had not gone fifty yards farther before another made his appearance from among the trees and hastened towards me, waving his arms and gesticulating as he came. This individual was well-dressed and of gentlemanly appearance. His clothes and linen, however, were much soiled, as if he had been sleeping out for several nights. When he came closer, it needed only a glance on my part to tell that he was mad.

"You will excuse me, sir, I hope," he said, approaching me and rubbing his hands one over the other as he did so, "but you do not happen to have seen my wife and children, I suppose? They left me yesterday morning, and though I have hunted all through the West End I have been unable to find them. There is a strange disease abroad, they tell me, but of course that would not be likely to affect them. Do you think so?"

"I regret to say that I have not seen them," I answered, and tried to pass him and continue my walk. He, however, was not to be denied, but kept pace with me, mincing along by my side, rubbing his hands together as before, and looking sideways into my face with an air of entreaty that was inexpressibly touching.

"It is really extremely awkward, 'pon my soul it is," he said. "I am quite worn out with looking for them, and where to try next I do not know." He was silent for a few paces, and then returned to his former topic. "Perhaps you have not heard that there has been considerable sickness in London of late? The plague they call it, but for my part I do not believe it. Would you like to hear my name for it? Then you shall. Between man and man I call it the devil, but mum's the word on that score. You will, of course, see why?"

Here he came a little closer and shook his head solemnly at me.

"Don't let there be any mistake about it," he said. "The devil is at the bottom of it; but mum's the word. And now good-morning. Time is money with me, and I must continue my search."

Then, lifting his hat, he made me a low bow, and ran away across the grass in the direction of Sutherland House.

Reaching the Mall, I crossed into St. James's Park and passed over the bridge which spans the lake. Here the water-birds were swimming about as happily as if nothing out of the common were occurring in the great city around them. At last I reached the office for which I was making. The Home Secretary at the time was a man I had known all my life, an upright, honest Englishman in every sense of the word, beloved by everybody, and respected even by his political opponents. If any man would listen to my story, I felt convinced he would be that one. When, however, I reached the office, what a change was there! Only the day before, as I still imagined, the place had been teeming with life, every room filled with clerks, and exhibiting all the machinery of a great Government office. Now, at first glance, it appeared deserted. I entered the hall in which I had been accustomed to inquire from the porter for my friend, only to find it occupied by a sergeant of the Guards, who rose on seeing me.

"What do you want?" he inquired brusquely.

"I desire to see the Home Secretary without loss of time," I answered. "I am the bearer of most important information, and it is most imperative that I should see him at once."

"What is the information?" the man inquired suspiciously. "The Home Secretary sees no one except on the most urgent business now."

"My business *is* the most urgent possible," I returned. "If you will take my name to him, I feel sure he will see me."

"I shall do nothing of the kind," replied the sergeant, "so you had better take yourself off. We don't want any of your kind about here just now. There's enough trouble without having you to look after."

"But I must see him!" I cried in despair. "You don't know what you are doing when you try to stop me. I have a confession to make to him, and make it I will at any hazard. Take me to him at once, or I shall find him myself."

The man was moving towards me with the evident intention of putting me into the street, when a door opened and the Home Secretary, Sir Edward Grangerfield, stood before me. When last I had seen him at the Duchess of Amersham's ball—I remembered that he congratulated me on my engagement on that occasion—he had looked in the prime of life. Now he was an old man, borne down by the weight of sorrow and responsibility which the plague had placed upon his shoulders. From the way he looked at me, it was plain he did not recognise me.

"Sir Edward," I said, "is it possible I am so much changed that you do not know me? I am Cyril Forrester."

"Cyril Forrester!" he cried in amazement, coming a step closer to me as he spoke. "Surely not? But it is, I see. Why, man, how changed you are! What brings you here, and what is it you want with me? I have not much time to spare. I have an appointment with the Public Health Commission in a quarter of an hour."

"So much the better," I answered, "for you will then be able to acquaint them with the circumstances I am about to reveal to you. Sir Edward, I must have a few moments' conversation with you alone. I have a confession to make to you—the most hideous tale to pour into your ears that ever man confided to another." Then, recollecting myself, I continued : "But it must not be here. It must be in the open air, or I shall infect you."

He looked at me in a curious fashion.

"You need have no fear on that score," he said. "I have had the plague, and have recovered from it. So far it has not been known to attack any one twice. But since you wish to speak to me alone, come with me."

With this he led me down the long passage to an office at the farther end. Like the others, this one was also deserted. Once inside, he closed the door.

"Be as brief as you can," he said, "for during this terribly trying period my time is not my own. What is it you wish to say to me?"

"I wish to confess to you," I said, and my voice rang in my ears like a death-knell, "that I am the cause of the misery under the weight of which England and Europe is groaning at the present time."

Once more Sir Edward looked at me as he had done in the passage outside.

"I am afraid I do not quite understand," he said, but this time in a somewhat different tone. "Do you mean that you wish me to believe that you, Cyril Forrester, are the cause of the plague which is decimating England in this terrible manner?"

"I do," I answered, and then waited to hear what he would say.

In reply he inquired whether I had suffered from the disease myself.

"I was the first to have it," I answered. "My story is an extraordinary one, but I assure you every particular of it is true. I was inoculated with the virus while I was in Egypt—that is to say, in the Queen's Hall of the Great Pyramid of Gizeh. I afterwards nearly died of it in an Arab tent out in the desert beyond Luxor. Later on I was taken by a man, of whom I will tell you more presently, to Constantinople, thence through Austria and Germany, and finally was smuggled across the Channel into England."

"And who was the man who inoculated you?" inquired the Home Secretary, still with the same peculiar intonation. "Can you remember his name?"

"He is known in England as Pharos the Egyptian," I replied—"the foulest fiend this world has ever seen. In reality he is Ptahmes the Magician, and he has sworn vengeance on the human race. Among other things

he was the real murderer of Clausand, the curiosity
dealer, in Bonwell Street last June, and not the in-
offensive German who shot himself after confessing
to the crime at Bow Street. He smuggled me into
England from Hamburg, and the night before last
he took me all through London—to the Antiquarian
Club, the Renaissance Theatre, the House of Commons,
the Occidental Music Hall, to the Duchess of Amersham's ball, to Covent Garden, and to many other
places. Every one I spoke to became infected, and
that, I assure you, on my word of honour, was how the
plague originated here. Oh, Sir Edward, you cannot
realize what agonies I have suffered since I became
possessed of this terrible knowledge!"

A short silence followed, during which I am convinced I heard my companion say very softly to himself,
"That settles it."

Then, turning to me, he continued : "You say you
were at the Duchess of Amersham's ball the night
before last? Do you mean this?"

"Of course I do," I replied. "Why, you spoke to
me there yourself, and congratulated me upon my
engagement. And, now I come to think of it, I saw
you talking with Pharos there."

"Quite right," he said. "I did speak to Monsieur
Pharos there. But are you sure it was the night before
last? That is what I want to get at."

"I am as sure of that as I am of anything in this
world," I replied.

"What you tell me is very interesting," he said,
rising from his chair—"very interesting indeed, and I
am sincerely obliged to you for coming to me. Now,

if you will excuse me, I must be going, for, as I told you, I have a meeting of the Health Commission to attend in a few minutes. If I were you, I should go back to my house and keep quiet. There is nothing to be gained by worrying oneself, as you have evidently been doing."

" I can see that you do not believe what I have told you," I cried with great bitterness. " Sir Edward, I implore you to do so. I assure you, on my honour as a gentleman, I will swear, by any oath you care to name, that what I say is true in every particular. Pharos is still in London, in Park Lane, and if you are quick you can capture him. But there is not a moment to lose. For God's sake believe me before it is too late ! "

" I have listened to all you have said, my dear Cyril," he answered soothingly, " and I can quite understand that you believe it to be true. You have been ill, and it is plain your always excitable imagination has not yet recovered its equilibrium. Go home, as I say, and rest. Trust me, you will soon be yourself once more. Now I must go."

" Oh, heavens ! how can I convince you ? " I groaned, wringing my hands. " Is there nothing I can say or do that will make you believe my story ? You will find out when it is too late that I have told you the truth. Men and women are dying like sheep to right and left of us, and yet the vile author of all this sorrow and suffering will escape unpunished. Is it any use, Sir Edward, for me to address one last appeal to you ? "

Then a notion struck me. I thrust my hand into my coat pocket and produced the prescription which

Pharos had given me for Valerie in Hamburg, and which, since it had done her so much good, I had been careful not to let out of my possession.

"Take that, Sir Edward," I said. "I came to make my confession to you because I deemed it my duty, and because of the load upon my brain, which I thought it might help to lighten. You will not believe me, so what can I do? This paper contains the only prescription which has yet been effectual in checking the disease. It saved the life of Valerie de Vocxqal, and I can vouch for its efficacy. Show it to the medical authorities. It is possible it may convince them that I am not as mad as you think me."

He took it from me, but it was plain to me, from the look upon his face, that he believed it to be only another part of my delusion.

"If it will make your mind any easier," he said, "I will give you my word that it shall be placed before the members of the Commission. Iı they deem it likely that any good can result from it, you may be sure it will be used."

He then wished me good-bye, and, with a feeling of unavailing rage and disappointment in my heart, I left the Offices and passed out into Whitehall. Once more I made my way into St. James's Park, and reaching a secluded spot, threw myself down upon the turf and buried my face in my arms. At first I could think of nothing but my own shame; then my thoughts turned to Valerie. In my trouble I had for the moment forgotten her. Coward that I was, I had considered my own before her safety. If anything happened to me, who would protect her? I was still debating this with myself when my ears caught the sound of a footstep on the hard ground, and then the rustle of a dress. A moment later a voice sounded in my ears like the sweetest music. "Thank God!" it said, "oh! thank God! I have found you."

Her cry of happiness ended in a little choking sob, and I turned and looked up to discover Valerie, her beautiful eyes streaming with tears, bending over me.

"How did you find me?" I inquired, in a voice that my love and longing for her rendered almost inaudible. "How did you know that I was here?"

"Love told me," she answered softly. "My heart led me to you. You forget the strange power with which I am gifted. Though I did not see you leave the house, I knew that you were gone, and my instinct warned me not only where you were going, but what you were going to do. Cyril, it was brave of you to go."

"It was useless!" I cried. "I have failed. He would not believe me, Valerie, and I am lost eternally!"

"Hush!" she said. "Dear love, you must not say such things. They are not true. But rise. You must come to him. All this morning he has not been at all the same. I do not know what to think, but something is going to happen, I am certain."

There was no need for her to say to whom she referred.

I did as she commanded me, and side by side we crossed the park.

"He has made arrangements to leave England this afternoon," she continued, as we passed into Piccadilly.

"The yacht is in the Thames, and orders have been sent to hold her in readiness for a long voyage."

"And what does he intend doing with us?"

"I know nothing of that," she answered. "But there is something very strange about him to-day. When he sent for me this morning, I scarcely knew him, he was so changed."

We made our way along the deserted streets and presently reached Park Lane. As soon as we were inside the house, I ascended the stairs beside her, and it was not until we had reached the top floor, on which Pharos's room was situated, that we paused before a door. Listening before it, we could plainly hear some one moving about inside. When we knocked, a voice I failed to recognise called upon us to enter. It was a strange picture we saw when we did so. In a large armchair before a roaring fire, though it was the middle of summer, sat Pharos, but so changed that I hardly knew him. He looked half his usual size; his skin hung loose about his face, as if the bones had shrunken underneath it; his eyes, always so deep-set in his head, were now so much sunken that they could scarcely be seen, while his hands were shrivelled until they resembled those of a mummy more than a man. The monkey also, which was huddled beside him in the chair, looked smaller than I had ever seen it. As if this were not enough, the room was filled with Egyptian curios from floor to ceiling. So many were there, indeed, that there barely remained room for Pharos's chair. How he had obtained possession of them, I did not understand; but since Sir George Legrath's confession, written shortly before his tragic death by his own hand, the mystery has been solved, and Pharos confronts us in an even more unenviable light than before. Hating, loathing, and yet fearing the man as I did, there was something in his look now that roused an emotion in me that was almost akin to pity.

"Thou hast come in time," he said to Valerie, but in a different voice and without that harshness to which we had so long grown accustomed. "I have been anxiously awaiting thee."

He signed to her to approach him.

"Give me your hand," he whispered faintly. "Through you it is decreed that I must learn my fate. Courage, courage—there is naught for thee to fear!"

Taking her hand, he bade her close her eyes and describe to him what she saw. She did as she was ordered, and for upwards of a minute perfect silence reigned in the room. The picture they made—the worn-out, shrivelled body of the man and the lovely woman—I cannot hope to make you understand.

"I see a great hall supported by pillars," she said at last, speaking in that hard, measured voice I remembered to have heard on board the yacht. "The walls are covered with paintings, and two sphinxes guard the door. In the centre is an old man with a long white beard, who holds his arms above his head."

"It is Paduamen, the mouthpiece of the gods," moaned Pharos, with a look of terror in his face that there was no disguising. "I am lost for ever—for ever; not for to-day, not for to-morrow, but for all time! Tell me, woman, what judgment the Mighty Ones pronounce against me?"

"Hush—he speaks!" Valerie continued slowly ; and then a wonderful thing happened.

Whether it was the first warning of the illness that was presently to fall upon me, or whether I was so much in sympathy with Valerie that I saw what she and Pharos saw, I cannot say; at any rate, I suddenly found myself transported from Park Lane away to that mysterious hall below the Temple of Ammon, of which I retained so vivid a recollection. The place was in semi-darkness, and in the centre, as Valerie had described, stood the old man who had acted as my guide on the other occasion that I had been there. His arms were raised above his head, and his voice when he spoke was stern yet full of sadness.

" Ptahmes, son of Netruhôtep," he was saying, " across the seas I speak to thee. For the second time thou hast been found wanting in the trust reposed in thee. Thou hast used the power vouchsafed thee by the gods for thine own purposes and to enrich thyself in the goods of the earth. Therefore thy doom is decreed, and in the Valley of Amenti thy punishment awaits thee. Prepare, for that time is even now upon thee."

Then the hall grew dark, there was a rushing sound as of a great wind, and once more I was back in Park Lane. Pharos was crouching in his chair, moaning feebly, and evidently beside himself with terror.

"What more dost thou see?" he said at length, and his voice was growing perceptibly weaker. "Tell me all."

There was another pause, and then Valerie spoke again.

"I see a rocky hillside and a newly opened tomb. I see three white men and five Arabs who surround it. They are lifting a mummy from the vault below with cords."

On hearing this Pharos sprang to his feet with a loud cry, and for a moment fought wildly with the air. Meanwhile the monkey clung tenaciously to him, uttering strange cries, which grew feebler every moment. Valerie, released from her trance, if by such a name I may describe it, and unable to bear more, fled the room, while I stood rooted to the spot, powerless to move hand or foot, watching Pharos with fascinated eyes.

As if he were choking, he tore at his throat with his skeleton fingers till the blood spurted out on either side. Little by little, however, his struggles grew weaker, until they ceased altogether, and he fell back into his chair to all intents and purposes a dead man, with the dying monkey still clinging to his coat.

After all I had lately gone through, the strain this terrible scene put upon my mind was too great for me to bear, and I fell back against the wall in a dead faint.

*   *   *   *   *

When I recovered from the attack of brain fever which followed the ghastly event I have just described, I found myself lying in my bunk in my old cabin on board the yacht. Valerie was sitting beside me, holding my hand in hers and gazing lovingly into my face. Surprised at finding myself where I was, I endeavoured to obtain an explanation from her.

"Hush," she said, "you must not talk! Let it suffice

that I have saved you, and now we are away from England, and at sea together. Pharos is dead, and the past is only a bitter memory."

As she spoke, as if to bear out what she had said, a ray of sunshine streamed in through the porthole and fell upon us both.

THE END.